Alcock, Alfred

A Descriptive Catalogue of the Indian deep-Sea Fishes in the Indian Museum

Alcock, Alfred

A Descriptive Catalogue of the Indian deep-Sea Fishes in the Indian Museum

Inktank publishing, 2018

www.inktank-publishing.com

ISBN/EAN: 9783750147362

A
DESCRIPTIVE CATALOGUE
OF THE
INDIAN DEEP-SEA FISHES
IN THE
INDIAN MUSEUM.

BEING A REVISED ACCOUNT OF THE DEEP-SEA FISHES

COLLECTED BY THE

ROYAL INDIAN MARINE SURVEY SHIP
INVESTIGATOR

BY

A. ALCOCK, M.B., C.M.Z.S., F.G.S.,

INDIAN MEDICAL SERVICE, SUPERINTENDENT OF THE INDIAN MUSEUM AND PROFESSOR OF ZOOLOGY IN THE MEDICAL COLLEGE, CALCUTTA; FORMERLY NATURALIST TO THE MARINE SURVEY OF INDIA.

CALCUTTA:
PRINTED BY ORDER OF THE TRUSTEES OF THE INDIAN MUSEUM.

1899.

Price Five Rupees.

Preface.

The following extract from the Prefatory Note to the *Account of the Deep Sea Madreporaria collected by the R. I. M. S. Investigator* will serve to explain how the collection of Deep-Sea Fishes described in the present volume came to be made and to be presented to the Indian Museum.

"In the year 1871 the Council of the Asiatic Society of Bengal appointed Dr. T. Oldham, Dr. F. Stoliczka and Mr. J. Wood-Mason to form a sub-committee to report upon the desirability of moving the Government of India to undertake deep-sea dredging in Indian waters.

"The sub-committee drew up an elaborate *Memoir* on the subject, in which definite proposals for deep-sea dredging were embodied: this Memoir was submitted to Government, and a copy of it along with a copy of the letter with which it was forwarded, is published in the *Proceedings of the Asiatic Society of Bengal* for 1871.

"The Government received the proposals of the Council of the Asiatic Society with cordial approval: it gave a small grant-in-aid of carrying them into immediate effect, and when, in 1874, the present Marine Survey Department was established, it sanctioned the appointment, upon the staff of the Survey, of a Surgeon-Naturalist—an appointment that had also been strongly advocated by the organizer and first head of the Department, Commander Dundas Taylor, I. N.

"But in the early days of the Survey (1874-1881) neither machinery nor vessels capable of deep-sea research were available, so that Surgeon (now Lieutenant-Colonel) J. Armstrong, I.M.S., the first Surgeon-Naturalist of the Department, had to report that it was "quite impossible to carry into execution the scheme of deep-sea dredging originally proposed by the Council of the Asiatic Society of Bengal," and had to confine himself to the Zoology of the shallow-water and littoral, although he did occasionally manage to dredge in water as deep as 100 fathoms.

"However, in 1876, when it had been decided to construct a special vessel for the accommodation of the Marine Survey, the Council of the Asiatic Society again addressed the Government of India, and asked that provision for deep-sea dredging might not be forgotten in the plans for the new vessel. In reply the Government authorized the Council of the Society to confer with the Dockyard authorities on the subject of such equipment.

"The Council thereupon appointed a sub-committee, consisting of Dr. John Anderson, then Superintendent of the Indian Museum, and Messrs. J. Wood-Mason (then Deputy Superintendent of the Indian Museum), W. T. Blanford, H. F. Blanford, and H. B. Medlicott, for the purpose of advising the Dockyard authorities in this direction.

"The result of this and other measures was that when, in 1881, the new vessel *Investigator* was ready for sea, she was properly provided with the means of undertaking deep-sea research as opportunity should occur.

"Before this, however, Dr. Armstrong had left the Survey, and it was not until the end of the year 1884, when Commander A. Carpenter, R. N., was appointed to the command of the 'Investigator,' and Surgeon (now Major) G. M. J. Giles, I.M.S., to the post of Surgeon-Naturalist, that deep-sea dredging became a recognized, if subordinate, branch of the ship's routine.

"Since 1885 the Zoological collections made by the 'Investigator' have been accumulating year by year in the Indian Museum, where, in accordance with the recommendations of the Council of the Asiatic Society of Bengal, they have been deposited.

"It must not, however, be supposed that deep-sea dredging occupies a very large part of the attention of the officers of the Survey; since, as a rule, it is only possible when the ship is proceeding to and returning from her systematic surveys of the shores and shallows. It is rarely indeed that as many as twenty deep-sea hauls are made in one year.

"From October 1888, when regular records began to be kept, up to the present time, 118 more or less successful hauls have been made in depths of over a hundred fathoms (100–1997 fms.).

"As regards the 'Investigator' herself, she is a paddle-steamer of 580 tons, and for a few facts as to her history and equipment I may refer to a paper in the *Scientific Memoirs of the Medical Officers of the Army of India* for 1898."

With regard to the contents of the present volume on the Deep-Sea Fishes, I may state that the species not here described for the first time have already been noticed in the following papers :—

Journ. As. Soc. Bengal: Vol. LVIII. pt. 2, 1889, pp. 279–295, pl. xvi–xviii, and pp. 296–305, pl. xxii; Vol. LXIII. pt. 2, 1894, pp. 115–137, pl. vi-vii; and Vol. LXV. pt. 2, 1896, pp. 301–338.

Ann. Mag. Nat. Hist., (6) IV. 1889, pp. 376–399 and 450–461; (6) VI. 1890, pp. 197–222, pl. viii-ix, and pp. 295–311; (6) VIII. 1891, pp. 16–34 and 119–138, pl. vii–viii; (6) X. 1892, pp. 345–365, pl. xviii, and pp. 207–214; (6) XVI. 1895, pp. 144–146; and (7) II. 1898, pp. 136–156.

Proc. Zool. Soc. 1891, pp. 226–227.

All but four of the new species described in the above-cited papers have been figured in the Illustrations of the Zoology of the R. I. M. S. Investigator, Fishes, pls. I–XXVI (and XXVII–XXXV *in the press*).

As it is intended that those plates should be bound up with the present Catalogue, together with a small appendix on the Shore Fishes discovered by the Investigator, no special illustrations have been prepared for this volume.

I have however added (facing page 12) a chart, compiled from plate ii of Dr. Ernst Koken's *Die Vorwelt und ihre Entwickelungsgeschichte*, which is meant to elucidate the theories upheld in the Investigator Reports as to the origin and past geographical relations of the fauna of the Indian Oligobenthus.

For the opportunity of making this chart and for help in compiling it, I am indebted to Mr. T. H. Holland of the Indian Geological Survey.

To explain an apparent want of uniformity in the plan of this Catalogue, I must mention that I have intentionally omitted diagnoses of the families and genera, and of the one or two species, heretofore well known to inhabit Indian seas. The Catalogue is designed to meet the wants of students of the Indian fauna, and it would have been superfluous to reprint information that can be found recorded in Day's standard volumes on the Fishes of India.

I cannot let this volume go out without acknowledging the essential and fundamental obligations that it owes to the *Catalogue of the Fishes in the British Museum*, to the *Introduction to the Study of Fishes*, and to the *Report on the Deep Sea Fishes collected by H. M. S. Challenger*.

In any scheme of classification the compass and standing of the various units will vary with individual opinion; but the value and influence of a well-organized system of broad, clear, consistent generalizations must always last, and I am happy to add my tribute of regard to the author of the works in which these qualities are so conspicuously manifest.

A. Alcock, Major, I. M. S.,
Superintendent of the Indian Museum.

INTRODUCTION.

The Fishes included in this Catalogue were all of them dredged by the R. I. M. S. "Investigator," in deep water, between the meridians of 65° and 99° E. and the parallels of 5° and 24° N., during the years 1885–1899.

They number, exclusive of a few mangled remains that cannot be identified with certainty, 169 species, namely :—

Chondropterygii	... ...	9 species.
Acanthopterygii	... ...	46 ,,
Anacanthini	... ...	55 ,,
Physostomi	... ...	57 ,,
Plectognathi	... ...	2 ,,

Of these—126 species have, so far as is known, been taken only by the "Investigator;" while 43 species are believed to be identical with species found in other parts of the world, the identities having been assured by actual comparison of specimens in 13 instances.

It will be interesting, to begin with, to inquire into the geographical distribution of these 43 species and to see if they throw any light on the outside relations of the Fish-fauna of the Indian seas.

It appears that the following 23 of them, or over thirteen per cent. of the whole, are common to these seas and the Atlantic, and many of them to certain very definite areas of that Ocean :—

Setarches Güntheri Johns.
* *Hoplostethus mediterraneum* C. V. (Also in the Mediterranean).
Trachichthys Darwinii Johns.
Polymixia nobilis Lowe.
* *Antigonia capros* Lowe.
{ *Bembrops caudimacula* Stdr.
(= **Hypsicometes gobioides* G. & B.).
Chiasmodus niger Johns.
Chaunax pictus Lowe.
* *Dicrolene intronigra* G. & B.
Diplacanthopoma brachysoma Gthr.
{ * *Macrurus cavernosus* G. & B.
(probably identical with the Mediterranean *Hymenocephalus italicus* Giglioli).
Macrurus lævis Lowe. (Also in the Mediterranean).
Bathygadus longifilis G. & B.
* *Argyropelecus hemigymnus* Cocco. (Also in the Mediterranean).

---

* Species marked with an asterisk have been compared with actual specimens from other localities.

1

* *Sternoptyx diaphana* Herm.
Cyclothone elongata (Gthr.).
Cyclothone microdon (Gthr.).
Chauliodus Sloanii Bl. Schn. (Also in the Mediterranean).
* *Neoscopelus macrolepidotus* Johns.
Platytroctes apus Gthr.
* *Synaphobranchus pinnatus* Gronov.
Uroconger vicinus Vaillant.
? *Leptoderma macrops* Vaillant.

The remaining 20 are Indo-Pacific species.

Very significant, to my mind, is the occurrence in these seas—it also occurs in Japan, where it was originally found—of *Bembrops caudimacula* (=*Hypsicometes gobioides* G. & B.). Hardly less significant is the distribution, having regard to its mode of life, of *Chaunax pictus*.

Bembrops caudimacula, which is undoubtedly the young of *Bembrops gobioides*, appears to be common off the West Indies and neighbouring coasts of North America at depths of 68 to 324 fathoms, and a good number of specimens have been taken in the Andaman Sea at 107 to 194 fathoms. It is a Trachinoid fish with a large flat head and a big shovel mouth, very much the form of *Platycephalus*, and is undoubtedly—like most of the members of its family—a dweller on or near the bottom. A fish that most commonly lives near the 100-fathom limit cannot be truly called bathybial, nor would anyone who has handled *Bembrops* be likely to decide that it belonged to the nectic fauna; so that some other explanation must be found for its peculiar geographical distribution. And if this explanation will also serve to throw some light on the distribution of, *e.g.*, *Lobotes surinamensis*, which is so far from being pelagic or nectic that it enters brackish water; and if it will also enable us to better understand the curious distribution, *e.g.*, of *Symbranchus*, of the *Chromides*, and of the *Cyprinodontidæ*, its probability will be enhanced.

The hypothesis that appears to offer the most satisfactory explanation is, that a very considerable part of the fish-fauna of the Oriental region originated from, and to a certain extent is a remnant of, the fauna of the Tertiary Mediterranean of Professor Suess—of a Mediterranean that extended from the present Gulf of Mexico, through the present Mediterranean basin, far into the Eastern Hemisphere.

In the *Account of the Deep Sea Madreporaria collected by the Investigator*, pp. 5–10, I have discussed some evidence in favour of this hypothesis that is afforded by certain other elements of the marine fauna; and in the *Account of the Deep Sea Brachyura collected by the Investigator*, pp. 2, 3, 82, 85, I have added some further confirmatory evidence, derived from the present distribution of

* Species marked with an asterisk have been compared with actual specimens.

certain genera and species of Crabs; so that the evidence to be adduced from the fish-fauna will already have been corroborated from several other marine groups.

It is no part of my plan, in this series of Reports, to refer to the evidence that lies outside the boundaries of the "Investigator" collections; but no one who remembers the singular distribution of certain Mammals (*e.g.* the Tapirs), Birds (*e.g.* the Trogons, Barbets, and Whistling Teal), and Amphibia (*e.g.* the *Cæciliidæ*), and no one, more especially, who has considered the geographical range of a number of Indian Snake and Lizard families and genera too numerous to mention, can have failed to have suspicions of the former existence of some land connexion (which this sea-connexion implies) between the tropical and subtropical regions of America and the Old World — suspicions which the comfortable formula "similarity of conditions" alone will not satisfy.

Moreover, as regards marine fishes, the researches of Dr. Günther have familiarized us with the idea of a former direct and open connexion between the Mediterranean and Japanese Seas (*Introd. Study of Fishes, p.* 270).

The testimony supplied by the Indian fish-fauna favourable to the hypotheses in question may be briefly summarized as follows :—

A. The Marine Fishes. The total number of genera of Indian marine fishes is about 350, of which

(1) about 28 per cent. are common to the *Atlantic*, the *Mediterranean* and the *Indo-Pacific*:

(2) nearly 6 per cent. are common to the *Atlantic*, the *Red Sea*, and the *Indo-Pacific*, to the exclusion of the Mediterranean:

(3) nearly 20 per cent. are common to the *Atlantic* and *Indo-Pacific*, to the exclusion of the Mediterranean and Red Seas:

(4) nearly 3 per cent. are common to the Mediterranean and Indo-Pacific to the exclusion of the Atlantic.

That is to say, taking the Atlantic and Mediterranean as one integral region, over 56 per cent. of the genera of Indian marine fishes are also found in that region.

Not only so, but a considerable number of *species* are common to the two regions, and although it may be argued that most of these—such as the Sword-fishes, the Pilot fish, the Tunnies, the Sucker fish, the *Sternoptychidæ*, and even certain *Clupeidæ* and *Berycidæ*—are oceanic forms of unlimited range, yet this objection cannot, I think, apply to such species as *Lobotes surinamensis*, *Bembrops caudimacula*, *Chaunax pictus*, or *Macrurus cavernosus*, or to *Sargus noct* and *Crenidens Forskalii*.

B. The Freshwater Fishes. Exclusive of certain immigrants from marine families, the freshwater fishes of India are Carps (which are nearer two-thirds than half the whole freshwater fish-fauna), *Siluridæ*, *Cyprinodontidæ*, *Chromides* and *Nandinæ, Symbranchidæ, Notopteridæ, Labyrinthici, Ophiocephalidæ, Rhynchobdellidæ.* Excluding the Carps and the *Nandinæ*, we have our attention at once attracted by certain curiosities of distribution.

For instance, in the small family of *Symbranchidæ*, we find *Symbranchus* with three species, one common in the jheels of the Oriental region, another common in tropical America. The third is from Indo-Australian waters.

Again, the *Cyprinodontidæ*, of which 2 genera and 5 species occur in India, have a most suggestive range, being found in tropical and temperate America, in tropical Africa and the regions of the Mediterranean basin, and in south-western Asia—one genus, *Cyprinodon*, being represented in India and all round the Mediterranean.

Again, the Siluroid genus *Arius* has a tropical distribution that fits in most remarkably with the theory of a tropical Mediterranean of wide extent east and west.

The same is the case with the *Chromides*, which are freshwater fishes of tropical America and Africa, and of which three species are found in India.

The other families—*Notopteridæ, Rhynchobdellidæ, Labyrinthici* and *Ophiocephalidæ*— do not extend farther to the west than Western Africa.

I may conclude this Introduction with some Tables of genera and species that are common, on the one hand to the Atlantic and Mediterranean and, on the other hand, to the seas of India. Of course many of these are widely ranging forms, and may be discounted; but, on the other hand, no mention is made of several characteristic Indo-Pacific genera that have been discovered, fossil, in the Tertiary deposits of Northern Italy, and a respectable number of forms that are common to the Atlantic, the Mediterranean and *Japan* are not included here.

I. *List of Genera and Species common to the* Atlantic, *the* Mediterranean, *and the* Indian *Fauna.*

1. Carcharias.
2. Zygæna.
i. „ blochii.
ii. „ tudes.
3. Lamna.
iii. „ spallanzanii.
4. Odontaspis.
5. Alopecias.
iv. „ vulpes.
6. Notidanus.
7. Scyllium.
8. Centrophorus.
9. Pristis.
v. „ pectinata.
vi. „ perrottoti (Atlantic *not* Med.).
10. Rhinobatis.
vii. „ halavi.
viii. „ columnae.
11. Raja.
12. Trygon.
ix. „ pastinaca.
x. „ bennettii (Atl. *not* Med.).
13. Pteroplatæa.
14. Myliobatis.
15. Rhinoptera.
16. Dicerobatis.
17. Serranus.
18. Chelidoperca.
19. Pristipoma.
xi. „ stridens (Med. *not* Atl.).

20. Lobotes.
xii. „ surinamensis.
21. Apogon.
22. Dentex.
23. Smaris.
24. Chætodon.
25. Sargus.
xiii. „ noct (Med. *not* Atl.).
26. Pagrus.
27. Chrysophrys.
28. Pimelepterus.
29. Sebastes.
30. Scorpæna.
31. Hoplostethus.
xiv. „ mediterraneum.
32. Umbrina.
33. Sciæna.
34. Sciænoides.
35. Histiophorus.
36. Trichiurus.
37. Thyrsites.
38. Caranx.
xv. „ carangus.
39. Naucrates.
xvi. „ ductor.
40. Echeneis.
xvii. „ remora.
xviii. „ naucrates.
41. Seriola.
42. Stromateus.
43. Coryphæna.
xix. „ hippurus.
44. Scomber.
45. Thynnus.
xx. „ thunnina.
xxi. „ pelamys.
46. Cybium.
47. Batrachus.
48. Lophius.
49. Trigla.
50. Peristethium.
51. Dactylopterus.
52. Gobius.
53. Callionymus.
54. Salarias.
55. Tripterygium.
56. Cepola.
57. Sphyraena.
58. Atherina.
59. Mugil.
60. Regalecus.
61. Heliastes.
62. Novacula.
63. Julis.
64. Coris.
65. Physiculus.
66 Fierasfer.
67. Ammodytes.
68. Macrurus.
69. Mystaconurus.
70. Malacocephalus.
xxii. „ lævis.
71. Arnoglossus.
72. Platophrys.
73. Solea.
74. Syngnathus.
75. Hippocampus.
xxiii. „ guttulatus.
76. Nerophis.
77. Balistes.
xxiv. „ maculatus (Atl. *not* Med.).
78. Ostracion.
xxv. „ nasus (Med. *not* Atl.).
79. Tetrodon.
80. Diodon.
xxvi. „ hystrix.
81. Orthagoriscus.
82. Argyropelecus.
xxvii. „ hemigymnus.
83. Chauliodus.
xxviii. „ sloanii.
84. Saurus.
85. Scopelus.
86. Chlorophthalmus.
87. Belone.
88. Hemiramphus.
89. Exocœtus.
xxix. „ evolans.
xxx. „ furcatus.
90. Stomias.
91. Clupea.
92. Engraulis.
93. Alepocephalus.
94. Anguilla.
95. Congromuræna.
96. Muræna.
xxxi. „ afra (Atl. *not* Med.).
97. Muraenesox.
98. Nettastoma.
99. Ophichthys.

II. *List of Additional Genera and Species common to the* ATLANTIC *the* RED SEA *and the* INDIAN *Fauna, excluding the Mediterranean.*

100. Tæniura.
101. Mesoprion.
102. Priacanthus.
103. Holacanthus.
104. Mulloides.
105. Upeneus.
106. Holocentrum.
107. Myripristis.
108. Acanthurus.
109. Opisthognathus.
110. Antennarius.
111. Periophthalmus.
112. Salarias.
113. Eleotris.
114. Glyphidodon.
115. Platyglossus.
116. Pseudoscarus.
117. Callyodon.
118. Monacanthus.
119. Albula.
xxxii. „ conorhynchus.

III. *List of Additional Genera and Species common to the* ATLANTIC *and the* INDIAN *Fauna excluding the Mediterranean.*

120. Galeocerdo.
121. Mustelus.
122. Centroscyllium.
123. Ginglymostoma.
124. Narcine.
125. Aetobatis.
xxxiii. „ narinari.
126. Dules.
127. Gerres.
128. Ephippus.
129. Lethrinus.
130. Setarches.
xxxiv. „ güntheri.
131. Trachichthys.
xxxv. „ darwinii.
132. Polymixia.
xxxvi. „ nobilis.
133. Melamphaes.
134. Bathyclupea.
135. Polynemus.
136. Otolithus.
137. Antigonia.
xxxvii. „ capros.
138. Micropteryx.
xxxviii. „ chrysurus.
139. Chorinemus.
140. Trachynotus.
xxxix. „ ovatus.
141. Psenes.
xl. „ regulus.
142. Elacate.
xli. „ nigra.
143. Malacanthus.
144. Chiasmodus.
xlii. „ niger.
145. Bembrops.
xliii. „ caudimacula.
146. Chaunax.
xliv. „ pictus.
147. Ceratias.
148. Onirodes.
149. Dibranchus.
150. Sicydium.
151. Fistularia.
152. Pomacentrus.
153. Cossyphus.
154. Bregmaceros.
155. Brotula.
156. Neobythites.
157. Dicrolene.
xlv. „ intronigra.
158. Diplacanthopoma.
xlvi. „ brachysoma.
159. Bassozetus.
160. Bathygadus.
xlvii. „ longifilis.
xlviii. Mystaconurus cavernosus.
161. Citharichthys.
162. Pseudorhombus.
163. Aphoristia.
164. Cynoglossus.
165. Doryichthys.
166. Neoscopelus.
xlix. „ macrolepidotus.
167. Bathypterois.
168. Arius.

169. Opisthopterus.
170. Raconda.
171. Chatoessus.
172. Spratelloides.
173. Elops.
l. „ saurus.
174. Pellona.
175. Megalops.
176. Sternoptyx.
li. „ diaphana.
177. Cyclothone.
lii. „ microdon.
liii. „ elongata.
178. Malacosteus.
179. Photostomias.
180. Bathytroctes.
181. Platytroctes.
liv. „ apus.
182. Xenodermichthys.
183. Leptoderma.
184. Halosaurus.
185. Nemichthys.
186. Synaphobranchus.
lv. „ pinnatus.
187. Uroconger.
lvi. „ vicinus.
188. Gymnomuræna.
lvii. Diodon maculatus.
189. Chilomycterus.

IV. *List of Genera and Species common to the* MEDITERRANEAN *and* INDIAN *Fauna, excluding the Atlantic.*

190. Lates.
191. Diagramma.
192. Crenidens.
lviii. „ forskalii.
193. Uranoscopus.
194. Lepidotrigla.
195. Cristiceps.
196. Synaptura.
197. Odontostomus.
198. Saurenchelys.

To sum up: if we estimate the number of Indian genera of marine fishes at 350, and of species at 1200, then over 56 per cent. of the genera and close on 5 per cent. of the species are also found in the Atlantic-Mediterranean region.

This does not include the Cephalochordate forms *Amphioxus* and *Asymmetron*.

Amphioxus occurs in the tropical and temperate parts of the Atlantic, in the Mediterranean, off the Indian and Ceylon coasts, and in the tropical and temperate parts of the Pacific.

Asymmetron has only been found (1) in the West Indies and (2) off the south-eastern coast of Papua. In the latter locality a species has recently been discovered by Dr. Arthur Willey, who was at once attracted by the singular fact of geographical distribution thus revealed.

List of the Indian Deep-Sea Fishes contained in the Collection of the Indian Museum.

[The references for the plates and figures are to the *Illustrations of the Zoology of the Investigator* for 1892, 1894, 1895, 1897, 1898, 1899, 1900.]

		Page.	Plate	Fig.
CHONDROPTERYGII :—				
i. Family Spinacidæ :—				
1.	*Centrophorus Rossi.*	13	XXVI	3
2.	*Centroscyllium ornatum.*	14	VIII & XXXV	2 & 1
ii. Family Scyllidæ :—				
3.	Scyllium canescens, Gthr.	16		
4.	*Scyllium hispidum.*	15	VIII	3
5.	*Scyllium quagga.*	17	XXVII	1
iii. Family Torpedinidæ :—				
6.	*Benthobatis Moresbyi.*	18	XXVI	1
iv. Family Rajidæ :—				
7.	*Raja mamillidens.*	19	VIII	1
8.	*Raja Powelli.*	20	XXVI	4
9.	*Raja Johannis-Davisi.*	21	XXVII	2
TELEOSTEI :—				
Acanthopterygii :—				
i. Family Serranidæ :—				
1.	*Chelidoperca investigatoris.*	23	X	1
2.	Synagrops philippinensis, (Gthr.).	24	XXVIII	1
3.	*Brephostoma Carpenteri.*	26	XVIII	2
ii. Family Scorpænidæ :—				
4.	Sebastes hexanema, Gthr.	27		
5.	Setarches Güntheri, Johns.	28	X	3
6.	*Pterois macrurus.*	30	XVIII	4
7.	*Minous inermis.*	30	XVIII	3
iii. Family Berycidæ :—				
8.	Monocentris japonicus, C. V.	32		
9.	Hoplostethus mediterraneum, C. V.	34	XIV	3
10.	Trachichthys Darwinii, Johns.	35		
11.	Trachichthys intermedius, Hector.	36		
12.	Melamphaes mizolepis, Gthr.	37		
13.	Polymixia nobilis, Lowe.	38		
iv. Family Kurtidæ :—				
14.	*Bathyclupea Hoskynii.*	40	XXVIII	2
v. Family Trichiuridæ :—				
15.	*Thyrsites bengalensis.*	42	XV	10
vi. Family Carangidæ :—				
16.	*Bathyseriola cyanea.*	43	XVIII	1
vii. Family Cyttidæ :—				
17.	Antigonia capros, Lowe.	44		

2

		Page.	Plate.	Fig.
12.	*Dicrolene nigricaudis.*	87 ...	II ...	4
13.	*Bassozetus glutinosus.*	88 ...	I ...	3
14.	*Dermatorus trichiurus.*	90 ...	I ...	1
15.	*Dermatorus melanocephalus.*	91 ...	XXI ...	4
16.	*Dermatorus melampeplus.*	92 ...	XVII ...	3
17.	*Glyptophidium argenteum.*	93 ...	II ...	3
18.	*Glyptophidium macropus.*	94 ...	XV ...	6
19.	*Lamprogrammus niger.*	95 ...	I ...	2
20.	*Lamprogrammus fragilis.*	96		
21.	*Tauredophidium Hextii.*	97 ...	XXI ...	3
22.	*Diplacanthopoma Rivers-Andersoni.* ...	99 ...	XVII ...	1
23.	DIPLACANTHOPOMA BRACHYSOMA, Gthr. ...	100 ...	XVII ...	2
24.	*Diplacanthopoma raniceps.*	101 ...	XXVI ...	2
25.	*Saccogaster maculata.*	102 ...	XXIX ...	2
26.	*Hephthocara simum.*	103 ...	XXII ...	3
iii.	Family Macruridæ :—			
27.	MACRURUS PARALLELUS, Gthr.	106		
28.	*Macrurus quadricristatus.*	106 ...	III ...	1
29.	*Macrurus flabellispinis.*	107 ...	XVI ...	2
30.	*Macrurus investigatoris.*	109 ...	III ...	4
31.	*Macrurus Petersonii.*	110 ...	III ...	5
32.	MACRURUS NASUTUS, Gthr.	111 ...	XIII ...	3
33.	*Macrurus semiquincunciatus.*	111 ...	XII ...	2
34.	*Macrurus polylepis.*	112 ...	XXIX ...	4
35.	*Macrurus pumiliceps.*	113 ...	XVI ...	3
36.	*Macrurus Hextii.*	113 ...	XII ...	3
37.	*Macrurus Wood-Masoni.*	114 ...	XIII ...	1
38.	*Macrurus macrolophus.* ...	115 ...	XII ...	1
39.	*Macrurus lophotes.*	116 ...	III ...	2
40.	*Macrurus Hoskynii.*	116 ...	IX ...	4
41.	MACRURUS CAVERNOSUS, G. & B. ...	117 ...	III ...	3
42.	MACRURUS LÆVIS, Lowe.	119		
43.	BATHYGADUS LONGIFILIS, G. & B. ...	120		
44.	*Bathygadus furvescens.*	121 ...	XVI	1
iv.	Family Ateleopodidæ :—			
45.	*Ateleopus indicus.*	123 ...	II ...	2
v.	Family Pleuronectidæ :—			
46.	*Chascanopsetta lugubris.*	125 ...	XV ...	3
47.	*Boopsetta prælonga.*	126 ...	XV & XVII ...	2 & 5
48.	*Boopsetta maculosa.*	127 ...	XV ...	1
49.	*Læops macrophthalmus.* ...	128 ...	XXIII ...	1
50.	*Solea umbratilis.*	129 ...	XV ...	4
51.	*Aphoristia Gilesii.*	131 ...	XIV	4
52.	*Aphoristia Wood-Masoni.*	131 ...	XVI	4
53.	*Aphoristia septemstriata.*	132 ...	II	1
54.	*Aphoristia trifasciata.* ...	133 ...	XV	5
55.	*Cynoglossus Carpenteri.* ...	133 ...	XXII	5

N. B.—The species of *Astronesthes* was mislaid among some specimens of Shore Fishes, and was only discovered after the text relating to the Stomiatidæ had been printed off.

Explanation of the Chart.

The Chart has been compiled from Plate II of Dr. Ernst Koken's *Die Vorwelt und ihre Entwickelungsgeschichte*, and shows the supposed coast-lines of the Tertiary Continents.

The present coast-lines are indicated by dotted lines.

The supposed Tertiary coast-lines of Koken are indicated by thick black lines.

The Great Inland Sea, stretching from the present Gulf of Mexico to the present Arabian Sea, is coloured dark blue.

The Chart is meant to elucidate the theory advanced in the text as to the origin of a considerable part of the Fish Fauna of India, especially that of the Oligobenthus.

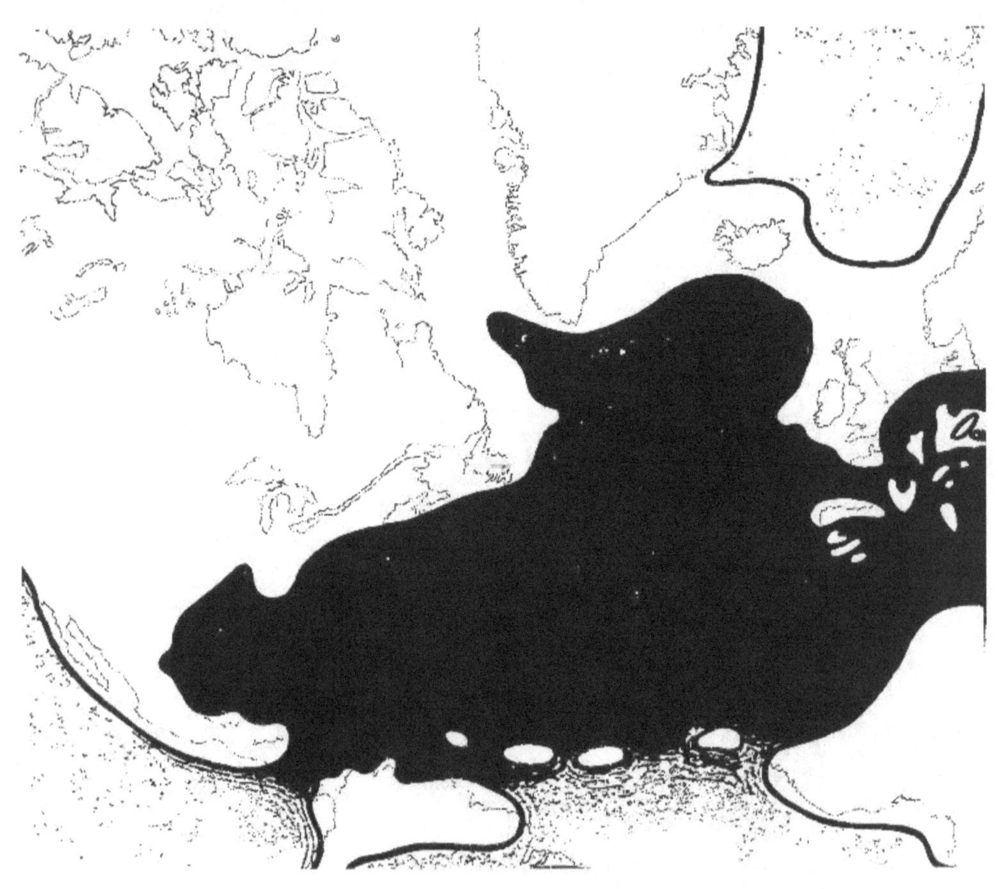

Sub-class CHONDROPTERYGII.

Order PLAGIOSTOMATA.

Sub-order SELACHOIDEI.

In the Fauna of British India, Fishes, Vol. I. p. 6, five families of Sharks are recorded for the seas of India, namely, *Carchariidæ, Lamnidæ, Rhinodontidæ, Notidanidæ, Scylliidæ.*

A sixth family, *Spinacidæ*, with two genera, has been discovered by the "Investigator" to be also represented.

Family *Spinacidæ*.

"Two dorsal fins: no anal. Mouth but slightly arched; a long deep "straight oblique groove on each side of the mouth. Spiracles present: "gill-openings narrow. Pectoral fins not notched at their origin. No nic-"titating membrane." *(Günther)*.

Key to the Indian genera of the family Spinacidæ.

Each dorsal fin with a spine: no lateral folds of skin along the belly:—

1. Upper teeth erect, with a single cusp: lower teeth oblique ... ... CENTROPHORUS.
2. Teeth equal in both jaws, very small, tricuspid ... CENTROSCYLLIUM.

CENTROPHORUS, Müller and Henle.

Centrophorus, Müller and Henle, Plagiostomen, p. 88: Günther, Catalogue of Fishes, VIII. 419 (*et synon.*).

"Two dorsal fins, each with a spine which is sometimes hidden below the "skin: no anal fin. Trunk elongate without lateral folds. Mouth wide, but "slightly arched: a long deep straight oblique groove on each side of the mouth. "Teeth of the lower jaw with the point more or less inclined backwards or out-"wards. Upper teeth erect, triangular or narrow-lanceolate, with a single cusp. "No membrana nictitans. Spiracles wide, behind the eye. Gill-openings narrow." (*Günther*).

1. *Centrophorus Rossi*, Alcock.

Centrophorus Rossi, Alcock, Ann. Mag. Nat. Hist. August, 1898, p. 143: ILLUSTRATIONS OF THE ZOOLOGY OF THE INVESTIGATOR, FISHES, PLATE XXVI. FIG 3.

Snout spathulate, much produced, its length measured from the most convex part of the upper jaw is one-eighth of the total, or more than $2\frac{1}{2}$ times the inter-narial space, or about three times the major diameter of the eye-ball. The nostrils, though completely ventral, cause a distinct notching of the margin of the snout seen from above.

Mouth crescent-shaped, considerably protractile, the distance between its angles is about two-thirds the length of the snout. The labial fold extends rather more than half-way between the angle of the mouth and the middle of the lower jaw.

Teeth of the upper jaw acute, triangular, in two series: those of the lower jaw very oblique, in a single series.

The posterior borders of all the fins are frayed or fringed, this not being due to abrasion. The angle of the pectoral is rounded; the extremity of the ventral is almost in the perpendicular with the after limit of the base of the second dorsal. The dorsal spines (measured obliquely as they stand) are not much more than half the greatest height of their fins, but their points project well beyond the skin; the second dorsal is a little larger than the first.

Scales minute, acutely and very elegantly tridentate, or anchor-shaped.

Colour uniform jet-black.

A single specimen, 10 inches long, from off the Travancore coast, 430 fath. Regd. No. $\frac{225}{1}$.

Named in memory of Captain Daniel Ross, who, according to Sir Clements Markham, was the first Indian "Marine Surveyor-General" (1823–1833) to introduce a really scientific method into marine surveying in India.

This species is closely related to the *Centrophorus calceus* Lowe and the *Centrophorus obscurus* Vaillant of the Atlantic-Mediterranean gate and to the *Centrophorus foliaceus* of the Japanese Sea.

CENTROSCYLLIUM, Müller and Henle.

Centroscyllium, Müller and Henle, Plagiostomen, p. 191: Günther Catalogue of Fishes, VIII. 425: Jordan and Evermann, Fishes of North and Middle America, I. p. 56: Goode and Bean, Oceanic Ichthyology, p. 11.

Paracentroscyllium, Alcock, Ann. Mag. Nat. Hist. Nov. 1889, p. 379.

"Two dorsal fins, each with a strong spine: no anal fin. Mouth crescent-"shaped: a straight oblique groove at each angle of the mouth. Teeth equal "in both jaws, very small, tricuspid. No membrana nictitans. Spiracles of "moderate width. Gill-openings rather narrow." (*Günther*).

Centroscyllium contains three species, *Centroscyllium fabricii* from Greenland, North America and the coast of "Sahara," *Centroscyllium granulatum* from the Falkland Is., and *Centroscyllium ornatum* from the Arabian Sea and Bay of Bengal, 690–620 and 405–285 fathoms.

2. ***Centroscyllium ornatum***, Alcock.

Paracentroscyllium ornatum, Alcock, Ann. Mag. Nat. Hist. Nov. 1889, p. 379: ILLUSTRATIONS OF THE ZOOLOGY OF THE INVESTIGATOR, FISHES, PL. VIII. FIG. 2 (young), pl. XXXV. fig. 1.

Centroscyllium ornatum, Alcock, Journ. As. Soc. Bengal, Vol. LXV. pt 2, 1896, pp. 308, 310.

All the tissues extremely fragile.

Head very large, very flat and depressed, branchial regions laterally expanded.

Snout much depressed, somewhat polygonal in outline: nostrils very large, situated on ventral surface of edge of snout. Under surface of snout with numerous rather large pores, two rows of which form an elegant Y- or V-shaped figure that extends between the nostrils.

Eyes very large, their major diameter four-fifths as long as the snout measured from the mouth, and a fifth the length of the head (branchial region included).

Spiracles rather small, about a third the major diameter of the eye, situated on the upper surface of the head, behind the eye.

Mouth crescentic, large, the distance between its angles being as long as, or slightly longer than the snout: minute tricuspid teeth in both jaws.

Body covered with minute extremely deciduous placoid scales, the spine of each scale with a stelliform base.

Dorsal spines very strong and acute, the 2nd nearly twice the size of the 1st. The 1st dorsal fin arises in advance of a point midway between the pectorals and ventrals, the 2nd arises immediately behind the level of the base of the ventrals.

Colours uniform jet-black, but the integument is very deciduous. In young specimens the hue is "deep violet black, lighter between the eyes; head with minute white spots arranged in the shape of a lute; ventrals with pale tips."

Bay of Bengal 405–285 fathoms: Arabian Sea 690–620 fathoms.

Regd. Nos. 11664, 11666: $\frac{64}{1}$ to $\frac{67}{1}$.

Family *Scylliidæ.*

SCYLLIUM, Cuv., M. & H.

3. *Scyllium hispidum*, Alcock.

Scyllium hispidum, Alcock, Ann. Mag. Nat. Hist., July, 1891, p. 21: ILLUSTRATIONS OF THE ZOOLOGY OF THE INVESTIGATOR, FISHES, PL. VIII. FIGS. 3, 3a.

Head broad and depressed. Snout flat, semicircular in outline, its length, measured from the convexity of the upper jaw, is half its greatest breadth and twice the width of the inter-narial space. Nasal valves separated by an interval almost equal to the maximum diameter of the nostril: each has a very short cirrus.

Eyeballs large, their major diameter being between two-thirds and three-quarters the length of the snout (measured as above).

Spiracles very small, their diameter less than half that of the pupil, situated immediately behind and below the eye.

Mouth large crescentic, a short labial fold at the angles only. Teeth in broadish bands in both jaws, small, mostly tricuspid (sometimes 5-cuspid) the middle cusp much the largest. Surface of palate and of tongue papillated.

The entire surface of the skin closely covered with minute stony tricuspid spines.

The first dorsal fin, which arises just ahead of the vertical through the after end of the base of the ventrals, is larger than the second, which is about opposite the anal: the base of the anal is about twice as long as that of either dorsal. The pectorals are at least twice as big as the ventrals, and the latter have a very oblique posterior margin.

Colours: dull stone-grey, rather lighter ventrally.

Andaman Sea, 188–220 fathoms, 185 fathoms, 370–419 fathoms, and 405 fathoms.

The largest specimen is a female 11 inches long.

Regd. Nos. 13120 type of male: $\frac{112}{1}$ type of female: $\frac{226}{1}$: $\frac{228}{1}$ – $\frac{231}{1}$: $\frac{382}{1}$ – $\frac{385}{1}$.

4. *Scyllium canescens*, Günther.

Scyllium canescens, Günther, Ann. Mag. Nat. Hist. (5) II. 1878, p. 18: Challenger Deep Sea Fishes, p. 1, pl. i., fig. A: Alcock, J. A. S. B., Vol. LXV., pt. 2, 1896, p. 310.

Differs from *S. hispidum*, if my identification be correct, in the following particulars:—

(1) the snout is slightly longer, relatively:

(2) the eye is slightly smaller:

(3) the labial folds at the angles of the mouth are slightly larger:

(4) teeth tricuspid, *the cusps subequal:*

(5) the body is covered with *simple stiff prickles:*

(6) the fins have much the same position, but the second dorsal is slightly larger than the first, and the base of the anal is not so extensive.

Colours in spirit blackish with a hoary gray surface. Some of the fins, as in some specimens of *Scyllium hispidum*, may be tipped with white behind.

A single small specimen from the Arabian Sea, 690–620 fathoms.

Regd. No. $\frac{68}{1}$.

[The type of this species was dredged by the Challenger, off the south-western coast of S. America at a depth of 400 fathoms.]

Distribution. Patagonian fjords: Arabian Sea: at considerable depths.

5. *Scyllium quagga*, n. sp.

ILLUSTRATIONS OF THE ZOOLOGY OF THE INVESTIGATOR, FISHES, PL. XXVII. FIG. 1.

Head broad, depressed. Snout flat, elliptical in outline with a bluntly acuminate tip; its length, measured from the convexity of the upper jaw is half its greatest breadth.

Nasal valves separated by an interval the width of which is rather more than two-fifths the length of the snout: each with a very short and inconspicuous cirrus.

Eyes large, their major diameter rather over two-thirds the length of the snout.

Spiracles small, their diameter about equal to that of the pupil; situated immediately behind and below the eye.

Mouth large, crescentic; a short labial fold at the angles only. Teeth in both jaws tricuspid, the middle cusp much the longest and most acute.

Body everywhere covered with minute scales, which are tricuspid or anchor-shaped, except on the throat and belly, where they are granular.

The dorsal fins are not very unequal: the first arises just in front of the vertical through the after end of the base of the ventrals: the second arises just in advance of the vertical through the after end of the anal.

Base of anal a little longer than that of either of the dorsals, between a half and two-thirds the length of the interval between itself and the caudal.

Posterior margin of ventrals very oblique.

Colours in spirit: very numerous well-defined alternate cross-bands of light and very dark brown, from snout to tip of tail, not passing on to ventral surface: the cross-bands are rather irregular in breadth, but the dark ones are usually the narrowest. The dark cross-bands are not broken up into spots, but are continuous stripes, and the light cross-bands are unspotted.

An apparently adult male is 11 inches long.

Off Malabar coast, 102 fathoms.

Regd. No. $\frac{751}{1}$.

This species comes nearest to *S. Bürgeri* M. & H.

Suborder BATOIDEI.

Family *Torpedinidæ.*

BENTHOBATIS, Alcock.

Benthobatis, Alcock, Ann. Mag. Nat. Hist. August, 1898, p. 144.

The whole animal invested in a loose, soft, naked, glandular skin.

Tail very distinct from the oval disk and *without distinct lateral folds*. Two dorsal fins on the tail; caudal fin well developed.

Nasal valves confluent into a quadrangular curtain.

Teeth flat, rhomboidal, with the posterior angle acutely produced.

Spiracles large, situated immediately behind the *inconspicuous and quite rudimentary eyes.*

A large electric organ between the head and either pectoral fin.

This curious blind torpedo differs from all other members of the family in having the eyes quite rudimentary and in the absence of lateral folds of skin on the tail. In general form it resembles *Narcine*, though the disk is not quite so broad. The teeth, like those of *Discopyge*, have the posterior angle produced, but more acutely than in *Discopyge*, judging from Tschudi's figure.

6. ***Benthobatis Moresbyi***, Alcock.

Benthobatis Moresbyi, Alcock, Ann. Mag. Nat. Hist. August, 1898, p. 145: Illustrations of the Zoology of the Investigator, Fishes, pl. XXVI. fig. 1.

The disk is oval, its long axis, which is fore and aft, is a little shorter than the tail: more than a third of its extent is pre-oral.

The eyes are represented by two small unpigmented spots, each not much bigger than the head of a pin, situated one in front of either spiracle; a slender optic nerve passes to each, and expands into a vesicle so small as to need a lens for its recognition.

The mouth is small and protractile; the teeth are small rhomboidal plates, with the posterior angle strongly and acutely produced, and are arranged in mosaic in about ten very oblique series in either jaw.

The gill-openings are large and well-spaced: the posterior one is nearer to the cloacal opening than to the mouth.

The dorsal fins are placed rather close together, the first being a little in front of the posterior limit of the ventrals, and, like the caudal, are thick and fleshy. The ventrals are of the usual shape; though they are separate, the skin between them is loose and copious. The whole animal is covered with a perfectly smooth, soft, glandular, purplish-black skin; scattered on the disk and round the edge of it are some small white pores, not much smaller than the eyes; in one specimen part of the tips of the second dorsal and caudal fins are white.

Two males (each about 14 inches long) and a young one, from off the Travancore coast, 430 fath.

Regd. Nos. $\frac{232}{1}$: $\frac{234}{1}$.

Named in memory of Capt. Moresby, of the Indian Navy, whose surveys (1834–38) in the seas where this curious fish is found are known to all readers of Darwin's 'Coral-Reefs.'

Family *Rajidæ.*

Raja, (Artedi) Cuvier.

Raja, Cuvier, Règne Animal, Poissons, p. 375.

Raja and *Uraptera*, Müller and Henle, Plagiostomen, pp. 132, 155.

Raja, Günther Catalogue of Fishes, VIII. 455.

Raja, Jordan and Evermann, Fishes of North and Middle America (Bull. U. S. Nat. Mus. No. 47, 1896) I. p. 66: Goode and Bean, Oceanic Ichthyology, p. 24.

"Tail very distinct from the disk, which is of rhombic shape, with a fold on "each side. Body generally rough or with spines, rarely entirely smooth. Two "dorsal fins, on the tail, without spine. Tail with a rudimentary caudal fin, or "without caudal. Each ventral fin divided into two by a deep notch. Nasal "valves separated in the middle, where they are without a free margin. Teeth "obtuse or pointed. Pectoral fins not extending forward to the extremity of the "snout. Sexes differing in the form of the teeth and in the dorsal spines."

(*Günther*).

Synopsis of the Indian species of Raja.

I. Snout short, slightly exsert: upper surface of disk covered with prickles, in addition to definitely placed spines: a single row of large spines on middle line of back and tail: dorsal fins very close together ... ... *R. mamillidens.*

II. Snout much exsert: upper surface of disk with definitely placed spines, but with few or no prickles: dorsal fins well separated :—

1. Snout, measured from mouth, about two-sevenths the greatest breadth of the disk in length: a short row of spines in the middle line of the nape, and several rows on the tail ... *R. Powelli.*

2. Snout, measured from mouth, about a third the greatest breadth of the disk in length: a single spine in the middle line of the nape: a single row of spines on the tail ... ... *R. Johannis-Davisi.*

7. *Raja mamillidens*, Alcock.

Raja mamillidens, Alcock, Ann. Mag. Nat. Hist. November 1889, p. 380: Illustrations of the Zoology of the Investigator, Fishes, plate VIII, fig. 1.

The disk, including the ventral fins, is about half the total length and its breadth is about the same: it is rhomboidal in shape, with the angles rounded: the anterior margin of the pectoral fin is slightly and broadly sinuous.

The snout is short, broad, and only slightly exsert, its length, measured from the mouth or from the eye, is not quite a fourth the greatest breadth of the disk, and is a little more than the distance between the outer margins of the nostrils.

Major diameter of orbit equal to the width of the inter-orbital space and much more than that of the spiracle.

Mouth crescentic. Teeth, in the female, having a globular base and a mamillary point: in twenty-four oblique rows in the upper and eighteen in the lower jaw.

The whole of the upper surface of the disk (including the ventral fins) and tail, and all the surfaces of the posterior half of the tail (including the dorsal and rudimentary caudal fins) are covered with small sharp close-set prickles: under surface of disk smooth and glandular.

A large spine at either angle of either orbit, and a pair of spines between the spiracles: one or two on each shoulder girdle, and a single row down the middle of the back from the occiput nearly to the first dorsal fin.

Dorsal fins adjacent but separate, the posterior the larger.

Colour in life—uniform jet black: in spirit, dark chocolate.

A single female specimen, 11½ inches long, from the Gulf of Manár, 597 fathoms.

Regd. No. 11769.

Apparently allied to the Mediterranean *Raja atrata*, M. & H.

8. *Raja Powelli*, Alcock.

Raja Powelli, Alcock, Ann. Mag. Nat. Hist., August, 1898, p. 145: Illustrations of the Zoology of the Investigator, Fishes, pl. XXVI. fig. 4.

The disk without the ventral fins is nearly half the total length, and its breadth is equal to its length with the ventrals: it is rhomboidal with the angles, except the rostral, rounded: the anterior margin of the pectoral fin is broadly sinuous.

The snout is rather slender and much exsert: its length, measured from the mouth, is two-sevenths the greatest breadth of the disk and is nearly half again as much as the distance between the outer margins of the nostrils.

Major diameter of orbit hardly equal to the width of the inter-orbital space, but considerably more than that of the spiracle.

Teeth in the female obtusely pointed or obscurely tricuspid; in about 55 transverse rows in either jaw. Mouth straight.

Both surfaces of the disk are smooth, except for some prickles near the edge of the snout and the edge of the anterior half of the pectoral fins.

Two or three spines on the anterior edge of the orbit and one near either postorbital angle: three in the middle line of the nape. Two or three series of spines extend from the hinder fourth of the disk to the first dorsal fin, there is a single short series between the dorsal fins, and the sides of the tail from end to end are thorny.

The distance between the two dorsal fins is greater than the length of either: the first dorsal is the higher, the second, which is confluent with the rudimentary caudal, is the longer.

Colours: upper surface warm brown with a pair of large ocelli behind the shoulder girdle: under surface dirty white.

A single female $12\frac{1}{2}$ inches long from the Gulf of Martaban 67 fathoms.

Regd. No. $\frac{235}{1}$.

Apparently allied to the Kerguelen *Raja murrayi*, Gthr.

Named after Lieutenant Powell of the Indian Navy: a colleague, in the old Marine Survey branch of the service, of Captain Moresby.

9. *Raja Johannis-Davisi*, n. sp.

ILLUSTRATIONS OF THE ZOOLOGY OF THE INVESTIGATOR, PL. XXVII, FIG. 2.

The disk without the ventral fins is nearly half the total length, and its breadth is much more than its length with the ventrals: it is rhomboidal with the angles, except the rostral, rounded, and with the two anterior sides much longer than the other two: the anterior margin of the pectoral fin is broadly sinuous.

Snout slender and much exsert: its length, measured from the mouth, is close on a third the greatest breadth of the singularly broad disk and is $1\frac{3}{4}$ times the distance between the outer margins of the nostrils.

Major diameter of orbit equal to the width of the interorbital space and nearly twice that of the spiracle.

Mouth straight: teeth obtusely pointed (male) in about 32 very oblique rows in the upper, and about 30 in the lower jaw.

Both surfaces of disk smooth, except for some star-shaped prickles on the ventral surface of the rostral cartilage and of the edges of the snout and adjacent part of the pectoral fins.

Two strong spines on the anterior margin and one at the posterior angle of either orbit: a very strong spine in the middle of the nape. An eminence but not a distinct spine on either side of shoulder and pelvic girdles. Tail smooth except for a mid-dorsal row of large spines which extend from its base to the second dorsal fin.

The distance between the two dorsal fins is rather more than half the length of the base of either: the two fins are of about equal size and the second is confluent with the caudal.

Colours: smoky black above, black mottled with white below.

A single male 8¼ inches long from off the Travancore coast 224–284 fathoms.

Regd. No. $\frac{477}{1}$.

Near the Mediterranean *Raja oxyrhynchus* L. Named after the celebrated Elizabethan navigator and explorer John Davis, who—though best known for his Arctic voyages—piloted three expeditions to the East Indies and lost his life in Indian seas.

Besides the Sharks and Rays just described, there is evidence of the existence of other species in the depths of these seas:—

(1) Off the Travancore coast, in 824 fathoms, an egg, with a very early embryo, of some gigantic species of, probably, *Raja* was dredged.

(2) Off the western coast of the Andamans, in 561 fathoms, an empty egg-capsule of, probably, *Callorhynchus* was taken.

(3) Off the Godavari Delta, in 410 fathoms, an empty egg-capsule of, probably, *Chimæra* was obtained.

Sub-class TELEOSTOMI.

Order Teleostei.

Sub-order Acanthopterygii.

Family *Serranidæ.*

Chelidoperca, Boulenger.

Chelidoperca, Boulenger, Catalogue of the Perciform Fishes in the British Museum, I. p. 304.

"Body compressed; scales rather large, rough and ciliated. Lateral line "complete, the tube with ascending tubule. Mouth large, protractile; maxil- "lary exposed; jaws with bands of villiform teeth, a few of the inner ones in "the middle of the upper jaw enlarged, depressible, hinged at the base; teeth "on vomer and palatines; tongue smooth. Head partly scaled; pre-opercle "serrated, without antrorse teeth on the lower border; opercle with two spines. "Gill-membranes separate; seven branchiostegals; pseudobranchiæ present; "gill-rakers rather long. Dorsal fins confluent, with X. 10 rays, the spinous "and soft portions subequal in length. Anal short with III. 6 rays. Pectorals "subsymmetrical, obtusely pointed, (with 17 rays).* Ventrals anterior to base "of pectorals, close together, with a strong spine. Posterior process of "premaxillaries not extending to the frontals; supra-occipital and parietal crests "short, smooth area of cranium extending posteriorly to a line connecting the "preopercular portions" (*Boulenger*).

* In the single Indian species the pectoral fin rays are 14 or 15 in number.

10. *Chelidoperca investigatoris,* (Alcock).

Centropristis investigatoris, Alcock, Ann. Mag. Nat. Hist., September, 1890, p. 109: ILLUSTRATIONS OF THE ZOOLOGY OF THE INVESTIGATOR, FISHES, PL. X. FIG. 1.

Chelidoperca investigatoris, Boulenger, Cat. Perciform Fishes, I. p. 305.

B. 7. D. X. 10. A. III. 6. L. lat. 42. L. tr $\frac{2\frac{1}{2}}{\frac{1}{10}}$.

Dorsal and ventral profiles quite symmetrical.

Height of the body between $3\frac{1}{2}$ and $3\frac{2}{3}$, length of the head, from the tip of the lower jaw to the tip of the operculum about $2\frac{1}{16}$, in the total, without caudal.

Head inclined to depression in its anterior half, deep, broad, and inflated in its branchial region, with the operculum prolonged; scaly, except on the snout and upper jaw.

Snout depressed, rounded; its tip formed by a prominent median knob on the projecting lower jaw; its extreme length (including the mandibular element) is equal to the major diameter of the eye and is less than its breadth.

Eyes in their long diameter $4\frac{2}{3}$ in the head-length; the upper border of the orbit enters the dorsal profile; the breadth of the interorbital space is one-third the length of the eye. Nostrils superior.

Mouth wide, oblique; jaws strong, the maxilla reaches the vertical through the posterior border of the orbit, the mandible closes outside the maxilla; teeth in villiform bands in the premaxilla and palatines and in a small patch on the vomer; small canines in the mandible and at the maxillary symphysis; tongue long and spathulate.

Gill-opening very wide; operculum with two flat spines; preopercular border rounded and serrated throughout; sub- and interoperculum large; pseudobranchiæ coarse; gill-rakers tuberculate.

Scales, except on the lateral line and in the row flanking the dorsal fin, large; finely ctenoid, except on the operculum; eight series on the cheek. Lateral line salient, with very small scales.

One dorsal, with its spinous and soft portions of equal extent, the fourth and fifth spines the greatest and one-fourth longer than the eye; the rays slightly increasing in length to the ninth, which is less than two-thirds of the maximum body-height and shorter than the corresponding anal ray. Caudal emarginate, with the upper lobe the longer, its basal half scaly; its length is about equal to that of the pectoral, which is rather longer than the postorbital portion of the head. Ventrals subjugular, the second ray almost as long as the pectoral fin.

Pyloric cæca few. Air-bladder small.

Colours in life :—Head and body bright pink, belly and throat white; a broad bright yellow band passes from the tip of the snout through the eye to the caudal fin; indefinite bright yellow markings on the cheeks, opercles, and fins. In spirit, faded yellow, with four incomplete cross bands of grey.

Total length $5\frac{1}{8}$ inches.

Two specimens from off the Ganjam coast, 98–102 fathoms.

Regd. No. 12820, 12821.

SYNAGROPS, Günther.

Synagrops, Günther, Challenger Deep-Sea Fishes, p. 16.
Melanostoma, Döderlein, Denk. Akad. Wien, XLVIII. 1884, p. 5 *(name pre-occupied)*.
Parascombrops, Alcock, Journ. As. Soc. Bengal, Vol. LVIII. pt. 2, 1889, p. 296.
Hypoclydonia, Goode & Bean, Oceanic Ichthyology, p. 236.

Body rather elongate, covered with large, thin, deciduous, cycloid scales. Muciferous cavities of the vertex of the head well developed. Seven branchiostegals: pseudobranchiæ present: edge of preoperculum more or less serrated: operculum with two weak points. Villiform teeth in (usually) narrow bands on the jaws vomer and palatines, with the addition of a pair of large canines in the upper jaw and an irregular row of canines in the lower jaw. Two separate dorsal fins, the first with nine slender spines: anal fin with two spines. An air-bladder. Pyloric cæca in small number.

This genus may probably prove to be identical with *Acropoma* Temm. and Schleg.

11. ***Synagrops philippinensis***, (Günther).

Acropoma philippinense, Günther, Challenger Shore Fishes, p. 51: Alcock, Journ. As. Soc. Bengal, Vol. LXII. pt. 2, 1894, p. 116.
Parascombrops pellucida, Alcock, Journ. As. Soc. Bengal, Vol. LVIII. pt. 2, 1889, p. 296, pl. xxii. fig. 1.
? *Melanostoma argyreum*, Gilbert and Cramer, Proc. U. S. Nat. Mus. Vol. XIX. 1896, p. 416, pl. xxxix. fig. 3.
Synagrops philippinensis, ILLUSTRATIONS OF THE ZOOLOGY OF THE INVESTIGATOR, FISHES, PL. XXVIII. FIG. 1.

B. 7. D. IX. I-9. A. II. 7. L. lat. *circ.* 28.

Body compressed, its greatest height between $3\frac{1}{3}$ and $3\frac{1}{2}$ in the total without the caudal.

Head, measured from the tip of the underhung lower jaw to the tip of the semimembranous prolongation of the opercle, $2\frac{1}{2}$ in the total without the caudal, compressed, the muciferous cavities of its vertex well developed and bounded by numerous low sharp crests, most of which are oblique: in the skin covering the vertex of the head numerous tiny scales are embedded and almost concealed.

Snout short, a large part of it is formed by the prominent lower jaw: its length, including the mandibular element, is less than that of the eye.

Eye of good size, its major diameter is equal to the depth of the caudal peduncle or to two-sevenths of the greatest body height, and is rather more than the greatest width of the inter-orbital space.

Mouth-cleft wide, very oblique; the maxilla reaching a little behind the middle of the pupil; the mandibles peculiarly emarginate on either side of the symphysis. Villiform teeth on premaxillæ, vomer, palatines and anterior part of lower jaw; in addition there is a pair of large canines at the symphysis of the upper jaw and a row of irregular (large and small) canines in the lower jaw, one of them being at the symphysis.

Gill-cleft wide: numerous gill-rakers, the longest of which are nearly two-thirds the major diameter of the eye, on the first branchial arch. Pseudobranchiæ large.

Preoperculum with a double border, the angle and the lower limb of the outer border strongly serrated, the angle of the inner border with three small spines. Operculum naked, with two weak points. Sub-operculum much prolonged behind the angle of the operculum.

Scales cycloid, large, very thin, extremely deciduous.

The dorsal fins are separated by an interspace equal to three-fourths the length of the eye: the spinous is considerably the higher: the 1st spine is small, the 3rd is the longest and is equal to two-thirds of the body height, the 4th is nearly as long. The 1st anal spine is short, the 2nd as long as the eye. Caudal forked almost to its base, forming two distinct lobes. Pectoral delicate; its length equals the distance from the tip of the snout to the anterior pre-opercular edge. Ventral long, reaching two-thirds of the distance to the anal: its spine is long, and has its outer edge closely sharply and evenly serrated.

Colours in life, transparent light brown suffused with pink from the blood-vessels: opercular and visceral regions like burnished silver.

The intestine is long and much coiled; and there are five very large pyloric cæca.

A small fish: adults of both sexes measure from 3 to 4 inches.

Common in the Bay of Bengal between 60 and 102 fathoms, also found between 145 and 250 fathoms.

Regd. Nos. 11829: 12437: 12720: 12723 *a–j*: 12856 *a–b*: 12857 *a–q*: 13503–13508, 13510.

I cannot see any difference between this and the species described and figured by Gilbert and Cramer under the name of *Melanostoma argyreum*.

Distribution. Bay of Bengal: East Indian Archipelago: (Hawaii).

4

BREPHOSTOMA, Alcock.

Brephostoma, Alcock, Ann. Mag. Nat. Hist., Nov., 1889, p. 383, and September, 1890, p. 201.

Head-bones and opercles unarmed; preoperculum with a double edge. Mouth edentulous. Eyes large. Two separate dorsal fins, the first with five spines. Anal fin with one spine and similar to second dorsal. Scales large, adherent, ctenoid. Seven branchiostegals. Pseudobranchiæ present. Pyloric cæca in moderate number. No air-bladder.

Its nearest relative is *Pomatomus*.

12. *Brephostoma Carpenteri*, Alcock.

Brephostoma carpenteri, Alcock, Ann. Mag. Nat. Hist., Nov. 1889, p. 383, and Sept. 1890, p. 201, pl. ix. fig. 4: ILLUSTRATIONS OF THE ZOOLOGY OF THE R. I. M. S. INVESTIGATOR, FISHES, PL. XVIII. FIG. 2.

B. 7. D. V. I. 10. A. I. 9. L. lat. 32–36. L. tr. $\frac{2}{\frac{1}{9}}$.

Body elongate, compressed, its greatest height slightly over one-fourth the total length without the caudal.

Head one-third the total length without the caudal, for the most part covered with somewhat deciduous scales.

Snout broadish and somewhat depressed, its tip formed by the symphysis of the lower jaw: its length, including the mandibular element, is about two-thirds the major diameter of the eye.

Eyes large, their major diameter more than a third the length of the head and about twice the breadth of the inter-orbital space: supra-orbital margin in the dorsal profile.

Mouth oblique; the upper jaw, which is much concealed by the extensive pre-orbitals, hardly reaching to the pupil; the lower jaw, the rami of which are very broad, closes inside the upper jaw except at the symphysis. No teeth. Tongue free, broad.

Gill-opening very wide, the bones of the gill-cover, like those of the face and jaws, thin and weak—almost membranous, quite unarmed; the preoperculum with a double edge. Gill-rakers of the outer side of the first arch long, close-set,—the longest being nearly half the length of the eye. Pseudobranchiæ large.

Scales strong, thick, very adherent, imbricate, the exposed surface studded with spines as in most species of *Macrurus*. The scales of the head, though otherwise similar to those on the body, are somewhat deciduous. Lateral line in the form of simple tubes with large round patent orifice: it extends half-way along the caudal fin.

Dorsal fins separated by a snout-length, the second much the higher; the first has five stout sharp spines, the three anterior a little longer than the snout; the second has one short spine and ten branched rays, and is invested at its base with scales. Anal with one spine and nine branched rays, situated opposite the second dorsal, and similar to it in every respect. Caudal short, forked; its proximal half scaly. Pectorals well developed, as long as the head without the snout. Ventrals thoracic, with one spine and five rays with scaly bases.

No air-bladder. Long pyloric cæca in moderate number. Colours in life, uniform jet-black.

A single specimen, 4 inches long, from Carpenter's Ridge (Lat. 6° 18′ to 16′ N., long. 90° 40′ to 44′ E.) 1370 to 1520 fathoms.

Regd. No. 12472.

Named after Captain Alfred Carpenter, R.N., D.S.O., Superintendent of the Indian Marine Survey from 1884 to 1889, who practically initiated, and who greatly developed, the deep-sea dredging operations of the "Investigator."

Family *Scorpænidæ.*

SEBASTES, Cuv. & Val.

13. *Sebastes hexanema*, Günther.

Sebastes hexanema, Günther, Challenger Shore Fishes, pl. xvii. fig. B, and Challenger Deep-Sea Fishes, p. 18: Alcock, Ann. Mag. Nat. Hist., July 1891, p. 23.

D. XI. I–9. A. III–5. Sc. *circ.* 53.

Height of the body about one-third, length of the head nearly half, the total length without the caudal.

Snout produced, its length is not quite equal to the major diameter of the eye, which is about two-sevenths the length of the head, and more than twice the width of the inter-orbital space (in young specimens).

Vertex of head with prominent spines and small scales and with three pairs of simple tentacles of good length—one at the anterior angles of the orbits, one above the middle of the eyes, and a third on the nape. (There are other small tentacles along the preopercular stay and along the lateral line, but they are liable to be lost by abrasion).

Mouth-cleft wide, the maxilla reaching nearly to the middle of the eye. Villiform teeth in the jaws, in a narrow band on the palatines, and in a **V**-shaped patch on the vomer. Tongue free, pointed.

The 3rd and 4th dorsal spines are the longest, about a third the length of the head, and shorter than the 2nd of the anal. Pectoral fin reaching to the anal.

Rose-coloured in life with indistinct dusky patches on the back and one on the first dorsal fin: these fade away in spirit.

Two specimens, the largest just over 3 inches long, from the Andaman Sea, 188–220 fathoms. They have been compared with one of the *Challenger* duplicates.

Regd. Nos. 13031, 13032.

Distribution: Andaman Sea: East Indian Archipelago.

SETARCHES, Johnson.

Setarches, Johnson, Proc. Zool. Soc. 1862, p. 177: Günther, Challenger Deep-Sea Fishes, p. 19: Goode and Bean, Oceanic Ichthyology, p. 262: Jordan and Evermann, Fishes of North and Middle America, II. p. 1860.

Bathysebastes, Steindachner and Döderlein, Denk. Ak. Wien, XLIX. 1885, p. 207.

? *Lioscorpius*, Günther, Challenger Shore Fishes, p. 40, and Challenger Deep-Sea Fishes, p. 20.

Head and body compressed: the vertex of the head with the muciferous cavities well developed but with few ridges, and those low and indistinct, and with no erect spines: occiput naked, without a groove. Preorbital and preoperculum armed with spines, operculum with two spines. Seven branchiostegals. Pseudobranchiæ present. Bands of villiform teeth on the jaws vomer and palatines.

Body covered with very small cycloid scales. Lateral line very wide, naked. Vertical fins not elongate. Dorsal fins separate but in contact, the first usually with eleven spines. Pectorals long and large, without separate appendages.

Pyloric appendages few.

14. *Setarches Güntheri*, Johnson.

Setarches Güntheri, Johnson, Proc. Zool. Soc., 1862, p. 177, pl. xxiii: Vaillant, Exp. Sci. Travailleur et Talisman Poissons, p. 373: Goode and Bean, Oceanic Ichthyology, p. 263.

Lioscorpius longiceps, Alcock, Ann. Mag. Nat. Hist., July 1891, p. 23; ILLUSTRATIONS OF THE ZOOLOGY OF THE INVESTIGATOR, FISHES, PL. X. FIG. 3. [It seems to me that *Lioscorpius longiceps* Günther, Challenger Shore Fishes, p. 40, pl. xvii. fig. C is little different from this species, for though the short description does not correspond the figure does.]

Scorpæna remigera, Gilbert and Cramer, Proc. U. S. Nat. Mus. Vol. XIX. 1896, p. 418, pl. xl.

B. 7. D. IX. I-10. A. III-5.

Height of the body from $\frac{1}{3}$ to $\frac{2}{7}$, length of the head about $\frac{4}{9}$ the total length without the caudal.

Head singularly large and clumsy looking, with cavernous bones and well-developed muciferous cavities, scaly on temples cheeks and opercles, naked elsewhere.

Three free divergent spines on edge of preorbital; four or five, of which the three upper are usually large, on the edge of the preoperculum; two on the operculum. Preopercular stay prominent, with or without a single small spine near its posterior end. No true spines on the top of the head, but two low ridges on the occiput and one behind either orbit end somewhat acutely, as also does a short ridge at the anterior supra-orbital angle and one above the middle of the orbit.

The snout (including the sharp knob at the mandibular symphysis which, fitting into a notch in the pre-maxillary, forms its tip) is about $3\frac{1}{2}$ in the length of the head. Nostrils of good size, a fleshy papilla above the anterior one (this is liable to loss by abrasion).

Major diameter of eye from $\frac{1}{4}$ to $\frac{1}{5}$ the length of the head: interorbital space a little wider than the eye, with three very characteristic mucous fossæ, one large and elliptical in the middle line posteriorly, two smaller and oval, side by side, anteriorly.

Mouth large, oblique, with prominent lower jaw; the maxilla reaches as far as the posterior border of the orbit. Villiform teeth on jaws vomer and palatines. Tongue ending in a small free spathulate tip.

Gill-opening wide. Pseudobranchiæ rather large. Gill-rakers on outer side of first arch rather short and distant.

Body covered with tiny cycloid scales. Lateral line broad, naked, with double tubule.

3rd, 4th and 5th dorsal spines the longest, the 3rd about as long as the snout, and not quite as long as the 3rd anal spine, which is the longest of that fin. Pectorals very large, reaching beyond the beginning of the anal, consisting of 21 or 22 rays. Ventrals reaching rather more than halfway to anal.

Colours red with minute black specks, and with some dusky markings that usually fade.

Most of our specimens come up with everted stomach and dislocated viscera, so that dissection is difficult. In two specimens I have counted 4 large pyloric cæca, and in one there was a small thick-walled air-bladder.

Andaman Sea 185 and 188–220 fathoms: Bay of Bengal, off Trincomali, 320–296 fathoms.

Largest specimen nearly $5\frac{1}{2}$ inches long.

Distribution: Madeira and C. Verde Is., Bay of Bengal, Andaman Sea, (East Indian Archipelago?), Hawaii: in moderate depths (up to about 300 fathoms).

Regd. Nos. 13036, 14131–14133, $\frac{154}{1}$, $\frac{236}{1}$–$\frac{243}{1}$.

PTEROIS, Cuv.

15. *Pterois macrurus*, Alcock.

Pterois macrurus, Alcock, Journ. As. Soc. Bengal, Vol. LXV. pt. 2, 1896, p. 303: ILLUSTRATIONS OF THE ZOOLOGY OF THE INVESTIGATOR, FISHES, PL. XVIII. FIG. 4.

D. XIII. 9. A. II. 7.

Length of the head about two-fifths, height of the body about one-third of the total without the caudal.

Snout deep, about as long as the eye, which is about one-fourth the length of the head. Supra-orbital ridges high, overhanging the deeply concave interorbital space, the width of which is about half the length of the eye. Preorbital with frill-like crests arranged in a star, and with a large tentacle overhanging the angle of the mouth. Crests of the head and cheek fairly well developed, serrated.

Scales finely ctenoid: in from 40 to 45 rows between the temple and the base of the caudal. The scales cover all parts of the head except the jaws, throat, and tip of the snout, and the middle line of the narrow interorbital space.

The pectorals reach to the base of the caudal: the ventrals reach just beyond the beginning of the anal. The caudal is pointed, one at least of its upper rays is produced as a slender filament which is as long as the body behind the eye: the rays below this gradually decrease in length.

Pseudobranchiæ singularly large. Three large pyloric cæca.

Colours in spirit: sepia with black cross-bars: vertical fins with dark spots which are distinct only along the upper edge of the caudal: pectorals and ventrals nearly black, with white spots.

Seven inches from tip of snout to tip of caudal filament.

Two specimens from off the Malabar coast, 68–148 fathoms; (six specimens from 45 fathoms).

Regd. Nos. 13823 to 13828: $\frac{480}{1}$.

MINOUS, Cuv. & Val.

16. *Minous inermis*, Alcock.

Minous inermis, Alcock, Journ. As. Soc. Bengal, Vol. LVIII. 1889, pt. 2, p. 299, pl. xxii. fig. 4: Ann. Mag. Nat. Hist., Sept. 1892, pp. 207–214: Journ. As. Soc. Bengal, Vol. LXIII. 1894, pt. 2, p. 116: ILLUSTRATIONS OF THE ZOOLOGY OF THE INVESTIGATOR, FISHES, PL. XVIII. FIG. 3.

B. 7. D. XI. 12. A. II. 10. P. 11/1. V. I. 5. C. 13.

Head and body compressed: height of body about a third, length of head about three-sevenths the total without the caudal.

Preorbital with two divergent spines on its edge: preoperculum with a large and a short spine at its angle and some dentations along its lower edge: operculum with two weak stays hardly projecting as spines. Preopercular stay crenate. Top of head eroded: two eroded and crenate ridges on occiput, one or either postorbital region: upper margin of orbit eroded and crenate.

Snout about as long as the eye, or rather more than a fourth the length of the head: interorbital space hardly narrower than the eye, traversed by ridges.

Mouth-cleft oblique, the maxilla reaches almost to the anterior margin of the pupil. A barbel about the middle of the limb of the lower jaw. Villiform teeth in the jaws and palatines.

Gill-opening wide: the posterior gill-cleft is a small foramen. Gill-rakers short, somewhat club-shaped.

Integument comparatively thin, without scales: it invests all the fins. The lateral line shows as 17 to 18 tubular papillæ.

All the fin-rays are simple. Dorsal fins continuous, the soft portion being the higher: all the spines are weak and flexible, the 1st being very small and the 2nd and 3rd somewhat isolated. Anal spines hidden, the 1st being visible only on reflecting the skin. Pectoral as long as the head: its free filament reaches to the 3rd anal ray. Ventral two-thirds or more as long as pectoral.

Colours in life:—rosy red with white and gray mottlings and minute black dots; throat and barbels white; pectoral, ventral, and anal fins edged with black, the posterior surface of the pectoral with small light spots.

Two large pyloric cæca: a small air-bladder.

Largest specimen about 4½ inches long.

Off Coromandel coast, 133, 70, and 60 fathoms. Off Malabar coast, 68–148 and 45 fathoms.

Regd. Nos. 12444, 12445: 13219: 13220–13223: 13511–13514: $\frac{461}{1}$-$\frac{476}{1}$.

This fish, wherever found—and it has been taken at five widely-distant stations on both coasts of the peninsula—is always more or less encrusted with the gymnoblastic Hydroid *Stylactis minoi*.

In the *Annals and Magazine of Natural History* for September 1892 I have given reasons for concluding that the relation between the Fish and the Hydroid is a definite commensalism, and not accidental or parasitic. Since that paper was published *Minous inermis* has twice been taken by the "Investigator,"—once off the Madras coast and once off the Konkan coast—and on both occasions *Stylactis minoi* was found on all the specimens captured.

For the description and figure of *Stylactis minoi* see Ann. Mag. Nat. Hist., Sept. 1892, pp. 212, 213.

Family *Berycidæ*.

When Day's latest volumes on the *Fishes of India* were published, in the *Fauna of British India* series, only two Indian genera of this family were known; I therefore give a synopsis of the genera now known to inhabit these seas.

Synopsis of the Indian genera of the family Berycidæ.

I. No barbels: eight branchiostegals:—
  1. Scales bony, forming a bony mail: ventrals consisting of a huge spine and 2 or 3 almost rudimentary rays ... ... Monocentris.
  2. Scales ctenoid: anal spines 3 or 4:—
    i. One dorsal: abdomen serrated: 6 soft rays in the ventrals:
      a. No teeth in the vomer ... ... Hoplostethus.
      b. Vomerine teeth ... ... Trachichthys.
    ii. Two dorsals: abdomen not serrated: 7 soft rays in the ventrals:—
      a. No preopercular spine ... ... *Myripristis*.
      b. A preopercular spine ... ... *Holocentrum*.
  3. Scales cycloid: anal spines feeble and few (1 or 2) ... Melamphaes.
II. Two barbels: four branchiostegals ... ... Polymixia.

Monocentris, Bl. Schn., Cuv. & Val.

Monocentris, Cuv. & Val., Hist. Nat. Poissons, IV. p. 461: Günther, Cat. Fishes. I. p. 8 *(ubi synon.)*.

Body deep, compressed, covered with a mail of large irregular bony scales: those in the middle line of the belly are large and strongly keeled.

Head large, the superficial bones, with the exception of the operculum, are sculptured to form wide deep muciferous cavities which are covered by spongy skin. Eye large. Snout blunt, rounded, overhanging the mouth. Mouth inferior, large, its cleft little oblique. Villiform teeth on jaws and palatines only.

Eight branchiostegals: large pseudobranchiæ: no large projecting spine at the angle of the preoperculum.

Two dorsal fins, the first consisting of a few large coarse isolated spines. Caudal emarginate but not deeply forked. Ventrals consisting of a huge spine and two or three small rays.

An air-bladder: a few large pyloric cæca.

17. *Monocentris japonicus* (Houtt.), Cuv. & Val.

Monocentris japonicus, Cuv. & Val., Hist. Nat. Poiss. IV. 461, pl. xcvii.: Temm. & Schleg. Faun. Japon., Poiss. p. 50, pl. xxii. fig. 1: Günther Catalogue of Fishes, vol. I. p. 9: Bleeker, Atlas Ichthyol. Vol. VIII. pl. ccclvi. fig. 4.

See also Castelnau, P. L. S. New South Wales, vol. III. 1878, p. 365: Hilgendorf, SB. Ges. nat. Freunde, Berlin. 1879, p. 22: Macleay, P. L. S. N. S. Wales, vol. V. 1880-81, p. 510: Steindachner and Döderlein, Denk. Ak. Wien, LXVII. 1883, p. 217: Nyström, Bihang Svensk. Vet.-Akad. Handl. XIII. iv. no. 4, 1887, p. 4.

B. 8. D. VI. 11. A. 10. P. 13 or 14. V. I. 2 or 3. L. lat. 16.

Height of the body nearly half the total length with the caudal, length of the head nearly half the total without the caudal.

Snout overhanging the mouth, blunt, rounded, about as long as the eye, which is about a fourth the length of the head: it, like the broad convex inter-orbital space and the vertex of the head, is occupied by large deep polygonal mucous cavities which are covered with thick spongy skin. The same sort of skin covers the cheek and opercles, with the exception of the operculum which is naked and coarsely striated. Nostrils large, situated near the lower angle of the orbit.

Mouth inferior, its cleft very slightly oblique: the maxilla is half as long as the head and completely overlaps the mandible. Broad bands of hard black villiform teeth in the jaws and palatines.

Gill-cleft wide. Gill-rakers coarse, those on the outer side of the 1st arch close set and more than half as long as the eye. Pseudobranchiæ very large. The operculum completed behind by a flap of thick skin.

Body covered with great irregular bony plates, many of which are acutely keeled: there are 15 rows of them round the body at the level of the 2nd dorsal spine,—the mid-ventral row, which are very strongly keeled, being unpaired.

First dorsal fin in the form of 6 coarse isolated spines, of which the first four are acute and fluted, and the last two are small truncated and eroded at tip. The 2nd dorsal and the anal are placed far back on the body. The caudal peduncle is formed very abruptly, its depth being less than a fifth the greatest body-height. Ventral spine a great fluted spike, about five-sixths as long as the head: it can be securely fixed like a bayonet, at right angles to the body.

Colours in spirit greenish-yellow, the bony dermal plates neatly outlined in black.

A single specimen, an adult female with ova, a little over six inches long, from the Gulf of Martaban, 67 fathoms.

Regd. No. $\frac{176}{1}$.

Distribution: Japanese Seas, Port Jackson, Andaman Sea, Mauritius.

HOPLOSTETHUS, Cuv. & Val., Gthr.

Hoplostethus, Cuv. and Val., Hist. Nat. Poiss. IV. p. 469: Günther Cat. Fishes I. p. 9 (*ubi synon.*) and Challenger Deep Sea Fishes, p. 20: Goode and Bean, Oceanic Ichthyology, p. 180: Jordan and Evermann, Fishes of North America I. p. 837.

"Body deep, compressed, covered with scales of moderate size and more or "less distinct ctenoid structure, rather irregularly arranged, those of the lateral "line being the largest.

"Head very large, the superficial bones being deeply sculptured to receive "wide muciferous cavities which are covered by thin skin only. Mouth very "wide, oblique; the jaws and palatine bones armed with villiform teeth, the "vomer being toothless. Eye very large. Eight branchiostegals; gill-openings

5

"very wide, gill-laminæ very short. Preoperculum armed with a flat spine. "Abdomen protected by dermal scutes which form a serrated edge. One "dorsal fin the anterior rays of which are spinous. Ventrals with six soft rays: "pectoral symmetrical. Caudal deeply forked. Air-bladder simple. Pyloric "appendages numerous." *Günther.*

18. ***Hoplostethus mediterraneum,*** Cuv. & Val.

Hoplostethus mediterraneum, Cuv. & Val. Günther, Challenger Deep-Sea Fishes, p. 21 *(ubi synon.)*.

See also Vaillant, Exp. Sci. Travailleur et Talisman, Poiss., p. 378: Günther, Ann. Mag. Nat. Hist. IV. 1889, p. 417: Carus, Prodr. Faun. Medit II. p. 616: Alcock, Journ. As. Soc. Bengal, Vol. LXIII. 1894, pt. 2, p. 116: Goode and Bean, Oceanic Ichthyology, p. 189, fig. 208: Jordan and Evermann, Fishes of North America, I. p. 837: R. Koehler, Campagne du *Caudan*, Poissons, p. 484.

Illustrations of the Zoology of the Investigator, Fishes, pl. XIV, fig. 3.

B. 8. D. VI. 13. A. III. 9. P. 13. V. I. 6. L. lat. 28-29.

Height of body rather over $2\frac{1}{3}$, length of head $2\frac{1}{2}$ in total without caudal.

As in *Monocentris* the head cheeks and preopercles are occupied by large deep square and rhomboidal muciferous cavities, which, however, are covered by a thin skin. A strong flat supra-clavicular spine, and a much stronger one at the angle of the preopercle.

Snout not overhanging the mouth, its length (including the prominent tip of the mandibular symphysis) is somewhat less than the diameter of the large round eye: the latter is about $3\frac{1}{4}$ to $3\frac{1}{2}$ in the length of the head and a little less than the width of the convex inter-orbital space. Nostrils large, situated near the upper angle of the orbit.

Mouth-cleft wide, very oblique (nearer the vertical than the horizontal); the lower jaw, though closing within the upper, distinctly prominent; the upper jaw nearly two-thirds the length of the head. Villiform teeth in the jaws, and in a short and narrow band in the palatines.

Gill-cleft wide: some gill-rakers on the outer side of the first arch are more than three-fourths the length of the eye: large pseudobranchiæ. Opercle striated.

Body covered with scales of uneven size, those of the lateral line, to the number of 28 or 29, being enlarged. On the back and tail, and on the throat and near the middle line of the belly, the scales are sharply granular, but behind the gill-opening and on the sides of the belly they are smooth. In the middle line of the belly the scales, to the number of 11 to 13, are enlarged and strongly keeled—the keels ending very acutely.

Pectorals large, reaching more than half-way along the anal. Ventrals reaching two-thirds of the way to the vent.

Colours in spirit, warm brown or plum-colour with a silvery sheen.

Six specimens, the largest nearly a foot long, from off Madras, 145–250 fathoms, off Trincomali, 320–296 fathoms, and off Travancore coast 224 to 430 fathoms.

Regd. Nos. 13711 : 14126–14129 : $\frac{246}{1}$: $\frac{531}{1}$.

Distribution: Atlantic coast of North America, between 11° and 40° N. lat.: off the European and African shores of the Atlantic from Ireland to Cape Verde: Mediterranean: Arabian Sea: Bay of Bengal: Japanese Seas. At moderate depths (about 150 to about 400 fathoms, where the depth has been recorded). In the Indian Museum there are also specimens from the Caribbean Sea and from the Gulf of Gascony.

TRACHICHTHYS Shaw, Cuv. & Val., Günther.

Trachichthys, Cuv. & Val., Hist. Nat. Poiss. III. p. 229: Günther, Cat. Fishes, I. p. 10 (*ubi synon.*), and Challenger Deep-Sea Fishes, p. 21: Goode and Bean, Oceanic Ichthyology, p. 187.

Trachichthys differs from *Hoplostethus* only in having villiform teeth on the vomer. The pyloric cæca (in some species) are less numerous, and there is a distinct spine on the operculum.

19. *Trachichthys Darwinii*, Johnson.

Trachichthys Darwinii, Johnson, Proc. Zool. Soc., 1866, p. 311, pl. xxxii.

Trachichthys japonicus, Steindachner & Döderlein, Denk. Ak. Wien, XLVII. 1883, p. 218, pl. ii.

Trachichthys Darwinii, Günther, Challenger Deep-Sea Fishes, p. 24 (*ubi synon.*): Alcock J.A.S.B. LXV. 1896, pt. 2, p. 314: Goode and Bean, Oceanic Ichthyology, p. 188, fig. 207.

B. 8. D. VIII. 13. A. III. 11. P. 15. V. I. 6. L. lat. 27–30.

Height of body about $2\frac{1}{5}$, length of head about $2\frac{1}{2}$ in the total length without the caudal.

Bones of vertex of head and of sub-orbital ring, but not of any part of the opercle, sculptured for muciferous cavities that are covered with a harsh skin in which tiny scales are embedded: the cheeks, the membranous edge of the operculum, and the middle line of the chin are also scaly. A flat supra-clavicular spine of no great size: a very strong flat spine at the angle of the preopercle: a stay, ending in a prominent spine, across the upper part of the operculum, which bone has a striated surface.

Snout (measured to the tip of the symphysis of the lower jaw) a little longer than the eye and about equal to the width of the interorbital space. Eye large, round, its diameter about one-fourth the length of the head. Nostrils very large, situated near the upper angle of the eye.

Mouth very wide and oblique, approaching the vertical: the lower jaw, though closing inside the upper, projecting: the upper jaw two-thirds as long as the head. Villiform teeth in jaws and vomer and in a long narrow band in the palatines: the inner row of teeth in the lower jaw and in the anterior half of the upper jaw considerably enlarged.

Gill-opening very wide: some of the gill-rakers on the outer side of the 1st arch are about two-thirds as long as the eye: large pseudobranchiæ.

Body closely covered with harsh ctenoid scales of irregular size and disposition. Those of the lateral line, to the number of 27 to 30, are enlarged. There are from 10 to 12 enlarged, strongly and acutely keeled, abdominal scutes.

3rd and 4th dorsal spines the longest, a little longer than the eye. The pectorals do not reach to the vent: the ventrals reach about two-thirds the way to the vent.

Colours in spirit: frosted, the cheeks and backs cinnamon, the operculum and gill-membranes dusky.

One specimen, a foot long, off Trincomali, 320–296 fathoms.

Regd. No. 14130.

Distribution: Madeira, Bay of Bengal, Japan.

20. *Trachichthys intermedius*, Hector.

Trachichthys intermedius, Hector, Trans. and Proc. New Zealand Inst. VII. 1874, p. 245, pl. xi: Günther, Challenger Deep-Sea Fishes, p. 24, pl. v. fig. D: Alcock, Ann. Mag. Nat. Hist., Dec. 1889, p. 380.

B. 8. D. VI. 13. A. III. 10–11. P. 18 or 19. V. I. 6. L. lat. 28.

Height of the body nearly half, length of the head two-fifths the total length without the caudal.

The skin covering the muciferous cavities of the head and cheeks is not scaly, nor is the middle line of the chin and the membranous edge of the operculum scaly. Supra-clavicular and preopercular spines sharp and prominent: spine at upper end of operculum not very prominent.

Snout much shorter than the eye: eye from a third to two-sevenths the length of the head and equal to the width of the interorbital space.

Cleft of the mouth oblique, but not approaching the vertical: none of the teeth are appreciably enlarged.

Only 9 keeled scutes in the middle line of the belly.

5th and 6th dorsal spines the longest,—a good deal longer than the eye. The pectorals reach well beyond the middle of the anal: the first two ventral rays almost reach the vent, the ventral spine is sharply serrated in the basal half.

Colours in spirit: warm brown, pectorals and ventrals much darker.

The characters noticed above are those that distinguish this species from *T. Darwinii.*

One specimen, $2\frac{3}{4}$ inches long, from the Bay of Bengal, 272 fathoms.

Regd. No. 11723.

Distribution: New Zealand Seas: Bay of Bengal.

MELAMPHAES, Günther.

Melamphaes, Günther, Cat. Fishes V. p. 433, and Challenger Deep-Sea Fishes, p. 26 (*ubi synon.*): Goode and Bean, Oceanic Ichthyology, p. 177.

Plectromus, Gill, Proc. U. S. Nat. Mus. VI. 1883, p. 257: Goode and Bean, Oceanic Ichthyology, p. 178: Jordan and Evermann, Fishes of North America, I. p. 840.

Scopelogadus, Vaillant, Exp. Sci. Travailleur et Talisman, Poiss. p. 140: Goode & Bean, Oceanic Ichthyology, p. 181.

"Head large and thick, with nearly all the superficial bones modified into "wide muciferous channels. Cleft of the mouth of moderate width, obliquely descending backwards, with the jaws nearly equal in front. A narrow band of "villiform teeth in both the jaws, palate toothless. Eight branchiostegals: "pseudobranchiæ present. No barbels. Opercles not armed. Scales large, "cycloid, rather irregularly arranged. One dorsal: caudal forked: anal spines "very feeble: ventrals with seven rays." (*Günther*).

Distribution: Atlantic, Indo-Pacific.

21. *Melamphaes mizolepis*, Günther.

Scopelus mizolepis, Günther Ann. Mag. Nat. Hist. 1878, Vol. II. p. 185.

Melamphaes mizolepis, Günther, Challenger Deep-Sea Fishes, p. 28: Alcock, Ann. Mag. Nat. Hist. Sept. 1890 p. 201.

B. 8. D. II.11. A. I.8. P.14. V. I.7.

Height of the body about two-sevenths, length of the head about two-fifths of the total length without the caudal.

Head very thick, with deep muciferous cavities: the bones of the cranium stout, the other bones thin and weak: snout short.

Eye very small, about one-seventh the length of the head, half that of the snout, and half the width of the interorbital space.

Mouth cleft wide, somewhat oblique, the maxilla reaching to the middle of the pupil, the lower jaw slightly prominent. A very narrow band of villiform teeth in both the jaws.

Gill-opening very wide: the gill-rakers on the outer side of the first arch are close-set and nearly as long as the eye. Posterior margin of the preoperculum subvertical.

Scales deciduous very large: [one left on the thorax of the single "Investigator" specimen measured quarter of an inch in its major diameter, the specimen itself being just over 3 inches long.]

The dorsal fin arises somewhat nearer to the tip of the snout than to the base of the caudal, and behind the base of the ventral, which is below that of the pectoral: the last dorsal ray is above the middle of the anal. Pectoral fin long, reaching nearly to the end of the anal.

Stomach very large: a few very large pyloric cæca.

Colour black.

A single specimen from the Bay of Bengal, off the Ganjam coast, 1310 fathoms.

Regd. No. 12834.

Distribution: East Indian Archipelago: Bay of Bengal: in deep water.

POLYMIXIA, Lowe.

Polymixia, Lowe, Trans. Camb. Phil. Soc., VI. 1838, p. 198: Günther, Cat. Fishes I. p. 16 (*et synon.*): Goode & Bean, Oceanic Ichthyology, p. 243 (*ubi synon.*): Jordan & Evermann, Fishes of North America, I. p. 854.

Body compressed, rather elongate. Eye large. Snout short. Mouth-cleft very slightly oblique: the upper jaw overhanging the lower. Villiform teeth in jaws, vomer, palatines, and pterygoids.

Two barbels on the throat.

Gill openings wide: only four branchiostegals: gill-cover unarmed, except that the edge of the preoperculum is finely serrated: pseudobranchiæ present.

Scales moderate: ctenoid. One long dorsal fin, beginning with about five spines. Ventrals with 6 or 7 rays. Caudal forked. Anal with 4 spines.

Delicate pyloric appendages in moderate number. A thin-walled air-bladder with more or less distinct vestiges of a pneumatic duct.

22. *Polymixia nobilis*, Lowe.

Polymixia nobilis, Lowe, Günther Cat. Fishes, I. p. 17, and Challenger Deep Sea Fishes, p. 34, pl. i. fig. B: *ubi synon.* (*Nemobrama Webbii* Val., *Polymixia lowei* and *japonica* Gthr., *Dinemus venustus* Poey): Alcock, Ann. Mag. Nat. Hist., Nov., 1889, p. 381, and July, 1891, p. 23: Goode and Bean, Oceanic Ichthyology, p. 243, fig. 241: Jordan and Evermann, Fishes of North America, I. pp. 854, 855 (*foot-note*).

B. 4. D. V. 30–38. A. III–IV. 14–18. V. I. 6–7. Sc. *circ.* 50. L. lat. *circ.* 36.

Height of the body about equal to the length of the head, which is a little over one-third the total without the caudal.

All parts of the head, except the snout, the suborbital space, the upper jaw, the middle line of the chin, and the border of the angle of the pre-operculum, are scaly.

Snout not much more than half the length of the eye, which is about one-third that of the head: interorbital space about a fourth of a head-length in width. Nostrils of good size, placed near the level of the middle of the eye.

Mouth-cleft large: the upper jaw reaches behind the posterior border of the orbit and so overhangs the lower that its teeth are quite outside the mouth when closed. Barbels about as long as the head without the operculum.

Gill-opening very wide: gill-rakers on the outer side of the 1st arch nearly half the length of the eye: pseudobranchiæ large.

Scales of moderate size, strongly ctenoid: about 36 of those of the lateral line are perforated.

The dorsal spines gradually increase in length to the last, which is about half the length of the anterior dorsal rays: the anterior third, or more, of the soft part of the dorsal is high, the posterior two-thirds or less is very low. The anal spines also gradually increase in length to the last, which is not nearly so long as the anterior anal rays: also the anterior half of the soft part of the anal is high, and the posterior half low.

Pectorals about three-fifths, ventrals about two-fifths the length of the head: the ventral spine and first ventral ray are very intimately adherent.

Colours in spirit silvery, the cheeks nape and back a warmish light-brown: tip of the elevated part of the dorsal fin black.

Five specimens from the Andaman Sea 185 to 405 fathoms: the largest is about 7½ inches long.

Regd. Nos. 11725: 13034: $\frac{162}{1}$: $\frac{244\text{-}245}{1\ \ 1}$

Distribution: West Indies: Madeira, Canaries and S. Atlantic: Mauritius: Andaman Sea: Japan.

I accept Dr. Günther's synonomy of the species. There is no doubt that our specimens are absolutely identical with *P. lowei* and *P. japonica*.

Family ***Kurtidæ.***

BATHYCLUPEA, Alcock.

Bathyclupea, Alcock, Ann. Mag. Nat. Hist., August, 1891, p. 130: Goode and Bean, Oceanic Ichthyology, p. 190: Jordan and Evermann, Fishes of North America, I. p. 834.

Head and body compressed: the head with the mucous cavities well developed. Mouth cleft oblique, or very oblique, with the lower jaw prominent. Minute villiform teeth in the jaws, palatines, and vomer. Gill-openings wide: seven branchiostegals: pseudobranchiæ present. Scales cycloid, deciduous: lateral line nearly straight.

One short dorsal fin, with the spines weak or absent, situated in the posterior half of the body. Anal long, with one spine. Pectorals large, the upper rays longest. Ventrals small, subjugular, with one spine and five rays. Caudal forked.

Pyloric appendages in moderate number.

Air-bladder with a persistent pneumatic duct.

Distribution : Andaman Sea, Bay of Bengal : Caribbean Sea.

I was led by a combination of external characters and by the presence of a persistent pneumatic duct, to place this genus among the *Clupeidæ*; but Messrs. Gill and Goode and Bean have quite properly removed it to the neighbourhood of the *Berycidæ*. They have made it the type of a distinct family (*Bathyclupeidæ*); but I prefer to emphasize its very obvious relations with *Kurtus* and *Pempheris* and to include it in the same family with them.

23. ***Bathyclupea Hoskynii***, Alcock.

Bathyclupea Hoskynii, Alcock, Ann. Mag. Nat. Hist., August, 1891, pp. 131, 132, fig. 4: ILLUSTRATIONS OF THE ZOOLOGY OF THE INVESTIGATOR, FISHES, PL. XXVIII. FIG. 2.

B. 7. D. 10. A. 33. P. 29. V. 6. L. lat. circ. 38.

Soft tissues fragile, bones thin.

Head and body compressed; the height of the latter almost exactly equals the length of the former, which is one-third the total without the caudal. The median abdominal line is neither keeled nor serrated. The mucous cavities of the skull are large.

Snout rectangular, formed in front by the lower jaw, which in repose is almost vertical; its length, including the mandibular element, is not quite equal to the diameter of the large lateral circular eye, which is one-third the length of the head; the width of the flat interorbital space is half the diameter of the eye. Nostrils small, almost superior.

Mouth wide, its cleft nearly vertical: length of the upper jaw two-fifths that of the head. Villiform teeth in narrow bands in the premaxillæ, mandible, and palatine, and in an inconspicuous V-shaped patch on the vomer. Tongue large, bilobed.

Gill-cleft very wide, the membranes entirely ununited; all the opercular bones well-developed, and the horizontal border of the preoperculum sharply serrated; four gills; the middle gill-rakers on the outer side of the first arch considerably elongated; pseudobranchiæ large.

Head naked. Body and nape covered with large cycloid scales, deciduous everywhere except on the lateral line. In the largest specimen a scale from the flank measures 10 millim. in the vertical and 7·5 millim. in the antero-posterior diameter. Each scale of the lateral line has a deep pocket on its inner side which opens externally by numerous fine pores.

The dorsal fin commences almost exactly midway between the tip of the snout and the tip of the upper lobe of the caudal fin; the length of its base is equal to that of the snout; it is roughly triangular and its height is a fifth greater than the diameter of the eye. The anal commences about an eye-diameter in advance of the dorsal and extends to within a very short distance (equal to three-fourths of an eye-diameter) of the base of the caudal. Caudal forked, its length is about one-sixth of the total. Pectorals extending a good deal beyond the origin of the anal. Ventrals very small, in close contact.

Stomach large, with a cæcal sac and a bunch of large pyloric appendages. A large air-bladder with a persistent pneumatic duct much like that of *Clupea*. Vertebrae 9 + 22.

Colours silvery grey becoming black along the back.

14 specimens, from the Andaman Sea, 185 fathoms, 188–220 fathoms, and 370–419 fathoms, and from off Madras 145–250 fathoms. The largest specimen, an adult female, is 8 inches long: the largest adult male is $6\frac{1}{2}$ inches long.

Registered Nos. 13111, 13112, 13114: 13641, 13642: $\frac{247}{1}$, $\frac{248}{1}$, $\frac{250 \text{ to } 252}{1}$, $\frac{254 \text{ to } 256}{1}$: $\frac{381}{1}$.

Named after the late Commander R. F. Hoskyn, R.N., who was Superintendent of the Marine Survey of India from October 1889 until his death on January 27th, 1892. Most of the success of the "Investigator" during those years was due to his good-natured sympathy, joined to a singular boldness and originality in handling the trawl.

Family *Trichiuridæ*.

Thyrsites, Cuv. & Val.

Thyrsites, Cuv. & Val., Hist. Nat. Poiss. VIII. p. 196: Günther, Cat. Fishes, II. p. 350.

"Body rather elongate: cleft of the mouth wide. The first dorsal continu-"ous, with the spines of moderate length and extending on to the second. Two "to six spurious fins behind the dorsal and anal. The greater portion of the "body naked. Several strong teeth in the jaws: teeth on the palatine bones. "No keel on the tail. Seven branchiostegals. Air-bladder present. Pyloric "appendages in moderate number." (*Günther*).

Subgenus Promethichthys, Gill.

Promethichthys, Gill, Mem. Ac. Nat. Sci. Vol. VI. 1893, 115, 123: Goode and Bean, Oceanic Ichthyology, p. 200: Jordan and Evermann, Fishes of North America, Vol. I. p. 882.

Two finlets behind the dorsal and two behind the anal fin. Ventrals represented by a pair of small spines. No dagger-shaped spine behind the vent. Scales very minute or absent. Lateral line undulating or bifurcating below the front part of the spinous dorsal.

6

24. *Thyrsites (Promethichthys) bengalensis,* Alcock.

Thyrsites bengalensis, Alcock, Journ. As. Soc. Bengal, Vol. LXIII. pt. 2, 1894, p. 117, pl. vi. fig. 1: ILLUSTRATIONS OF THE ZOOLOGY OF THE INVESTIGATOR, FISHES, PL. XV. FIG. 10.

This species may possibly be identical with the *T. prometheoides* of Bleeker, which I know only from the short description in Günther's *Catalogue*.

B.7. D.XVIII. $\frac{II}{13\text{-}14}$ I.I. A.II.11-12 I.I. P.14. V.I.

Length of head two-sevenths of the total (caudal included), and twice the greatest height of the body.

The snout, which has the usual Trichiurid form, is two-fifths of the head in length, and twice the diameter of the eye. The nostrils are small pores situated well in front of the eye.

The mouth is large, and the upper jaw-bones are massive: the maxilla reaches to a point midway between the anterior border of the orbit and the pupil. There is a single row of distant fang-like teeth in the premaxillary, which in front, to the number of three or four, are of great size: the mandibular teeth are similar in size form and arrangement, but only two—the front one on each side—are enlarged, and these but slightly. There is a single row of small sharp distant teeth on each palatine. Gill-opening extremely wide. Pseudobranchiæ large.

The head and body are invested in a thick silvery scaleless skin. The lateral line bifurcates at the level of the 5th or 6th dorsal spine, the upper branch running along the base of the dorsal fin, the lower descending with a curve to the middle line, or a little ventrad of it, and then taking a somewhat sinuous course to the caudal.

The longest (middle) spines of the long first dorsal fin are two-thirds the greatest body-height in length: the second dorsal, like the anal, is low and short: the two spurious finlets are incompletely isolated in both fins.

The caudal is large and deeply forked.

The delicate pectorals are not quite half as long as the head. The ventrals, which arise close together on the abdominal profile, a little in advance of the pectorals, are each reduced to a single fluted spine.

In correlation with the strong jaws and large fangs the stomach is huge, its length being one-third of the total (caudal included). In the specimen dissected there is a small air-bladder and seven large but delicate pyloric cæca.

Colours in spirit: burnished silver, with the mid-dorsal line, from snout to caudal, blue-black: fins hyaline, the spinous dorsal with a black edge which is broadest in front, the tips of the lobes of the caudal fin dusky.

Five specimens are in the Indian Museum, from off Madras 145–250 fathoms. The largest specimen is $5\frac{1}{4}$ inches long.

Regd. Nos. 13518, 13520–13522, 13524.

Family *Carangidæ.*

Bathyseriola, Alcock.

Bathyseriola, Alcock, Ann. Mag. Nat. Hist., Sept. 1890, p. 202.

Body fusiform but much compressed; edge of the belly sharp, grooved along the middle line. Scales small, deciduous, cycloid: lateral line unarmed. One dorsal fin with the spinous portion rather feeble: the soft portion, and the anal, long. No finlets. Anal spines forming an integral part of the anal fin. Ventral with a continuous membranous attachment to the belly.

Snout conical, cleft of mouth narrow: villiform teeth in the jaws only. Preopercular border entire: seven branchiostegals: pseudobranchiæ present.

No air-bladder. Pyloric appendages numerous. Vertebræ 10 + 14.

25. *Bathyseriola cyanea*, Alcock.

Bathyseriola cyanea, Alcock, Ann. Mag. Nat. Hist. Sept. 1890, p. 202; Illustrations of the Zoology of the Investigator, Fishes, pl. XVIII. fig. 1.

B. 7. D. VIII–IX. 24–25. A. III. 22. P. 22. V. I. 5.

Body oblong and compressed; its height about $3\frac{1}{4}$ in the total and one-ninth less than the length of the head.

Head compressed and thin in its lower, broad and heavy in its upper half; its muciferous cavities well developed. Snout rounded, a little inflated at the tip, the jaws equal in front; its length, which is hardly equal to its greatest breadth, is equal to the diameter of the eye. Eyes circular, their diameter not quite one-fourth of the length of the head; they are encircled by a sharp-edged adipose fold, widest fore and aft; interorbital space wider than the eye, convex from side to side. Nostrils large, situated almost superiorly at the tip of the snout.

Cleft of mouth narrow, the maxillary hardly reaching the vertical through the middle of the eye; jaw-bones weak, with a trenchant edge, which bears a narrow band of villiform teeth; tongue large and fleshy; buccal folds very broad. Gill-cleft wide; gill-membranes united only quite anteriorly; gill-covers with thin, almost membranous, bones, the operculum with two diverging weak stays above, the preoperculum bulging backwards as a large, striated, entire lobe; gill-laminæ broad, gill-rakers on the first arch long, close-set, acute; pseudobranchiæ fleshy. The mucosa of the whole pharynx black.

Scales extremely deciduous; the few that still adhere are small and membranous, and those of the lateral line, which are $\frac{1}{12}$ inch in their major diameter, have each a salient membranous tube.

The dorsal and anal fins have thick gelatinous bases; the dorsal spines are short and rather weak, and their interconnecting membrane is delicate; the anal spines are in close contact with each other and with the rest of the fin. Caudal symmetrically forked. Pectorals pointed, their length rather more than four-fifths the height of the body. Ventrals much shorter than the pectorals; they are adherent to the abdomen throughout their inner border, and can be retracted within a shallow furrow in the middle abdominal line.

Peritoneal cavity large, the membrane black; numerous pyloric cæca in an arborescent mass; no air-bladder. Vertebræ 10/14.

Colours in life, uniform bluish black, with an uneven silvery sheen.

In the Indian Museum are four adult specimens, the largest being nearly 7 inches long, from off the Ganjam coast 98–102 fathoms and off the Godavari coast, 240–276 fathoms.

Regd. Nos. 12816, 12817, 12819: 13035.

This species has affinities on the one hand with *Seriola* and on the other hand with the *Nomeidæ*.

Family *Cyttidæ*.

Antigonia, Lowe.

Antigonia, Lowe, Proc. Zool. Soc. 1843, p. 45.

Caprophonus, Müller and Troschel Horæ Ichthyol, iii. p. xxviii.

Hypsinotus, Temminck and Schlegel, Faun. Japon. Poiss. p. 84.

Antigonia, Günther, Cat. Fishes, ii. p. 497 and Challenger Deep-Sea Fishes, p. 44, (*ubi synon*): Steindachner and Döderlein, Denk. Ak. Wien, XLIX. 1885, p. 187: Goode and Bean, Oceanic Ichthyology, p. 229.

Body compressed and elevated (rhomboidal) covered with rather small spiny scales. One dorsal fin with eight spines: the soft portion, like the soft portion of the anal, long. Anal with three spines, which though continuous with, are somewhat isolated from, the soft portion. Ventrals composed of a spine and five rays.

Mouth small, little protractile; small teeth in the jaws only. Lower limb of preoperculum serrated. Six branchiostegals. Pseudobranchiæ present.

Pyloric appendages few. Air-bladder present, large.

26. *Antigonia capros*, Lowe.

Antigonia capros, Lowe, Proc. Zool. Soc. 1843, p. 85: Günther, Cat. Fishes, II. 497 and Challenger Deep-Sea Fishes, p. 44: Steindachner and Döderlein, Denk. Ak. Wien. XLIX. 1885, p. 187, pl. v: Goode and Bean, Oceanic Ichthyology, p. 229, fig. 235.

Caprophonus aurora, Müll. & Trosch. Hor. Ichth. III. p. xxviii., pl. v. fig. 1.

Hypsinotus rubescens, Temm. & Schleg. Faun. Japon. Poiss. p. 84, pl. xlii. fig. 2. Günther Challenger Shore Fishes, p. 44.

B. 6. D. VIII-IX. 27–34. A. III. 27–33.

The height of the body varies with age: in adults it is greater than the length without the caudal, in specimens about a third grown it equals the length of the body to the beginning of the caudal peduncle.

Head everywhere covered with harsh ctenoid scales; its length is from two-fifths to a third the total without the caudal. The superficial bones of the cranium are sculptured and striated: the edge of the preorbital is denticulated and the horizontal limb of the opercle serrated.

Snout about equal to the width of the inter-orbital space in length and rather shorter than the eye. Eye round, a third or more the length of the head. Nostrils almost superior.

Mouth-cleft very small, the maxilla not nearly reaching to the anterior border of the orbit. Gill-rakers short. Pseudobranchiæ very large.

Scales small, harsh, ctenoid; in from 60 to 65 rows between the gill-opening and the caudal fin. Small scales extend some way along the spines and rays of the dorsal and anal fins. Lateral line strongly curved.

2nd or 3rd dorsal spine the longest and by far the stoutest: its length is two-thirds that of the head and twice that of the longest soft rays. 1st anal spine the longest, about as long as the eye and about one-fourth longer than the longest soft rays. 12 or 13 rays in the pectoral: the upper, which are the longest, are more than three-quarters the length of the head. Ventral spine very strong, its length is equal to that of the snout and eye combined: its edge like the inner edge of the ventral rays is scabrous.

Colour in life red: in spirit light brown or yellow.

5 pyloric cæca, of which 2 are much enlarged.

Two specimens from off Trincomali 320 to 296 fathoms, and one from off the Malabar coast 68 to 148 fathoms.

Regd. Nos. 14134, 14135: $\frac{478}{1}$.

Distribution: West Indies, Madeira, East Indian Seas, Japan.

Family *Trachinidæ.*

URANOSCOPUS, CUV.

27. *Uranoscopus crassiceps*, Alcock.

Uranoscopus crassiceps, Alcock, Ann. Mag. Nat. Hist. Sept. 1890, p. 205: ILLUSTRATIONS OF THE ZOOLOGY OF THE INVESTIGATOR, FISHES, PL. X, FIG. 4.

B. 6. D. IV. $\frac{1}{13}$ A. 13. P. 18. V. I.5.

Length of the head $2\frac{1}{3}$ to two-fifths of the total without the caudal; its maximum breadth in repose (that is, when the opercles are not expanded for defence) is two-thirds its length; its greatest height (and that of the body) is about one-fourth the total length of the body without the caudal.

Bones of the head rugose: the antero-inferior angle of the preorbital produced and subacute: a spine on the lower border of the suboperculum and 4 or 5 along the lower border of the preoperculum. Two small coarse spines or tubercles on the supra-clavicular region: the clavicular spine about as long as the major diameter of the orbit. The points of the pubic bones project as a pair of spines between the clavicular symphysis.

Eye from a sixth to a seventh the length of the head, according to age, and rather less than the width of the inter-orbital space. A small filament in front of the nostril.

Lips rather fleshy, papillated, especially the lower lip. *A large prelingual filament, more than two-fifths the length of the head.* No barbel.

No scales on the throat and belly.

Nine pyloric appendages.

Colours in life: back dirty greenish, below marbled with lighter shades, belly silvery white, first dorsal black.

The type specimen is eight inches long.

Numerous specimens from off the Ganjam coast 98 to 102 fathoms, off the Coromandel coast 128 fathoms, and off the Malabar coast 45, 100 and 68 to 148 fathoms.

Regd. Nos. 12784–12786, 12788, 12791, 12797–12798, 12800, 12803, 13214, 13451, 13495, 13496, 13498–13500, 14093–14103: $\frac{481}{1}-\frac{484}{1}:\frac{689}{1}-\frac{723}{1}$.

In the original description, I stated that there is no prelingual filament; but, as a matter of fact, the prelingual filament is very large.

The nearest relative of this species seems to be *U. kaianus*, Günther (Challenger Shore Fishes, p. 43, pl. xix. fig. A).

It is a voracious species: in the stomach of the specimen dissected seven entire individuals of *Scopelus pterotus* were found.

Champsodon, Günther.

Champsodon, Günther, Proc. Zool. Soc. 1867, p. 102; Challenger Shore Fishes, p. 52: Goode and Bean Oceanic Ichthyology, p. 291.

Body elongate, compressed, covered with minute granular or spiny scales. Two indistinct lateral lines, with transverse branches that lodge minute gland-like papillæ.

Mouth wide, oblique: irregular cardiform and setiform teeth of unequal size in the jaws—largest in the lower jaw: cardiform teeth in two patches on the vomer. Eye lateral, directed somewhat upwards. Two naked spines on edge of preorbital bone.

Seven branchiostegals. Gill-openings very wide. Posterior border of preoperculum finely denticulated: a strong dagger-shaped spine at its angle.

Two dorsal fins, the first short, the second long and similar to the anal. Caudal forked. Pectorals small, median. Ventrals jugular, of good size.

An elongate air-bladder. A few large pyloric cæca.

28. ***Champsodon vorax***, Günther.

Champsodon vorax, Günther, P. Z. S. 1867, p. 102, and Challenger Shore Fishes, pp. 43, 52, 56, pl. xxiii. fig. A, and Challenger Deep-Sea Fishes, p. 40: Alcock, Journ. As. Soc. Bengal, Vol. LVIII. pt. 2, 1889, p. 302: ILLUSTRATIONS OF THE ZOOLOGY OF THE INVESTIGATOR, FISHES, PL. XXVIII. FIG. 5.

B. 7. D. V. 21. A. 19.

Length of head $3\frac{1}{2}$, height of body 5 to $5\frac{1}{4}$ in the total without the caudal.

All parts of the head, except the edge of the operculum, the throat and branchiostegal membranes, and the sides of the chin, are covered with very small granular scales, among which are some rows of tiny gland-like papillæ. The crown of the head is flat, and is traversed, from the snout backwards, by a pair of ridges, which are fairly parallel as far as the occiput and then diverge to end each in a supra-clavicular spinule. There are two diverging spines on the edge of the preorbital, two spinules on the lower edge of the interoperculum, and a long dagger-like spine at the angle of the preoperculum.

The snout, measured to the tip of the prominent lower jaw, is nearly twice the length of the eye, which, in the adult, is about one-fifth the length of the head. Inter-orbital space flat; its width equals the diameter of the eye. Pupil small. Nostrils almost superior, near the tip of the snout.

Mouth-cleft wide, very oblique, the lower jaw prominent, the maxilla reaches well behind the posterior border of the orbit. The larger teeth in the jaws are depressible.

Gill-opening extremely wide; gill-membranes quite free. Operculum thin, striated. Pseudobranchiæ small.

Body covered with minute ctenoid scales among which are some rows of small gland-like papillæ. Two indistinct lateral lines, with numerous transverse branches in which the gland-like papillæ are generally found.

First dorsal small, lower than the anterior part of the second dorsal, from which it is separated by about an eye-length. The pectorals, which are not much longer than the snout, arise high up on the side and consist of very slender branched rays. Ventrals rather longer than the head without the snout.

Six or seven large pyloric cæca.

Colours warm brown, gradually becoming whitish on the belly: the whole surface with a frosted appearance: first dorsal black.

The largest specimen in the Indian Museum—an adult female—is 5 inches long.

Numerous specimens from the Bay of Bengal 100 to 40 fathoms, and off the Malabar coast 124 to 28 fathoms.

Regd. Nos. 11663, 11831, 11832, 11835, 11923, 11924, 12438, 12506, 12948, 13935–13939, 14334–14350, $\frac{485}{1}$, $\frac{486}{1}$, $\frac{487}{1}$.

Distribution: East Indian Archipelago, Bay of Bengal, Arabian Sea.

In the Indian Museum is also one of the Challenger Duplicates from the East Indian Archipelago.

Bembrops, Steindachner.

Bembrops, Steindachner, SB. Ak. Wien, LXXIV. 1877, i. p. 211; Alcock, Journ. As. Soc. Bengal, Vol. LXIII. 1894, pt. 2, p. 118, and Vol. LXV. 1896, pt. 2, p. 316.

Hypsicometes, Goode, Proc. U.S. Nat. Mus. III. 1880, p. 347; Günther, 'Challenger' Deep-sea Fishes, p. 85; Jordan and Gilbert, Bull. U.S. Nat. Mus. XVI. p. 808; Goode and Bean, Oceanic Ichthyology, p. 290: Jordan & Evermann, Fishes of N. America, III., p. 2293.

Bathypercis, Alcock, Journ. As. Soc. Bengal, Vol. LXII. 1893, pt. 2, p. 177.

Body elongate, subcylindrical: head large, depressed. Snout broad spathulate: cleft of the mouth wide, oblique, with the lower jaw projecting: villiform teeth in the jaws vomer and palatines. Eyes large, close together, almost superior.

Gill-opening very wide, the membranes free. Seven branchiostegals. Opercle with 3 spines: angle of preoperculum feebly armed. Pseudobranchiæ large.

Scales large, cycloid or very finely ctenoid, rather deciduous. Lateral line continuous from occiput to caudal, the scales of its anterior portion keeled or feebly spinate. A small supra-clavicular spine.

Two separate dorsal fins, the first short, the second long. Anal similar to the 2nd dorsal. Ventrals jugular.

Pyloric appendages few. No air-bladder.

29. *Bembrops caudimacula*, Steindachner.

Bembrops caudimacula, Steindachner, Sitzungsb. Ak. Wien, LXXIV. 1877, i. p. 212: Alcock, Journ. As. Soc. Bengal, Vol. LXIII. pt. 2, 1894, p. 118.

Hypsicometes gobioides, Goode, Proc. U.S. Nat. Mus. III. 1880, p. 347, and Oceanic Ichthyology, p. 290, fig. 263: Günther, Challenger Deep-Sea Fishes, p. 85; Jordan and Evermann, Fishes of N. America III. p. 2294.

Bathypercis platyrhynchus, Alcock, J. A. S. B. Vol. LXII. pt. 2, 1893, p. 177, pl. ix. fig. 1.

Bembrops platyrhynchus, Alcock, J. A. S. B. Vol. LXIII. pt. 2, 1894, p. 118: Illustrations of the Zoology of the Investigator, Fishes, pl. XX. fig. 6.

B. 7. D. VI. 14. A. 16-17. P. *circ.* 25. V. I. 5. L. lat., from origin on occiput, 50.

Head large, broad, depressed, its extreme length, measured from the tip of the projecting mandible to the apex of the prolonged opercular flap is from two-fifths of to $2\frac{3}{4}$ in the total, caudal excluded. Body elongate, cylindrical, low, and tapering to the large caudal: its greatest height is about one-third the length of the head.

The snout is broad, much depressed, and spathulate, resembling the bill of *Bathypterois*; its extreme length is a little more than the major diameter of the orbit which is about one-fourth the extreme length of the head. Mouth-cleft wide, slightly oblique, the maxilla reaching nearly to the vertical through the middle of the eye, and ending in a fleshy horizontally-disposed barbel. Teeth in villiform bands on the jaws, vomer, and palatines. Tongue large, spathulate.

The large eyes are placed close together on the summit of the head, separated from each other by a narrow groove; but the visual axis is lateral. The gill-cleft is very wide, the gill-membranes being free of the isthmus throughout: the preopercular angle is spinate, and the operculum, which is prolonged in membrane nearly to the level of the 4th dorsal spine, has two spines above, and one belonging to the suboperculum below. Four gills with setiform gill-rakers and broad laminæ: pseudobranchiæ large.

The body, and the head and the snout above, are covered with rather large cycloid or finely ctenoid scales. The lateral line beginning on the occiput as a close-set row of weak re-curved spines, or strongly carinated scales, curves inwards towards the first dorsal fin and then downwards along the lower half of the tail, being salient but unarmed in this part of its course.

The first dorsal fin is short, and is separated from the second by four or five rows of scales: the second, which is much more elevated than the first, extends from the level of the vent to within an eye-length of the base of the caudal. The anal fin is similar to the second dorsal. The pectorals are large and long and reach to, or even beyond, the origin of the anal. The ventrals arise an eye-length in front of the pectorals and reach half-way to the anal.

Three rather large pyloric cæca.

Colours in spirit, yellowish brown with thirteen incomplete and indefinite darker cross-bands: a golden-green ocellus on the crown of the head and one in the apex of each opercle, but all these ocelli tend to fade away: spinous dorsal white at the base, black in the upper half.

In the young there is a large oval black and white ocellus in the upper part of the basal half of the caudal fin; but this gets broken up in older individuals.

An adult female in the Indian Museum is $8\frac{1}{2}$ inches long.

In the Indian Museum are 14 specimens from off the Coromandel coast 107 and 128 fathoms, from the Gulf of Manar 143 fathoms, and from the Andaman Sea 185 and 194 fathoms: [also a specimen labelled *Hypsicometes gobioides* from the Gulf of Mexico 280 fathoms].

Regd. Nos. 13437, 13493, 13494: $\frac{257-259}{1}$, $\frac{373}{1}$, $\frac{673-679}{1}$.

7

Distribution: Caribbean Sea and Atlantic coasts of N. America to 40° N., between 68 and 324 fathoms: Bay of Bengal and Andaman Sea 107 to 194 fathoms: Sea of Japan.

A series dredged in the Andaman Sea shows that *B. gobioides* is the adult of *B. caudimacula*. The latter name has the priority.

CHIASMODUS, Johnson.

Chiasmodus, Johnson, Proc. Zool. Soc. 1863, p. 408 and Ann. Mag. Nat. Hist. (3) XIV. 1864, p. 76: Günther, Cat. Fishes V. p. 435, and Challenger Deep-Sea Fishes, p. 99: Goode and Bean, Oceanic Ichthyology, p. 291 Jordan and Evermann, Fishes of N. America, III. p. 2291.

Ponerodon, Alcock, Ann. Mag. Nat. Hist. (6) VI. 1890, p. 203, and (6) VII. 1891, pp. 9, 10.

Pseudoscopelus, Lütken, Vid. Selsk. Skr. 1892, 6 Ræk. nat. math. Afd. VII. 6. pp. 285, 297.

Body elongate, naked. Eyes lateral. Two separate dorsal fins, of which the second is much the longer and is equal opposite and similar to the anal; ventrals thoracic; pectoral rays branched. Caudal forked, cleft of mouth extremely wide; jaws distensible and armed with canine teeth, as are also the palatines. Gill-openings very wide, the gill-membranes united only quite anteriorly; preoperculum with a (small) spine at its angle; seven branchiostegals; pseudobranchiæ. Lateral line single, uninterrupted. Abdominal cavity enormously distensible. An air-bladder. No pyloric cæca. No anal papilla. Vertebræ 14/24. Mucous system of the head well developed.

30. ***Chiasmodus niger***, Johnson.

Chiasmodus niger, Johnson, P. Z. S. 1863, p. 408 and Ann. Mag. Nat. Hist. (3) XIV. 1864, p. 76: Günther, Cat. Fishes, V. p. 435 and Challenger Deep-Sea Fishes, p. 99: Carte, P. Z. S. 1866, p. 35, pl. ii: Jordan and Gilbert, Cat Fish. N. America, p. 119: A. Agassiz, Bull. Mus. Comp. Zool. XV. 1888, p. 29, fig. 208: Goode and Bean, Oceanic Ichthyology, p. 292, fig. 264.

Ponerodon vastator, Alcock, Ann. Mag. Nat. Hist. (6) VI. 1890, p. 203, pl.ix. fig. 5.

Chiasmodus niger, Alcock, ILLUSTRATIONS OF THE ZOOLOGY OF THE INVESTIGATOR, FISHES, PL. XXVIII. FIG. 3.

B.7. D.X.29. A.29. V.I.5.

Body somewhat elongate and compressed, its height being $4\frac{1}{4}$ in the total without the caudal.

Head low, long, and compressed, its length being $3\frac{1}{4}$ in the same standard; its surface is studded with pores, those on the crown being elliptical and arranged in numerous longitudinal rows. A very large pore, almost as big as the anterior nostril, in front of the upper angle of the orbit.

Snout depressed, tapering, and rounded, its length being twice the diameter of the eye and about one-fourth the length of the head; the lower jaw projects slightly. Eyes lateral, small, circular, deep-set; interorbital space nearly twice the diameter of the eye and nearly flat from side to side; it is traversed by two anteriorly-converging ridges which enclose a V-shaped space. Nostrils large, superior, situated near the tip of the snout.

Cleft of mouth oblique, extremely wide, the maxilla which is a very slender bone, reaches almost to the angle of the preoperculum. Depressible hinged fangs in two rows—those of the inner row being much the larger—in both jaws: a row of distant, fixed, recurved teeth in each palatine. The front tooth on each side of both jaws is also fixed. Tongue free, thin, almost spathulate.

Gill-openings wide; gill-covers thin and flexible, the preoperculum with a very oblique edge, a small, stout, obliquely decurrent spine at its angle, and a thick muscular covering; gill-membranes attached only quite anteriorly; four gills, the last gill-cleft a small foramen, branchial arches extremely weak and flexible; no gill-rakers; pseudobranchiæ well developed.

Skin entirely scaleless, thin, covered with a uniformly thick adherent layer of mucus; a single lateral line of pores, which follows the dorsal profile from occiput to base of caudal.

Two dorsal fins, separated by an interval equal to two-thirds the length of the snout: the first, which begins slightly in advance of the vertical through the base of the pectoral, consists of ten slender but well-ossified spines, of which the longest (third) is barely as long as the snout and eye combined; the second contains twenty-nine slender articulated rays, branched at the tip and decreasing regularly in length from before backwards, the longest (second) being about half the length of the head. Anal equal, opposite and similar to the second dorsal. Caudal symmetrically forked. Pectorals slender, as long as the post-orbital portion of the head, all the rays branched. Ventrals thoracic, equal in length to the eye and snout combined.

The abdomen is a great elastic sac, which extends behind the normally situated vent into the tail; it contains a vast collapsed stomach, but no pyloric cæca. There is an air-bladder similar to that of *Champsodon*.

There are 14 abdominal and 24 caudal vertebræ.

Colours in life: blotchy violet-black to black.

In the Indian Museum is a single specimen, just over six inches long, from the Bay of Bengal, off the Godavari coast, 920 to 690 fathoms.

Regd. No. 12836.

Distribution: West Indies, North and Mid Atlantic, Madeira, Bay of Bengal.

Dr. Günther places *Chiasmodus* among the *Gadidæ*, but I feel pretty sure that its place in the system is close to *Champsodon*.

Family *Pediculati*.

When the second volume of the *Fishes*, in the *Fauna of British India*, was published in 1889, only two genera of Pediculates were known to occur in Indian Seas, namely, *Antennarius* and *Halieutæa*.

We now know of nine Indian genera, which are shown in the following table.

Synopsis of the Indian genera of the family Pediculati.

I. Gills three and a half or two and two halves: no pseudobranchiæ: an air-bladder: no pyloric cæca. Body compressed and elevated: the spinous dorsal consists of 3 isolated spines, of which the first is a rostral tentacle ... ... *Antennarius.*

II. Gills three: small pseudobranchiæ present: no air-blader: two pyloric cæca. Head and anterior part of body depressed, disk-like: the spinous dorsal consists of from 3 to 6 spines, of which the first 3 are long isolated tentacles ... ... LOPHIUS.

III. Gills two and a half: no air-bladder: no pyloric cæca:—

1. Body elevated: mouth-cleft oblique or nearly vertical: the spinous dorsal consists of 1 or 2 unprotected tentacles. No pseudobranchiæ:—

i. Ventral fins present ... ... CHAUNAX.

ii. Ventral fins absent:—

a. Skin covered with prickles ... ... CERATIAS.

b. Skin smooth ... ... ONIRODES.

2. Head and anterior part of body depressed, disk-like: mouth horizontal: the spinous dorsal consists of a single tentacle lodged in a bony cavity above the mouth. Pseudobranchiæ rudimentary, but distinct ... ... *Halieutæa.*

IV. Gills two: no pseudobranchiæ: no air-bladder: no pyloric cæca. Head, *etc.*, depressed, disk-like: mouth-cleft horizontal, not wide: the spinous dorsal consists of a single tentacle lodged in a bony cavity above the mouth:—

1. Soft dorsal fin present:—

i. Teeth in the jaws only ... ... DIBRANCHUS.

ii. Teeth in the jaws, vomer, and palatines ... ... MALTHOPSIS.

2. No soft dorsal fin ... ... HALICMETUS.

LOPHIUS, Artedi.

Lophius, Artedi, Genera Piscium p. 62: Cuv. and Val. Hist. Nat. Poiss. XII. p. 339: Günther, Cat. Fishes, II. p. 178: Goode and Bean, Oceanic Ichthyology, p. 485:

Lophius and *Lophiomus*, Jordan and Evermann, Fishes N. America III. pp. 2713, 2714.

Head exceedingly large, forming a broad disk with the eyes on its upper surface. Mouth exceedingly wide, the lower jaw projecting: jaws and palate with cardiform teeth. Skin naked: bones of the head with numerous spines. The three anterior dorsal spines, which are situated on the head, are isolated and are modified to form tentacles: the posterior dorsal spines vary in number from one to three, and when numbering three form a continuous fin. Soft dorsal and anal short. Gills three. Pseudobranchiæ present, small. Pyloric appendages two.

Distribution. American, European, and African coasts of N. Atlantic: Mediterranean: Seas of India and Archipelago: Seas of China and Japan.

Key to the Indian species of the genus Lophius.

I. Six dorsal spines, the last 3 of which form a continuous fin:—
  1. Pectorals broad: 3rd dorsal spine a simple filament ... *L. indicus.*
  2. Pectorals narrow: 3rd dorsal spine fringed with tags of skin ... ... *L. gracilimanus.*

II. Five dorsal spines, the last 2 rudimentary and hidden beneath the skin ... ... *L. mutilus.*

III. Four dorsal spines, the 4th not hidden ... ... *L. lugubris.*

31. ***Lophius indicus,*** Alcock.

Lophius indicus, Alcock, Journ. As. Soc. Bengal, Vol. LVIII. pt. 2, 1889, p. 302: Illustrations of the Zoology of the Investigator, Fishes, pl. XIX. fig. 3.

B. 6. D. I. I. I. III. 8-9. A. 6-7. P. *circ.* 23. V. I. 5.

Disk subcircular, half the total length, caudal included, fringed all round with tassels of skin which also extend along the sides of the tail and caudal fin and on to the dorsal surface of the pectoral fins.

Two spines on the preorbital, and two on the elevated upper border of the orbit. Humeral spine coarse, multifid.

Eyes very small, their diameter being about one-tenth the length of the cephalic disk and about two-thirds the width of the interorbital space.

Tongue hyoid and neighbouring parts of branchial arches coloured much like the body.

Depressible teeth of unequal size in 2 or 3 irregular series in both jaws, the inner series the largest (especially in the lower jaw) and most regular. Two teeth on either side of the vomer, and three or four along each palatine.

First and third dorsal spines the longest,—rather over two-fifths the length of the disk: the first spine a bristle ending in a large tuft, the second fringed throughout, the third a simple bristle. Of the next three connected spines the first is much the longest, the 2nd and 3rd being short. Caudal about a fifth the total length (itself included). Pectorals broad and fan-like, all but the first one or two and the last five or six rays being of approximately equal length.

Colour in life, dorsal surface dark grey or brown with either a network of fine black lines or numerous small black rings: ventral surface colourless.

In the Indian Museum are eight specimens, the largest being just over five inches long.

Malabar coast, 28 fathoms, Bay of Bengal 25 to 60 fathoms, Gulf of Martaban 67 fathoms, Andaman Sea 90 fathoms.

Regd. Nos. 12450, 12451, 12504, 13216, $\frac{261-263}{1}$, $\frac{413}{1}$.

This species is very closely related to, and may possibly be only a dwarf variety of, *Lophius setigerus* Wahl, the common Fishing-frog of Japan.

32. *Lophius gracilimanus*, n. sp.

ILLUSTRATIONS OF THE ZOOLOGY OF THE INVESTIGATOR, FISHES, PL. XXIX. FIG. 3.

B. 6. D. I. I. I. III. 8. A. 6. P. *circ.* 18. V. I. 5.

Disk elliptical, nearly half the total length, caudal included, fringed as in the preceding species, but more scantily.

Two spines on the preorbital, supra-orbital margin elevated and dentated. Humeral spine truncated and bifid at tip.

Eyes of moderate size, their major diameter about one-sixth the length of the disk and nearly equal to the width of the interorbital space.

Hyoid and neighbouring parts of branchial arches not or only slightly pigmented.

Teeth as in the preceding species, except that the premaxillary teeth beyond the vicinity of the symphysis become a single series.

Second dorsal spine the longest, its length being at least three-quarters that of the disk: the first dorsal spine is a bristle ending in a small tassel, the second is a simple bristle, and the third which is little shorter than the second is fringed throughout its length. Of the next three connected spines the first is the longest, but the 2nd and 3rd are also of good length. Caudal a fourth the total length (itself included). Pectorals narrow, pointed.

Colours, mottled dark sepia to blue-black.

Only one of the pyloric cæca is large.

Three specimens, the longest a little over four and a quarter inches long, from off the Malabar coast 68 to 148, and 100 fathoms.

This species is distinguished from *L. indicus* by the larger eye, the narrow pointed pectoral fin, the long caudal fin, and the different form and length of the isolated dorsal spines.

Regd. Nos. $\frac{488-490}{1}$, $\frac{672}{1}$.

33. *Lophius mutilus*, Alcock.

Lophius mutilus, Alcock, Journ. As. Soc. Bengal, Vol. LXII. pt. 2, 1893, p. 179: ILLUSTRATIONS OF THE ZOOLOGY OF THE INVESTIGATOR, FISHES, PL. X. FIG. 2.

B. 6. D. I. I. I. II *rudimentary*. 8–9. A. 5. P. *circ.* 15. V. I.5.

Cephalic disk subcircular, not quite half the total length caudal included, scantily fringed—like the sides of the tail and the dorsal surface of the pectoral fins—with slender tassels.

A single distinct spine on the preorbital: three teeth on the sharp overhanging upper border of the orbit. Humeral spine trifid.

Eyes large, their diameter being a fifth the length of the disk and equal to the width of the interorbital space.

Hyoid and neighbouring parts of branchial arches dusky, but not distinctly pigmented.

Small depressible fangs of unequal size in three irregular series in the mandible, in two series near the symphysis of the upper jaw, but in a single series along the greater part of the upper jaw. A pair of rigid fangs on each side of the vomer, and five or six along each palatine.

The third dorsal spine is much the longest, being as long as the cephalic disk: all three are plain bristles. The second portion of the spinous dorsal consists of two small spines only visible after dissection. Caudal about a fourth the total length (itself included). Pectorals narrow.

Colours in spirit, mottled brown.

A single specimen, $5\frac{1}{4}$ inches long, from the Bay of Bengal, off the Madras coast, 128 fathoms.

Regd. No. 13438.

This species is at once distinguished by the rudimentary second part of the spinous dorsal.

34. *Lophius lugubris*, Alcock.

Lophius lugubris, Alcock, Journ. As. Soc. Bengal, Vol. LXIII. pt. 2, 1894, p. 118: ILLUSTRATIONS OF THE ZOOLOGY OF THE INVESTIGATOR, FISHES, PL. XIV. FIG. 1.

B. 6. D. I. I. I. I. 7-8. A. 5-6. P. *circ.* 13. V. I.5.

Cephalic disk subcircular, about half the total length, caudal included, scantily fringed with slender tassels as in *Lophius mutilus.*

A single distinct spine on the preorbital; 3 teeth on the sharp overhanging upper border of the orbit. Humeral spine trifid.

Eyes moderate, their diameter about a seventh the length of the disk, and rather less than the width of the interorbital space except at its fore end.

Hyoid and neighbouring parts of mouth slightly dusky, not distinctly pigmented.

Teeth as in *Lophius mutilus.*

All the dorsal spines are simple filaments: the third is much the longest, being as long as or even longer than the cephalic disk. The second part of the dorsal fin consists of a single short slender filament, about twice as long as the eye. Caudal rather more than a fourth the length of the total (itself included). Pectorals narrow.

Colours in spirit, dark sepia mottled with black.

Three specimens, the largest $5\frac{1}{2}$ inches long, from off Colombo, 143 and 142 to 400 fathoms.

Regd. Nos. 13467, $\frac{670}{1}$, $\frac{671}{1}$.

This species is distinguished from *L. mutilus* by the smaller eye, and by the second portion of the spinous dorsal fin, which consists of a single filament. In one of the specimens this filament is not present, or any trace of it.

Ceratias, Kröyer.

Ceratias, Kröyer, Naturhist. Tidsskr. 1844-45, p. 639: Günther, Cat. Fishes, III. p. 205 and Challenger Deep Sea Fishes, p. 52.

Ceratias. Diceratias, Mancalias, Typhlopsaras, Cryptopsaras, Gill: Goode and Bean, Oceanic Ichthyology, pp. 488–491 (subgenera).

Ceratias and *Mancalias* (p. 2729), *Cryptopsaras* (p. 2731), Jordan and Evermann, Fishes of N. America, Vol. III.

Head enormous, body and tail short; both often elevated and compressed. Skin with minute scutes or prickles. Mouth very large, approaching the vertical, the mandible projecting. Depressible teeth of unequal size in the jaws and sometimes on the vomer. Eyes small.

Gills two and a half. No pseudobranchiæ.

Spinous dorsal reduced to one or two spines, which are generally modified into tentacles. Soft dorsal and anal short.

Ventrals absent.

Distribution: Arctic and North Atlantic: Seas of India and Archipelago Japanese Seas.

Subgenus Diceratias.

Two dorsal spines situated on the anterior part of the head. Vomerine teeth present. No pyloric appendages.

35. *Ceratias (Diceratias) bispinosus*, Günther.

Ceratias bispinosus, Günther, Challenger Deep Sea Fishes, p. 53. Alcock, Illustrations of the Zoology of the Investigator, Fishes, pl. XXXV. fig. 2.

D. I.I. 6. A. 4. C. 9. P. 14.

The height of the body, when the stomach is empty, is about half the total, caudal included.

Head much larger than the body and tail combined. Each frontal bone with a strong outstanding spine, situated above and behind the eye.

On top of the snout are the two isolated dorsal spines, the anterior of which bears a long stout tentacle (about a third as long as the body) ending in a fleshy knob, while the second is almost a rudiment.

Eye small, subcutaneous, about a third as long as the snout: in front of it is a tubular nostril.

Mouth-cleft enormous, the length of the maxilla being nearly one-third of the total, caudal included. A series of large and small depressible teeth in each jaw: a few large teeth, decreasing in size from without inwards, on each side of the vomer.

Skin of head and body covered with minute prickles.

Dorsal and anal fins placed close to the caudal, which is very large and is pointed.

Colour black.

A single specimen, $5\frac{1}{2}$ inches long, from off the Malabar coast, 636 fathoms.

Regd. No. 14008.

Distribution: Banda Sea, Arabian Sea.

ONIRODES, Lütken.

Oneirodes, Lütken, Oversigt Dansk. Vid. Selsk. Forhandl. 1871, p. 56: Gill, Proc. U. S. Nat. Mus. I. 1878, p. 227: Günther, Challenger Deep Sea Fishes, p. 56: Jordan and Gilbert, Bull. U. S. Nat. Mus. XVI. p. 848: Goode and Bean, Oceanic Ichthyology, p. 492: Jordan and Evermann, Fishes of N. America III. p. 2732.

Paroneirodes, Alcock, Ann. Mag. Nat. Hist. Sept. 1890, p. 206.

Head enormous, body and tail short, both compressed and elevated. Skin naked. Mouth large, oblique, the lower jaw a little prominent. Depressible teeth of unequal size in the jaws and on the vomer. Eyes small.

Gills two and a half. No pseudobranchiæ.

Spinous dorsal reduced to two spines, which are modified into tentacles. Soft dorsal and anal short.

Ventrals absent. No pyloric cæca.

Distribution: off coasts of Greenland: Bay of Bengal in deep water.

36. ***Onirodes glomerosus***, Alcock.

Paronirodes glomerosus, Alcock, Ann. Mag. Nat. Hist. Sept. 1890, p 206, pl. ix. fig 6: ILLUSTRATIONS OF THE ZOOLOGY OF THE INVESTIGATOR, PL. XXVIII. FIG. 4.

D. 1.1. 6. A. 4. C. 8.

When captured the form of the body was ovoid, though unstable; hardened in spirit it becomes compressed and oval. The length of the head is five eighths, its greatest height nine-sixteenths of the total, without the caudal. The eye is small, being deeply buried beneath a circular patch of transparent (unpig-

8

mented) skin; above each eye is a prominent, coarse, procumbent spine. Mouth moderately large, its cleft obliquely ascending; the length of the maxilla is one-third that of the head; a narrow band (?) of small teeth in each jaw and on the vomer; tongue large; only the floor of the mouth pigmented.

Gills $2\frac{1}{2}$; gill-opening a small circular aperture just beneath the root of the pectoral fin.

Skin thin and perfectly smooth and scaleless; it is protected by a thick coat of mucus.

Two clavate cephalic tentacles, the first being rather more than twice the length of the second, situated close together in the after part of the interorbital space, with luminous organs imbedded in their enlarged tips. Second dorsal and anal placed far back on the tail, almost in contact with the caudal, which is pointed and in length a little more than one-fourth of the total; all the rays of the vertical fins simple; pectorals very short, pointed; ventrals absent.

Colours:—Body and fins jet-black; in spirit the tip of the cephalic tentacles become white. Pharyngo-branchial and peritoneal membranes unpigmented.

One specimen, $1\frac{1}{6}$ inch long from the Bay of Bengal, 1260 fathoms.

Regd. No. 12840.

Chaunax, Lowe.

Chaunax, Lowe, Trans. Zool. Soc. III. 1849, p. 339: Günther, Cat. Fishes, III. p. 200 and Challenger Deep Sea Fishes, p. 58: Goode and Bean, Oceanic Ichthyology, p. 487: Jordan and Evermann, Fishes N. America, III. p. 2726.

Head enormous, cuboidal. Skin covered with minute prickles. Mouth-cleft wide, approaching the vertical, the lower jaw heavy and prominent. Bands of small teeth in the jaws and palate.

Spinous dorsal reduced to a short tentacle situated on the snout. Soft dorsal of moderate length. Anal short. Ventrals present.

Gills two and a half: no pseudobranchiæ. No pyloric cæca.

37. *Chaunax pictus*, Lowe.

Chaunax pictus, Lowe, Trans. Zool. Soc. III. 1849, p. 339, pl. li: Günther, Cat. Fishes, III. p. 200 and Challenger Deep Sea Fishes, p. 58, pl. x. fig. A: Goode, Proc. U. S. Nat. Mus. III. 1881, p. 470: Jordan and Gilbert, Bull. U. S. Nat. Mus. XVI. p. 846: Vaillant, Exp. Sci. Travailleur et Talisman, Poiss. p. 343, pl. xxviii. figs. 1-11: Alcock, Ann. Mag. Nat. Hist. Nov. 1889, p. 381: Goode and Bean, Oceanic Ichthyology, p. 487, fig. 398.

Chaunax fimbriatus, Hilgendorf, Sitzungsb. Ges. Naturf. Freunde, 1879, p. 80: Steindachner and Döderlein, Denk. Ak. Wien XLIX. 1885, p. 191.

B. 7. D. I. 11. A. 6–7. P. 11. V. 4. C. 8.

Shape like that of *Diodon* or *Tetrodon*.

The great cuboidal head is at least half the total length without the caudal, and its greatest height, behind the eyes, is from a third to two-fifths the same measure.

Eyes large, subcutaneous, lateral although placed high up near the dorsal profile.

Snout short, squarish, underhung by the massive square-cut lower jaw. Nostrils two tiny pores situated near the edge of the snout. On the top of the snout, folding backwards on to a shallow smooth depression of the skin, is a tentacle, about half as long as the eye, ending in a leaf-like tassel: this represents the first dorsal fin.

Mouth-cleft wide, the length of the maxilla being two-ninths the total without the caudal.

Skin extremely loose, covered with minute granules or prickles which are finest on the throat and belly, traversed by chain-like rows of mucous pores as follows :—

(1) one extending, on each side, from the snout over the eye, and then curving downwards to run along the ventral surface of the tail and on to the base of the caudal:

(2) one extending from the tip of the chin, on each side, along the lower border of the head, to near the gill-opening:

(3) one across the head ("like a headstall") behind the level of the eyes from (2) to (2):

(4) one on each side from the snout, in continuation of (1), round and across the cheek, to (3):

(5) one across the chin from (2) to (2).

Pectorals fairly broad, ventrals small and narrow.

Colours in spirit, either uniform light yellow, or light yellow with large faint-brown spots; throat white.

In the Indian Museum are numerous specimens from the Bay of Bengal 193, 272 and 145 to 250 fathoms, and two from off Colombo 142 to 400 fathoms and 480 fathoms.

Regd. Nos. 11687, 11690, 11693–11695, 11719, 11720, 13468, 13483–13492, $\frac{528}{1}$.

Distribution: West Indies and neighbouring Atlantic coasts of America, Madeira, C. Verde and neighbouring coasts of Africa: Arabian Sea, Bay of Bengal: Fiji, Japan: at moderate depths, 130 to about 400 fathoms.

HALIEUTÆA, Cuv. and Val.

Diagnosis, *etc.*, recorded in the *Fishes of India.*

Key to the Indian species of the genus Halieutæa.

I. Under surface of disk covered with a thick, perfectly smooth, glandular skin ... ... *H. fumosa.*

II. Under surface of disk finely granular; interorbital space decidedly concave:—

1. Four rays in the dorsal fin ... ... *H. stellata.*
2. Five rays in the dorsal fin... ... ... *H. nigra.*

III. Under surface of disk with stellate spines; interorbital space hardly concave; five rays in the dorsal fin ... ... *H. coccinea.*

38. ***Halieutæa stellata***, Wahl.

Synonomy recorded in the *Fishes of India.*

B. 6. D. 4. A. 4. P. 13. V. I. 5. C. 9.

Tail, including the caudal fin, about three-fourths the length of the disk.

Disk broader than long, very little elevated anteriorly. Dorsal surface covered with stout sharp spines having a broad star-shaped base. The spines on the edge of the disk and along the side of the tail are bifid or multifid, and usually have numerous short filaments between them.

Skin of the under surface of the disk finely granular.

Eyes between $\frac{1}{8}$ and $\frac{1}{9}$ the length of the disk in diameter, and about a diameter apart. Interorbital space decidedly concave.

Rostral tentacle three-lobed.

Caudal about $\frac{2}{9}$ the total length (itself included), not quite as long as the pectoral. Ventrals moderately broad, between $\frac{1}{2}$ and $\frac{2}{3}$ the length of the pectorals.

Parietal peritoneum moderately pigmented.

Colours in life, pink: in spirit the dorsum is light brown with some black streaks and patches.

Has been taken in the Bay of Bengal at 98 to 102 fathoms and off the Malabar coast at 68 to 148 fathoms.

Distribution: Seas of India, Malay Archipelago, China, and Japan.

39. ***Halieutæa nigra***, Alcock.

Halieutæa nigra, Alcock, Ann. Mag. Nat. Hist. July, 1891, p. 24: ILLUSTRATIONS OF THE ZOOLOGY OF THE INVESTIGATOR, FISHES, PL. XIX. FIG. 2.

B. 6. D. 5. A. 4. C. 9. P. 13. V. I. 5.

Differs from *H. stellata* in the following particulars :—

(1) the cephalic disk is circular and is decidedly elevated anteriorly, and there are no cutaneous filaments along its edge, except at the chin :

(2) the eyes are about $\frac{1}{7}$ the length of the disk, and are rather more than a diameter apart :

(3) the caudal is $\frac{1}{4}$ the total length (itself included) :

(4) the ventrals, which are only about half the length of the pectorals, are slender.

Colours in life, blue-black with jet black vermicular lines on the dorsal surface : in spirit bluish with the black lines more distinct.

A single specimen, just over $2\frac{1}{2}$ inches long, from the Andaman Sea, 188 to 220 fathoms.

Regd. No. 13027.

It is quite possible that this is only a variety of *H. stellata*.

40. ***Halieutæa coccinea***, Alcock.

Halieutæa coccinea, Alcock, Ann. Mag. Nat. Hist., Nov. 1889, p. 382 : ILLUSTRATIONS OF THE ZOOLOGY OF THE INVESTIGATOR, FISHES, PL. XIX. FIG. 1.

B. 6. D. 5. A. 4. C. 9. P. 13-14. V. I. 5.

Differs from *H. stellata* in the following particulars :—

(1) the cephalic disk is circular and is distinctly elevated anteriorly, and the cutaneous filaments on its edge are few and inconspicuous :

(2) the spines of the dorsal surface have needle-like points, and the under surface of the disk is well covered with stellate spines : [in the young the spines of the under surface are scattered and very small] :

(3) the interorbital space is but slightly concave and its width is much more than a diameter of the eye :

(4) the caudal is about a fifth the total length :

(5) the ventrals are slender :

(6) the parietal peritoneum and branchial mucosa are jet black and particularly thick.

Colours in life : "dorsum bright pink, with fine black vermicular lines ; under surface crimson" : in spirit white, with the black lines very distinct and the black peritoneum and branchial mucosa showing through on both sides of the disk.

Numerous specimens from the Andaman Sea, 265 and 185 fathoms : the largest is just over 7 inches long.

Regd. Nos. 11741 : $\frac{264\text{-}281}{1}$.

This species may perhaps be only a variety of *H. stellata*. An accident to the unique specimen known in 1889 led me to describe the rostral tentacle as bilobed: in the specimens received since then the tentacle has the usual three-lobed form.

41. *Halieutæa fumosa*, Alcock.

Halieutæa fumosa, Alcock, Journ. As. Soc. Bengal, Vol. LXIII. pt. 2, 1894, p. 119: ILLUSTRATIONS OF THE ZOOLOGY OF THE INVESTIGATOR, FISHES, PL. XIV. FIG. 2.

B. 6. D. 4. A. 4. C. 9. P. 13. V. I. 5.

Differs from *H. stellata* in the following particulars:—

(1) the spines of the dorsal surface are mere spinules, though their bases are pyramidal or star-shaped: the filaments along the edge of the disk and sides of tail are excessively delicate:

(2) the skin of the under surface of the disk is thick, gelatinous and absolutely smooth:

(3) the length of the eye is between $\frac{1}{7}$ and $\frac{1}{8}$ that of the disk, and the interorbital space is slightly concave:

(4) caudal one-fourth the total length, and equal to the pectorals:

(5) ventrals slender, more than $\frac{2}{3}$ the length of the pectorals.

Colours in spirit: upper surface smoky blue, becoming hyaline near the edge of the disk; under surface grey, finely and closely speckled with silver; dorsal fin blackish; pectorals and caudal with a broad black cross-band and commonly a milk-white tip.

Numerous specimens, from the Bay of Bengal, 145 to 250 fathoms, and off the Malabar coast, 68 to 148 fathoms. The largest is about 4 inches long.

Regd. Nos. 13716–13720, 13722–13725, 13727, 12823, $\frac{491-492}{1}$.

It is quite possible that this species also is merely a variety of *H. stellata*.

DIBRANCHUS, Peters.

Dibranchus, Peters, Monatsb. Akad. Berlin, 1875, p. 736: Gill, Proc. U. S. Nat. Mus. I. 1878, p. 231: Günther, Challenger Deep Sea Fishes, p. 59: Goode and Bean, Oceanic Ichthyology, p. 50? Jordan and Evermann, Fishes of North America, III. p. 2743.

Head and anterior part of body forming a large subtriangular or ovate disk the edge of which is armed with horizontal spines. Skin beset with spines having stelliform bases, or with tubercles and granules.

Cleft of mouth horizontal, of moderate width. Minute teeth in the jaws only.

Forehead with a transverse bony bridge forming a cavern above the mouth, in which a retractile tentacle, that represents the 1st dorsal fin, is lodged.

Soft dorsal and anal short.

Two gills (on the 2nd and 3rd branchial arches). No pseudobranchiæ.

No air-bladder: no pyloric appendages.

Distribution: West Indies and Atlantic coasts of the United States: Cape Verde and neighbouring coasts of Africa: Arabian Sea, Bay of Bengal, Andaman Sea. At moderate depths.

42. ***Dibranchus nasutus***, Alcock.

Dibranchus nasutus, Alcock, Ann. Mag. Nat. Hist, July 1891, p. 24, pl. vii, fig. 1: ILLUSTRATIONS OF THE ZOOLOGY OF THE INVESTIGATOR, FISHES, PL. XX, FIG. 2.

B. 6. D. 6. A. 4. C. 9. P. 12–13. V. I. 5.

Disk, measured to the gill-opening, shorter than the tail (including caudal), its cranial portion very slightly elevated.

The frontal bridge projects considerably beyond the mouth, forming a snout.

The rostral tentacle ends in a pair of fleshy balls, with a pair of filaments above and between them.

Eyes about one-sixth the length of the disk and not much more than one diameter apart anteriorly.

Dorsal surface closely covered with rigid spines having a stelliform base: ventral surface much more sparsely beset with similar but smaller spines or acute tubercles.

Dorsal fin in the anterior half of the tail, but some distance behind the gill-opening: anal fin entirely behind the dorsal.

Caudal fin $4\frac{2}{3}$ in the total length, equal to the pectorals. Ventrals narrow, nearly as long as the pectorals.

Colour in life, blue black to jet black.

The largest specimen is not quite $3\frac{1}{4}$ inches long.

Andaman Sea, 188 to 220 and 405 fathoms: off Travancore coast, 406 fathoms.

Regd. Nos. 13028, 14116–14118, $\frac{153}{1}$.

43. ***Dibranchus micropus***, Alcock.

Dibranchus micropus, Alcock, Ann. Mag. Nat. Hist., July 1891, p. 25, pl. vii. figs. 2, 2*a*, 2*b*,: ILLUSTRATIONS OF THE ZOOLOGY OF THE INVESTIGATOR, FISHES, PL. XX, FIG. 1.

B. 6. D. 5. A. 4. C. 9. P. 15. V. 5.

Disk as long as, or longer than, the tail, its cranial portion very decidedly elevated.

Edge of the frontal bridge flush with the chin, not projecting.

The rostral tentacle ends in a pair of fleshy lobes, surmounted by a third, median, foliaceous fimbriated lobe.

Eyes between a sixth and a seventh the length of the disk, somewhat more than two diameters apart.

Dorsal surface closely covered with spines which have a stelliform base and a flexible, almost setaceous, shaft; on the tail they are almost rigid: ventral surface with similar but smaller bristle-like spines.

Dorsal fin close behind the gill-opening, anal fin not entirely behind the dorsal.

Caudal fin $4\frac{1}{4}$ to $4\frac{1}{2}$ in the total length, equal to the pectorals. Ventrals very small, not a third the length of the pectorals.

Colour in life, uniform blue black.

The largest specimen is not quite 3 inches long.

Bay of Bengal, off Vizagapatam coast, 240 fathoms; Andaman Sea, 370 to 419 and 405 fathoms; off Travancore coast, 406 fathoms.

Regd. Nos. 13029, 13030, 14120, $\frac{116}{1}$, $\frac{377}{1}$.

MALTHOPSIS, Alcock.

Malthopsis, Alcock, Ann. Mag. Nat. Hist., July 1891, p. 26.

Head and anterior part of body forming a large depressed sub-triangular disk. Bones of the snout produced to form a sharp projecting spine, overhanging a cavity above the mouth, in which a retractile tentacle is lodged.

Skin more or less beset with large conical striated tubercles.

Mouth-cleft rather narrow, horizontal. Villiform teeth on the jaws vomer and palatines.

Soft dorsal and anal short.

Two gills (on the 2nd and 3rd branchial arches). No pseudobranchiæ.

No air-bladder: no pyloric appendages.

Distribution: Indian Seas, Mid Pacific. At moderate depths.

44. *Malthopsis lutea*, Alcock.

Malthopsis lutea, Alcock, Ann. Mag. Nat. Hist., July 1891, p. 26, pl. viii. figs. 2, 2*a*: ILLUSTRATIONS OF THE ZOOLOGY OF THE INVESTIGATOR, FISHES, PL. XIX. FIG. 4.

B. 5. D. 5. A. 4. C. 9. P. 11. V. 1.5.

Disk not quite as long as the tail (caudal included), its cranial part moderately elevated. Snout projecting horizontally or obliquely upwards as a stout striated spine.

Beneath this nasal prolongation is a deep narrow vault, flanked on each side by a pair of large, almost confluent nostrils, and containing a short, fleshy, clavate tentacle.

Eyes large, lateral, nearly circular; their diameter is about one-seventh of the total length, caudal not included; they are strongly convergent and anteriorly are barely half a diameter apart; the anterior limit of the orbit is in the same vertical line with the anterior limit of the mouth.

The mouth-cleft, which is horizontal, is about two-thirds of an eye-diameter in width. Teeth villiform, in bands in the jaws and in broad patches on the vomer and anterior ends of the palatines.

Gill-cleft a small foramen, in width about one-fifth of an eye-diameter, situated superiorly in the axilla; two gills; no pseudobranchiæ. Sub-operculum prolonged and ending in a stout trifid or multifid spine.

Body more or less covered with hard granular adherent plates, each with a large radially-striated conical tubercle in its centre. On the dorsal surface of the cephalic disk they are of moderate size, in contact along the middle line, but distant and slightly sunken laterally; on the ventral surface of the cephalic disk they are very few and distant (except on the belly, where they may be numerous) and sunken; on the tail they are large and in close contact throughout.

The dorsal fin is in the anterior half of the tail, the anal is completely behind the dorsal: the ventrals are very long, nearly equal to the pectorals, which are equal to the caudal, which is two-ninths of the total.

Colours in life: pinkish yellow; some specimens with a few irregular dark rings on the dorsum of the cephalic disk.

Five abdominal and thirteen caudal vertebræ, the neural spines of the former fused into a trenchant ridge as in *Malthe* and *Halieutæa*.

The largest specimen is $3\frac{1}{2}$ inches long.

Andaman Sea, 185, 188 to 220, and 405 fathoms.

Regd. Nos. 13014–13016, 13018–13020: $\frac{286}{1}$, $\frac{288-290}{1}$, $\frac{292}{1}$: $\frac{130-135}{1}$.

Halicmetus, Alcock.

Halicmetus, Alcock, Ann. Mag. Nat. Hist., July 1891, p. 319.

Head and anterior part of body forming a large depressed sub-triangular disk. Front with a transverse bony bridge roofing in a cavity that lies above the mouth and lodges a fleshy retractile tentacle representing the spinous dorsal fin.

Skin covered with granules and tubercles.

Mouth-cleft rather narrow, horizontal. Villiform teeth in jaws vomer and palatines.

No dorsal fin whatever (except the rostral tentacle): anal fin very short.

Two gills (on the 2nd and 3rd branchial arches). No pseudobranchiæ.

No air-bladder: no pyloric appendages.

45. *Halicmetus ruber*, Alcock.

Halicmetus ruber, Alcock, Ann. Mag. Nat. Hist., July 1891, p. 27, pl. viii. figs. 1, 1*a-b*. ILLUSTRATIONS OF THE ZOOLOGY OF THE INVESTIGATOR, FISHES, PL. XIX. FIG. 5. ("*Halieutæa coccinea*," Goode and Bean, Oceanic Ichthyology, fig. 410.)

B. 6. D. 0. A. 3-4. C. 9. P. 11. V. I.5.

Disk not quite as long as the tail (caudal included), its cranial part little elevated.

The truncated snout is occupied by a bony rugose orbital bridge, beneath which is a cavity lodging a fleshy tentacle which ends in three lobes, the middle (superior) lobe being crested by a pair of papillæ or small bifid filament. The eyes are about one-seventh the length of the disk and are about half a diameter apart anteriorly.

The nostrils are minute papillæ situated on each side of the rostral tentacle, almost within the subrostral cavity.

Mouth horizontal, with the lower jaw slightly projecting; its cleft is a little wider than the eye. Villiform teeth in bands in the jaws vomer and on the anterior ends of the palatines.

Gill-cleft a small foramen, less than half an eye-diameter in width, situated superiorly in the axilla. The sub-operculum ends in a stout multifid spine.

Surface of the body uniformly invested with minute close-set graniform spines, which also cover the eyes up to the corneal margin. The edge of the cephalic disk bears in addition large finely granular multifid spines in three longitudinal series, and the tail is clad with large granular conical tubercles—of which there are five longitudinal series on each side—in close contact. There are also some smaller tubercles scattered on the dorsal surface of the disk.

Fins in form and position as in *Halieutæa*, *Malthopsis*, &c., but the soft dorsal, as well as the spinous, is entirely wanting, and the anal is almost rudimentary. The pectorals, which are about a third longer than the ventrals and a little longer than the caudal, are nearly one-fifth the total length.

Colours in life, uniform light pink.

Five abdominal and thirteen caudal vertebræ.

The largest specimen, a gravid female, is nearly $3\frac{1}{2}$ inches long.

Andaman Sea, 188 to 220, and 405 fathoms: Arabian Sea, off Travancore coast, 406 fathoms.

Regd. Nos. 13025, 13026: 14122–14125 : $\frac{284}{1}$.

Family *Cottidæ.*

Trigla, Artedi.

46. *Trigla hemisticta*, Temm. & Schleg.

Synonomy and diagnosis recorded in the *Fishes of India*, p. 791, and Fauna of British India, *Fishes* II. p. 241.

Bay of Bengal, off Ganjam coast, 98 to 102 fathoms.

Regd. Nos. 12748, 12751, 12752, 12757, 12761, 12762, 12766, 12767, 12773, 12774, 12776, 12777.

Lepidotrigla, Günther.

Lepidotrigla, Günther, Cat. Fishes, II. p. 196.

"Head parallelopiped, with the upper surface and the sides entirely bony: "the enlarged infra-orbital covering the cheek. Body with scales of moderate "size, regularly arranged. Two dorsals, the first much shorter than the second. "Three pectoral filaments. Villiform teeth in both the jaws and on the vomer, "none on the palatine bones. Air-bladder generally with lateral muscles, often "divided into two lateral halves. Pyloric appendages in moderate number." (*Günther*).

47. *Lepidotrigla spiloptera*, Günther.

Lepidotrigla spiloptera, Günther, Challenger Shore Fishes, p. 42, pl. xviii. fig. C; and Challenger Deep Sea Fishes, p. 64.

B. 7. D. IX. 15. A. 15. L. lat. 60.

Scales feebly serrated, those of the lateral line unarmed, those that immediately flank the dorsal fins with well developed spines.

Profile of snout concave: pre-orbital projecting as a broad spine, about half as long as the eye. Interorbital space very concave, its width is nearly equal to the vertical diameter of the eye. A deepish transverse groove behind the orbits, not well marked in the young.

The 1st dorsal spine, which is the highest, is not very much more than half the length of the head. Pectoral fin reaching to the 4th or 5th anal ray.

Colours in life: reddish; pectoral dark blue on its inner surface, with numerous white spots and a white margin.

One specimen, nearly four inches long, from the Gulf of Martaban 67 fathoms.

Regd. No. $\frac{294}{1}$.

This species was taken by the Challenger in the seas of the East Indian Archipelago at 140 fathoms.

48. *Lepidotrigla spiloptera* var. *longipinnis*, Alcock.

Lepidotrigla spiloptera, var. *longipinnis*, Alcock, Ann. Mag. Nat. Hist., Dec. 1890, p. 429.

Only differs from the type in the great length of the pectoral fins, which reach to, or beyond, the 9th anal ray.

Largest specimen five inches long.

Off Ganjam coast 18 fathoms, Gulf of Martaban 67 fathoms, Andaman Sea 55 fathoms, off Malabar coast 68 to 148 fathoms and 100 fathoms.

Regd. Nos. 12925, $\frac{295}{1}$, $\frac{416-417}{1}$, $\frac{499-527}{1}$, $\frac{680-688}{1}$.

Family *Cataphracti*.

Peristethium, Lacépède.

Diagnosis, etc., recorded in the *Fauna of British India, Fishes*, II. p. 241.

Key to the Indian species of the genus Peristethium.

I. Pre-opercular ridge not prolonged to form a spine ... *P. Rivers-Andersoni.*
II. Pre-opercular ridge prolonged to form a spine :—
  1. Preorbital processes long, narrow, spathulate *P. serrulatum.*
  2. Preorbital processes short, broad, triangular :—
    i. Twenty rays in the soft dorsal ... ... *P. investigatoris.*
    ii. Fifteen rays in the soft dorsal ... ... *P. Halyi.*

49. *Peristethium Rivers-Andersoni*, Alcock.

Peristethus Rivers-Andersoni, Alcock, Journ. As. Soc. Bengal, Vol. LXIII. pt. 2, 1894, p. 121, pl. vi. figs. 2, 2a, 2b.

B. 7. D. VI. 22. A. 21. L. lat. 32.

The length of the narrow sub-spathulate pre-orbital processes is nearly equal to the distance between their base and the anterior border of the orbit: each has, on the upper surface near its base, a recurved upstanding spine.

The pre-opercular ridge is remarkably salient but is sharply truncated, not forming a spine. The opercular ridge forms a short blunt spine.

The lower jaw is thickly fringed with small tentacles. The long labial tentacles when laid back hardly surpass the angle of the mouth.

The interorbital space, the breadth of which is equal to the major diameter of the orbit, is deeply concave, and is traversed fore and aft by a deep median groove. Each supra-orbital margin is surmounted posteriorly by a strong recurved spine, and there is a similar spine on each side of the occiput.

The body-shields are in four rows on each side: each shield is strongly carinated, the carina being produced behind into a strong spine; and in the case of the shields of the posterior third of the lateral line the carinæ are slightly produced and pointed in front also.

The length of the anterior ventral shields is more than twice their greatest breadth.

Colours in spirit: body flesh-coloured; the pectorals with a broad jet-black band in their posterior half and with a milk-white tip; the spinous dorsal black in its upper half, and the soft dorsal with a black edge.

Length $3\frac{1}{2}$ inches.

Off Colombo, 142 to 400 fathoms. One specimen.

Regd. No. 13469.

Named after Captain A. R. S. Anderson, I.M.S., Surgeon-Naturalist to the Marine Survey of India from 1893 to 1899.

50. ***Peristethium serrulatum***, Alcock.

Peristethus serrulatum, Alcock, Ann. Mag. Nat. Hist., August 1898, p. 153: ILLUSTRATIONS OF THE ZOOLOGY OF THE INVESTIGATOR, FISHES, PL. XXV. FIGS. 2, 2a.

B. 7. D. VII. 22. A. 21. L. lat. 33.

The length of the narrow spathulate preorbital processes is equal to more than two-thirds the distance between their base and the anterior border of the orbit.

Pre-opercular ridge sharply serrulate, ending in a curved rather narrow spine, which is nearly as long as the eye. All the bony ridges of the head are finely serrulate or serrate; in addition there are, on either side, a preorbital, a post-orbital, an occipital, a post-temporal and an opercular spine, and on the forehead there are at least five small spines.

Interorbital space concave, less than the major diameter of the eye.

The large labial tentacles, when laid back, reach to the after limit of the orbit.

All the shields of the body carry a stout recurved spine—eight rows in all; those of the posterior third of the lateral line are not simple spines, but are acutely produced both forwards and backwards. The anterior ventral plates are nearly twice as long as broad and nearly twice as long as the posterior ventral plates.

Colours in spirit: flesh-colour, rather dusky dorsally; distal half of pectorals and edges of vertical fins blackish.

Length nearly six inches.

Andaman Sea, 185 fathoms.

Regd. Nos. $\frac{296}{1}$, $\frac{297}{1}$.

51. *Peristethium investigatoris*, Alcock.

Peristethus investigatoris, Alcock, Ann. Mag. Nat. Hist., August 1898, p. 152: ILLUSTRATIONS OF THE ZOOLOGY OF THE INVESTIGATOR, FISHES, PL. XXV. FIGS. 1, 1*a*.

B. 7. D. VII. 20. A. 21. L. lat. 35-36.

The length of the broad triangular preorbital processes is equal to considerably less than half the distance between their base and the anterior border of the orbit.

Preopercular ridge trenchant, ending in a sharp spine, which is about two-thirds as long as the eye.

A spine at the posterior angle of the orbit, one on either side of the occiput, one on either post-temporal region, one at the upper angle of the operculum; in young specimens *only* there are three small inconspicuous tubercles, disposed in a triangle, on the forehead.

Interorbital space concave, less than the major diameter of the eye.

The large labial tentacles, when laid back, reach far behind the posterior border of the orbit.

All the shields of the body carry a stout recurved spine—eight rows in all.

The anterior ventral plates are irregular in shape, their greatest length, measured diagonally, is nearly twice their breadth, and is half again as much as the greatest length of the posterior ventral plates.

Colours in life: adults red, young dusky violet; pectorals, first dorsal, and distal half of labial tentacles black, second dorsal with a black edge.

The largest specimen is a little over 6 inches long.

Andaman Sea, 188 to 220 and 405 fathoms: off Travancore coast, 224 to 284 fathoms.

Regd. Nos. 13037, 13038, $\frac{121}{1}$, $\frac{140}{1}$, $\frac{529}{1}$, $\frac{530}{1}$.

This species appears to be near *P. platycephalum* Goode and Bean, from Barbados.

Family *Gobiidæ*.

Gobius, Artedi.

52. *Gobius cometes*, Alcock.

Gobius cometes, Alcock, Ann. Mag. Nat. Hist., Sept. 1890, p. 208, pl. viii. fig. 2; Illustrations of the Zoology of the Investigator, Fishes, pl. XX. fig. 3.

B. 5. D. VI. 10-11. A. 10-11. L. lat. 23-24. L. tr. 5-6. C. 18–20. P. 23. V. I.5.

Length of the head about $2\frac{2}{3}$, height of the body about $4\frac{1}{2}$ in the total without the caudal.

Snout broad, its length about two-thirds that of the eye. Eyes entering the dorsal profile, separated by a very narrow shallow groove, their major diameter about $3\frac{2}{3}$ in the length of the head.

Mouth cleft oblique, the lower jaw a little prominent, the maxilla reaching the vertical through the middle of the eye.

In each jaw an inner band of villiform teeth, and an outer regular row of slightly enlarged, acute, slightly curved teeth; tongue large and fleshy.

Gill-covers large, the suboperculum much larger than the operculum; gill-laminæ broad; gill-rakers small and weak.

Scales large (0·23 inch in the vertical, 0·18 inch in the antero-posterior diameter) microscopically ctenoid; they cover the crown of the head as far as the eyes, leaving the cheeks and opercles scaleless; there are five or six rows of scales between the second dorsal and the anal fins.

All the fins are elongated; the second and third dorsal spines are about half as long as the head; the rays of the feathery second dorsal and anal increase in length from before backwards as far as the antepenultimate ray, which is almost as long as the head. The caudal is long and pointed, its longest rays, which are on the dorsal aspect, are nearly one-third the total length. The ventrals are united, but are not adherent to the abdomen; their length is about equal to the height of the body. Pectorals with a long fleshy base, their longest (middle) rays are equal to the length of the head without the snout.

Intestine short; anal papilla long and slender. A large thin-walled air-bladder is present. Vertebræ 11/13.

Colours in life:—Transparent grey, with seven broad bright-yellow cross bands not quite reaching the middle line of the abdomen, and the gills showing through the gill-cover as a bright pink blotch. Second dorsal and caudal fins beautifully pencilled black and white like a feather, anal with a broad dark border, ventrals blue-black. In spirit the yellow cross-bands almost entirely fade.

Length between 4 and 5 inches.

Very numerous specimens from off the Ganjam coast, 98 to 102 fathoms. and 107 fathoms.

Regd. Nos. 12729 *et seq.*

Amblyopus, Cuv. & Val.

53. *Amblyopus arctocephalus*, Alcock.

Amblyopus arctocephalus, Alcock, Ann. Mag. Nat. Hist., Dec. 1890, p. 432: Illustrations of the Zoology of the Investigator, Fishes, pl. XX, fig. 7 (*eye far too distinct*).

D. VI. 43. A. 41. Scales 50–60 rows.

Head angular, its opercular region somewhat inflated, its vertex compressed into a sharp carina, its length one-sixth of the total, caudal included.

Body compressed, its height, which is 7 to $7\frac{1}{2}$ in the total, caudal included, diminishes very slightly from nape to base of caudal. Eyes completely hidden and aborted, though the optic nerve is distinct.

Snout broad, with the lower jaw prominent. Mouth-cleft oblique, rather wide, the length of the maxilla being $2\frac{2}{3}$ in that of the head; the upper lip with a short broad barbel on each side; the mandibular symphysis prominent. In each jaw a row of small, close, even, acute teeth, and external to these in the front of the premaxilla, on each side, two large canines, and in the mandible five, of which two are lateral and one (the largest) median.

Head naked; body covered with thin, smooth, hardly imbricate scales, which increase in size from before backwards.

Dorsal and anal fins low, enveloped in skin, confluent with the pointed caudal. Pectorals with the four or five upper rays as long as the maxilla, the lower rays extremely short. Ventrals jugular, small, cohering; their length varies from nearly two-thirds to not quite one-third the body-height.

Stomach large, saccular; no pyloric cæca. A large, globular, thick-walled air-bladder. Anal papilla large, bilobed. Eleven abdominal, seventeen caudal vertebræ.

Colours in life mottled pink, fins hyaline.

Length 5 inches.

Off Orissa coast, 50 fathoms, off Vizagapatam, coast 20 to 25 fathoms, off Indus Delta 137 to 131 fathoms.

Regd. Nos. 12926–12931, 13457–13459, $\frac{300}{1}$, $\frac{302-306}{1}$.

In the drawing the artist has mistaken the dissected orbit for the eye. As a matter of fact the eye-ball is indistinguishably fused with the connective-tissue of the orbit, though the optic nerve is of normal size.

CALLIONYMUS, Linn.

54. *Callionymus carebares,* Alcock.

Callionymus carebares, Alcock, Ann. Mag. Nat. Hist., Sept. 1890, p. 209: ILLUSTRATIONS OF THE ZOOLOGY OF THE INVESTIGATOR, FISHES, PL. XX, FIG. 4.

B. 7. D. IV. 9. A. 9. C. 9 + *r*. P. 21. V. I. 5.

The upcurved branchiostegal rays are prolonged considerably beyond the suboperculum, so that the extreme length of the head is about two-fifths of the total without the caudal. The height of the body is about one-sixth of the same measure, and is less than the height of the head.

Eyes large, their major diameter being rather over one-fourth of the extreme head-length and one-fourth longer than the snout; they are separated by a narrow shallow groove.

Floor of the mouth dusky.

Preopercular spine upcurved, very fine and acute; its length is two-thirds the long diameter of the eye; its base is advanced forwards as a sharp spine of considerable length; and on its upper border, close behind the angle of the preoperculum, are one or sometimes two spinelets.

The gill-opening is not much smaller than the orbit and is rather more on the side than on the top of the head; the branchial arches are slender and flexible, the gill-rakers almost rudimentary.

The skin is loose and very thin. Lateral line single. The first dorsal fin is lower than the second, its spines decreasing in length from before backwards; the height of the second dorsal and of the anal is not quite twice the greatest body-height; the length of the caudal is rather more than one-fourth of the total in the female and about one-fourth the total in the male; the pectorals are rather shorter than the ventrals, which are as long as the postorbital portion of the head and reach to or just beyond the origin of the anal, when laid back.

The intestine is convoluted; the anal papilla is very slender, and in the male it is very much longer than it is in the female. Vertebræ 8/13.

Colours in life:—the upper half of the head and body and all the fins range from sepia-grey to blotchy black, and the ventral surface of the body is transparent and colourless; the first dorsal fin has in the male a central black patch, and in the female a central, black, white-edged ocellus.

Total length 5 inches.

Numerous specimens, from off the Ganjam coast, 98 to 102 fathoms, and from off the Malabar coast 100 fathoms.

Regd. Nos. 1270 *et seq.*, $\frac{724-749}{1}$.

In this species the secondary sexual characters are developed in the female, not the male.

10

55. *Callionymus kaianus*, Gthr.

Callionymus kaianus, Günther, Challenger Shore Fishes, p. 44, pl. xix. fig. B.

D. IV. 9. A. 9. C. 10. P. 21. V. I.5.

Length of the head nearly a third, height of the body about a ninth of the total length without the caudal. Eyes as long as or a little longer than the snout, one-fourth the length of the head; separated by a very narrow bridge.

Preopercular spine shorter than the eye; its base is advanced forwards as a sharp spine; on its upper edge are two spinelets, the anterior of which is very small.

Gill-opening a small aperture, not half the diameter of the eye, on the upper side of the neck.

Lateral line single.

The anterior dorsal spine is prolonged, especially in the male, in which sex it is not much shorter than the head. The rays of the second dorsal fin, in both sexes, are as long as the postorbital portion of the head. The middle caudal rays are prolonged in both sexes, being between a third and a fourth the total length (caudal included).

The ventrals are a little longer than the pectorals; in the female, but not in the male, they reach beyond the origin of the anal.

Anal papilla large in the male.

Colours: reddish, with irregular large rounded violet spots along the middle of the body: a lunate black spot, in both sexes, between the 3rd and 4th dorsal spines; second dorsal with a series of large subocellated bands, which are very conspicuous in the male.

Two specimens, adult male and female, from off the Malabar coast 102 fathoms. The male is 7 inches long.

Regd. Nos. $\frac{752}{1}$, $\frac{753}{1}$.

Distribution: Sea of New Guinea: Arabian Sea.

A large number of young, which may perhaps belong to this species, were taken off the Malabar coast in 56 to 58 fathoms.

Suborder Anacanthini.

Anacanthini Gadoidei.

The Gadoidei of the *Fauna of British India*, include two families (*Gadidæ* and *Ophidiidæ*), three genera exclusive of *Ammodytes*, and five species only.

To these we have now to add two families (*Macruridæ* and *Atelcopodidæ*), seventeen genera, and forty-four species, all of which have been brought to light by the dredge of the "Investigator."

The following synopsis shows the inter-relations of the Indian families of the Gadoidei :—

I. At least two dorsal fins: scales present: the ventrals in all Indian species contain six rays or more: air-bladder and pyloric appendages generally present :—
  1. Second dorsal fin well developed: a normal caudal fin in all the known Indian species ... ... GADIDÆ.
  2. Second dorsal more or less rudimentary: the tail tapers to a filament ... ... MACRURIDÆ.

II. One dorsal fin: the ventrals consist of one or two filaments, or may be wanting :—
  1. Dorsal fin short, corresponding with the first dorsal fin of *Macruridæ*: each ventral consists of one filament. No scales: no air-bladder: no pyloric cæca ... ... ATELEOPODIDÆ.
  2. Dorsal fin long, occupying the greater part of the back: ventrals, when present, consisting of one or two filaments. Scales generally present, and air-bladder also. Pyloric appendages present or not ... ... OPHIDIIDÆ.

Family *Gadidæ*.

Two genera are now known to inhabit the seas of India.

I. First dorsal fin above the pectorals, and consisting of several rays: an air-bladder ... ... PHYSICULUS.

II. First dorsal consisting of a single ray placed on the occiput ... BREGMACEROS.

BREGMACEROS, Thompson.

56. *Bregmaceros Macclellandii*, Thompson.

Diagnosis and synonomy in *Fauna of British India, Fishes*, II. p. 433.

Numerous specimens from the Bay of Bengal, 10, 65, 95 and 145 to 250 fathoms; from off the Andamans; and from off the Malabar coast 56 to 58 fathoms.

Regd. Nos. 11830, 12387, 12475, 13442–13447, 13563–13587, $\frac{580}{1}$.

PHYSICULUS, Kaup.

Physiculus, Kaup, Wiegmann's Archiv. f. Naturges. 1858, p. 88: Günther, Challenger Deep Sea Fishes, p. 87: Goode and Bean, Oceanic Ichthyology, p. 365: Jordan and Evermann, Fishes of N. America, III. p. 2547.

Physiculus and *Pseudophycis*, Günther, Cat. Fishes, IV. pp. 348, 350: *vide* Challenger Deep Sea Fishes, p. 87.

Body elongate, covered with small scales. A separate caudal fin. Two dorsals and one anal fin. Ventrals with a narrow flat base; composed of several rays. A band of villiform teeth in the jaws: no teeth on the vomer or palatines. Chin with a barbel. Seven branchiostegals. Small glandular pseudobranchiæ in some of the species.

Distribution: West Indies, Madeira and neighbouring parts of Atlantic, Mediterranean: India, Australia, Japan.

Key to the Indian species of the genus Physiculus.

I. First ray of the dorsal fin prolonged: the longest ventral ray reaches only just beyond the origin of the anal ... ... *P. roseus.*

II. Dorsal fin not prolonged: the longest ventral ray reaches far beyond the origin of the anal ... ... *P. argyropastus.*

57. *Physiculus roseus,* Alcock.

Physiculus roseus, Alcock, Ann. Mag. Nat. Hist., July, 1891, p. 28: ILLUSTRATIONS OF THE ZOOLOGY OF THE INVESTIGATOR, FISHES, PL. XI, FIG. 2: Journ. As. Soc. Bengal, Vol. LXIII, pt. 2, 1894, p. 122.

B. 7. D. 6–7/57. A. 55. V. 7.

Head and trunk broad; tail compressed, higher than the trunk anteriorly. Length of the head very nearly one-fourth of the total, including the caudal; greatest height of the body, just behind the origin of the dorsal fin, about one-sixth of the total.

Snout depressed, broader than long, obtusely rounded; its length, which is equal to the major diameter of the eye and slightly exceeds the width of the flat interorbital space, is one-fourth that of the head. Nostrils superior, situated immediately in front of the orbit.

Mouth wide, oblique, with the upper jaw overlapping the lower; the maxilla reaches beyond the vertical through the middle of the orbit. Teeth villiform, in broadish bands in the jaws only.

Barbel stout, about as long as the eye.

Gill-openings very wide. Small glandular pseudobranchiæ.

Body and head covered with a thick mucilaginous skin, which is invested everywhere with small deciduous scales, of which there appear to be six rows between the first dorsal fin and the lateral line. The dorsal and anal fins, which are invested with a fold of thick scaleless skin, extend to within an eye-length of the caudal. The first dorsal, which is separated from the second only by a notch, begins in the vertical through the base of the pectoral; its first ray is prolonged and nearly equals the postrostral portion of the head in length. The ventrals arise on flattened bases; their outer ray is prolonged only just beyond the origin of the anal. The pointed pectorals arise on oblique bases; their length is about equal to that of the head behind the eye.

The vent is situated well in advance of the origin of the anal fin, but behind the base of the pectorals, and there is a small postanal papilla. A large simple air-bladder.

Colours in life uniform rose-red.

Length 7 inches.

From the Andaman Sea, 185 and 188 to 220 fathoms.

Regd. Nos. 13047 : $\frac{322-324}{1}$.

58. ***Physiculus argyropastus***, Alcock.

Physiculus argyropastus, Alcock, Journ. As. Soc. Bengal, Vol. LXII. pt. 2, 1893, p. 180, pl. ix. fig. 2, and Vol. LXIII. pt. 2, 1894, p. 122 : Illustrations of the Zoology of the Investigator, Fishes, pl. XXII. fig. 1.

B. 7. D. 9/55. A. 57. V. 6.

Differs from *P. roseus* in the following particulars :—

(1) the length of the head is more than a fourth of the total, caudal included :

(2) the length of the snout is barely equal to the width of the inter-orbital space and exceeds the major diameter of the eye, which is about a fifth the length of the head :

(3) the maxilla reaches nearly to the posterior border of the orbit :

(4) the first dorsal is not prolonged, its length being less than a third that of the head :

(5) the vent is situated between the bases of the pectoral fins :

(6) the upper rays of the pectoral fin are as long as the head behind the middle of the eye :

(7) the prolonged ventral ray reaches to the 6th or 7th anal ray, or even beyond :

(8) the margin of the air-bladder is fimbriated.

Colours in spirit light pinkish brown with a silvery sheen : belly throat and gill-membranes black.

Length 9 inches.

Bay of Bengal 107 and 128 fathoms : Gulf of Manár, 180 to 217 fathoms.

Regd. Nos. 13439–13441, 13541–13545, 13549, $\frac{23}{1}$.

Family ***Ophidiidæ***.

Excluding *Ammodytes*, the genera included in the *Fishes of India* are two, namely *Brotula* with 3 species, and *Fierasfer* with a single species.

The 'Investigator' has since brought to light thirteen more genera and 23 more species, a few, indeed, of which belong to the fauna of the abysses, but the majority of which are inhabitants of moderate depths.

Synopsis of the Indian genera of the family Ophidiidæ.

* Vent situated at the throat ... ... [*Fierasfer*].

* Vent situated at least about a head-length behind the gill-opening :—

** Barbels present, on the chin ... ... [*Brotula*].

** No barbels :—

I. Caudal completely free ... ... [DINEMATICHTHYS].

II. Caudal more or less united with the dorsal and anal fins :—

A. Head more or less scaly. Oviparous :—

1. Eyes well developed :—

i. Bones of the head firm, without spines (except perhaps on the gill-covers) : greatest height of the body from a fourth to a seventh the total length : preoperculum of moderate size :—

a. Pectorals entire :—

α. Lateral line distinct, extending well on to the tail :—

κ. Pyloric cæca very small : pseudobranchiæ consisting of 2 or 3 filaments ... NEOBYTHITES.

γ. Pyloric cæca large : pseudobranchiæ absent ... ... PYCNOCRASPEDUM.

β. Lateral line indistinct or absent ... BASSOGIGAS.

b. Lower pectoral rays prolonged and more or less detached from each other and from the rest of the fin ... ... DICROLENE.

ii. Bones of the head thin and soft ; greatest body-height an eighth to an eleventh of the total length, the tail ending in a long lash : preoperculum very large and expanded :—

a. No spines on the head (except one on the operculum) ... ... BASSOZETUS.

b. Bones of the head with spiny crests ... DERMATORUS.

iii. Bones of the head thin and soft, with frill-like crests : greatest body-height about a sixth the total length : preoperculum of moderate size :—

a. No lateral line ; ventral fins consisting of one or two filaments ... ... GLYPTOPHIDIUM.

b. No ventral fins : lateral line peculiarly large and conspicuous ... ... LAMPROGRAMMUS.

2. No eyes : gill-covers armed with enormous spines ... TAURENOPHIDIUM.

B. Head covered with a peculiar loose glandular scale-less skin. Viviparous :—

1. Ventral fins consisting each of a single filament, which however may be made up of more than one ray :—

i. Scales of the body imbricate : none of the teeth enlarged ... ... DIPLACANTHOPOMA.

ii. Scales not or hardly imbricate : some of the teeth enlarged ... ... SACCOGASTER.

2. No ventral fins ... ... HEPHTHOCARA.

NEOBYTHITES, Goode & Bean.

Neobythites, Goode and Bean, Proc. U. S. Nat. Mus. VIII. 1886, p. 600: Günther, Challenger Deep Sea Fishes p. 100.

Pycnocraspedum, Alcock, Ann. Mag. Nat. Hist., Nov. 1889, p. 386.

Monomitopus, Alcock, Ann. Mag. Nat. Hist., Oct. 1890, p. 297.

Neobythites, (p. 325), *Dicromita* (p. 319), *Benthocometes* (p. 327), *Bassogigas*, (p. 328), Goode and Bean, Oceanic Ichthyology: Jordan and Evermann, Fishes of N. America, III. pp. 2512, 2506, 2514, 2515.

Body elongate, compressed; head not compressed, its bones firm: both head and body covered with small cycloid scales: tail not filamentous.

Lateral line never continued to the end of the tail, sometimes very indistinct.

Snout slightly overhanging the lower jaw; without barbels. Mouth wide. Villiform teeth in bands on the jaws and palatines, and in a Λ-shaped band or a patch on the vomer.

Eye of moderate size.

Gill-openings wide: operculum with a spine, which is usually long sharp and styliform, but may sometimes be weak and flat. Eight branchiostegals. Pseudobranchiæ rudimentary (usually consisting of 2 or 3 filaments) or absent.

Dorsal and anal fins more or less confluent with the caudal. Each ventral fin consists of two rays which may either be intimately fused to form a single filament, or (more commonly) be separate in all or part of their extent: the ventral fins are inserted, either close together or some little distance apart, just behind the clavicular symphysis.

Air-bladder present. Pyloric cæca usually present.

Another character by which spirit specimens of *Neobythites* may be recognized is that the dorsal profile of the cranium and snout form a single common curve of no great convexity.

Distribution: Atlantic: Indo-Pacific. At moderate depths usually.

Key to the Indian species of the genus Neobythites.

I. The lateral line runs halfway along the tail, or further: pectoral fins broad and short: pyloric cæca present:—
    1. A strong sharp styliform spine at the upper angle of the operculum: numerous long gill-rakers along the outer side of the 1st branchial arch: each pseudobranch consists of two small filaments: pyloric cæca very short:—
        i. Very short pyloric cæca in a ring round the pylorus and in two short rows along the mesenteric attachment of the neighbouring part of the intestine:—
            a. Two spines or spinules at the angle of the preoperculum:—
                α. Each ventral fin consist of 2 rays coherent only in their basal moiety ... ... *N. macrops.*

β. Each ventral fin consists of 2 rays coherent throughout so as to form a single filament ... *N. conjugator.*

b. No spines or spinules at the angle of the preoperculum ... ... *N. steatiticus.*

ii. Short pyloric cæca in a ring round the pylorus only: angle of preoperculum merely excised: each ventral fin consists of a single filament ... ... *N. nigripinnis.*

2. A flat weak point at the upper angle of the operculum: only 4 or 5 long gill-rakers on the outerside of the 1st branchial arch: no pseudobranchiæ whatever: pyloric cæca large [PYCNOCRASPEDUM] *N. squamipinnis.*

II. The lateral line is indistinguishable and appears to be present only close to the head: pectoral fins long and feathery: no pyloric cæca [BASSOGIGAS] ... ... *N. pterotus.*

The Indian species of *Neobythites* are so much alike that it will be sufficient to give a diagnosis of one, and then to note merely the specific differences of the others.

59. *Neobythites macrops*, Gthr.

Neobythites macrops, Günther, Challenger Deep Sea Fishes, p. 102, pl. xx. fig. A: Alcock, Ann. Mag. Nat. Hist. (6) IV. 1889, p. 385 and VIII. 1891, p. 30.

D. *circ.* 100. A. *circ.* 80. P. *circ.* 26. V. 2 coherent at base.

(1) Length of head $4\frac{1}{2}$ to $4\frac{2}{3}$ in the total. (2) Greatest body height about equal to the length of the head without the snout.

(3) Snout broad, rounded, hardly overhanging the upper jaw, as long as the eye and about equal to the width of the flat interorbital space.

(4) Major diameter of eye about two-ninths the length of the head.

(5) Nostrils rather far apart,—one in front of the eye, the other, subtubular, near the edge of the snout.

(6) Upper jaw half as long as the head, overhanging the lower jaw. Teeth in broad bands in the jaws, in a Λ-shaped patch on the vomer, and in an elliptical patch on each palatine. None of the teeth in any way enlarged.

(7) Opercular spine long and sharp. (8) A spinule at the angle of the preoperculum and another a short distance above it. (9) Gill-rakers on the outer side of the first branchial arch numerous, of good length. (10) Each pseudobranch consists of 2 filaments.

(11) Body, head, and bases of fins covered with small scales, of which there are 8 or 9 series between the 1st dorsal ray and the lateral line. (12) The lateral line extends more than halfway along the tail.

(13) The dorsal and anal fins are confluent with the caudal: the longest dorsal rays are equal to between a third and a fourth the greatest body height.

(14) The distance between the first anal ray and the base of the pectoral fin is equal to the length of the head without the snout.

(15) Pectorals pointed, their length is equal to the post-orbital portion of the head.

(16) The ventrals are bifid but at some considerable distance from their base, the inner branch being considerably the longer and both branches being slender. The total length of the ventrals is equal to the length of the head behind the middle of the eye.

(17) Pyloric cæca extremely short, in a ring round the pylorus and in two short series along the mesenteric attachment of the neighbouring part of the gut.

Colours in spirit, yellowish grey mottled with brown; some large black blotches on the dorsal fin.

The largest specimen in the Indian Museum—an adult—is $8\frac{1}{2}$ inches long.

Andaman Sea, 188 to 220, 271, and 405 fathoms: Arabian Sea, off Travancore coast, 224 to 284 fathoms.

Regd. Nos. 11646, 11647, 11649: 13053—13056, 13060, 13062—13064, 13066: $\frac{151}{1}$, $\frac{156}{1}$, $\frac{585}{1}$.

Distribution: Fiji Is.: Andaman Sea.

60. *Neobythites conjugator*, Alcock.

Neobythites conjugator, Alcock, Journ. As. Soc. Bengal, Vol. LXV. 1896, pt. 2, p. 304: ILLUSTRATIONS OF THE ZOOLOGY OF THE INVESTIGATOR, FISHES, PL. XVII. FIG. 4.

D. *circ.* 90. A. *circ.* 72. P. *circ.* 28. V. 2 (fused to form a single filament). Scales 100–110 rows.

This species differs from *N. macrops* only in the following particulars, which for easy reference are numbered to correspond with the numbers relating to the diagnosis of that species.

(1) Length of head about $4\frac{3}{4}$ in total.

(6) The outer row of teeth in the upper jaw is distinctly enlarged.

(15) The pectorals are hardly half as long as the head.

(16) The ventrals are half the length of the head: each consists of two rays intimately fused to form a single filament.

Colours in spirit, sepia; caudal, distal two-thirds of pectorals, and outer part of dorsal and anal fins black.

Length 9 inches.

Off Ceylon, 296–320 fathoms: off Travancore coast 406 fathoms.

Regd. Nos. $\frac{56}{1}$ – $\frac{59}{1}$.

11

61. *Neobythites nigripinnis*, Alcock.

Sirembo nigripinnis, Alcock, Ann. Mag. Nat. Hist., Nov. 1889, p. 384.
Monomitopus nigripinnis, Alcock, Ann. Mag. Nat. Hist., Oct. 1890, p. 295: Illustrations of the Zoology of the Investigator, Fishes, pl. XI, fig. 3 (*lateral line incorrect*).

D. 95-100. A. 85–88. P. 28. V. I.

Differs from *N. macrops* in the following particulars:—

(3) The snout, though as long as the eye, is only about $\frac{2}{3}$ to $\frac{3}{4}$ the width of the interorbital space in length.

(6) The upper jaw is rather more than half the length of the head.

(8) The preopercular angle is excised, and the angles bounding the excision are pronounced but are not distinct spines.

(12) The lateral line extends only about halfway along the tail.

(15) The pectorals are not half the length of the head.

(16) Each ventral is a single slender filament not half as long as the head.

(17) There is a ring of short pyloric cæca round the pylorus only.

Colours in spirit, sepia; fins black.

Length 9 inches.

Arabian Sea, 719, 740 and 824 fathoms; Bay of Bengal, 561, 599, 753 and 696 fathoms; Andaman Sea, 490 fathoms.

Regd. Nos. 11764, 12864, 13448, 13449, 13464, 13536–13540, $\frac{10}{1}$, $\frac{11}{1}$, $\frac{328}{1}$, $\frac{329}{1}$, $\frac{331-333}{1}$.

62. *Neobythites steatiticus*, Alcock.

Neobythites steatiticus, Alcock, Journ. As. Soc. Bengal, Vol. LXII, pt. 2, 1893, p. 181, pl. ix, fig. 3: Illustrations of the Zoology of the Investigator, Fishes, pl. XXI, fig. 2 (*lateral line drawn too long*).

D. *circ.* 85. A. *circ.* 65. P. *circ.* 22. V. 2 (coherent at base).

Differs from *N. macrops* only in the following particulars:—

(1) Length of head about $3\frac{3}{4}$ in the total.

(4) Major diameter of the eye about one-sixth the length of the head.

(6) The bands of teeth in the jaws are not very broad.

(8) There are no spinules at the angle of the pre-operculum, which is rounded.

(13) The longest dorsal rays are about two-fifths of the greatest body height.

(14) The distance between the first anal ray and the base of the pectoral fin is equal to the length of the post-orbital portion of the head.

(15) Pectorals rounded, their length not much more than half that of the head.

(16) The ventrals are equal in length to the post-orbital portion of the head: each consists of two stout filaments—the inner of which is slightly the longer—bound together in their basal half.

Colours in spirit: creamy yellow, clouded marbled and mottled like soap-stone with shades of light brown; a large oval ocellus, consisting of a black centre and a creamy white ring, on the dorsal fin between the 20th and 30th rays or beyond: anal jet black with a milk-white border.

Length 7 inches.

Bay of Bengal, 107, 128 and 145 to 250 fathoms.

Regd. Nos. 13435, 13474, 13476, 13478—13482.

63. *Neobythites (Bassogigas) pterotus*, Alcock.

Neobythites pterotus, Alcock, Ann. Mag. Nat. Hist., Sept. 1890, p. 210; Oct. 1890, p. 297; July 1891, p. 30: ILLUSTRATIONS OF THE ZOOLOGY OF THE INVESTIGATOR, FISHES, PL. XI. FIG. 4 (*female*), AND PL. XXIX. FIG. 1 (*male*).

D. *circ.* 120. A. *circ.* 95. P. 18. V. 2.

Differs from *N. macrops* in the following particulars:—

(1) Length of head about a sixth of the total: (2) greatest body height equal to the length of the head.

(3) Snout nearly twice as long as the eye and about three-fourths the width of the interorbital space; somewhat overlapping the upper jaw.

(4) Major diameter of the eye about a seventh the length of the head.

(5) Anterior nostril large, not subtubular though pierced in a circumscribed patch of naked skin.

(6) Upper jaw more than half the length of the head.

(8) No spinules at the angle of the preoperculum.

(12) Lateral line either absent, or present only quite near the head: (thirty rows of scales between the base of the dorsal and the vent).

(13) The longest dorsal rays are half the greatest body height.

(14) The distance between the base of the pectoral and the first ray of the anal fin is $1\frac{1}{3}$ times the length of the head.

(15) Pectorals feathery: in the male they are $1\frac{2}{3}$ times the length of the head, in the female they are as long as the head behind the anterior nostril.

(16) Each ventral consists of two rays which are separate from their base; the inner ray, which is the longer, is about two-fifths the length of the head. In the male both rays have spathulate tips.

(17) Pyloric cæca absent.

Colours: body brown; head, abdomen, and all the fins black.

The largest specimen is nearly a foot long.

Bay of Bengal, 1310 and 1748 fathoms: Arabian Sea, 1000 fathoms.

Regd. Nos. 12832, 12863, 13046.

As in *N. squamipinnis*, the basal half or more of the dorsal and anal fins is particularly fleshy and scaly.

64. *Neobythites (Pycnocraspedum) squamipinnis*, Alcock.

Pycnocraspedum squamipinne, Alcock, Ann. Mag. Nat. Hist., Nov. 1889, p. 386.
Neobythites squamipinnis, Alcock, Journ. As. Soc. Bengal, Vol. LXIII. pt. 2, 1894, p. 123; ILLUSTRATIONS OF THE ZOOLOGY OF THE INVESTIGATOR, FISHES, PL. XXI. FIG. 1.

Differs from *N. macrops* in the following particulars:—

(1) The length of the head is about $3\frac{1}{2}$ in the total.

(2) The greatest body height is about equal to the length of the head behind the eye.

(3) The length of the snout though about equal to that of the eye, is only between two-thirds and three-fourths that of the interorbital space.

(4) Major diameter of eye between a fifth and a sixth the length of the head.

(5) Anterior nostril not subtubular.

(6) The teeth in the vomer and palate bones, though disposed in the same way are in narrow bands.

(7) Opercular spine flat short and weak: (8) two or three rather indistinct points at the angle of the preoperculum: (9) only four or five enlarged gill-rakers on the outer side of the 1st branchial arch. (10) Pseudobranchiæ entirely absent.

(16) The ventral fins though otherwise similar are not half the length of the head.

(17) Thirteen large long pyloric cæca.

Colours in spirit; yellowish or greenish grey, fins darker.

The largest specimen is $11\frac{1}{2}$ inches long.

Bay of Bengal 193 and 145 to 250 fathoms.

Regd. Nos. 11700, 11701, 13525, 13526.

The vertical fins are more thickly sealed than usual, in this species, and the caudal, though confluent with the dorsal and anal fins at its base, is free in a considerable part of its extent.

Subgenus DICROLENE, Goode & Bean.

Dicrolene, Goode and Bean, Bull. Mus. Comp. Zool X. 1883, p. 202, and Oceanic Ichthyology, p. 337 : Günther Challenger Deep-Sea Fishes, p. 107 : Jordan and Evermann, Fishes N. Amer. III. 2522.

Pteroidonus, Günther, Challenger Deep-Sea Fishes, p. 106 : Goode and Bean, Oceanic Ichthyology, p. 337.

Paradicrolene, Alcock, Ann. Mag. Nat. Hist., Nov. 1889, p. 387.

Differs from *Neobythites* only in having the lower pectoral rays, to the number of 6 to 10, prolonged, and more or less isolated from each other and from the rest of the pectoral fin, as free filaments. This one character is, in any case, insufficient to justify the separation of *Dicrolene* from *Neobythites;* but the character itself is variable, for not only in the young of one species, but also in the adults of another species, the lower pectoral rays are, for a considerable distance, united to one another and to their pectoral fin by membrane.

Key to the species of Dicrolene.

I. Pectoral filaments free and independent in the adult : no circumscribed cross-band on the tail :—

1. Twenty-seven rows of scales between the dorsal fin and the vent ... *D. intronigra.*
2. Thirty-four rows of scales between the dorsal fin and the vent ... *D. multifilis.*

II. Pectoral filaments inter-connected by membrane in their basal moiety : a broad black cross-band, involving also the dorsal and anal fins, on the posterior third of the tail ... ... *D. nigricaudis.*

65. ***Dicrolene intronigra***, Goode & Bean.

Dicrolene intronigra, Goode and Bean, Bull. Mus. Comp. Zool. X. 1883, p. 202, and Oceanic Ichthyology, p. 338, fig. 297 A, B : Günther, Challenger Deep Sea Fishes, p. 107 : Vaillant, Exp. Sci. Travailleur et Talisman, Poissons, p. 258, pl. xxiii, fig. 2.

Paradicrolene Vaillanti, Alcock, Ann. Mag. Nat. Hist. (6) VI. 1890, p. 297.

D. *circ.* 100. A. *circ.* 85. P. 18-19/8-9. V. 2.

(1) Length of head one-fifth the total or less : (2) greatest height of the body equal to the length of the head without the snout.

(3) Snout broad, rounded, hardly overhanging the upper jaw, as long as the eye, but hardly equal to the width of the inter-orbital space. Nostrils rather large and far apart, one being in front of the eye, the other near the edge of the snout.

(4) Major diameter of eye two-ninths to one-fourth the length of the head.

(5) Upper jaw decidedly more than half the length of the head, overhanging the lower jaw. Villiform teeth in broadish bands on the jaws and palatines and in a narrow Λ-shaped patch on the vomer : none of the teeth enlarged.

(6) Opercular spine a long sharp style : three spinules at the angle of the preoperculum.

(7) Gill-rakers on the outer side of the first branchial arch numerous and of good length. Each pseudobranch consists of two small filaments.

(8) Body, head, and bases of fins covered with small scales, of which there are about twenty-seven rows between the dorsal fin and the vent. Lateral line very indistinct, apparently not continued halfway along the tail.

(9) Dorsal and anal fins confluent with the caudal: the longest dorsal rays are about two-fifths the greatest body height.

(10) The distance of the 1st anal ray from the base of the pectoral is slightly more than the length of the head.

(11) Each pectoral consists of two portions,—a normal, pointed, upper portion which is a little longer than the head, and a lower portion consisting of eight or nine free filamentous rays the longest of which (2nd and 3rd) are from $1\frac{1}{2}$ times to twice the length of the head.

(12) Each ventral consists of two entirely separate rays, the inner and longer of which is equal to the length of the head behind the middle of the eye.

(13) There are a few extremely short almost rudimentary pyloric cæca.

Colours in spirit, yellowish brown: gill-membranes, pectoral fins and their free filaments, ventrals, and outer part of dorsal and anal fins, black.

The largest specimen is 10 inches long.

In the Indian Museum are 4 specimens from the Andaman Sea, 669 fathoms, and the Arabian Sea, 406 and 740 fathoms, (besides a specimen from the Atlantic, presented by the Smithsonian Institution).

Distribution: West Indies and Atlantic coasts of the United States: Atlantic coasts of Morocco and north-west Africa: Arabian Sea. At considerable depths.

Regd. Nos. 12862, $\frac{12}{1}$, $\frac{13}{1}$, $\frac{750}{1}$.

66. ***Dicrolene multifilis***, Alcock.

Paradicrolene multifilis, Alcock, Ann. Mag. Nat. Hist., Nov. 1889, p. 387 and Nov. 1892, p. 348: ILLUSTRATIONS OF THE ZOOLOGY OF THE INVESTIGATOR, PL. XI. FIG 1.

D. *circ.* 100. A. *circ.* 85. P. 18/8–10. V. 2.

Differs from *Dicrolene intronigra* only in the following particulars, which are numbered to correspond with the paragraphs relating to the diagnosis of that species:—

(1) The length of the head is about two-ninths of the total.

(4) The major diameter of the eye is not quite two-ninths the length of the head.

(8) Scales in 34 or 35 rows between the dorsal fin and the vent: the lateral line ends in the last third of the tail.

(10) The distance of the 1st anal ray from the base of the pectoral is equal to the length of the head without the snout.

(11) The pectoral filaments are never as much as twice the length of the head.

(12) The inner ray of the ventral fin is not half the length of the head.

Colours in spirit yellowish or sepia, fins dark grey.

A mature female is only $6\frac{1}{2}$ inches long.

Bay of Bengal, 193 and 231 to 258 fathoms: Andaman Sea, 271 fathoms.

Regd. Nos. 11648, 11704, 11707, 11715–11717, 13166–13169.

67. *Dicrolene nigricaudis*, Alcock.

Paradicrolene nigricaudis, Alcock, Ann. Mag. Nat. Hist., July 1891, p. 30; ILLUSTRATIONS OF THE ZOOLOGY OF THE INVESTIGATOR, FISHES, PL. II FIG 4.

D. *circ.* 90. A. *circ.* 75. P. 19-20/6-7. V. 2.

Differs from *Dicrolene intronigra* only in the following particulars:—

(1) The length of the head is two-ninths of the total.

(3) The length of the snout is quite equal to the width of the interorbital space.

(4) The major diameter of the eye is not quite two-ninths the length of the head.

(8) There are 30-31 rows of scales between the dorsal fin and the vent. The lateral line is very distinct: it runs four scales below the first dorsal ray and ends in the posterior fourth of the tail.

(10) The distance between the first anal ray and the base of the pectoral fin is equal to the length of the head.

(11) The pectorals are as long as the postrostral portion of the head: their free rays are connected with one another for a considerable distance, and with the rest of the fin, by membrane, and are never more than $1\frac{2}{3}$ times as long as the head.

(12) The inner ray of the ventral fin is equal in length to the postorbital portion of the head.

(13) The intestinal wall round the pylorus is puckered, but there are no distinct cæcal pouches.

Colours in spirit, brown: the posterior third of the tail, including the corresponding parts of the dorsal and anal fins, is black: the caudal fin and pectoral filaments are white.

The largest specimen, which is not far off maturity, is a little over 8 inches long.

Andaman Sea, 188 to 220 fathoms: Arabian Sea, off Travancore coast, 224 to 284 fathoms.

Regd. Nos. 13040, 13044, $\frac{581-584}{1}$.

Bassozetus, Gill.

Bassozetus, Gill, Proc. U. S. Nat. Mus. VI. 1883, p. 259: Goode and Bean, Oceanic Ichthyology, p. 321: Jordan and Evermann, Fishes of North America, III. p. 2507.

Bathyonus, Goode and Bean, Proc. U. S. Nat. Mus. VIII. 1886, p. 603: Günther, Challenger Deep Sea Fishes, p. 321.

? *Moebia*, Goode and Bean, Oceanic Ichthyology, p. 331: Jordan and Evermann, Fishes of North America, III. p. 2510.

I follow Goode and Bean in substituting the name *Bassozetus* for *Bathyonus*, but the fact remains that *Bassozetus* was quite insufficiently characterized by its author.

Head and body compressed, the body low and very elongate, the end of the tail lash-like: the bones of the head soft, almost membranaceous. Both head and body covered with small, deciduous, cycloid scales.

Lateral line indistinguishable.

Snout hardly overhanging the lower jaw, somewhat depressed; without barbels. Mouth wide. Villiform teeth in bands on the jaws and palatines and in a Λ-shaped band on the vomer.

Eye small.

Gill-openings wide: operculum with a feeble spine above. Eight branchiostegals. Pseudobranchiæ rudimentary or absent. Preoperculum large, usually extending far back over the other opercular bones, its edge entire.

Dorsal and anal fins confluent with the caudal The ventrals arise close together at the clavicular symphysis: each consists of either one or two filaments.

Air-bladder present. No pyloric cæca.

This genus is very closely related to *Neobythites*, from which it only differs in the following particulars:—

(1) the tail is long and lash-like and the body altogether lower and more elongate:

(2) the bones of the head are very thin and soft:

(3) the angle of the preoperculum forms a sort of semicircular lobe extending some way over the other opercular bones.

Distribution: Atlantic and Indo-Pacific, at great depths. *Nematonus* and *Mixonus* are probably not distinct from *Bassozetus*.

68. ***Bassozetus glutinosus*** (Alcock).

Bathyonus glutinosus, Alcock, Ann. Mag. Nat. Hist., Sept. 1890, p. 211: Illustrations of the Zoology of the Investigator, Fishes, pl. I. fig. 3.

D. *circ.* 125. A. *circ.* 105. P. 29-30. V. 1.

Length of the head about one-fifth the total: greatest height of the body three-fifths the length of the head.

Snout depressed, rounded, somewhat inflated at the tip; its length, which is less than its breadth, is nearly one-fifth the length of the head. Eyes situated in the uppermost part of the anterior third of the head, their major diameter being one-tenth to one-eleventh of the head-length and one-third the width of the convex interocular space. Nostrils large, one at the antero-superior limit of the orbit, the other midway between the first and the tip of the snout. Mouth wide, oblique; the maxilla, which is half as long as the head, completely encloses the mandible in repose; villiform teeth in narrowish bands in the jaws, palatines, and vomer, the last arranged in a V with incurved limbs.

Gill-covers large; the preoperculum overlaps large portions of all the other opercular bones, extending almost to the hinder edge of the operculum; the operculum with a feeble flat spur at the postero-superior angle, and another below concealed by the overlying preoperculum; seventeen long scabrous gill-rakers on the first branchial arch, besides some rudimentary ones above; no pseudobranchiæ.

Scales small, thin, deciduous; there are twenty-five rows between the dorsal fin and the vent.

All the fin-rays delicate. The dorsal and anal fins are thick and fleshy; the highest rays of the dorsal—near the middle of the fin—are higher than the corresponding anal rays, and measure nearly half the maximum body-height; the dorsal begins well in advance of the gill-opening. Caudal very narrow, its length nearly one-twelfth of the total; it is confluent with the other vertical fins only at its base. Pectorals entire, pointed, half as long as the head. Ventrals consisting each of a single filament, which is as long as the postorbital portion of the head.

Colours in spirit: head belly and pectorals black, body brown, vertical fins light grey.

The largest specimen is about $7\frac{1}{2}$ inches long.

Bay of Bengal, off the Ganjam coast, 1310 fathoms: Arabian Sea, off Malabar coast, 636 and 891 fathoms.

Regd. Nos. 12824, 12825, 12827: 14006, 14007, $\frac{22}{1}$.

Dermatorus, Alcock.

Dermatorus, Alcock, Ann. Mag. Nat. Hist., Oct. 1890, p. 298.
Celema, Goode and Bean, Oceanic Ichthyology, p. 329.

Head and body compressed, the body low and very elongate, the end of the tail lash-like.

The bones of the head, though thin, are fairly firm, and are armed with numerous upstanding spines.

12

Both head and body are covered with small deciduous cycloid scales—so deciduous on the head that except in very well preserved specimens that part may be thought to be naked.

Lateral line indistinguishable.

Snout hardly overhanging the lower jaw, depressed; without barbels. Mouth very wide. Villiform teeth in bands on the jaws and palatines; few and scattered, deciduous or absent, on the vomer.

Eye of moderate size.

Gill-openings wide: gill covers armed with spines. Eight branchiostegals. Pseudobranchiæ rudimentary or absent. Preoperculum expanded much as in *Bassozetus*. The gill-rakers on the outer side of the first branchial arch are long and most curiously compound.

Dorsal and anal fins confluent with the caudal. The ventrals arise close together at the clavicular symphysis: each consists of a single filament, which may be bifid at its extremity.

Air-bladder small. Pyloric cæca absent or quite rudimentary.

This genus is very closely related to *Bassozetus*, from which it only differs in the following particulars:—

(1) the bones of the head are firmer and are armed with numerous spines:

(2) the teeth on the vomer are few and scattered, or are entirely wanting.

Alcockia Goode and Bean, Oceanic Ichthyology, p. 329, probably should be united with *Dermatorus*.

Key to the species of Dermatorus.

I. Spines of the head rigid: diameter of eye about two-ninths the length of the head: some vomerine teeth present ... ... *D. trichiurus.*

II. Spines of the head weak and flexible: diameter of eye a sixth or a seventh the length of the head:—

    1. Some vomerine teeth ... ... *D. melanocephalus.*
    2. No vomerine teeth ... ... *D. melampeplus.*

69. *Dermatorus trichiurus*, Alcock.

Dermatorus trichiurus, Alcock, Ann. Mag. Nat. Hist., Oct. 1890, p. 298: ILLUSTRATIONS OF THE ZOOLOGY OF THE INVESTIGATOR, FISHES, PL. I, FIG. 1.

D. 160 + *x*. A. 140 + *x*. P. *circ*. 16. V. 1. (split at the end).

Head between a sixth and a seventh the total length: greatest height of the body equal to the length of the head behind the posterior border of the pupil.

Two small preorbital spines. A strong recurved spine at the anterior angle of the orbit from which two irregular series of spines pass backwards to the supraclavicular angle. In addition both edges of a broad mucous channel excavated in the edge of the preoperculum are spinate, and there is an acute spine at the upper angle of the operculum.

Snout depressed; its length is a little more than that of the eye and equal to the width of the interorbital space. A large nostril in front of the eye, and a smaller one midway between it and the edge of the snout.

Diameter of the eye about two-ninths the length of the head.

The length of the upper jaw is nearly two-thirds that of the head. Teeth in narrow bands in the jaws and palatines; few and scattered on the vomer.

About 20 long gill-rakers on the outer side of the first branchial arch. Each pseudobranch consists of two inconspicuous papillæ.

Scales in about 20 rows between the dorsal fin and the vent. No lateral line.

The rays of the vertical fins are weak: the first anal ray is a little less than a head-length behind the axilla. Pectorals pointed, as long as the post-orbital portion of the head. Each ventral consists of a filament, as long as the post-rostral portion of the head, split into two near its end.

The intestine is puckered round the junction with the pylorus, but there are no distinct cæca.

Colours in spirit: head and belly black, body light brown, fins light grey.

An adult female is a little over 7 inches long.

Arabian Sea, 1000 and 931 fathoms.

Regd. Nos. 12865 : $\frac{19-21}{1}$.

This species may probably prove to be identical with the previously described *Porogadus nudus* Vaillant (Exp. Sci. Travailleur et Talisman, Poissons, p. 262, pl. xxiv. fig. 2).

70. *Dermatorus melanocephalus*, Alcock.

Dermatorus melanocephalus Alcock, Ann. Mag. Nat. Hist., July 1891, p. 32: ILLUSTRATIONS OF THE ZOOLOGY OF THE INVESTIGATOR, FISHES, PL. XXI. FIG. 4.

Differs from *D. trichiurus* only in the following particulars:—

(1) the bones of the head are thin and soft and the spines are all weak and flexible, bending, instead of pricking the hand as they do in *D. trichiurus;* there are no spines on the edge of the preoperculum:

(2) the diameter of the eye is only one-sixth the length of the head and half that of the snout:

(3) the long gill-rakers on the outer side of the first branchial arch are less numerous: and there are no pseudobranchiæ:

(4) the pyloric cæca are somewhat less rudimentary.

An adult female is nearly 8 inches long.

Bay of Bengal, 1644 and 1748 fathoms.

Regd. No. 13073.

This species may very probably prove identical with *Porogadus subarmatus* Vaillant (*op. cit.* p. 265, pl. xxiv. fig. 3).

71. *Dermatorus melampeplus*, Alcock.

Dermatorus melampeplus, Alcock, Journ. As. Soc. Bengal, Vol. LXV. pt. 2, 1896, p. 305: ILLUSTRATIONS OF THE ZOOLOGY OF THE INVESTIGATOR, FISHES, PL. XVII. FIG. 3.

Differs from *D. trichiurus* in the following particulars :—

(1) As in *D. melanocephalus* the spines of the head are weak and flexible; but there are some on the edge of the preoperculum :

(2) the eye is half the length of the snout and less than a sixth the length of the head :

(3) there are no teeth on the vomer.

Colour uniform black.

Length a little over 9 inches.

One specimen from off the Malabar coast, 931 fathoms.

Regd. No. $\frac{60}{1}$.

GLYPTOPHIDIUM, Alcock.

Glyptophidium, Alcock, Ann. Mag. Nat. Hist., Nov. 1889, p. 390, and Journ. As. Soc. Bengal, Vol. LXV. pt. 2, 1896, p. 309.

Body elongate, compressed, of good height; tail long, tapering to a lash-like filament: head compressed, with soft, almost membranaceous, frilled and crested bones. Both head and body covered with thin caducous scales.

Lateral line absent.

Snout not overhanging the lower jaw, without barbels. Mouth wide: villiform teeth in bands on the jaws and palatines and in a Λ-shaped band on the vomer.

Eye of good size.

Gill-openings wide: operculum with a feeble flat spine. Eight branchiostegals. Each pseudobranch consists of from 6 to 12 rather long lax filaments.

Dorsal and anal fins confluent with the caudal.

The ventral fins arise close together just behind the clavicular symphysis: each consists of either 1 or 2 filamentous rays.

Air-bladder present. Pyloric appendages small, almost rudimentary.

The tail is so extremely slender and filiform that the end of it is often lost, and when the caudal fin grows again it appears to be free from the other vertical fins.

The lash-like tail, the frilled crests of the head bones, and the comparatively large pseudobranchiæ distinguish *Glyptophidium*. In no other Indian Ophidioid do the pseudobranchiæ consist of more than 2 small filaments.

Key to the species of Glyptophidium.

I. Each ventral consists of a single filament ... ... *G. argenteum.*
II. Each ventral consists of two filaments ... ... *G. macropus.*

72. *Glyptophidium argenteum*, Alcock.

Glyptophidium argenteum, Alcock, Ann. Mag. Nat. Hist., Nov. 1889, p. 390: ILLUSTRATIONS OF THE ZOOLOGY OF THE INVESTIGATOR, FISHES, PL. II. FIG. 3.

Length of the head about a fifth the total, greatest body height (at the shoulder) equal to the length of the head without the snout. The body rapidly tapers to a long filamentous tail.

Length of the snout equal to the major diameter of the eye (which is nearly a fourth the length of the head), barely equal to the width of the interorbital space.

The upper jaw overlaps the lower, except at the tip, where a sharp knob at the mandibular symphysis projects slightly: its length is half that of the head. Villiform teeth in a broadish band on the upper jaw, in a narrow band on the lower jaw, in a slightly curved narrowly-elliptical band on the palatines, and in a Λ-shaped band on the vomer.

Three weak points at the angle of the preoperculum. Numerous long gill-rakers on the outer side of the 1st branchial arch. Each pseudobranch consists of about a dozen filaments.

Scales rather large, excessively thin and deciduous,—more especially on the head, so that in specimens that are not exceptionally well preserved the head appears naked.

Dorsal and anal fins confluent with the caudal, the rays of the anal being much shorter than those of the dorsal and the rays of all three being very slender: the longest dorsal rays are nearly half the body height.

Pectorals pointed, a little longer than the head without the snout, the rays very slender and about 22 in number.

Each ventral consists of a single slender ray which is about as long as the post-orbital portion of the head.

A few rudimentary cæca round the pylorus only.

Colours in spirit: blackish, silvered over; fins blackish grey.

Numerous specimens, the largest $9\frac{1}{2}$ inches long.

Andaman Sea, 271 and 405 fathoms: off Travancore coast, 360 and 406 fathoms.

Regd. Nos. 11661, $\frac{14}{1}-\frac{17}{1}$, $\frac{125}{1}$, $\frac{144}{1}$, $\frac{160}{1}$, $\frac{161}{1}$, $\frac{164}{1}$, $\frac{334}{1}$, $\frac{336}{1}$, $\frac{337}{1}$.

73. *Glyptophidium macropus*, Alcock.

Glyptophidium macropus, Alcock, Journ. As. Soc. Bengal, Vol. LXIII, pt. 2, 1894, p. 122, pl. vi. fig. 3: Illustrations of the Zoology of the Investigator, Fishes, pl. XV. fig. 6.

Differs from *G. argenteum* only in the following particulars:—

The length of the head is only about a fourth the total.

The angle of the preoperculum is notched, the angles of the notch being rounded off.

Each pseudobranch consists of from 5 to 8 filaments.

The length of the pectorals is equal to that of the head behind the middle of the eye.

Each ventral consists of two rays of which the inner one is an eye-length longer than the head.

The pyloric cæca are longer.

The largest specimen is $5\frac{1}{2}$ inches long.

Colours in spirit: head, iris and body silvery, the body finely speckled with black: vertical fins greyish with blackish tips, pectorals blackish, ventrals milk white.

Bay of Bengal, 145 to 250 fathoms.

Regd. Nos. 13529–13535.

Lamprogrammus, Alcock.

Lamprogrammus, Alcock, Ann. Mag. Nat. Hist., July 1891, and Journ. As. Soc. Bengal, Vol. LXV. pt. 2, 1896, p. 309.

Body elongate, compressed, of good height; tail long, tapering to a lash-like filament: head compressed, with soft, almost membranaceous, frilled and crested bones: both head and body covered with thin deciduous scales.

Lateral line broad, very conspicuous, continued at least halfway along the tail; its scales much enlarged, each being furnished with a (luminous) gland.

Snout not overhanging the jaws, without barbels. Mouth wide. Villiform teeth in bands on the jaws and palatines and in a Λ-shaped band on the vomer.

Eye of moderate size.

Gill-openings wide: operculum with a feeble flat spine. Eight branchiostegals. No pseudobranchiæ.

Dorsal and anal fins confluent with the caudal.

No ventral fins.

A small air-bladder present. Pyloric appendages few and small.

The curious *Halosaurus*-like lateral line and the absence of ventral fins and pseudobranchiæ distinguish this genus from *Glyptophidium*, which it otherwise closely resembles.

Key to the species of the genus Lamprogrammus.

I. The angle of the preoperculum is simply notched ... ... *L. niger*.
II. Three weak flat teeth at the angle of the preoperculum ... ... *L. fragilis*.

74. *Lamprogrammus niger*, Alcock.

Lamprogrammus niger, Alcock, Ann. Mag. Nat. Hist., July 1891, p. 33, fig. 2: ILLUSTRATIONS OF THE ZOOLOGY OF THE INVESTIGATOR, FISHES, PL. I. FIG. 2.

D. *circ.* 110. A. *circ.* 90. P. 17. V. 0.

Length of the head about one-fifth of the total, greatest body height (at the shoulder) equal to the length of the head without the snout.

Length of the snout about twice that of the eye, less than the width of the convex interorbital space.

The major diameter of the eye is an eighth or a ninth the length of the head.

The upper jaw, the length of which is half that of the head, overlaps the lower. Villiform teeth in a broad band in the upper jaw, in a narrow band on the lower jaw and on each palatine, and in a narrow broken Λ-shaped band on the vomer.

Angle of the preoperculum notched, the angles of the notch rounded off. About ten long gill-rakers on the outer side of the first branchial arch.

Body and head covered with deciduous, almost membranaceous, scales of moderate size.

The scales of the very conspicuous lateral line are adherent and greatly enlarged; they lie beneath a continuous sheath of black skin, which is loopholed over a long narrow groove with raised margins situated along the vertical diameter of each scale. These grooves are filled with an opaque white substance, which probably has a luminous function. The lateral line, in fact, is exactly similar to that of several species of *Halosaurus*.

The rays of the fins are weak and are damaged beyond description by capture: those of the dorsal fin are much more strongly developed than those of the anal. The pectorals appear to be short.

Six small pyloric cæca.

Colour: jet black.

The largest specimen is $15\frac{1}{2}$ inches long.

Bay of Bengal, near the Andamans, 561 fathoms: Andaman Sea, 405 fathoms.

Regd. Nos. 13048, 13049.

75. ***Lamprogrammus fragilis***, Alcock.

Lamprogrammus fragilis, Alcock, Ann. Mag. Nat. Hist., Nov. 1892, p. 348.

D. *circ.* 90. A. *circ.* 75. P. 17. V. 0.

Differs from *L. niger* only in the following particulars:—

The greatest height of the body is equal to the length of the head.

The major diameter of the eye is between a sixth and a seventh the length of the head.

The upper jaw is not quite half as long as the head.

There are three weak teeth at the angle of the preoperculum.

The scales of the lateral line lie beneath a continuous tube of black skin which is traversed along the middle by a continuous bright stripe.

The pyloric cæca are a little longer.

Colour: jet black.

The largest specimen is 2 feet long.

Bay of Bengal, off Godávari coast, 678 fathoms: Arabian Sea, off Travancore coast, 406 fathoms.

Regd. Nos. 13171: $\frac{1}{1}$ - $\frac{8}{1}$.

TAUREDOPHIDIUM, Alcock.

Tauredophidium, Alcock, Ann. Mag. Nat. Hist., Sept. 1890, p. 212.

Body elongate, compressed: head large and broad, not compressed; its bones firm: both head and body covered with small cycloid scales.

Eyes atrophied and completely hidden beneath the skin.

Operculum and preoperculum armed with enormous spines.

Lateral line indistinguishable.

Snout broad, not overhanging the jaws; without barbels. Mouth wide. Villiform teeth in bands on the jaws and palatines, and in a Λ-shaped band on the vomer.

Gill-openings wide: eight branchiostegals. Pseudobranchiæ rudimentary or absent.

Dorsal and anal fins confluent with the caudal. The ventrals arising far apart, on distinct bony bases, about midway between the pectorals and the clavicular symphysis: each consists of two filaments.

An air-bladder and pyloric cæca present.

76. *Tauredophidium Hextii*, Alcock.

Tauredophidium Hextii, Alcock, Ann. Mag. Nat. Hist., Sept. 1890, p. 213, pl. viii. fig. 1: Illustrations of the Zoology of the Investigator, Fishes, pl. XXI. fig. 3.

D. 64. A. 58. C. 10. P. 18. V. 2.

Head broad, pyramidal, its length about a fourth of the total, its bones hard and firm. Greatest height of the body nearly equal to the length of the head.

The operculum, which is a short narrow bone, is armed with a great thick spine half as long as the head: at the angle of the preoperculum are three similar spines, the middle and longest one of which is three-fourths the length of the opercular spine. The occipital crest projects as a coarse subcutaneous eminence, and behind it the first (?) neural spine projects similarly but more strongly.

The eyes are completely atrophied; the small orbital cavities are hidden beneath thick scaly skin, and are filled with connective tissue, deeply imbedded in which is a small pigmented eyeball about the size of an ordinary pin-head. Nostrils large. Muciferous cavities of snout and mandible well developed and opening to the exterior by pores. Mouth large, its cleft nearly horizontal; maxilla more than half the length of the head, much expanded behind, completely including the lower jaw in repose. Teeth in narrowish villiform bands in jaws, vomer, and palatines. Ten long pointed scabrous gill-rakers on the first brancial arch, besides some rudimentary ones above and below.

Scales in 22 rows between the dorsal fin and the vent.

Vertical fins united; the dorsal begins just behind the vertical through the base of the pectoral, its longest rays—about the middle of the fin—are rather over one-third the maximum body-height and exceed the corresponding anal rays in length. Caudal long and pointed. Pectorals entire, pointed, as long as the head without the operculum. Ventrals separated from each other by an interspace equal to one-third the length of the head; each consists of two

13

filaments, of which the inner is much the longer, reaching beyond the origin of the anal fin.

A bunch of about six slender cæca situated above the pylorus.

Colours in the fresh state:—uniform chocolate; fins blackish; throat and belly black, owing to the pigmentation of the peritoneum.

The largest specimen is just over four inches long.

Bay of Bengal, off Ganjam coast, 1310 fathoms.

Regd. No. 12829, 12830.

Named after Rear-Admiral Sir John Hext, R. N., formerly Director of the Royal Indian Marine, who was always a good friend to the Zoological department of the "Investigator."

DIPLACANTHOPOMA, Günther.

Diplacanthopoma, Günther, Challenger Deep-Sea Fishes, p. 115: Goode and Bean, Oceanic Ichthyology, p. 318.

Body elongate, compressed, covered with small thin imbricate scales. Head broad, somewhat depressed, covered with a thick, glandular, scaleless skin, sharply defined from the scaly skin of the trunk: its bones firm.

Lateral line indistinct and incomplete (or absent?).

Snout broad, depressed, slightly overhanging the lower jaw; without barbels. Mouth wide: villiform teeth in bands on the jaws and palatines and in a Λ-shaped band on the vomer.

Eye of moderate size.

Gill-openings wide: operculum with two radiating ridges each ending in a spine: free edge of preoperculum rounded, unarmed. Eight branchiostegals (in two species), but the branchiostegal membranes are so thick that the rays cannot be counted without reflecting the skin. No pseudobranchiæ.

Dorsal and anal fins confluent with the caudal. The ventrals arise close together a short distance behind the clavicular symphysis: each consists of a single filament, which sometimes is made up of two (or more?) rays intimately fused together throughout their extent.

Air-bladder present. No pyloric cæca.

In one of the three known species of this genus the female is viviparous, and in another species the male has a peculiarly elaborate penis.

Key to the species of Diplacanthopoma.

I. The two spines of the operculum are hidden in loose skin: length of the adult female about six inches ... ... *D. raniceps*.

II. The two opercular spines project freely:—
   1. Adult female about four inches long ... ... *D. brachysoma*.
   2. Adult female about fifteen inches long ... ... *D. Rivers-Andersoni*.

Except in point of size, the species of *Diplacanthopoma* hardly differ from one another.

77. *Diplacanthopoma Rivers-Andersoni*, Alcock.

Diplacanthopoma Rivers-Andersoni, Alcock, Ann. Mag. Nat. Hist. Aug. 1895, p. 144: ILLUSTRATIONS OF THE ZOOLOGY OF THE INVESTIGATOR, FISHES, PL. XVII. FIG. 1.

Eight branchiostegals.

Head about a fourth the total length: greatest height of the body, at the shoulder, equal to the length of the head without the snout.

Snout depressed, on a very much lower plane than the occiput, its length as much exceeds that of the eye as it falls short of the width of the interorbital space. Nostrils large: one immediately in front of the eye, the other near the edge of the snout.

Major diameter of the eye between a sixth and a seventh the length of the head.

Upper jaw half as long as the head, overlapping the lower jaw. Jaw-teeth in broadish bands, palatine and vomerine teeth in narrowish bands.

The spines of the operculum project freely. Only three enlarged gill-rakers on the outer side of the first arch, and those entirely in the upper half of the arch.

The bases of the dorsal and anal fins are invested in a thick scaleless glandular skin similar to that of the head. The anal begins a head length behind the axilla. Pectorals and ventrals of no great length.

Each ventral fin consists of a single stout fluted filament, looking like two or more rays intimately fused together.

Colours in spirit: body purplish brown; head and fins much darker.

A single specimen from off the Indus Delta: length a little over 15 inches.

The specimen is a pregnant female: the ovaries open on a fleshy cushion, behind the vent.

Regd. No. 14136.

The *ovaries* consist of a densely packed mass of embryos and ova enclosed in a thin but extremely tough capsule. The capsule is abundantly supplied with blood by the ramifications of a large branch of the mesenteric artery.

There is no attachment or adhesion of any kind between the ovarian capsule and its contents.

The embryos form a thick surface layer immediately beneath the capsule, enclosing a central mass of largish (a little over 1 millim. diameter) ova, which consist entirely of yolk-spherules, without any trace of an embryo or even of a germinal area.

Whether these unchanged ova would have developed subsequently to the birth of the present superficial layers of embryos, or whether they were destined for the intra-ovarian nourishment of the present embryos, are questions which it is impossible in an isolated case to discuss; but from their large size, which precludes any suggestion of immaturity, it would seem probable that they were intended for present use rather than for a future brood.

The *embryos*, which are long and eel-like—6 to 8 millim. long—lie matted together, firmly adhering to one another by their tails, by means of a coagulated secretion.

The vertical fins only are represented by a median fold of integument, which runs from the occiput, round the tip of the tail, to the vent. This fold of integument consists of very numerous layers of large-nucleated cells. The remains of the yolk-sac are enclosed in the abdomen, causing a bulging of the abdominal wall along its whole length, from the throat to the vent; but there is no vitelline constriction or pedicle.

I am inclined to think that the vertical fold of the integument, which is really only an extended sheet of embryonic cells, is an absorbent (nutritive) surface, somewhat as in the embryos of certain fishes of the family *Embiotocidæ*, in which the interradial membranes of the vertical fins have been shown to act as a fœtal placenta.

In the present case, however, there is no vascular connexion, at any rate on the fœtal side; and I am inclined to think that the nutrient material is absorbed not so much from the thin tough ovarian capsule as from the ovary itself, perhaps from those ova in which no trace of a germinal vesicle can be found.

An embryo taken at random measures 8 millim., namely 2 millim from the snout to the vent and 6 millim. from the vent to the tip of the tail.

78. ***Diplacanthopoma brachysoma***, Günther.

Diplacanthopoma brachysoma, Günther, Challenger Deep Sea Fishes, p. 115, pl. xxiii. fig. C: Goode & Bean, Oceanic Ichthyology p. 319: Alcock, Illustrations of the Zoology of the Investigator, Fishes, pl. XVII. fig. 2, (*specimen with an injured tail*).

Differs from *D. Rivers-Andersoni* only in the following particulars:—

The branchiostegal rays appear to be only six in number.

The snout, though otherwise similar, is only as long as the eye.

The diameter of the eye is nearly a fourth that of the head.

The distance between the 1st anal ray and the axilla is less than the length of the head.

The ventral fins arise nearer to the clavicular symphysis: though stout, they are not fluted.

The colour is light brown fading on the head and belly: the fins are grey.

The size is much smaller: a gravid female in the Museum collection is only $4\frac{1}{4}$ inches long.

Andaman Sea, 490 fathoms.

Regd. No. 11768.

Distribution: off Atlantic coast of Brazil, 350 fathoms: Andaman Sea, 490 fathoms.

79. *Diplacanthopoma raniceps,* Alcock.

Diplacanthopoma raniceps, Alcock, Ann. Mag. Nat. Hist., Aug. 1898, p. 154: ILLUSTRATIONS OF THE ZOOLOGY OF THE INVESTIGATOR, FISHES, PL. XXVI. FIG. 2, 2a.

Differs from *D. Rivers-Andersoni* only in the following particulars:—

The head is conical, the slope from the occiput to the tip of the snout being gentle and not abrupt, the whole head being frog-like.

The length of the snout is equal to the diameter of the eye, which is nearly a fourth the length of the head.

The spines of the operculum hardly project through the skin.

The ventrals arise nearer the clavicular symphysis: each consists of a stout filament, more than half as long as the head, and flattened and broadened in the middle of its course: each is made up of at least two intimately-fused rays.

The size is much smaller, a gravid female in the collection is not quite six inches long.

Colours in spirit as in *D. Rivers-Andersoni.*

Andaman Sea, 405 fathoms.

Regd. Nos. $\frac{117}{1}$, $\frac{118}{1}$, $\frac{139}{1}$.

The male is furnished with a most elaborate copulatory organ, which is almost as long as the snout. It is hollow and is lined and strengthened by the peritoneum, which is as thick and tough as leather. The intestine opens at its base, and the testes are prolonged into its cavity. Its free end has almost the consistence of cartilage and is thrown into several broad rigid lip-like folds which inclose two deep cavities. From the smaller (anterior) cavity a pair of papillæ project, and into the larger (posterior) cavity the testes open.

The corresponding organ of the female, though smaller than that of the male, is large. It is a hollow cone, lined by peritoneum, and lodging the ends of the ovaries, which open by a large common orifice at its spongy tip.

Subgenus SACCOGASTER.

Saccogaster, Alcock, Ann. Mag. Nat. Hist., Nov. 1889, p. 389.

Differs from *Diplacanthopoma*, which it very closely resembles, *only* in the following characters:—

The scales are not, or hardly, imbricate, so that the peculiar scale-less skin of the head is not so abruptly demarcated from the integument of the body.

A row of teeth in the mandible, and a few teeth near the symphysis of the upper jaw are enlarged.

The operculum has two radiating ridges but they do not end in spines.

The only known species is viviparous.

80. *Diplacanthopoma (Saccogaster) maculatum*, Alcock.

Saccogaster maculata, Alcock, Ann. Mag. Nat. Hist., Nov. 1889, p. 389; and July 1891, p. 30, pl. vii. fig. 3: Proc. Zool Soc., 1891, pp. 226, 227, fig: ILLUSTRATIONS OF THE ZOOLOGY OF THE INVESTIGATOR, FISHES, PL. XXIX. FIG. 2.

Eight branchiostegals.

Length of head $3\frac{1}{2}$ to 4 in the total: greatest body-height (except in the pregnant female) equal to the postorbital portion of the head.

Snout depressed, not overhanging the lower jaw, its length is half again that of the eye and equal to the width of the interorbital space. Nostrils inconspicuous; one in front of the eye, the other near the edge of the snout.

Diameter of the eye about a tenth the length of the head.

Upper jaw half as long as the head.

Two or three gill-rakers on the outer side of the first branchial arch are somewhat enlarged, as in *Diplacanthopoma*.

The bases of the dorsal and anal fins are invested in a thick scaleless glandular skin. The first anal ray is a head-length behind the axilla.

The fleshy bases of the pectorals are particularly long: the fin is about as long as the postorbital portion of the head. The ventrals arise a short distance behind the clavicular symphysis; each consists of a single filament not half as long as the head.

Colours: light brown, the scales showing as white dots, head and fins darker.

The largest specimen is 4 inches long.

Bay of Bengal, 193, 240, 145 to 250, and 195 to 210 fathoms.

Regd. Nos. 11673, 11674, 13045, 13527, 13528.

The male is furnished with a penis that consists of a large bilobed papilla with a pore, or genital opening, between the lobes. Sometimes there is also a long filament between the lobes.

The female is viviparous as in *D. Rivers-Andersoni.*

HEPHTHOCARA, Alcock.

Hephthocara, Alcock, Ann. Mag. Nat. Hist., Nov. 1892, p. 349.

Body elongate, compressed, tail tapering to a filament, covered with small thin deciduous slightly imbricate scales. Head large and broad, covered with a thick gelatinous scaleless skin; its bones thin.

Lateral line indistinguishable.

Snout broad, depressed, not overhanging the jaws; without barbels.

Mouth wide, with oblique cleft; the lower jaw slightly prominent. Villiform teeth in the jaws and palatines and in a crescent on the vomer.

Eye of moderate size.

Gill-openings wide: operculum with two feeble radiating ridges, the upper of which ends in a spine. Eight branchiostegals. No pseudobranchiæ.

Dorsal and anal fins confluent with the caudal.

No ventral fins.

Air-bladder present. No pyloric cæca.

The only known species is viviparous.

Hephthocara differs from *Diplacanthopoma*, to which it is very closely related, in the absence of ventral fins and in having a long lash-like tail.

81. ***Hephthocara simum***, Alcock.

Hephthocara simum, Alcock, Ann. Mag. Nat. Hist., Nov. 1892, p. 349, PL. xviii. fig. 1: ILLUSTRATIONS OF THE ZOOLOGY OF THE INVESTIGATOR, FISHES, PL. XXII. FIG. 3.

Head large, deep, broad, much inflated posteriorly; its length is from 4 to 5 in the total; its greatest height, which is more than the greatest height of the body, is nearly equal to its length; its bones are wafer-like and smooth; its integument is smooth and scaleless and, in life, forms a thick mucous cap of gelatinous consistence.

The small snub snout, the end of which is formed by the projecting mandible, is equal in length to the width of the interocular space, this being rather more than twice the major diameter of the deep-set eye, which again is about one-seventh the length of the head. The nostrils are inconspicuous and are situated one in front of the angle of the eye, the other at the tip of the snout.

Mouth large, with its cleft oblique, and with the mandible projecting beyond the thin broad maxilla, which last is a little more than half as long as the head.

Villiform teeth in broadish bands in the premaxillæ and mandible, and in very narrow bands on the palatines and expanded head of the vomer.

The edge of the preoperculum is smooth. As in *Diplacanthopoma* and *Saccogaster* there are only three enlarged gill-rakers on the outer side of the first branchial arch, and these are in the upper half of the arch.

The fin-rays are all extremely delicate; the dorsal fin, which begins about a snout-length behind the level of the gill-opening, and the anal, which begins nearly a head-length behind the same level, are confluent with the caudal at its base. The narrow pointed pectorals are a little longer than the combined eye and snout. There are no traces of ventrals.

Colour: uniform sepia, fins black.

The largest specimen, which is a gravid female, is a little over 11 inches long.

Off Travancore coast, 824 and 902 fathoms: Gulf of Manár, 7° 58′ N., 937 fathoms: Bay of Bengal, near the Andaman Islands, 606 fathoms.

Regd. Nos. 13172, $\frac{339}{1}$, $\frac{340}{1}$, $\frac{372}{1}$, $\frac{590}{1}$.

This species is viviparous in almost exactly the same way as *Diplacanthopoma Rivers-Andersoni*.

Family *Macruridæ*.

Head large, with the muciferous cavities well developed; trunk short: tail long, compressed, gradually tapering to a filament. Scales present on the body and generally on the head. Two dorsal fins, the first, which arises just behind the head, being short; the second, which arises either immediately or a short distance behind the first, being continued to the tip of the tail. Anal nearly similar in extent to the second dorsal. No caudal. Ventral fins thoracic or jugular, composed of several (6-12) rays. No pseudobranchiæ. Six or seven branchiostegals. Air-bladder present. Pyloric appendages numerous.

This family has been added to our knowledge of the Indian Fauna by the researches of the "Investigator." Eighteen Indian species, belonging to two genera, are now known. Of these, thirteen seem to be peculiar to Indian waters, and five occur in other seas. The five that are found elsewhere are *Macrurus (Coelorhynchus) parallelus* and *Macrurus nasutus* from Japan; *Macrurus (Mystaconurus) cavernosus* (probably identical with *Macrurus italicus* of the Mediterranean) and *Bathygadus longifilis* which are also known from the West Indian and Madeiran regions; and *Macrurus (Malacocephalus) laevis* from the North Atlantic and Brazil coast.

Key to the Indian genera of the family Macruridæ.

I. Snout projecting beyond the mouth: rays of the anal fin better developed than those of the second dorsal: gill-rakers on the outer side of the first branchial arch tuberculiform ... ... MACRURUS.

II. Snout not projecting beyond the mouth: rays of the second dorsal fin better developed than those of the anal: gill-rakers on the outer side of the first branchial arch long and setiform ... ... BATHYGADUS.

MACRURUS, Bloch, Günther.

Macrurus, Günther, Challenger Deep-Sea Fishes, pp. 122–124.

Macrurus, Coelorhynchus, Coryphaenoides, Hymenocephalus, Lionurus, Trachonurus, Cetonurus, Chalinura, Optonurus, Malacocephalus, Nematonurus, Moseleya, Abyssicola, Goode and Bean, Oceanic Ichthyology, pp. 390–417.

Malacocephalus, Moseleya, Nematonurus, Albatrossia, Bogoslovius, Chalinura, Coryphaenoides, Hymenocephalus, Macrourus, Coelorhynchus, Trachonurus, Lionurus, Jordan and Evermann, Fishes N. America, pp. 2560–2592.

Head short and thick with the muciferous cavities well developed; tail long and tapering.

The snout usually projects well beyond the mouth, which may be either quite inferior or lateral and subterminal. Teeth in the jaws only. A barbel at the symphysis of the lower jaw.

Gill-openings wide, the gill-membranes slightly united in front. The first branchial arch is broadly connected by membrane with the outer wall of the gill-chamber, so that the slit between that arch and the gill-cover is very much narrower than the other branchial clefts. The gill-rakers on the outer side of the first branchial arch are mere scabrous tubercles.

Scales either strongly and typically ctenoid or, more rarely, cycloid. No scaleless fossa on the side of the nape.

Second dorsal fin separated from the first by an interval; its rays, or at least its anterior rays, are more or less rudimentary. Anal rays much better developed than those of the second dorsal. Ventrals arising below, or slightly in advance of, the pectorals.

Key to the Indian subgenera of Macrurus (adapted from Dr. Günther).

I. Villiform teeth in bands in both jaws: scales imbricate and spinigerous:—
  1. Dorsal spine serrated: mouth inferior ... MACRURUS.
  2. Dorsal spine smooth:—
    i. Mouth inferior; the infraorbital region divided into a vertical and a subhorizontal portion by a longitudinal ridge ... ... COELORHYNCHUS.
    ii. Mouth wide, in the ordinary lateral position ... MYSTACONURUS.

II. Teeth in two series in the upper jaw and in a single series in the lower jaw. [Dorsal spine smooth: mouth lateral: scales imbricate and spinigerous] ... ... MALACOCEPHALUS.

Subgenus Cœlorhynchus, Günther.

Mouth comparatively small, entirely inferior, on the lower side of the head. a longitudinal ridge dividing the infraorbital region into a vertical and a sub-horizontal portion. Teeth in bands in both jaws. Scales imbricate, with strong serrated keels; no series of enlarged dorsal scales. Dorsal spine smooth.

Key to the Indian species of the subgenus Cœlorhynchus.

I. Scales of the body with subparallel spiny ridges: pyloric cæca 12 in number: seven branchiostegals ... ... *M. parallelus.*

II. Scales of the body with radiating spiny ridges: pyloric cæca about 40 in number: six branchiostegals:—

1. Body-scales with 5 spiny ridges: 6 to 6½ series of scales between the first dorsal fin and the lateral line ... *M. quadricristatus.*
2. Body-scales with 8 or 9 spiny ridges: 4 to 5 series of scales between the first dorsal fin and the lateral line *M. flabellispinis.*

82. ? *Macrurus (Cœlorhynchus) parallelus*, Günther.

Macrurus (Cœlorhynchus) parallelus, Günther, Challenger Deep-Sea Fishes, p. 125, pl. XXIX. fig. A: Alcock, Ann. Mag. Nat. Hist., (6) IV. 1889, p. 391, and Journ. As. Soc., Bengal, Vol. LXIII. pt. 2. 1894. p. 126.

B. 7. D. 10. A. 90. P. 16. V. 7.

Scales with usually 5 spiny ridges which are nearly parallel to one another, and of which the middle one is the strongest.

Twelve pyloric cæca.

Two young specimens in extremely bad preservation possess the above characters, and are therefore referred, though with hesitation, to *M. parallelus* Gthr.

Gulf of Manár, 597 fathoms.

Regd. Nos. 11760, 11761.

Distribution: New Zealand waters; Japan; Gulf of Manár.

83. *Macrurus (Cœlorhynchus) quadricristatus*, Alcock.

Macrurus (Cœlorhynchus) quadricristatus, Alcock, Ann. Mag. Nat. Hist., August, 1891, p. 119: Journ. As. Soc. Bengal, Vol. LXIII. pt. 2, 1894, p. 126: Illustrations of the Zoology of the Investigator, Fishes, pl. III, fig. 1.

B. 6. D. 11. A. *circ.* 90. P. 16. V. 7.

Head much exceeding the trunk in all three dimensions: tail low, compressed, tapering.

Length of the head nearly a third the total: greatest height of the body barely equal to the length of the snout.

Length of the snout nearly half that of the head, twice the major diameter of the eye and twice the width of the interorbital space.

The suborbital crest is strongly salient and serrated and terminates acutely at the preopercular angle. The posterior half of the head is longitudinally traversed on each side by two strongly serrated ridges, one extends from the interorbital space to the occiput, the other from the supra-orbital ridge to the shoulder.

Nostrils situated immediately in front of the eye; the posterior is very large.

The mouth is a small, completely inferior, crescentic orifice; its front limit is in the vertical through the anterior nostril, and the maxilla reaches a little behind the vertical through the middle of the eye. Villiform teeth in bands in the jaws, the outer row in the upper jaw slightly enlarged. Barbel slender, less than half the eye in length.

Gill-rakers in the form of tubercles.

Scales of the head with about 3, scales of the body with about 5, thin salient slightly-divergent serrated crests. 6 or $6\frac{1}{2}$ series of scales between the last ray of the first dorsal fin and the lateral line.

The first spine of the first dorsal fin is very small, the second is smooth throughout. The interval between the first and the very inconspicuous second dorsal is hardly half the extent of the base of the first. Pectorals narrow and pointed, their length slightly exceeds that of the postorbital portion of the head. Ventrals with the outer ray prolonged well beyond the origin of the anal.

Stomach large, siphonal; very many long slender cæca in a thick cluster round the pylorus; a thin-walled air-bladder.

Colours in life:—Chocolate; body and tail with numerous broad black cross bands, which do not reach the mid-abdominal line. In spirit the colouration is unchanged, but much lighter.

The largest specimen is 7 inches long.

Andaman Sea, 185, 188 to 220, and 405 fathoms.

Registered Nos. 13070–13072, $\frac{342}{1}$.

84. ***Macrurus (Cœlorhynchus) flabellispinis***, Alcock.

Macrurus (Cœlorhynchus) flabellispinis, Alcock, Journ. As. Soc. Bengal, Vol. LXIII, pt. 2, 1894, pp. 123, 126. Illustrations of the Zoology of the Investigator, Fishes, Pl. XVI, figs. 2, 2a.

B. 6. D. 1/8. A. 95. P. 16. V. 7.

Differs from *M. quadricristatus* in the following particulars:—

(1) the length of the snout is about two-fifths that of the head:

(2) the suborbital crest ends bluntly, and the four crests on the nape are low and inconspicuous:

(3) the mouth is much larger, the maxilla reaching almost to the posterior border of the orbit:

(4) the scales of the head have from 3 to 8, those of the body have 8 or 9, strongly-radiating serrated crests; and there are 4 or $4\frac{1}{2}$ rows of scales between the last ray of the first dorsal fin and the lateral line:

(5) the interval between the two dorsal fins is longer than the base of the first:

(6) the pectorals are decidedly shorter than the postorbital portion of the head, and the prolonged first ventral ray does not reach to the anal fin.

There are about 40 long pyloric cæca, and there is a thin-walled air-bladder.

Colours: dark stone-grey; fins and gill-membranes black.

Length 19 inches.

Arabian Sea, 719 fathoms.

Regd. No. 13472.

Subgenus Macrurus, Gthr.

Mouth small or moderate, entirely inferior, the infraorbital ridge distinct. Teeth in bands in both jaws. Scales imbricate with spines or serrated keels: no series of enlarged dorsal scales. Dorsal spine serrated.

The following key is substituted for that given by me in J. A. S. B. Vol. LXIII. pt. 2, 1894, pp. 126-127, which was reprinted by Goode and Bean in *Oceanic Ichthyology*, p. 532.

Key to the Indian species of the subgenus Macrurus.

I. Seven branchiostegals: vent between the ventral fins:—
  1. Eight rays in the ventral fin:—
    i. Scales with strong serrated (parallel) ridges: barbel hardly half as long as the eye ... ... *M. investigatoris.*
    ii. Scales with spinelets: barbel at least as long as eye ... *M. Petersoni.*
  2. Ten rays in the ventral fin: scales with densely packed spinelets *M. nasutus.*
  3. Eleven or twelve rays in the ventral fin:—
    i. Length of the head about a fifth of the total:—
      a Scales with about fifteen series of capillary spinelets *M. semiquincunciatus.*
      b. Scales with about seven series of capillary spinelets *M. polylepis.*
    ii. Length of head about an eighth the total: scales with from three to eight (usually six) series of short spinelets ... *M. pumiliceps.*

II. Six branchiostegals: vent immediately in front of the first ray of the anal fin:—
  1. Seven rays in the ventral fin ... ... *M. Hextii.*

2 Eight (rarely 9) rays in the ventral fin:—
   i. Second spine of the first dorsal fin remarkably prolonged:—
      a. Scales with twelve to seventeen rows of spinclets ... *M. macrolophus.*
      b. Scales with five or six very short series of spinelets *M. lophotes.*
   ii. Second spine of the first dorsal fin not abnormally long ... *M. Wood-Masoni.*
3 Nine rays in the ventral fin: one or more of the spinelets of the middle series in each scale much enlarged ... ... *M. Hoskynii.*

The species of *Macrurus* so much resemble each other, that it will be sufficient to describe one species and then to give only the differential points of the others, leaving the points of agreement to be understood. The commonest of the Indian species—*M. investigatoris*—may be first described.

85. ***Macrurus (Macrurus) investigatoris,*** Alcock.

Macrurus investigatoris, Alcock, Ann. Mag. Nat. Hist., Nov. 1889, p. 391: Journ. As. Soc. Bengal, Vol. LXIII. pt. 2, 1894, p. 126. ILLUSTRATIONS OF THE ZOOLOGY OF THE INVESTIGATOR, FISHES, PL. III. FIG. 4.

B. 7. D. $r+11$. A. *circ.* 100. P. 20-21. V. 8 (rarely 9).

Length of the head rather over a fifth of the total. Greatest height of the body (at the eminence of the first dorsal fin) equal to the length of the head behind the anterior nostril.

Snout almost as long as the eye, overlapping the mouth; with 3 well developed tubercles (median and lateral): nostrils in a scaleless fossa, the posterior much the larger.

Major diameter of the eye $3\frac{1}{2}$ in the length of the head: width of interorbital space about two-thirds the length of the eye.

Mouth rather small, completely inferior: the upper jaw, which overlaps the lower and is about as long as the snout, about reaches to the middle of the eye. Teeth in the jaws in broadish bands, none of the teeth enlarged.

Barbel slender, hardly half as long as the eye.

Scales on all parts except the mouth, throat, and gill-membranes. Scales of the body of moderate size; each with from 9 to 13 quite similar, nearly parallel, longitudinal ridges which project slightly—sometimes not at all—beyond the edge of the scale. To the naked eye the ridges appear entire, but they are really finely serrated.

Five rows of scales between the last ray of the first dorsal fin and the lateral line.

First spine of the first dorsal fin rudimentary; second spine about as long as the head without the snout.

Pectorals pointed; as long as the head behind the middle of the eye.

Outer ray of the ventral fins filamentous, slightly longer than the pectorals.

Vent situated between the ventral fins. About twelve long filiform pyloric cæca.

Disctinctive colours: first dorsal fin black with white root and tip.

Bay of Bengal 193, 240, 270, and 320 to 296 fathoms: Andaman Sea, 265, 271, 405, 490 fathoms.

Regd. Nos. 11654, 11655, 11658, 11676, 11679, 11766, 11772, 12447, 13177, $\frac{47}{1}$, $\frac{48}{1}$, $\frac{120}{1}$, $\frac{123}{1}$, $\frac{145}{1}$, $\frac{148}{1}$, $\frac{152}{1}$, $\frac{158}{1}$.

86. ***Macrurus (Macrurus) Petersonii,*** Alcock.

Macrurus petersonii, Alcock, Ann. Mag. Nat. Hist., Aug. 1891, p. 124: Journ. As. Soc. Bengal, Vol. LXIII. pt. 2, 1894, p. 127: ILLUSTRATIONS OF THE ZOOLOGY OF THE INVESTIGATOR, FISHES, PL. III. FIG. 5.

? *Macrurus (Chalinurus) hispidus*, Alcock, Ann. Mag. Nat. Hist., Nov. 1889, p. 397: Illustrations of the Zoology of the Investigator, Fishes pl. xiii. fig. 2 (*is probably the young of M. Petersonii*).

B. 7. D. *r*+10. A. *circ.* 100. P. 18–20. V. 8.

Differs from *M. investigatoris* only in the following particulars:—

The snout is quite as long as the eye, and its tubercles are not very much pronounced.

The eye is about a fourth the length of the head, and very little more than the width of the interorbital space.

The mouth is large, and the upper jaw, which is much longer than the snout, reaches behind the middle of the eye. The outer row of teeth in the upper jaw are enlarged.

The barbel is at least as long as the eye.

The scales are covered, but not very densely, with sharp conical spinelets, not in rows, some of which project beyond the edge of the scale. Some scales along the edge of the gill-opening, and in a patch immediately behind the first dorsal fin, are quite smooth.

Six rows of scales between the last ray of the first dorsal fin and the lateral line.

Second dorsal spine as long as the head behind the middle of the eye.

Length of pectorals about equal to the postorbital portion of the head.

Outer ventral ray hardly prolonged, its length not much more than two-fifths that of the head.

Over twenty longish vermiform pyloric cæca of great delicacy.

Distinctive colouration: head and iris silvery; first dorsal black with white base and tip.

Length of adult, $9\frac{1}{2}$ inches.

Andaman Sea, 185 and 188 to 220 fathoms.

Named after Mr. E. Peterson, for many years gunner of the *Investigator*, who in his zeal for zoology, was once nearly wound round the surging-drum of the dredging-winch, and once fell overboard among sharks.

Regd. Nos. 13117, 13118, $\frac{343-346}{1}$, $\frac{348}{1}$.

87. *Macrurus (Macrurus) nasutus*, Günther.

Macrurus nasutus, Günther, Ann Mag. Nat. Hist., 1877, Vol. XX. p. 440: Challenger, Deep-Sea Fishes, p. 132, Pl. XXX. fig. B.

Macrurus brevirostris, Alcock, Ann. Mag. Nat. Hist. (6) IV. 1889, p. 393; Journ. As. Soc. Bengal, Vol. LXIII. pt. 2, 1894, p. 127. ILLUSTRATIONS OF THE ZOOLOGY OF THE INVESTIGATOR, FISHES, PL. XIII. FIG. 3.

B. 7. D. *r*+11. A. *circ.* 110. P. 20-21. V. 10.

Differs from *M. investigatoris* only in the following particulars :—

The head is between a fifth and a sixth of the total.

The median tubercle of the snout is prominent, but the lateral tubercles are indistinct.

Major diameter of eye about $3\frac{1}{3}$ in the length of the head.

Outer row of teeth of the upper jaw considerably enlarged.

Barbel decidedly more than half as long as the eye.

Scales very closely covered with sharp conical spinelets of equal size, not arranged in rows, some of them projecting beyond the edge of the scale.

Five and a half or six rows of scales between the last ray of the first dorsal fin and the lateral line.

2nd dorsal spine a little longer than the head.

About 35 large long pyloric cæca.

Largest specimen, 11 inches long.

Andaman Sea, 490 fathoms: Arabian Sea, off Travancore coast, 738 fathoms.

Regd. Nos. 11762, 13115.

(In the Indian Museum is also one of the "Challenger" duplicates from Japan).

88. *Macrurus (Macrurus) semiquincunciatus*, Alcock.

Macrurus semiquincunciatus, Alcock, Ann. Mag. Nat. Hist., Nov. 1889, p. 392; Journ. As. Soc. Bengal, Vol. LXIII. pt. 2, 1894, p. 127. ILLUSTRATIONS OF THE ZOOLOGY OF THE INVESTIGATOR, FISHES, PL. XII. FIG. 2.

B. 7. D. *r*+11. A. *circ.* 100. P. 21. V. 11.

Differs from *M. investigatoris* only in the following particulars :—

The median tubercle of the snout is not very prominent and the lateral ones are very indistinct.

The major diameter of the eye is $3\frac{2}{3}$ in the length of the head.

Outer row of teeth in the upper jaw considerably enlarged.

Barbel stout, as long as the eye.

Scales of the body small, densely covered with sharp capillary spinelets some of which project far beyond the edge of the scale.

Eight rows of scales between the last ray of the first dorsal fin and the lateral line.

2nd spine of the dorsal fin as long as the head.

Twenty-two long vermiform pyloric cæca.

Largest specimen 10 inches long.

Andaman Sea 130 to 250 fathoms: Bay of Bengal, 240 and 410 fathoms.

Regd. Nos. 11660, 13133, 13173.

Palatksy, quoted by Goode and Bean in *Oceanic Ichthyology* p. 531, has changed the name of this species to *M. sesquiuncciatus*. The word *sesquiuncciatus*, if it has any meaning, might mean 'an ounce and a half.' The name *semiquincunciatus* was meant to express the fact that the rows of spinelets on the scales are arranged like the *principes* and *hastati* of the Roman legion,—that is to say *in quincuncem*, but without the *triarii*, or in a semi-quincunx. The idea may perhaps be a little far-fetched, but the etymology appears to me to be perfectly correct.

89. ***Macrurus (Macrurus) polylepis,*** Alcock.

Macrurus polylepis, Alcock, Ann. Mag. Nat. Hist., Nov. 1889, p. 395; Journ. As. Soc. Bengal, Vol. LXIII. pt. 2, 1894, p. 127. ILLUSTRATIONS OF THE ZOOLOGY OF THE INVESTIGATOR, FISHES, PL. XXIX. FIG. 4.

B. 7. D. r+11. P. 19. V. 11-12.

Differs from *M. investigatoris* only in the following particulars :—

The greatest body-height (at the eminence of the first dorsal fin) is only equal to the length of the head behind the middle of the eye.

Snout decidedly shorter than the eye, the median tubercle far more distinct than the lateral ones.

Major diameter of the eye nearly a third the length of the head, and nearly twice the width of the interorbital space.

Though the mouth is not large, the upper jaw is much longer than the snout and reaches behind the middle of the eye.

Outer row of teeth in the upper jaw much enlarged.

Barbel about as long as the eye.

Scales small, with about seven series of sharp capillary spinelets, some of which project beyond the edge of the scale.

Eight series of scales between the last ray of the first dorsal fin and the lateral line.

[2nd dorsal spine and pectoral fins broken at tip].

Outer ray of the ventral fin as long as the head behind the middle of the eye.

[Pyloric cæca present, of moderate size].

Largest specimen (immature) just over 6 inches long.

Bay of Bengal, 193 and 272 fathoms.

Regd. Nos. 11678, 11724.

90. ***Macrurus (Macrurus) pumiliceps***, Alcock.

Macrurus pumiliceps, Alcock, Journ. As. Soc. Bengal, Vol. LXIII. pt. 2, 1894, pp. 125, 127: ILLUSTRATIONS OF THE ZOOLOGY OF THE INVESTIGATOR, PL. XVI. FIG. 3.

B. 7. D. r+12. P. 18. V. 12.

Differs from *M. investigatoris* only in the following particulars:—

The head is just over an eighth the total length.

The greatest height of the body is equal to the length of the head.

The major diameter of the eye is almost a third the length of the head.

The upper jaw is a little longer than the snout.

The barbel is about three-quarters as long as the eye.

Scales with from 3 to 8 (usually 6) short rows of spinelets, which seldom project beyond the edge of the scale.

Lateral line indistinguishable.

2nd dorsal spine as long as the head.

The pectorals and the outer ray of the ventral fin are as long as the head without the snout.

Nine or ten very small pyloric cæca.

Largest specimen 11 inches long.

Arabian Sea, between Maldives and Travancore coast, 719 fathoms.

Regd. Nos. 13561, 13562.

[The number of rays in the anal fin is far over 100].

91. ***Macrurus (Macrurus) Hextii***, Alcock.

Macrurus Hextii, Alcock, Ann. Mag. Nat. Hist., Oct. 1890, p. 299; Journ. As. Soc. Bengal, Vol. LXIII. pt. 2, 1894, p. 126. ILLUSTRATIONS OF THE ZOOLOGY OF THE INVESTIGATOR, FISHES, PL. XII. FIG. 3.

B. 6. D. r+11. A. *circ.* 110. P. 21. V. 7.

Differs from *M. investigatoris* only in the following particulars:—

The snout is as long as the eye, and its tubercles are inconspicuous.

15

The major diameter of the eye is $4\frac{1}{4}$ to $4\frac{1}{2}$ in the length of the head and equal to the width of the interorbital space.

Mouth rather large, the upper jaw, which is as long as the snout *plus* half the eye, extending behind the middle of the eye.

Outer row of teeth in the upper jaw considerably enlarged, in the lower jaw slightly enlarged.

Barbel stout, three-fourths as long as the eye.

Scales closely covered with tiny capillary spinelets which are deciduous and do not project beyond the edge of the scale.

[Five rows of scales between the last ray of the first dorsal fin and the lateral line, as in *M. investigatoris*.]

Outer ventral ray as long as the head behind the anterior nostril.

Vent far behind the tip of the mass of the ventral fins.

Fourteen or fifteen very large pyloric cæca.

Length of largest specimen nearly 23 inches.

Arabian Sea, between the Laccadives and the Malabar coast, 360 and 1000 fathoms.

Regd. No. 12866. $\frac{361}{1}$.

The structure of the ovary and of the maturing ova in this species, have been described by me in Ann. Mag. Nat. Hist., Nov. 1892, pp. 351, 353.

92. *Macrurus (Macrurus) Wood-Masoni*, Alcock.

Macrurus Wood-Masoni, Alcock, Ann. Mag. Nat. Hist., Oct. 1890, p. 301; Nov. 1892, p. 353: Journ. As Soc. Bengal, Vol. LXIII, pt. 2, 1894, p. 123. ILLUSTRATIONS OF THE ZOOLOGY OF THE INVESTIGATOR, FISHES, PL. XIII, FIG. 1.

B. 6. D. $r+10$. A. *circ.* 105. P. 21. V. 8.

Differs from *M. investigatoris* only in the following particulars:—

The snout is about quarter again as long as the eye; all its tubercles are indistinct.

Major diameter of the eye $4\frac{1}{3}$ to $4\frac{1}{2}$ in the length of the head, and very slightly more than the width of the interorbital space.

Mouth rather large, the upper jaw slightly longer than the snout. Outer row of teeth in the upper jaw slightly enlarged.

Barbel a mere papilla hardly a quarter the length of the eye.

Scales covered with numerous close-set series of tiny spinelets.

Four or five rows of scales between the last ray of the first dorsal fin and the lateral line.

Outer ventral ray considerably shorter than the postorbital portion of the head.

Vent situated far behind the tip of the ventral fins.

11 or 12 long large pyloric cæca.

Largest specimen just over 19 inches long.

[The end of the 2nd dorsal spine is broken in all the specimens].

Arabian Sea, between the Malabar coast and the Laccadives, 360, 559, 902 and 1000 fathoms.

Regd. Nos. 12867, $\frac{356}{1}$, $\frac{358-360}{1}$.

93. *Macrurus (Macrurus) macrolophus*, Alcock.

Macrurus macrolophus, Alcock, Ann. Mag. Nat. Hist., Nov. 1889, p. 394; August, 1891, p. 121; Nov. 1892 p. 351, 352. fig. 1: Journ. As. Soc. Bengal, Vol. LXIII, pt. 2, 1894, p. 126. ILLUSTRATIONS OF THE ZOOLOGY OF THE INVESTIGATOR, FISHES, PL. XII. FIG. 1 (*the tail is a healed "stump" in this figure*).

B. 6. D. *r* + 9. A. *circ.* 85. P. 20-21. V. 8.

Differs from *M. investigatoris* only in the following particulars:—

The head is about two-ninths of the total length.

The greatest height of the body is equal to the postrostral portion of the head.

The snout is decidedly longer than the eye, and the lateral tubercles are indistinct.

Major diameter of the eye about $4\frac{1}{4}$ in the length of the head.

Outer row of teeth in upper jaw slightly enlarged.

Barbel very inconspicuous, not a third as long as the eye.

Scales with 12 to 17 rows of spinelets, the rows converging towards the middle line of the scale, the last in each row projecting far beyond the edge of the scale.

[Five rows of scales between the last dorsal ray and the lateral line, as in *M. investigatoris*].

Second spine of the first dorsal fin much prolonged,—$1\frac{1}{2}$ to $1\frac{2}{3}$ times as long as the head.

Pectorals as long as the postorbital portion of the head.

Outer ventral ray about as long as the head behind the middle of the eye.

Vent behind the mass of the ventral fins.

About 10 or 11 slender pyloric cæca.

The largest specimen (adult) is 11 inches long.

Bay of Bengal, 240 and 410 fathoms: Andaman Sea, 265 and 370 to 419 fathoms: Arabian Sea, off Travancore and Malabar coast, 360 and 406 fathoms.

Regd. Nos. 11776, 13130, 13175, $\frac{37}{1} - \frac{46}{1}$, $\frac{340}{1} - \frac{351}{1}$, $\frac{353}{1}$.

94. ***Macrurus (Macrurus) lophotes***, Alcock.

Macrurus lophotes, Alcock, Ann. Mag. Nat. Hist., Nov. 1889, p. 385; Journ. As. Soc. Bengal, Vol. LXIII. pt. 2, 1894, p. 126. ILLUSTRATIONS OF THE ZOOLOGY OF THE INVESTIGATOR, FISHES, PL. III. FIG. 2.

B. 6. D. *r* + 11-12. V. 8-9.

Differs from *M. investigatoris* only in the following particulars :—

The greatest height of the body is equal to the length of the head without the snout.

The snout is nearly half again as long as the eye.

The barbel is not a quarter the length of the eye.

Outer row of teeth in the upper jaw slightly enlarged.

Scales small, with 5 or 6 very short series of spinelets, the last in each series projecting beyond the edge of the scale.

Five or six rows of scales between the last ray of the first dorsal fin and the lateral line.

2nd dorsal spine nearly twice as long as the head.

Vent situated behind the mass of the ventral fins.

The number of pyloric cæca is unknown, the specimens being far too much damaged for dissection.

Length of the immature specimens, five inches.

Bay of Bengal " Swatch of No-ground " 405 to 285 fathoms.

Regd. Nos. 11670, 11671.

95. ***Macrurus (Macrurus) Hoskynii***, Alcock.

Macrurus Hoskynii, Alcock, Ann. Mag. Nat. Hist., Sept. 1890, p. 214: Journ. As. Soc. Bengal, Vol. LXIII. pt. 2, 1894, p. 126. ILLUSTRATIONS OF THE ZOOLOGY OF THE INVESTIGATOR, FISHES, PL. IX. FIG. 4.

B. 6. D. *r* + 10. P. 19-20. V. 9.

Differs from *M. investigatoris* only in the following particulars :—

Snout slightly but distinctly longer than the eye.

Major diameter of the eye $4\frac{1}{2}$ in the length of the head : interorbital space one-fourth again as broad as the major diameter of the eye.

Outer row of teeth in the upper jaw slightly enlarged.

Barbel not a fourth as long as the eye.

Scales with 13 to 18 short series of acute conical spinelets, the last spinelet of the middle series greatly enlarged above the others.

Four rows of scales between the last ray of the first dorsal fin and the lateral line.

2nd dorsal spine almost as long as the head.

Outer ventral ray as long as the head behind the middle of the snout.

Vent situated behind the tips of the mass of the ventral fins. Nine pyloric cœca.

One specimen just over 14 inches long. In the fresh state it emitted a powerful and disagreeable musky odour.

Bay of Bengal, 1310 fathoms.

Regd. No. 12833.

Subgenus Mystaconurus, Günther.

Mouth wide, in the ordinary lateral position, the infra-orbital ridge quite indistinct and not marking off two distinct planes. Teeth in bands in both jaws. Scales imbricate, spinigerous; no series of enlarged dorsal scales. Dorsal spine smooth.

---

96. ***Macrurus (Mystaconurus) cavernosus***, Goode and Bean.

[*an Macrurus (Mystaconurus) italicus*, Giglioli.]

Bathygadus cavernosus, Goode and Bean, Proc. U. S. Nat. Mus. VIII. 1885, p. 598: Günther, Challenger Deep Sea Fishes, p. 156.

Hymenocephalus cavernosus, Goode and Bean, Oceanic Ichthyology, 1896, p. 408, fig. 341.

Macrurus (Mystaconurus) heterolepis, Alcock, Ann. Mag. Nat. Hist., Nov. 1889, p. 396; Aug. 1891, p. 122: Journ. As. Soc. Bengal, Vol. LXV. pt. 2, 1896, p. 309. Illustrations of the Zoology of the Investigator, Fishes, pl. III, fig. 3.

B. 7. D. *r* + 10-11. A. *circ*. 100. P. 13-14. V. 10-11.

Length of the head not quite a fifth of the total: greatest height of the body not quite equal to the length of the head without the snout: tail lash-like.

Snout about three-quarters as long as the eye, distinctly but not very greatly overhanging the mouth, with median and lateral angles but not tubercles. Nostrils as in all the previous species.

Major diameter of the eye about $3\frac{1}{2}$ in the length of the head and about four-fifths the width of the interorbital space.

Mouth wide, the upper jaw, which is about half as long as the head, reaching the level of the posterior border of the orbit. Villiform teeth in rather narrow tapering bands in both the jaws: none of the teeth enlarged.

Barbel very slender and inconspicuous, not half as long as the eye.

Scales apparently absent from the head; large thin and very deciduous on the body. The scales on the anterior half of the trunk and posterior half of the tail are smooth and cycloid; but between these parts—at any rate in adults—the scales bear 6 or 7 series of rather distant granules or semi-erect spinules.

Seven rows of scales between the last ray of the first dorsal fin and the lateral line.

1st dorsal spine rudimentary; the second is as long as the head without the snout.

Pectorals narrow, pointed; about as long as the postorbital portion of the head.

Outer ray of the ventral fins filamentous, nearly as long as the head without the snout.

Vent situated behind the mass of the ventral fins, immediately in front of the 1st anal ray. 12 or 13 not very long pyloric cæca.

Colours in life: head and iris silvery, body pinkish brown with a silvery sheen, throat and belly black: first dorsal white, with a black patch about the middle.

Length between 6 and 7 inches.

In some specimens there is a curious circular spot or pimple in the middle line of the belly in front of the ventral fins.

Andaman Sea, 188 to 220, 240, 265, 271 and 405 fathoms: Gulf of Manár, 180 to 217 fathoms.

Regd. Nos. 11644, 11774, 12449, 13551–13560, $\frac{24}{1}$ - $\frac{28}{1}$, $\frac{124}{1}$, $\frac{126}{1}$, $\frac{157}{1}$.

Distribution: G. of Mexico, 227 fathoms: G. of Manár and Andaman Sea, 180 to 405 fathoms.

I am satisfied by actual comparison of our specimens with one received from the Smithsonian Institution (and now in the Indian Museum collection), that the species described by me as *Mystaconurus heterolepis* is the same as Goode and Bean's *Hymenocephalus cavernosus:* and I believe that both these names will prove to be synonyms of Giglioli's *Hymenocephalus italicus* from the Mediterranean.

Subgenus Malacocephalus, Gthr.

Mouth wide, in the ordinary lateral position, the infra-orbital ridge quite indistinct. Teeth in the upper jaw in two rows; in a single row in the lower jaw. Scales imbricate, spinigerous. Dorsal spine smooth.

97. *Macrurus (Malacocephalus) lævis*, Lowe.

Macrurus lævis, Lowe, Proc. Zool. Soc. 1843, p. 92.

Malacocephalus lævis, Günther, Cat. Fishes, Vol. IV. p. 397; Lütken, Vid. Meddel. Nat. Foren., Kjobenhavn 1872, p. 1.

Macrurus lævis, Günther, Challenger Deep-Sea Fishes, p. 148, pl. xxxix. fig. B: Smitt, Hist. Scandinavian Fishes by Fries, Ekström & Sundevall, II. p. 593, fig. 141: Alcock, Ann. Mag. Nat. Hist., Nov. 1889, p. 398; and Aug. 1891, p. 123: Goode and Bean, Oceanic Ichthyology, p. 415: Koehler, Résult. Sci. "Caudan," Poissons, Fasc. III. p. 492.

Malacocephalus lævis, Gilbert & Cramer, Proc. U. S. Nat. Mus. XIX. 1896, p. 432.

B. 7. D. *r* + 11-12. A. *circ.* 200. P. 17. V. 9.

Head nearer a sixth than a fifth the total length: greatest body-height equal to the length of the head behind the anterior nostril: tail peculiarly low, long and tapering.

Snout blunt-pointed; the median tubercle hardly, and the lateral tubercles not at all, distinguishable; slightly projecting beyond the mouth; nearly as long as the eye. Nostrils, as usual, in a scaleless fossa high up in front of the eye.

Major diameter of the eye a third to three-sevenths the length of the head, barely equal to the width of the flat interorbital space.

Mouth wide; the upper jaw, which is half as long as the head, reaches behind the middle of the eye. Teeth of the upper jaw in two rows—an inner row smaller and closer-set, and an outer row more distant and much larger. A single row of large rather irregular teeth in the lower jaw.

Barbel about two-thirds as long as the eye.

Scales on all parts, except the mouth throat and branchiostegal membranes and certain definite patches to be presently noticed near the ventral fins. Those of the head are rough and very small: those on the body are small and are covered with very short bristle-like spinelets.

Eleven or 12 rows of scales between the last ray of the first dorsal fin and the lateral line.

First dorsal spine rudimentary; the second a little longer than the post-orbital portion of the head.

Pectorals rather narrow, pointed, about the same length as the second dorsal spine.

Ventrals very short; the outer ray very slightly prolonged—about as long as the eye.

The vent lies at the end of an oval naked depression between the ventral fins: there is a second naked fossa, but with its long diameter transverse, just in front of, or between, the bases of the ventral fins.

There are 60 or more slender pyloric cæca.

Andaman Sea, 188 to 220, 265, and 370 to 419 fathoms: Arabian Sea, between the Maldives and Cape Comorin, 719 fathoms.

Regd. Nos. 13116, 13517, $\frac{379}{1}$, $\frac{380}{1}$.

Distribution: off the coast of Brazil; North Sea, Bay of Biscay, Madeira and North Atlantic; Mediterranean (?); Arabian Sea, Andaman Sea, Hawaii (Sandwich Is.).

I have compared our specimens with the figures and descriptions given by Günther and by the authors of the *History of Scandinavian Fishes*, and I am perfectly sure that they are one and the same species.

BATHYGADUS, Günther.

Bathygadus, Günther, Ann. Mag. Nat. Hist., II. 1878, p. 23: Challenger Deep-Sea Fishes, p. 154: Goode and Bean, Oceanic Ichthyology, p. 420; Jordan and Evermann, Fishes N. America, III. p. 2563.

Head short and thick with the muciferous cavities well developed: tail long and tapering.

Snout not projecting beyond the mouth, which is large and lateral, with the jaws even in front. Villiform teeth in narrow bands in the jaws only. Barbel present or absent.

Gill-openings wide, the gill-membranes slightly united in front. No membranous connexion or diaphragm between the first branchial arch and the wall of the gill-chamber. Numerous long setiform gill-rakers on the outer side of the first branchial arch.

Scales small, deciduous, cycloid.

Second dorsal fin almost continuous with the first, its rays are well developed. Anal rays feeble. Ventrals arising below the pectorals.

Key to the Indian species of Bathygadus.

I. Barbel present: anterior dorsal, upper pectoral and outer ventral rays very greatly prolonged ... ... *B. longifilis.*

II. No barbel: anterior dorsal, upper pectoral and outer ventral rays slightly prolonged ... ... *B. furvescens.*

98. *Bathygadus longifilis*, Goode & Bean.

Bathygadus longifilis, Goode and Bean, Proc. U. S. Nat. Mus. VIII. 1885, p. 599, and Oceanic Ichthyology, 1896, p. 422: Günther, Challenger Deep-Sea Fishes, p. 157: Alcock, Ann. Mag. Nat. Hist. (6) VI. 1890, p. 302, and VIII. 1891, p. 123.

Bathygadus multifilis, Günther, Challenger Deep-Sea Fishes, p. 155.

Hymenocephalus longifilis, Vaillant, Exp. Sci. Travailleur et Talisman, Poiss. p. 218, pl. xxiii. fig. 1.

B. 7. D. *v* + 10 + *circ.* 140. P. 13–15. V. 8.

Head and body compressed. Head about a sixth the total length: greatest height of the body about equal to the length of the head behind the anterior nostril.

Snout barely longer than the eye, which is nearly a fourth the length of the head and slightly more than the width of the interorbital space. Nostrils in a scaleless fossa in front of the eye; the posterior the larger.

Mouth wide, the maxilla, which is decidedly more than half as long as the head, reaching the level of the posterior border of the orbit: villiform teeth in bands of moderate breadth in the jaws.

Barbel slender, from half to nearly two-thirds the length of the head.

Operculum with two feeble points, which are often subcutaneous and indistinguishable: angle of preoperculum full and rounded. Very numerous long close-set gill-rakers on the outer side of the first branchial arch.

Deciduous cycloid scales on the head and body: six rows of them between the last ray of the first dorsal fin and the lateral line.

First dorsal ray rudimentary, the second is produced to a filament and is about twice as long as the head, or even longer. The longest rays of the 2nd dorsal fin are about as long as the snout and eye combined.

Upper pectoral ray nearly three times, outer ventral ray nearly twice as long as the head.

About 20 long rather slender pyloric cæca.

The largest specimen is a little over a foot long.

Bay of Bengal, off west coast of Andamans, 683 fathoms: Arabian Sea, in the neighbourhood of the Laccadives and Maldives, 459, 636, and 740 fathoms.

Regd. Nos. 12860, 12861, 13132, 14004, $\frac{168}{1}$, $\frac{172}{1}$.

Distribution: Atlantic coasts of N. America; Atlantic coasts of Morocco; Arabian Sea and Bay of Bengal; off Philippine Islands.

99. ***Bathygadus furvescens***, Alcock.

Bathygadus furvescens, Alcock, Journ. As. Soc. Bengal, Vol. LXIII. pt. 2, 1894, p. 128: ILLUSTRATIONS OF THE ZOOLOGY OF THE INVESTIGATOR, FISHES, PL. XVI. FIG. 1 (*first dorsal, upper pectoral and outer ventral rays broken*).

B. 7. D. r + 9-10. P. 15. V. 8.

Differs from *B. longifilis*, Goode and Bean, only in the following particulars:—

Length of head from a fifth to a sixth (young) the total.

Snout distinctly though not very greatly longer than the eye.

Major diameter of the eye a fourth (young) to a fifth (adult) the length of the head.

No barbel.

Seven rows of scales between the last ray of the first dorsal fin and the lateral line.

Second dorsal spine from a half to two-thirds the length of the head. The upper pectoral rays vary from about two-thirds (adults) the length of the head to the entire length of the head (young). The outer ventral ray is about equal to the post-orbital portion of the head in the adult, but is equal to the post-rostral portion of the head in the young.

There are 20 very large pyloric cæca.

The longest specimen is $20\frac{1}{2}$ inches in length.

Arabian Sea, 406, 480, 719 fathoms; Gulf of Manár, 142 to 400 fathoms; Bay of Bengal, 410 fathoms; Andaman Sea 405 fathoms.

Regd. Nos. 13213, 13470, 13550, $\frac{30-33}{1}$, $\frac{143}{1}$, $\frac{155}{1}$, $\frac{587-589}{1}$.

This species may possibly be identical with *B. melanobranchus* Vaillant.

Family *Ateleopodidæ.*

Head rather large, with the muciferous cavities fairly well developed; trunk short; tail long, compressed, gradually tapering to a filament.

A single, short, dorsal fin, situated above the pectorals. A long anal fin, continuous with the caudal.

Ventrals jugular.

No pseudobranchiæ: no air-bladder: no pyloric appendages.

This is another family which has been found to range into Indian waters since the publication of the *Fishes* and *Fauna of India.*

Ateleopus, Schleg.

Ateleopus, Temminck and Schlegel, Faun. Japon., Poiss, p. 255: Günther, Cat. Fishes IV., p. 398.

Skeleton semi-cartilaginous.

The snout projects well beyond the mouth, which is small, quite inferior and strongly protractile downwards. Teeth villiform, minute; in a band in the upper jaw only, or in both jaws: palate smooth. No barbel.

Gill-openings fairly wide, the gill-membranes slightly united anteriorly. The first branchial arch is rather broadly connected, at its upper part, by membrane, with the wall of the gill-chamber, so that the slit between that arch and the gill-cover is narrower than the other branchial clefts. Gill-rakers on the outer side of the first branchial arch cartilaginous, tuberculiform. Eight branchiostegals.

Head and body covered with a thick, gelatinous, scaleless skin.

The ventrals arise immediately behind the clavicular symphysis: each consists of a single stout filament made up of two intimately coherent rays.

Distribution: Japan, Andaman Sea, Laccadive Sea.

100. *Ateleopus indicus*, Alcock.

Ateleopus indicus, Alcock, Ann. Mag. Nat. Hist., Aug. 1891, p. 123: ILLUSTRATIONS OF THE ZOOLOGY OF THE INVESTIGATOR, FISHES, PL. II, FIG. 2.

B. 8. D. 8. A. + C. 76–80. P. 12. V. 2 (fused to form a single ray).

Length of the head about equal to that of the rest of the trunk, and contained about $5\frac{3}{4}$ times in the total: greatest height of the body, at the shoulder, equal to the length of the head behind the middle of the snout.

The broadly-pointed, depressed, projecting, marginally-inflated snout is one-third of the head in length and twice the major diameter of the oval eye; about half its extent is preoral. The nostrils, which are very large, are situated superiorly immediately in front of the eye.

The mouth is a small, quite inferior, crescentic orifice, in width hardly more than equal to the diameter of the eye-ball, its angle barely reaching the vertical through the anterior border of the orbit, though the maxilla reaches nearly to the vertical through the middle of the orbit; it is strongly protractile downwards, and looks as if adapted for suction. There is a short band of very minute teeth in the inner aspect of the upper jaw; but the lower jaw is quite toothless.

Gill-rakers short, coarse, cartilaginous.

Head, body, and fins uniformly invested with a soft, thick, gelatinous, scaleless skin. The lateral line follows the dorsal curve of the trunk, and then runs along the middle of the tail.

The base of the dorsal fin is about three-quarters as long as the snout: the height of the fin is about equal to the length of the head. The longest rays of the anal fin are about equal to the postorbital portion of the head.

Pectorals pointed; their length is almost equal to that of the dorsal fin.

Each ventral consists of a stiffish cartilaginous rod, about half as long as the head, and made up of two intimately coherent rays.

Stomach long, simple; intestine short and wide, opening in front of the first anal ray. The ovaries in the adult female consist of a pair of thin-walled sacks loosely filled with largish eggs (over 1 millim. in diameter in spirit) and opening by a common orifice behind the vent.

Colours: mottled dark brown to purple-black; all the fins except the ventrals black.

The largest specimen, an adult female, is 15 inches long.

Andaman Sea, 188 to 220 and 405 fathoms: Arabian Sea, off Travancore coast, 224 to 284 fathoms.

Regd. Nos. 13069, $\frac{141}{1}$, $\frac{456-458}{1}$, $\frac{460}{1}$.

Anacanthini Pleuronectoidei.

To the 8 genera and 39 species recorded in the *Fauna of British India* the "Investigator" has added 8 more genera and 24 more species. Not all of these, however, belong to the fauna of the deep-sea.

The following is a synopsis of the genera of Pleuronectidæ at present known to inhabit Indian seas. Those that are represented in the depths are marked with an asterisk: those that have recently been added to the Indian fauna by the "Investigator," are marked with a dagger.

I. Jaws and dentition nearly equally developed on both sides:—
- 1. The dorsal fin begins on the neck ... ... PSETTODES.
- 2. The dorsal fin begins in front of the eyes, on the snout:—
  - i. Eyes on the left side: lateral line with a curve above the pectoral fin:—
    - *a.* Eyes not widely separated: teeth minute, equal, in a single series: maxilla about a third the length of the head ... ... ARNOGLOSSUS.†
    - *b.* Eyes not widely separated: teeth unequal, in a single series: maxilla nearly half as long as the head ... ... PSEUDORHOMBUS.
    - *c.* Eyes not widely separated: teeth large, unequal, in a single series: maxilla about three-quarters the length of the head ... ... *CHASCANOPSETTA.†
    - *d.* Eyes separated by a concave space, which is usually of considerable width ... RHOMBOIDICHTHYS.
    - *e.* Eyes as in Rhomboidichthys: *no scales* PSETTYLLIS.†
  - ii. Eyes on the left side: lateral line nearly straight ... CITHARICHTHYS.
  - iii. Eyes on the right side: lateral line nearly straight, slightly ascending anteriorly: mouth small ... SAMARIS.†
  - iv. Eyes on the right side: lateral line with a wide curve anteriorly: mouth large ... ... BRACHYPLEURA.†

II. Jaws and dentition much more developed on the blind side:—
- 1. Caudal fin independent:—
  - i. Eyes on the left side: lateral line with a curve above the pectoral: pectorals well developed ... ... *LÆOPS.†
  - ii. Eyes on the right side: lateral line with a curve above the pectoral: pectorals well developed ... ... *BOOPSETTA.†
  - iii. Eyes on the right side: lateral line straight: pectorals absent or present ... ... SOLEA and *ACHIRUS.
- 2. Vertical fins confluent with the caudal:—
  - i. Eyes on the right side: pectorals present or absent ... SYNAPTURA.
  - ii. Eyes on the left side: pectorals absent:—
    - *a.* No lateral line ... ... *APHORISTIA.†
    - *b.* Two or three lateral lines on the left side: lips with tentacles ... ... PLAGUSIA.
    - *c.* Two or three lateral lines on the left side: lips without tentacles ... ... *CYNOGLOSSUS.

Family *Pleuronectidæ.*

Chascanopsetta, Alcock.

Chascanopsetta, Alcock, Journ. As. Soc. Bengal, Vol. LXIII, pt. 2, 1894, p. 128.
Pelecanichthys, Gilbert and Cramer, Proc. U. S. Nat. Mus. XIX. 1896, p. 432.

Mouth very wide, the maxillary being very much more than half the length of the head. Jaws and teeth equally developed on both sides, each jaw being armed with a single row of long slender depressible teeth. Eyes on the left side. The dorsal fin commences near the tip of the snout, its rays, and those of the anal, being simple, slender, and scaleless. Caudal free. Scales minute, membranous, hardly imbricate. Lateral line with a strong curve above the pectoral. Gill-openings wide, the gill-membranes united in front. Gill-rakers none. Seven branchiostegals. Pseudobranchiæ large.

101. *Chascanopsetta lugubris*, Alcock.

Chascanopsetta lugubris, Alcock, Journ. As. Soc. Bengal, Vol. LXIII, pt. 2, 1894, p. 129, pl. vi. fig. 4: Illustrations of the Zoology of the Investigator, Fishes, pl. XV. fig. 3.

B. 7. D. 115. A. 80. C. 16. V. 6.

Body long, low, tapering, the dorsal profile considerably more convex than the ventral. The greatest height of the body is about one-fourth, and the length of the head about one-fifth of the total, caudal included.

Mouth-cleft very wide, oblique, with the lower jaw strongly projecting: the maxilla, which is hardly expanded posteriorly, is about three-quarters the length of the head,—reaching nearly to the angle of the properculum. Each jaw is armed with a single row of sharp curved teeth of two sizes, the larger fairly regularly alternating with the smaller: those of the lower jaw are very close-set, and are strongly depressible inwards across the floor of the mouth: those of the upper jaw are more distant, not so strongly depressible, and rather smaller. Tongue large, free, with a long styliform point. The rami of the lower jaw are capable of very wide divarication.

The eyes, which are on the left side, are large (their major diameter being about two-sevenths of the length of the head), close-set (less than a-third of a diameter apart), and nearly equal in front. The snout proper is short—about two-thirds the length of the eye. The nostrils are small pores situated in front of the interorbital space.

The gill-openings are wide, the gill-membranes being free posteriorly: the gill-arches are extremely weak and slender, the gill-laminæ are delicate, and there are no gill-rakers.

The body and the post-orbital portion of the head are covered with minute membranous hardly imbricating scales, which are somewhat enlarged along the lateral line. The lateral line on both sides has a strong sinuous curve above the pectoral fin.

The fin-rays are weak and filiform: the dorsal begins in front of the eye, on the snout. The caudal peduncle is strongly constricted, and expands again at the insertion of the fin, which is long and pointed,—$6\frac{1}{2}$ in the total length. The pectorals are slender: that on the coloured side is much larger than its fellow, its upper rays being nearly as long as the caudal. Both ventrals are well developed.

Colours: dull dusky brown, the peritoneum showing through as a black patch; iris and fins black; tongue dusky brown.

The largest specimen is $8\frac{3}{4}$ inches long.

Bay of Bengal, off Madras coast, 145 to 250 fathoms: Gulf of Manár, 143 fathoms.

Regd. Nos. 13728, 13729: $\frac{591-593}{1}$.

Boopsetta, Alcock.

Boopsetta, Alcock, Journ. As. Soc. Bengal, Vol. LXV. pt. 2, 1896, p. 305.

Cleft of the mouth very narrow: teeth in the jaws only, in broadish villiform bands on the blind side, gradually becoming obsolescent on the coloured side. Eyes on the right side, very large, almost in contact, the upper bulging beyond the dorsal profile, the lower in advance of the upper. The dorsal fin begins above the middle of the upper eye. Both pectorals and both ventrals well developed. Scales of moderate size, stout ctenoid* and adherent on the coloured side, thin cycloid and deciduous on the blind side. Lateral line with a strong curve above the pectoral.

Gill-openings somewhat contracted, the membranes very broadly united below the isthmus: gill-rakers numerous, of good length, pointed. Six branchiostegals.

Closely allied to *Pleuronectes*.

102. *Boopsetta prælonga*, Alcock.

Pœcilopsetta prælonga, Alcock, Journ. As. Soc. Bengal, Vol. LXIII. pt. 2, 1894, p. 130, pl. vii. fig. 2: Illustrations of the Zoology of the Investigator, Fishes, pl. XV. fig. 2 (*young*).

Boopsetta umbrarum, Alcock, Journ. As. Soc. Bengal, Vol. LXV. pt. 2, 1896, p. 305: Illustrations of the Zoology of the Investigator, Fishes, pl. XVII. fig. 5.

B. 6. D. 60. A. 51. C. 18. P. *d.* 8, *s.* 6. V. 6. L. lat. *circ.* 110.

Height of the body one-third, length of the head one-fourth the total, without the caudal.

* In the young the scales on both sides are cycloid.

The mouth is short and broad, the cleft approaching the vertical, the maxilla being a little over three-fourths the length of the eye, which is slightly more than one-third the length of the head. The teeth are in broad villiform bands in the jaws on the blind side, the bands gradually becoming narrow and disappearing on the coloured side. The upper eye bulges very strongly beyond the general dorsal profile. The length of the snout—*i.e.*, of the space between the front wall of the lower orbit and the tip of the knob of the mandibular symphysis—is less than half the length of the eye.

The body, and the head excepting only the snout throat and gill-membranes, are covered with scales.

The rays of the vertical fins are stout, the longest are more than two-fifths the greatest body-height. The caudal is large, with a distinct though broad peduncle. The dorsal begins just behind the middle of the eye.

The coloured pectoral is rather longer than its fellow, the latter being more than half the length of the head. The coloured ventral is rather longer than its fellow, the latter being as long as the eye.

Colours in spirit: right side blackish-brown, with traces of six opalescent cross-bands: irides and coloured pectoral fin blue-black, the pectoral with a narrow white cross-stripe. Vertical fins (on coloured side), and right ventral, almost black, tipped with milk white. Left side rather dusky.

In the young, both sides are coloured, being grey with numerous large black blotches, disposed in series.

The largest specimen is $6\frac{1}{4}$ inches long.

Gulf of Manár, 142 to 400 and 180 to 217 fathoms: Andaman Sea, 185 fathoms.

Regd. Nos. 13733, 13734, $\frac{61}{1}$, $\frac{363-365}{1}$, $\frac{367}{1}$, $\frac{643-646}{1}$.

103. ***Boopsetta maculosa***, Alcock.

Pœcilopsetta maculosa, Alcock, Journ. As. Soc. Bengal, Vol. LXIII. pt. 2, 1894, p. 130, pl. vii. fig. 1. Illustrations of the Zoology of the Investigator, Fishes, pl. XV. fig. 1.

B. 6. D. 56. A. 46. C. 18. V. 5.

Differs from *B. prælonga* only in the following particulars, specimens of about the same size being compared :—

The height of the body is half the total length without the caudal.

The maxilla is almost as long as the eye, which is a third as long as the head.

The dorsal fin begins above the middle of the eye: and the longest rays are barely a fourth the greatest height of the body.

The pectorals are only about as long as the eye.

The largest specimen is nearly $4\frac{1}{4}$ inches long, and is not adult.

Colours of the young: both sides of the body grey with numerous large dark grey and black blotches disposed in series: caudal with two black blotches: right pectoral with a black blotch.

Judging from the analogy of *B. prælonga* the coloration of the adult would be different.

Bay of Bengal, off Madras coast, 145–250 fathoms: Andaman Sea, 185 fathoms.

Regd. Nos. 13732, $\frac{368}{1}$.

LÆOPS, Günther.

Læops, Günther, Challenger Shore Fishes, p. 29.
Scianectes, Alcock, Ann. Mag. Nat. Hist., Sept. 1890, p. 216.

Body elongate-oval or piriform: head small. Cleft of the mouth very narrow, with the dentition much more developed on the blind side than on the coloured: palatine and vomerine teeth none. Eyes on the left side. The dorsal fin begins in front of the eye. Scales small, thin, deciduous. Lateral line with a curve above the pectoral.

Gill-openings moderately broad, the membranes united anteriorly and rather broadly. Gill-rakers sufficiently numerous, short, pointed. Six branchiostegals.

This genus is represented in India by 3 species, only one of which is an inhabitant of the deep-sea. Of the other two, one is hardly distinguishable from *Læops parviceps*, Günther.

104. ***Læops macrophthalmus***, Alcock.

Scianectes macrophthalmus, Alcock, Journ. As. Soc. Bengal, Vol. LVIII, pt. 2, 1889, p. 292, pl. xvi. fig. 4: Ann. Mag. Nat. Hist., Sept. 1890, p. 216: ILLUSTRATIONS OF THE ZOOLOGY OF THE INVESTIGATOR, FISHES, PL. XXIII. FIG. 1.

B. 6. D. 85–88. A. 68. C. 17. P. *s.* 14. *d.* 12. V. 6. L. lat. *circ.* 95.

Body piriform, very delicate, its greatest height about $2\frac{1}{2}$ in the total without caudal. The length of the head is one-third, or rather less, of the same standard. Snout obtuse, about half as long as the eye. Eyes close together, separated by a salient decliving ridge, the lower slightly in advance; their major diameter rather more than one-fourth the length of the head. Cleft of the mouth nearly vertical; length of the maxilla a little more than one-fourth that of the head; the lower jaw projecting in repose. Villiform teeth in a band on the blind side of each jaw.

Opercles thin; the branchiostegal rays prolonged.

Scales minute, thin, smooth, deciduous. Lateral line salient, curved above the pectoral, continued right along the caudal fin.

The longest dorsal rays are about half the length of the head and are slightly shorter than the corresponding anal rays.

The coloured (left) pectoral, which is more developed than its fellow, is nearly two-thirds the length of the head.

The coloured ventral is in the same line as the anal; its longest rays are equal to the major diameter of the eye.

Colours: left side dark sepia; vertical fins and left ventral black; left pectoral grey and black; edge of branchiostegal membrane, on left side, black.

The largest specimen is nearly 5 inches long.

Bay of Bengal, 100, 98 to 102, and 107 fathoms: Arabian Sea, off Malabar coast, 100 fathoms.

Regd. Nos. 11721, 12805–12809, 13632, 13633, $\frac{660-669}{1}$.

After renewed examination I am convinced that the vomerine teeth, the supposed presence of which led me to keep this species distinct from *Læops*, are not true teeth, but are only irregularities of the surface of the bone.

Solea, Cuv., Gthr.

105. ***Solea umbratilis***, Alcock.

Solea (Achirus) umbratilis, Alcock, Journ. As. Soc. Bengal, Vol. LXIII. pt. 2, 1894, p. 131, pl. vii. fig. 3: Illustrations of the Zoology of the Investigator, Fishes, pl. XV. fig. 4.

D. 70. A. 50. C. 18. P. 0. V. 5. L. lat. *circ.* 80.*

The height of the body is $2\frac{1}{3}$ in the total without the caudal. The length of the head is sometimes a little more, sometimes a little less than a third of the total without the caudal (in adults). The snout is but slightly hooked: its length is twice that of the eye and from two-sevenths to a quarter that of the head. The eyes are nearly or quite a diameter apart. The nostril of both sides is a slender tube. The mouth-cleft reaches to the posterior limit of the lower eye.

No pectoral fins whatever.

Ventral fins symmetrical, separated from the anal by more than an eye-length.

Colours in spirit: warm olive brown, with numerous large black blotches which form four or five irregular transverse series and three irregular longitudinal series: dorsal and anal fins bluish-black or black: underside smoky in rather more than the posterior half. The black blotches are sometimes circumscribed by a light areola.

* From its commencement behind the upper eye.

Length (of a nearly adult female) $4\frac{1}{4}$ inches.

Bay of Bengal, off Madras coast 107 and 91 fathoms: Arabian Sea, off Kattiwar coast, 82 fathoms, and off Malabar coast, 100 and 68 to 148 fathoms.

Regd. Nos. 13615–13618, 13621–13628, $\frac{50-54}{1}$, $\frac{595-642}{1}$.

In form and colour this species at first sight resembles *Solea cyanea* (Ann. Mag. Nat. Hist., Dec. 1890, p. 439), from which it is distinguished—specimens of equal size being compared—by the much larger head and mouth, by the larger and more widely separated eyes, and by the fewer rays in the dorsal and anal fins. It is however closely allied to *Solea cyanea*, and also to *Solea melanosticta*, Peters (MB. Ak. Berl., 1876, p. 845), and *Solea kaiana*, Gthr. (*'Challenger'* Shore fishes, p. 49, pl. XXI., fig. C.)—all being comparatively deep-water forms of the East Indian Seas.

APHORISTIA, Kaup.

Aphoristia, Kaup, Archiv. für Naturges. XXIV. 1858, i. p. 106: Günther, Cat. Fishes, IV. p. 490: Goode and Bean, Oceanic Ichthyology, p. 458.

Symphurus, Rafinesque, Jordan and Evermann, Fishes N. Amer. III., p. 2704.

Body elongate, lanceolate. Mouth narrow, more developed on the blind (right) side, where alone there are minute teeth in the jaws. Snout hardly hooked. Eyes on the left side. The dorsal fin begins above the middle of the eye: it and the anal are confluent with the caudal. No pectoral fins. Only one ventral—the left—present. Scales of moderate size, ctenoid. No lateral line.

Gill-openings narrow, the gill-membranes rather broadly united. Gill-rakers minute.

Distribution: West Indies and American coasts of North Atlantic; Bay of Bengal, Andaman Sea, and Gulf of Manár.

Key to the Indian species of Aphoristia.

I. Height of the body rather more than a fourth of the total length: no cross-stripes: some coloration on the right side:—
   1. Eyes so far forward that the mouth-cleft reaches to at least the middle of the lower one: the origin of the anal is hardly an eye-length behind the base of the ventral ... *A. Gilesii.*
   2. The mouth-cleft does not reach to the middle of the lower eye: the origin of the anal is at least two eye-lengths behind the base of the ventral ... ... *A. Wood-Masoni.*

II. Height of the body a fourth, or less than a fourth of the total length: dark cross-bands on the left side, no coloration on the right side:—
   1. Length of the head a fourth of the total: 3 (sometimes 4) cross-bands ... ... *A. trifasciata.*
   2. Length of the head a fifth of the total: 7 (sometimes 6) cross-bands ... ... *A. septemstriata.*

106. *Aphoristia Gilesii*, Alcock.

Aphoristia Gilesii, Alcock, Journ. As. Soc. Bengal, Vol. LVIII. pt. 2, 1889, p. 293, pl. xvii. fig. 2: ILLUSTRATIONS OF THE ZOOLOGY OF THE INVESTIGATOR, FISHES, PL. XIV. FIG. 4.

D. 97-98. A. 83–85. C. 14. V. 4. Scales about 90 transverse rows behind head: about 38 longitudinal series behind gill-opening.

Length of the head a fifth, greatest body height $3\frac{1}{2}$ to $3\frac{2}{3}$ in the total length without the caudal.

Snout between a fifth and a sixth the length of the head: the posterior nostril is a pore immediately in front of the inter-orbital space, the anterior is a slender tube situated above the lip midway between the eye and the tip of the snout. No nostrils on the blind side.

Eyes well within the anterior third of the head; their major diameter is about two-thirds the length of the snout and hardly an eighth the length of the head: they lie not very far apart, between the same verticals.

Mouth-cleft nearly horizontal, about two-ninths the length of the head, reaching to or slightly beyond the middle of the eye.

Body and every part of the head except the edges of the mouth, covered with scales, which are sharply ctenoid on the coloured side and less strongly ctenoid on the blind side.

The longest rays of the dorsal fin are a little more than a third the greatest body-height in length.

The anal fin begins about an eye-length behind the base of the ventral, which arises between the after border of the gill-covers.

Colours: left side dark brown with numerous close fine parallel longitudinal lines: right side grey with irregular dark brown patches.

The largest specimen is over $5\frac{1}{4}$ inches long.

Bay of Bengal, 193 and 210 fathoms.

Regd. Nos. 11684, 13630.

Named after Major G. M. J. Giles, I. M. S., who was Surgeon-Naturalist to the Marine Survey from 1884 to 1888.

107. *Aphoristia Wood-Masoni*, Alcock.

Aphoristia Wood-Masoni, Alcock, Journ. As. Soc. Bengal, Vol. LVIII. pt. 2, 1889, p. 294: ILLUSTRATIONS OF THE ZOOLOGY OF THE INVESTIGATOR, FISHES, PL. XVI. FIG. 4.

D. 90–98. A. 78–84. C. 14. V. 4. Scales about 90 transverse rows behind head: about 34 longitudinal series behind gill-opening.

Except in the following particulars this species agrees with *A. Gilesii*:—
The length of the snout is between a fourth and a fifth that of the head.

The eyes are only just within the anterior third of the head, and their diameter is not much more than half the length of the snout.

The mouth-cleft is a fourth the length of the head and does not reach to the middle of the eye.

The longest dorsal rays are not a third the greatest body height.

The anal fin begins a snout length behind the base of the ventral.

Colours: left side as in the preceding species, but the ground-colour is lighter: on the right side the fine parallel lines may be as distinct as they are on the left.

The largest specimen is nearly $5\frac{1}{2}$ inches long.

Andaman Sea, 490 fathoms: Bay of Bengal, 475 fathoms.

Regd. Nos. 11765, 13180.

Named after my predecessor James Wood-Mason. He was deputed as Naturalist with the "Investigator" in April and May 1888.

108. *Aphoristia septem-striata*, Alcock.

Aphoristia septem-striata, Alcock, Ann. Mag. Nat. Hist., Aug. 1891, p. 125: ILLUSTRATIONS OF THE ZOOLOGY OF THE INVESTIGATOR, FISHES, PL. II. FIG. 1.

D. 97. A. 80. C. 12. V. 4. Scales from 92 to 100 transverse rows behind the head: about 40 longitudinal series behind the gill-opening.

Except in the following particulars this species agrees with *A. Gilesii*:—

The greatest height of the body is a fourth of the total length.

The length of the snout is between a fourth and a fifth that of the head.

The eyes are only just within the anterior third of the head and are almost in contact.

The mouth-cleft is about a fourth the length of the head and does not reach to the middle of the eye.

The longest dorsal rays are about a third the greatest body-height.

The anal fin begins rather more than a snout-length behind the base of the ventral.

Colours: left side warm brown, with six or seven broad dark cross-bands: right side colourless.

The largest specimen is $4\frac{1}{2}$ inches long.

Andaman Sea, 188 to 220 fathoms: Gulf of Manár, 142 to 400 fathoms.

Regd. Nos. 13109, 13110, 13613, 13614.

109. *Aphoristia trifasciata,* Alcock.

Aphoristia trifasciata, Alcock, Journ. As. Soc. Bengal, Vol. LXIII. pt. 2, 1894, p. 132, pl. vii. fig. 4. ILLUSTRATIONS OF THE ZOOLOGY OF THE INVESTIGATOR, FISHES, PL. XV. FIG. 5.

D. 87–89. A. 75–77. C. 12. V. 4. Scales 80–82 transverse rows behind the head: 38–40 longitudinal series behind the gill-opening.

Except in the following particulars this species agrees with *A. Gilesii*:—

The length of the head is a fourth of the total, without the caudal, as also is the greatest height of the body. The eyes are in contact.

The mouth-cleft is about a fourth the length of the head and reaches considerably behind the middle of the eye.

The longest dorsal rays are about two-fifths the greatest body-height.

The anal fin begins a snout-length behind the base of the ventral.

Colours: left side warm brown with 3 broad blackish cross-bands: right side colourless.

The largest specimen is $4\frac{1}{2}$ inches long.

Bay of Bengal, off Madras coast, 145 to 250 and 195 to 210 fathoms.

Regd. Nos. 13595–13606, 13608–13612.

This species and the last are both akin to *Symphurus leei* Jordan and Bollman, *Symphurus fasciolaris* Gilbert, and *Symphurus atramentatus* Gilbert.

CYNOGLOSSUS, Ham. Buch., Gthr.

110. *Cynoglossus Carpenteri,* Alcock.

Cynoglossus Carpenteri, Alcock, Journ. As. Soc. Bengal, Vol. LVIII. pt 2, 1889, p. 287, pl. xviii. fig. 1: ILLUSTRATIONS OF THE ZOOLOGY OF THE INVESTIGATOR, FISHES, PL. XXII. FIG. 5.

D. *circ.* 105. A. *circ.* 85. C. 12. V. 4. Scales about 95 rows from top of gill-opening to caudal.

Body lanceolate: tail tapering. The height of the body is about the same as the length of the head, or from $3\frac{1}{2}$ to $3\frac{2}{3}$ in the total without the caudal.

The snout is obtusely triangular and about a third the length of the head: the rostral hook ends in the vertical through the anterior border of the eye. Two nostrils: the posterior, which is a pore lying behind a papilla, is situated in front of the interorbital space; the anterior, which is tubular, is situated a little in advance of the lower eye.

Eyes prominent, about half a diameter apart: the lower one, which is slightly the larger and slightly posterior, is about one-eleventh the length of the head in its major diameter.

Mouth large; its angle is nearly an eye-length behind the posterior border of the lower orbit, and about equidistant between the tip of the snout and the edge of the gill-cover. Minute teeth in the posterior two-thirds of the jaws on the blind side only. Lips not fringed.

The opercle is conspicuously expanded below and behind, and the branchiostegal rays and membrane extend a considerable distance behind its edge, giving the appearance of a broad fringe.

The integument is invested with small strong scales, which on the blind side and anterior half of the coloured side are cycloid, and on the posterior half of the coloured side sharply ctenoid. Three lateral lines on the left side, the middle separated from the upper by 16 or 17, and from the lower by 22 to 24 rows of scales at the respective points of greatest divergence: none on the right. Those on the left side are connected by an irregular cross line on the head.

The longest rays of the dorsal and anal fins are about equal to the snout. The ventral fin is almost indistinguishably confluent with the anal.

Colours in spirit: warm brown, the opercles and caudal blackish: right side colourless.

Length 6 to 8 inches.

Bay of Bengal, 68, 98 to 102, and 107 fathoms: Arabian Sea, off Malabar coast, 100 fathoms.

Regd. Nos. 12433, 12434, 12726 *a* to *g*, 12727 *a* to *k*, 12728 *a* to *h*, 13589–13594, $\frac{647-659}{1}$.

Sub-order PHYSOSTOMI.

Family ***Sternoptychidæ.***

Eight species of this family, belonging to six genera, are now known to inhabit the seas of India. They probably all belong to the "Necton," though they probably live below the depths to which daylight penetrates.

Body naked, or with very thin and deciduous scales. Barbels none. Margin of the upper jaw formed by the maxilla and premaxilla, both of which are toothed. Gill-opening very wide, the opercular apparatus not always completely developed. Pseudobranchiæ present or absent. Air-bladder simple, if present. Adipose fin present, but generally small. Series of phosphorescent bodies along the ventral aspect of the body.

Synopsis of the Indian Genera of the family Sternoptychidæ.

Sternoptychina.

I. Body short and elevated, its height more than half its length without the caudal. Pseudobranchiæ present:—
  1. Dorsal fin preceded by a large triangular transparent osseous plate: no teeth on the vomer:—
    i. Body hatchet shaped ... ... ARGYROPELECUS.
    ii. The ventral constriction between the body and the tail is filled by a curious transparent fold of skin supported by long interhæmal rays ... ... STERNOPTYX.
  2. Dorsal fin preceded by a forked spine: teeth on the vomer ... POLYIPNUS.

Chauliodontina.

II. Body very low and elongate. No pseudobranchiæ :—

1. Dorsal fin in the after half of the body, arising opposite the origin of the anal: anal long ... ... CYCLOTHONE.
2. Dorsal fin in the middle of the body, well in advance of the anal: anal moderately long ... ... PHOTICHTHYS.
3. Dorsal fin placed far forward, hardly a head-length behind the occiput: anal short: no gill-rakers ... ... CHAULIODUS.

ARGYROPELECUS, Cocco.

Argyropelecus, Cocco, Giorn. Sci. Sicil. 1829: Cuvier and Valenciennes. Hist. Nat. Poiss. XXII. p. 392: Günther, Cat. Fishes, V. p. 389: Goode and Bean, Oceanic Ichthyology, p. 125: Jordan and Evermann, Fishes N. Amer., p. 603.

Pleurothyris, Lowe, Fishes of Madeira, p. 64.

Head and body elevated and compressed: tail narrow, abruptly delimited from the trunk, like the handle of a hatchet. Body covered with a thin silvery skin, which is superficially wrinkled, as if thin scales had been loosely attached to it. Series of "bull's-eye"-like luminous organs along the ventral border of head, body, and tail. A series of imbricate scutes forms a serrature along the middle line of the belly, from the throat to the ventral fins.

Cleft of the mouth wide, vertical, with the lower jaw prominent, and the margin of the upper jaw formed by the premaxilla and maxilla: minute teeth in a single row in the jaws and palatines. The jaw-bones, like all the bones of the head, are very thin, but well-ossified.

Eyes rather large, lateral but directed upwards and very close together.

Gill-opening very wide, very long gill-rakers on the outer side of the first branchial arch. Nine branchiostegals. Pseudobranchiæ present.

Dorsal fin short, situated about the middle of the back, preceded by a thin transparent triangular osseous plate in which the ends of several neural spines are visible. Anal short. Caudal forked. Adipose dorsal rudimentary.

Pectorals well developed, situated near the ventral profile: ventrals small: both the humeral arch and the pubic bones project strongly, as flat spines, in the middle line of the belly.

An air-bladder. Four pyloric appendages.

Distribution: Atlantic, Mediterranean, Bay of Bengal.

111. *Argyropelecus hemigymnus*, Cocco.

Argyropelecus hemigymnus, Cocco, Giorn. Sci. Sicil. 1829: Bonaparte, Faun. Ital. Pesc., text: Cuv. & Val., Hist. Nat. Poiss. XXII., p. 398: Günther, Cat. Fishes, V., p. 385, and Challenger Deep-Sea Fishes, p. 167: Vaillant, Exp. Sci. Travailleur et Talisman, Poiss., p. 103: Goode and Bean, Oceanic Ichthyology, p. 126, fig. 147: Jordan and Evermann, Fishes N. Amer. p. 604.

Sternoptyx mediterranea, Cocco, Giorn. Il Faro, 1838, IV., p. 7, fig. 2: Bonaparte, Faun. Ital. Pesc., fig.

Sternoptyx hemigymnus, Cuvier, Règne Animal, Poiss., pl. 103, fig. 3.

B. 9. D. 7-8. A. 11. P. 9. V. 5.

Greatest height of the body about $2\frac{1}{2}$ times the greatest height of the tail, and about half the total length without the caudal fin. Major (vertical) diameter of eye from half to two-fifths the length of the head. A small spine at the posterior corner of the mandible, and another at the angle of the preoperculum. Tail without spines.

The pectoral fin extends nearly to the origin of the anal.

Bay of Bengal, 1803 fathoms.

Distribution: Atlantic, Mediterranean, Bay of Bengal. Regd. No. 13119.

Besides the "Investigator" specimen there are several specimens from the Mediterranean in the Indian Museum.

STERNOPTYX, Hermann.

Sternoptyx, Hermann, Naturforscher, 1781, XVI: Cuvier & Valenciennes, Hist. Nat. Poiss, XXII., p. 412: Günther, Cat. Fishes, V., p. 386, and Challenger Deep-Sea Fishes, p. 168: Goode and Bean, Oceanic Ichthyology, p. 123: Jordan and Evermann, Fishes N. Amer., p. 603.

Form of the body as in *Argyropelecus*, but with a peculiar drag downwards and forwards, and with the wide corner between the ventral angle of the trunk and the tail filled up by a curious transparent fold of skin supported by long interhaemal rays. Body covered with a skin like that of *Argyropelecus*, but not quite so brilliant. Series of luminous organs as in *Argyropelecus*, but less conspicuous and less "bull's-eye"-like. The middle line of the belly between the humeral and pelvic spines is trenchant, not serrated.

Mouth as in *Argyropelecus*, but not quite so wide: palatines toothless.

Eyes large, lateral, without any upward cast.

Gill-opening wide: a few rather distant gill-rakers on the outer side of the first branchial arch are elongate. Branchiostegals five. Pseudobranchiæ present.

Dorsal fin short, situated farther back than in *Argyropelecus*, preceded by a thin triangular osseous plate which has a serrated edge but no series of independent spines. Anal long, extending from near the vent to near the caudal; its rays are feeble. Caudal forked. The anal is preceded by a pair of little spines similar to those at the pectoral and pubic symphyses.

Pectorals well developed, not far from the ventral profile. Ventrals small.

Distribution: Atlantic, Arabian Sea, Western Pacific.

112. ***Sternoptyx diaphana***, Hermann.

Sternoptyx diaphana, Hermann, see Günther, Cat. Fishes, V., p. 387 and Challenger Deep-Sea Fishes, p. 169, pl. xlv, figs. D, D': Vaillant, Exp. Sci. Travailleur et Talisman, p. 102: A. Agassiz, Bull. Mus. Comp. Zool. XV., p. 22, fig. 195: Goode and Bean, Oceanic Ichthyology, p. 124, fig. 146: Jordan and Evermann, Fishes, N. Amer., p. 603: Collett, Hirondelle Poissons (Monaco, 1896), p. 125.

B. 5. D. 9–12. A. 12. P. 10. V. 3.

Greatest height of the body twice that of the tail (not including the transparent fold that fills up the corner between the tail and the belly), and more than two-thirds the total length without the caudal. Diameter of the circular eye nearly half the length of the head.

Besides the spines connected with the fins and the pectoral and pelvic arches, there are a pair of spines on the occiput, a pair on the nape, one at the angle of the preoperculum and one at the posterior end of the mandible.

The pectorals are short, being about half again as long as the eye. The ventrals are very short and narrow.

Arabian Sea: off Malabar coast, 912 to 931 fathoms.

Distribution: Atlantic, Arabian Sea, Western Pacific.

Regd. No. $\frac{49}{1}$.

Besides the "Investigator" specimen there is one of the "Challenger" duplicates in the Indian Museum.

POLYIPNUS, Günther.

Polyipnus, Günther, Challenger Deep-Sea Fishes, p. 170 (1887): Goode and Bean, Oceanic Ichthyology, p. 128.

Form of the body as in *Argyropelecus* but without the abrupt ventral constriction between the body and the tail. Body covered with a thin silvery burnished skin, like that of *Argyropelecus*, and with large extremely thin excessively deciduous scales. Series of conspicuous luminous organs along the ventral border of the head, body, and tail, and also on the sides of the head and belly. A series of scutes form a serrature along the mid-ventral line from the pectoral symphysis to the base of the caudal, the series being broken by the ventral and anal fins.

Mouth as in *Sternoptyx*, but the teeth in the jaws appear to be in more than one series, at any rate anteriorly, and there are teeth on the vomer.

Eyes large, lateral.

Gill-opening wide, numerous very long gill-rakers on the outer side of the first branchial arch. Pseudobranchiæ present. Branchiostegals six (?)

Dorsal fin beginning about the middle of the body, rather short, preceded by a small bifurcate spine but not by any large triangular osseous plate. Anal rather short. Caudal forked. Adipose dorsal present.

Pectorals well developed, situated near the ventral profile: ventrals small: the humeral and pelvic symphyses project in the middle line of the belly, but not so strongly as in *Argyropelecus*.

An air-bladder.

Distribution. Tropical Pacific, Andaman Sea.

113. *Polyipnus spinosus*, Günther.

Polyipnus spinosus, Günther, Challenger Deep-Sea Fishes, p. 170, pl. li. fig. B: Alcock, Ann. Mag. Nat. Hist., Dec. 1889, p. 398, and Aug. 1891, p. 126: Gilbert and Cramer, Proc. U. S. Nat. Mus. XIX., 1896, p. 416.

D. 12-13. A. 15-16. P. 12. V. 5.

Body oval, its greatest height between two-thirds and three-fourths its length without the caudal. Major diameter of eye vertical, more than half the length of the head. Snout very short. Nostrils large, situated close together on top of the snout, the posterior the larger.

The upper part of the head is narrow compressed and concave, and is bounded on each side by a serrated ridge that ends in a large sharp semi-recumbent spine. The edge of the preoperculum is serrated near the angle, which is occupied by a claw-like spine pointing vertically downwards. The lower edge of the mandible is finely serrated and ends in a spinule.

The scutes along the mid-ventral line are spiny.

The dorsal fin is preceded by a small forked spine: the adipose dorsal occupies the middle of the space between the dorsal and caudal. The pectoral reaches almost as far as the base of the ventrals.

The luminous organs are as follows, on each side:—

(1) a series of six small ones in the intervals between the bases of the branchiostegal rays:

(2) a series of six larger ones along the isthmus:

(3) a series of ten still larger ones along the abdomen between the humeral symphysis and the base of the ventral fin:

(4) a series of five between the ventral and the anal:

(5) a series of twelve above the anal fin:

(6) a series of four or five along the ventral border of the caudal peduncle:

(7) a small one at the anterior angle and a small one at the posterior angle of the eye:

(8) a very large one below the middle of the orbit, on the preoperculum:

(9) a small one on the suboperculum:

(10) two above the base and three behind the base of the pectoral fin, these form a second tier on the abdomen:

(11) one behind the gill-opening and one much further back, forming a third tier on the abdomen.

The scales are extremely thin and deciduous: one from the side of the trunk is 7·5 millim. in vertical and about 2·5 millim. in horizontal diameter; one from the middle of the tail is 6·5 millim. and not quite 2 millim. in its diameters.

The largest specimen is between 2 and $2\frac{1}{2}$ inches long.

CYCLOTHONE, Goode & Bean.

Cyclothone, Goode and Bean, Bull. Mus. Comp. Zool. X., 1883, p. 221, and Oceanic Ichthyology, p. 90: Jordan and Evermann, Fishes N. Amer., p. 681.

Sigmops, Gill, Proc. U. S. Nat. Mus. VI., 1883, p. 256.

Neostoma, Vaillant, Exp. Sci. Travailleur et Talisman, Poiss., p. 96.

Body elongate, compressed, without scales. Series of inconspicuous luminous spots along the ventral aspect of the body from the chin to the caudal fin. Head compressed, the bones thin but ossified. Cleft of mouth oblique, extremely wide, the maxilla, which extends nearly to the angle of the preoperculum, forming much the greater part of the margin of the upper jaw; the lower jaw projecting. Both jaws with a single series of needle-like teeth, large ones usually alternating with small ones. Teeth on the palatine and pterygoid bones usually present. Eye moderate, or small.

Gill-openings very wide: numerous long bristle-like gill-rakers. No pseudobranchiæ. Branchiostegals numerous.

Dorsal fin short or of moderate length, situated in the after half of the body, arising opposite the origin of the anal. Anal long. Caudal forked. Adipose fin, when present, small. Pectorals and ventrals well developed.

A long slender air-bladder is present in one of the Indian species.

Distribution: Atlantic, Antarctic, Indo-Pacific.

114. ***Cyclothone elongata*** (Gthr.).

Gonostoma elongatum, Günther, Ann. Mag. Nat. Hist. II. 1878, p. 187; and Challenger Deep-Sea Fishes, p. 173, pl. xlv., fig. B: Alcock, Ann. Mag. Nat. Hist. (6) VIII., 1891, p. 127, and X., 1892, p. 354.

Sigmops stigmaticus, Gill, Proc. U. S. Nat. Mus. VI., 1883, p. 256.

Cyclothone elongata, Goode and Bean, Oceanic Ichthyology, p. 101, fig. 119: Jordan and Evermann, Fishes N. Amer., p. 583.

B. 11. D. 13. A. 29-30. P. 11-12. V. 7-8.

Length of the head two-ninths, height of the body one-seventh of the total length without the caudal.

Length of the eye about two-thirds that of the snout, between a seventh and an eighth that of the head, less than the width of the interorbital space. Nostrils small, situated on top of the snout; the posterior the larger.

Mouth-cleft extremely wide, the maxilla reaching to the angle of the preoperculum. About 14 or 15 large needle-like teeth (two or three of which belong to the premaxilla) with minute teeth between them, on each side of the upper jaw; about ten large teeth, with small teeth between them, on each side of the lower jaw. Small teeth on the palatines and pterygoids, the anterior palatine tooth somewhat enlarged.

Gill-laminæ very short; gill-rakers numerous, long and bristle-like. Branchiostegals very short.

The dorsal fin commences nearly opposite the commencement of the anal, and is higher than the body below it. The anal ends a short distance in front of the caudal; its anterior portion (about 13 rays) is much the highest. Caudal forked.

Pectorals narrow, arising near the ventral profile, two-thirds as long as the head, and reaching two-thirds the way to the base of the ventrals. Ventrals narrow, nearly two-thirds as long as the pectorals; almost, but not quite, reaching to the vent.

The body is covered with a black skin which is scaleless, and is coated in life with thick tenacious mucus.

Two rows of luminous organs run along each side of the ventral border of the body.

In the lower series are 4 in front of the pectoral, 10 between the pectoral and ventral, 4 between the ventral and anal, and 22 above the anal fin.

The upper series, which are much the most conspicuous, consist of twelve organs and extend from the pectoral to the vent.

In addition, there are small organs in each of the spaces between the bases of the branchiostegal rays; a large one below each eye, one near the upper end of the preoperculum, one on each side of the mandibular symphysis and a short series on both the dorsal and ventral edges of the caudal peduncle.

In life, the luminous organs are bright rose-pink, with silvery margins.

The vent is midway between the root of the caudal fin and the eye. An air-bladder is present, and six large pyloric cæca.

A fine male and a female with ripe ovaries from the Arabian Sea, in the neighbourhood of the Laccadive Islands, 738 and 1200 fathoms. In both the length is $7\frac{3}{4}$ inches.

Distribution: New Guinea and Banda Sea: Arabian Sea: off Atlantic coasts of North America.

The female, taken off Minnikoy, when the dredge was shot in 1200 fathoms, was alive and active when taken from the dredge, and lived on board for about quarter of an hour afterwards; so that it is most improbable that it came from any great depth. No display of luminosity was observed, though it was watched for.

I have described the ovaries, and the microscopic structure of the stomach, in Ann. Mag. Nat. Hist. for November 1892. The ovaries are long narrow tubes in which the developing ova form a closely-pleated band with very little interstitial stroma.

In the stomach the submucous coat is of remarkable thickness, and consists of a network of connective tissue of great regularity, the meshes of which are crammed with leucocytes: the microscopic appearance is very much like that of the cortex of mammalian lymphatic gland.

Regd. Nos. 13122, 13181.

115. *Cyclothone microdon* (Günther).

Gonostoma microdon, Günther, Ann. Mag. Nat. Hist. II. 1878, p. 188, and Challenger Deep-Sea Fishes, p. 175: Alcock, Ann. Mag. Nat. Hist. Dec. 1889, p. 309: Lutken, Vid. Selsk. Skr. (6) Nat. Math. Afd. VII, 1892, 6, p. 280, pl. ii. figs. 4, 5.

Cyclothone lusca, Goode and Bean, Bull. Mus. Comp. Zool. X, 1883, p. 221: A. Agassiz, Bull. Mus. Comp. Zool. XV. 1888, p. 22, fig. 196.

Cyclothone microdon, Goode and Bean, Oceanic Ichthyology, p. 99, fig. 114: Jordan and Evermann, Fishes N. Amer. p. 582: Collett, "Hirondelle" Poissons (Monaco, 1896) p. 130.

B. 9. D. 12-13. A. 17-21. P. 9-10 V. 5?

The chief differences, besides the much smaller size and much shorter anal fin, that separate this species from *C. elongatum*, are the following:—

The eye is minute.

The teeth in the upper jaw are numerous, and gradually increase in size from before backwards, one or two in the premaxilla and a few in the posterior half of the maxilla being slightly enlarged: the teeth in the lower jaw, which are also extremely numerous and close set, also gradually increase in size from before backwards.

The narrow ventrals reach beyond the vent.

There are no glandular (luminous) masses on the edges of the caudal peduncle.

Bay of Bengal, off Andaman Is. 485 fathoms: Andaman Sea, 265 fathoms.

Regd. Nos. 12455, 12468.

Besides the "Investigator" specimens there are several of the "Challenger" duplicates in the Indian Museum.

Photichthys, Hutton.

Phosichthys, Hutton, Cat. Fishes New Zealand, p 55.

Photichthys, Günther, Challenger Deep-Sea Fishes, p. 177: Goode and Bean, Oceanic Ichthyology, p. 104.

Body elongate compressed, with thin extremely deciduous scales. Series of conspicuous luminous organs extending along the ventral aspect of the body from the chin to the caudal fin. Head compressed, the bones thin but ossified. Cleft of mouth oblique, extremely wide, the maxilla, which extends nearly to the angle of the preoperculum, forming the greater part of the margin of the upper jaw; the lower jaw projecting. Both jaws with a single series of teeth. A fang on either side of the head of the vomer. Teeth on the palatines and sometimes on the pterygoids. Eye moderate.

Gill-openings very wide: numerous long bristle-like gill-rakers. No pseudobranchiæ. Branchiostegals numerous.

Dorsal fin short, in the middle of the body, standing above the interval between the ventrals and the anal. Anal rather long. Caudal forked. Adipose dorsal small. Pectorals and anals well developed.

A long slender air-bladder present.

Distribution. Seas of India and New Zealand.

Photichthys differs from Cyclothone (1) in having scales, though they are thin and deciduous, (2) in the very conspicuous luminous organs, (3) in the position of the dorsal fin, which stands over the space between the ventrals and the anal instead of commencing opposite the origin of the anal.

116. *Photichthys corythæolus*, Alcock.

Diplophos corythæolum, Alcock, Ann. Mag. Nat. Hist. August, 1898, p. 147: ILLUSTRATIONS OF THE ZOOLOGY OF THE INVESTIGATOR, FISHES, PL. XXV. FIG. 3.

B. 12. D. *circ.* 11. A. *circ.* 24. P. 10. V. 7.

Length of head about one-fourth, height of body between one-fifth and one-sixth of the total without the caudal.

The snout, which has the lower jaw prominent, is hardly longer than the eye, which is not quite a fourth the length of the head. The eyes are not quite a diameter apart.

The maxillary almost reaches to the preopercular angle. There is a single row of small, rather distant, acicular fangs of unequal size in either jaw, and a row of close-set acicular teeth on part of the palatines; the whole surface of the mesopterygoids is studded with sharp little denticles; and there is a fang on either side of the head of the vomer.

Gill-openings extremely wide; four gills with short laminæ; gill-rakers, especially those on the first arch, long and bristle-like.

The body has evidently been covered with large thin and deciduous scales.

The dorsal fin arises about an eye-length behind the base of the ventrals, and its last few rays are just above the first few anal rays; its first ray is slightly nearer to the snout than to the base of the caudal. The long anal fin approaches within less than half a head-length of the base of the caudal. The pectorals are on almost the same plane as the ventrals, and these arise about midway between the base of the former and the origin of the anal.

The luminous organs, which are of the "bull's eye" type, are disposed as follows on either side:—

(1) one at the mandibular symphysis:

(2) one between the bases of all the branchiostegal rays:

(3) 12 or 13 between the tip of the isthmus and the base of the pectoral:

(4) eight between the pectoral and the ventral:

(5) eight between the ventral and the anal:

(6) 15 along the bases of the anal rays:

(7) eight between the anal and the caudal.

The above form the lowermost tier.

The upper tier consists of 17 between the gill-opening and the level of the anal fin, where it stops.

In addition, there are some luminous organs on the head, notably one at the anterior angle of the orbit.

Length 5 inches.

Andaman Sea, 185, 188 to 220, and 405 fathoms.

Regd. Nos. 13076, 13077, $\frac{127}{1}$, $\frac{150}{1}$, $\frac{314}{1}$, $\frac{315}{1}$.

Chauliodus, Bl. Schn.

Chauliodus, Schneider, Bloch, Syst. Ichth. p. 430: Günther, Cat. Fishes, V., p. 392: Goode and Bean, Oceanic Ichthyology, p. 96: Jordan and Evermann, Fishes N. Amer., p. 585.

Body elongate, compressed, covered with exceedingly thin and deciduous scales. Head elevated, compressed, with the bones thin but ossified, and the gill-cover very narrow. Series of luminous spots along the ventral aspect of the body from the chin to the caudal fin. Cleft of the mouth extremely wide, the upper jaw, about half of the edge of which is formed by the premaxilla, reaching almost to the angle of the preoperculum; the mandible projecting. About four enormous fangs in each premaxilla, and about five fangs, the anterior one of which is more than half the length of the head, in the mandible: none of these fangs are received within the mouth. Edge of maxilla finely denticulated: palatine with a single series of small teeth: no teeth on the tongue. Eye of moderate size.

Gill-opening very wide: no gill-rakers: no pseudobranchiæ. Branchiostegals numerous.

Dorsal fin short, placed far forwards on the body, hardly a head-length behind the head. Anal fin also short, placed far back near the caudal. Caudal forked. Adipose dorsal small, opposite the anal. Pectorals and ventrals well developed, the ventrals long.

A long slender thin-walled air-bladder.

Distribution: Atlantic, Mediterranean, Arabian Sea and Bay of Bengal, Western Pacific.

117. *Chauliodus Sloanii*, Bl. Schn.

Chauliodus sloanii, Schneider, Bloch, Syst. Ichth. p. 430: Cuvier and Valenciennes, Hist. Nat. Poiss. XXII. p. 383; Günther, Cat. Fishes, V. p. 392, and Challenger Deep-Sea Fishes, p 179: Goode and Bean, Bull. Essex Inst. XI. 1879, p. 22: Goode, Proc. U. S. Nat. Mus. III. 1880, p. 483: Facciola, Nat. Sicil. II. p. 206: Vinciguerra, Ann. Mus. Genov. (2) II. p. 469: A. Agassiz, Bull. Mus. Comp. Zool. XV. 1888, p. 32, fig. 214: Carus, Prodr. Faun. Medit. II. p. 570: Alcock, Ann. Mag. Nat. Hist. (6) IV. 1889, p. 309; VIII. 1891, p. 127: X. 1892, p. 355: Goode and Bean, Oceanic Ichthyology, p. 96, fig. 115: Jordan and Evermann, Fishes N. Amer. p. 585.

Chauliodus setinosus, Schneider op. cit pl. lxxxv: Bonaparte, Faun. Ital. Pesc. fig.

Chauliodus Schneideri, Risso, Faun. Eur. Merid. III. p 442 fig. 37.

Stomias Schneideri (*Stomias boa*) Cuvier, Règne An., Poiss., pl. 97, fig. 3 (too many teeth and luminous spots).

? *Chauliodus Macouni*, Bean, Proc. U. S. Nat. Mus. 1890, p. 44.

B. 16–18. D. 6. A. 12. P. 12-13. V. 7. L. lat. 56.

Head much compressed squarish, its length, which is not much more than its height, is from a sixth to a seventh of the total, without the caudal. Eye circular, about as long as the snout proper, between a third and a fourth the length of the head. Lower jaw prominent beyond the snout.

The dorsal fin begins less than a head-length behind the occiput; the filamentous first ray is from twice the length of the head to more than half the body in length.

The longest ventral rays are nearly twice as long as the pectorals and about a third as long again as the head.

Scales hexagonal. The luminous organs are disposed, on each side, as follows, and are conspicuous :—

(1) a series between the bases of the branchiostegals :

(2) a series of 61 in a lower tier from the chin to the caudal, of which 30 are between the chin and the ventrals :

(3) a series of 38 between the base of the pectoral and the anus, of which 17 are between the base of the pectoral and the base of the ventral.

(4) one below the eye, and (5) one in the upper part of the suboperculum.

Besides these there are countless tiny spots, in rows and clusters, all along the abdominal line from the chin to the caudal.

Colours in spirit, silvery more or less; fins white.

A ripe female in the Indian Museum is six inches long, but there is a mutilated specimen much longer.

Gulf of Manár, 597 fathoms; Bay of Bengal, 922 and 1590 fathoms; Laccadive Sea.

Distribution : as for the genus.

Regd. Nos. 11731–11733, 12473, 12837, 12838.

In one specimen dissected there were 3 large pyloric cæca, in another 3 large ones and a small one.

The ova are not arranged in a pleated band in the ovaries as they are in *Gonostoma.*

The stomach is much like that of *Gonostoma*, having a remarkably thick submucous coat, which, under the microscope, has much the structure of the cortex of mammalian lymph-gland.

118. *Chauliodus pammelas*, Alcock.

Chauliodus pammelas, Alcock, Ann. Mag. Nat. Hist., Nov. 1892, p. 355: ILLUSTRATIONS OF THE ZOOLOGY OF THE INVESTIGATOR, FISHES, PL. XXX, FIG. 4.

B. 16. D. 6. A. 12. P. 11-12. V. 7.

Differs from *C. Sloanii* in the following points:—

The length of the eye is considerably more than that of the snout proper, and is a third that of the head.

The skin is naked, although it is mapped out into rhomboidal and hexagonal depressions each of which has a luminous spot in the centre, and in life was covered with a thick coat of transparent mucus tissue full of capillary blood-vessels.

The luminous organs are much less conspicuous.

The body fins and iris are uniform jet black, which has not altered after nearly seven years' immersion in spirit.

Length 10 inches.

Arabian Sea, in the neighbourhood of Minnikoy, 1370 fathoms.

Regd. No. 13183.

This is undoubtedly a good species.

Family *Stomiatidæ.*

Skin generally naked, sometimes with thin deciduous scales. A hyoid barbel, which may be either free or attached to the mandibular symphysis. Margin of the upper jaw formed by the premaxilla and maxilla, which are both toothed. Opercular apparatus little developed or rudimentary. Gill-opening, like the mouth-cleft, very wide. Pseudobranchiæ none. Adipose fin present or absent. Air-bladder present or absent.

The presence of four representatives of this family has been brought to light by the "Investigator."

I have followed Dr. Günther in keeping this family distinct. My own opinion is that it might be united with the *Sternoptychidæ.*

19

Synopsis of the Indian genera of Stomiatidæ.

I.	Pectorals present: hyoid barbel free: skin mapped out into subhexagonal areolæ: teeth on the palatines and vomer	STOMIAS.
II.	Pectorals rudimentary: skin perfectly smooth and scaleless: hyoid barbel attached to the mandibular symphysis: no teeth on the palate ...	MALACOSTEUS.
III.	Pectorals absent: skin perfectly smooth and scaleless: hyoid barbel attached to the mandibular symphysis: teeth on the palatines ...	PHOTOSTOMIAS.

STOMIAS, Cuv., Gthr.

Stomias, Cuvier, Règne Animal, Poiss. p. 232: Günther, Cat. Fishes, V. p. 426: Goode and Bean, Oceanic Ichthyology, p. 107: Jordan and Evermann, Fishes of N. Amer. p. 588.

Body low, elongate, compressed, vent situated at no great distance from the caudal fin. Skin with subhexagonal impressions in which deciduous scarcely-imbricate scales may be present. Head compressed, with the snout very short and the mouth-cleft oblique and very wide. Teeth pointed, unequal in size, those of the premaxilla and mandible the longest; maxilla finely denticulated: vomer with a pair of fangs: palatines and tongue with smaller pointed teeth. Eye of moderate size. A fleshy barbel in the centre of the hyoid region. Opercle narrow, incomplete.

Dorsal opposite the anal, close to the caudal. Pectorals and ventrals narrow, the ventrals situated very far back in the posterior third of the body. No adipose dorsal.

Series of phosphorescent dots along the lower side of the head body and tail.

An air-bladder. No pyloric appendages.

Distribution: North Atlantic and West Indies; Atlantic gate of Mediterranean; Mediterranean; Arabian Sea.

Key to the Indian species of the genus Stomias.

I.	Height of the body about a twelfth of the total length (with caudal) ...	*S. nebulosus.*
II.	Height of the body about a sixteenth of the total length (with caudal) ...	*S. elongatus.*

119. ***Stomias nebulosus,*** Alcock.

Stomias nebulosus, Alcock, Ann. Mag. Nat. Hist., Dec. 1889, p. 451. ILLUSTRATIONS OF THE ZOOLOGY OF THE INVESTIGATOR, FISHES, PL. VII. FIG. 1.

This species may prove to be identical with the West Indian *S. affinis.*

D. 17. A. 21. P. 6. V. 5.

Length of the head one-ninth, height of the body one-twelfth of the total. Snout shorter than the large eye.

Cleft of mouth oblique, enormous; the limbs of the mandible widely distensible. Teeth fixed; upwards of twenty-five small, unequal, and curved in each premaxilla, and about the same number, in the form of minute, close-set, even serrations, in each maxilla; a fang on each side of the vomer; one or two moderate-sized teeth in the palatines. The teeth of the lower jaw are very large, curved and acute, and stand out laterally, eight or nine on each side, almost at right angles to the jaw.

Barbel about as long as the head and ending in three longish filaments.

The bony part of the opercle is reduced to a small preoperculum.

The surface of the body is covered with a tenacious slime. There are no scales, but the body is mapped with regular rows of hexagonal depressions, each with a minute central white point.

A salient white line, composed of a multitude of (luminous?) specks, runs along the mid-ventral line, from the throat to the anal fin. Two rows of luminous organs on each side of the abdomen, the lower one extending from the isthmus to the base of the caudal, the upper extending from the base of the pectoral to the origin of the anal.

Those of the lower row are disposed as follows:—6 from the isthmus to the base of the pectoral, 34 from the pectoral to the base of the ventral, 9 from the ventral to the anal, 15 above the course of the anal,—in all 64.

Those of the upper row are 35 or 36 in number.

The dorsal fin begins in the last fifth of the body, a little in rear of the commencement of the anal, which is also the deeper. Caudal not forked. The pectorals arise on very narrow bases near the ventral profile; their length is equal to the height of the body. The ventrals are also narrow and are exceedingly prolonged, reaching beyond the origin of the anal.

Colours in spirit:—Uniform black; fins and barbel white, with black tips.

Two specimens, rather mutilated, the longer $3\frac{1}{2}$ inches.

Gulf of Manaar, 597 fathoms.

Regd. Nos. 11734, 11735.

120. *Stomias elongatus*, Alcock.

Stomias elongatus, Alcock, Ann. Mag. Nat. Hist., August, 1891, p. 129.

D. 19. A. 21. P. 6. V. 6.

Length of the head one-tenth, height of the body one-fifteenth of the total without the caudal. Eye longer than the snout, not quite a fourth the length of the head.

The widely-distensible mandible projects much beyond the upper jaw. Five large, distant, fixed fangs in each premaxilla, as well as a freely movable one near the symphysis; a few minute, inconspicuous, distant denticulations in the maxillæ; eight or nine moderate-sized laterally-projecting fangs on each limb of the mandible, decreasing in size from before backwards; a fang on each side of the vomer, and two small, distant, incurved teeth on each palatine.

The barbel, which is as long as the caudal fin, is trifid at its extremity. Opercular bones membranaceous.

No scales; the body, which is coated with tenacious mucus, is mapped out into silvery hexagonal areolæ. There are on each side along the ventral surface of the body two rows of small luminous organs; the internal extends from the mandibular symphysis to the base of the caudal, but, owing to the denudation of the integuments of the tail, the number of its constituents cannot be determined beyond the origin of the anal fin, up to which point there are 57, namely, to the base of the pectorals 9, to the base of the ventrals 51, to the origin of the anal 57; the external extends from the base of the pectoral to the origin of the anal, and numbers 45. There is a single luminous organ on the barbel and a row along the base of the branchiostegal rays. The dorsal fin arises at the level of the third anal ray. Caudal pointed, its length is about one-twelfth of the total. The pectorals, which arise near the ventral profile, are equal in length to the caudal. The ventrals are very long, reaching to the sixth anal ray.

Colours in the fresh state:—jet black, with silvery hexagonal markings. A long slender air-bladder is present.

One specimen, a little over 5 inches long.

Arabian Sea, off the Laccadives, 738 fathoms.

Regd. No. 13075.

MALACOSTEUS, Ayres.

Malacosteus, Ayres, Journal Boston Soc. Nat. Hist. 1849, p. 53: Günther, Cat. Fishes, V. p. 427, and Challenger Deep Sea Fishes, p. 212: Goode and Bean, Oceanic Ichthyology, p. 113: Jordan and Evermann, Fishes N. America, p. 592.

Differs from *Stomias* in the following respects:—

The body is not so low and elongate, and the skin is perfectly smooth and scaleless. The head is not so much compressed, and the gape is even wider, the ends of the jaws extending beyond the root of the pectoral. There are no teeth on the palate. The opercle is membranaceous. The pectorals are rudimentary, and the ventrals are not placed so far back, being well in front of the posterior third of the body.

Distribution: Atlantic; Andaman Sea; off Philippines.

121. *Malacosteus* sp.

? *Malacosteus niger*, Ayres, *l. c.* pl. v. Goode and Bean, Oceanic Ichthyology, p. 114, fig. 138.

? *Malacosteus indicus*, Günther, Alcock, Ann. Mag. Nat. Hist., (6) IV. 1889, p. 452; ILLUSTRATIONS OF THE ZOOLOGY OF THE INVESTIGATOR, FISHES, PL. XXXIII. FIG. 4.

A species of *Malacosteus* was dredged in the Andaman Sea in 650 fathoms. It is represented by a single damaged specimen, and appears to be identical with *Malacosteus indicus* Günther, of the Challenger Report, p. 214, pl. liv. fig. B.

At the same time, judging from the descriptions and figures of the two species, it seems to me that *Malacosteus indicus* and *Malacosteus niger* are the same.

The following is a brief description of the "Investigator" specimen, so far as description is possible :—

D. 18. A. 20. P. 3. V. 6.

The gill-cleft is so wide, and the neck so narrow, that the head can be turned completely upside down over the back without hurting the specimen.

Length of jaws and mouth-cleft more than a third of the distance between the tip of the snout and the origin of the anal fin.

There is almost no snout distinct from the rim of the orbit: eye between a third and a fourth the length of the lower jaw.

The largest teeth are a pair of curved outstanding fangs at the fore end of the mandible. Of the lateral mandibular teeth two exceed the others in size, the anterior one being not very far from the mandibular symphysis, the posterior one being a good way back.

Skin smooth, soft, black, everywhere covered with tiny white dots. A large petal-shaped luminous organ, as long as the orbit, beneath the eye, and a smaller oval one on the cheek near the middle of the upper jaw.

Dorsal and anal fins nearly equal and opposite, close to the caudal. Caudal small, its peduncle narrow,—the height midway between the anal and the caudal fin being about half an eye-length. The ventrals arise about an eye-length behind the middle of the body.

Length $3\frac{1}{4}$ inches.

Regd. No. 11642.

PHOTOSTOMIAS, Collett.

Photostomias, Collett, Bull. Soc. Zool France, 1889, p. 291, and Hirondelle Poissons (Monaco, 1896), p. 131: Goode and Bean, Oceanic Ichthyology, p. 114.

Thaumastomias, Alcock, Ann. Mag. Nat. Hist., Sept. 1890, p. 220.

Body elongate, compressed, scaleless, with the vent not far distant from the caudal fin. Head compressed, with the cranium small, the snout short, and the cleft of the mouth exceedingly wide. A long elastic muscular band passing from the hyoid bone to the inner aspect of the mandibular symphysis. Teeth acute, unequal, in single series in premaxillæ, maxillæ, mandibles, and palatines; none on the tongue. Eye moderate. Gill-covers rudimentary. One dorsal fin opposite to the anal, situated in the posterior fourth of the body, near the caudal. No adipose dorsal. No pectoral fins. Ventral fins situated in the anterior half of the body. Gill-openings very wide. No air-bladder.

A large luminous organ behind the orbit: two long rows of small luminous organs on either side of the body, on the ventral aspect, from the gill-opening to or nearly to the caudal fin.

Distribution: North Atlantic and Azores; both sides of the Bay of Bengal.

122. *Photostomias atrox* (Alcock).

Thaumastomias atrox, Alcock, Ann. Mag. Nat. Hist., Sept. 1890, p. 220, pl. viii fig. 7, and Aug. 1898, p. 147: ILLUSTRATIONS OF THE ZOOLOGY OF THE INVESTIGATOR, FISHES, PL. XXX, FIG. 2. [See also Goode and Bean, Oceanic Ichthyology, fig. 141, which, however, has been incorrectly copied from my figure in the Annals and Magazine of Natural History, a second large post-orbital luminous organ, of which there is no trace either in the specimen or in my drawing and description, having been added.

D. 23. A. 25. C. *circ.* 25. P. 0. V. 6.

Length of the head one-fifth, height of the body one-tenth, of the total without the caudal.

Snout truncated, broad, with a slightly concave vertical profile, its length one-third the diameter of the eye. Eye large, circular, its diameter about one-fourth the length of the head; interorbital space wider than the eye, convex. On each side there are two luminous organs, one about the size and shape of a caraway-seed, below and partly in front of the eye, the other large, salient, slipper-shaped, and more than one-third the length of the head, lying parallel with the upper jaw behind the eye. Mouth enormous, its cleft as long as the head; its floor is completely wanting except quite anteriorly, its place being taken by a long elastic muscular band which extends from the tip of the hyoid to the inner surface of the mandibular symphysis; the mouth-cleft and the gill-cleft being thus continuous beneath, almost divide the head from the rest of the body; the lower jaw projects beyond the upper. Teeth, everywhere except in the maxilla, in the form of slender acute rigid fangs; in each premaxilla eight or nine, and three remote stouter ones at the symphysis; in each half of the mandible an uneven row of over twenty, and five (one median flanked on each side by a pair) of superior size at the symphysis; in each palatine a row of seven or eight, increasing in size from before backwards, and a patch on the upper pharyngeal bones; maxillary teeth in the form of even, close-set, recurved serrations, of which there are over thirty in each bone.

Gill-cleft extremely wide and oblique, its superior limit being above the middle of the eye; gill-cover reduced apparently to a narrow straight preoperculum, very obliquely articulated, furnished with a narrow membranous fringe; four branchial arches, extremely weak and flexible, bearing very narrow laminæ; gill-rakers rudimentary.

Body scaleless. Skin thick, soft, velvety, and uniformly covered with adherent tenacious mucus; apparently no lateral line. Besides the large luminous glands already described, there are two regular rows of minute luminous organs along the ventral half of the body on each side: the upper, numbering about fifty, extending from the gill-opening to the base of the caudal; the lower, numbering about forty, skirting the ventral profile from the isthmus to the fifth anal ray; a few similar luminous organs on the crown of the head.

The dorsal fin begins slightly in advance of the posterior fifth of the body, and is equal and opposite to the anal. The longest (central) anal rays are a little longer than the corresponding dorsal rays, and are equal to the depth of the tail at their point of origin. The caudal is deeply forked, with the lower lobe the broader and longer and about $\frac{1}{22}$ of the total length.

Pectorals absent. The ventrals arise in the anterior half of the body, their point of origin being $1\frac{1}{3}$ times as far from the vent as from the margin of the gill-cleft; the two outer rays are thickened, coherent throughout, and prolonged, their length being two-fifths of the total length including the caudal; the inner rays are short, weak, and inconspicuous.

Stomach siphonal, its *cul-de-sac* extending halfway along the abdominal cavity; intestine straight, opening at the origin of the anal fin. No pyloric cæca.

Colours intense black: the large postocular luminous organs very conspicuous, one being naked and rose pink in colour, the other being silvery and almost entirely covered by a fold of black skin. The small luminous organs were not visible until after immersion in spirit.

The largest specimen is just under 5 inches long.

Bay of Bengal, off Ganjam coast, 1310 fathoms, and off the Andamans, 606 fathoms.

Regd. Nos. 12835, $\frac{374}{1}$.

Family *Scopelidæ*.

In the *Fauna of British India* four genera and six species are recorded. We now know of six more genera and thirteen more species, all belonging to the deep sea.

In the following synopsis the genera added to the Indian list by the *Investigator* are marked with an asterisk, and those that are represented in the deep sea by a dagger.

Synopsis of the Indian genera of Scopelidæ.

I. Pseudobranchiæ well developed :—
- 1. Body scaly, without phosphorescent spots :—
  - i. Maxilla not dilated posteriorly :—
    - *a.* Dorsal in front of the ventrals : some of the teeth enlarged and barbed at point : eyes with a strong upward cast ... ... *SCOPELARCHUS.†
    - *b.* Dorsal fin above or behind the ventrals : none of the teeth barbed : eyes quite lateral :—
      - *α.* Teeth on each palatine in a single band ... *Saurus.*
      - *β.* Teeth on each palatine in a double band ... *Saurida.*
  - ii. Maxilla rudimentary or absent : some of the teeth barbed at point : caudal three-lobed ... ... *Harpodon.*†
  - iii. Maxilla dilated behind :—
    - *a.* Eyes lateral, very large : no prolonged rays ... *CHLOROPHTHALMUS.†
    - *b.* Eyes very small : some of the rays of the pectoral (and also sometimes of the caudal and anal fins) enormously prolonged ... ... *BATHYPTEROIS.†
- 2. Body scaly, with phosphorescent spots :—
  - i. Snout high, short, bluntly rounded : mouth-cleft nearly reaching the angle of the preoperculum : anal fin close behind the dorsal ... ... *Scopelus.*†
  - ii. Snout depressed, rather long : mouth-cleft wide, but not nearly reaching the angle of the preoperculum : anal a considerable distance behind the dorsal ... ... *NEOSCOPELUS.†
- 3. Body naked : some enormous fangs in the mandible, vomer and palatines ... ... *ODONTOSTOMUS.†

II. Pseudobranchiæ rudimentary : otherwise closely related to *Neoscopelus* *SCOPELENGYS.†

SCOPELARCHUS, Alcock.

Scopelarchus, Alcock, Journ. As. Soc. Bengal, Vol. LXV. pt. 2, 1896, p. 306.

Body elongate, compressed, covered with scales which, except on the lateral line, where they are adherent, are deciduous.

Cleft of mouth very wide : premaxilla very long, tapering, firmly attached to the long slender maxillæ. A single row of small teeth in the premaxilla : a double row of teeth in the mandible, the inner row being large depressible and barbed at tip ; an incompletely double series of similarly enlarged teeth on either palatine, and a long narrow row of almost similar teeth on the tongue and hyoid. Eye large. Gill-openings very wide, gill-membranes not attached to the isthmus, branchiostegals not very numerous (about 6?); pseudobranchiæ large.

The dorsal fin is short, it arises well in the anterior third of the body (measured with the caudal) and all its extent lies between the pectorals and ventrals: the anal is long, occupying the greater part of the tail. Pectorals large. Ventrals with 8 rays. An adipose dorsal fin. Caudal forked. No luminous spots.

This is a remarkable generalized form of Scopeloid, showing affinities with *Saurus*, *Chlorophthalmus*, *Scopelus*, *Odontostomus*, and *Paralepis*. To casual view it looks just like a *Scopelus* devoid of luminous organs.

123. ***Scopelarchus Güntheri***, Alcock.

Scopelarchus Güntheri, Alcock, Journ. As. Soc. Bengal, Vol. LXV. pt. 2, 1896, p. 307: Illustrations of the Zoology of the Investigator, Fishes, pl. XVII. fig. 7.

D. 9. A. 26. P. 19. V. 8. L. lat. (of enlarged adherent scales) *circ.* 50.

Head and body compressed: shape as of *Scopelus*.

Length of head (with gill-cover) not quite one-fourth, height of body about two-elevenths of the total (without caudal). Snout about three-fourths the length of the eye: the lower jaw in repose fitting within the upper. The eyes are large—about one-third the length of the head—they are separated from one another by a mere linear space, and their visual axis is rather more superior than lateral.

The mouth-cleft forms a slightly oblique sweep, and the maxilla extends a considerable distance behind the posterior border of the orbit.

The scales of the lateral line are much enlarged, and their vertical diameter is much greater than their antero-posterior diameter; each is chambered, the chamber opening dorsally and ventrally.

The first dorsal ray arises about an eye-length behind the base of the pectorals, the last stands a little in advance of the base of the ventrals. The first anal ray arises near the middle of the body (measured with the caudal), the last is less than an eye-length distant from the rudimentary rays at the base of the caudal. The adipose fin stands in the posterior third of the distance between the dorsal and caudal.

Pectorals broad and falciform, reaching to the base of the ventrals, which are small and do not nearly reach the anal.

Colours in spirit white, occiput and caudal peduncle black.

A single specimen, an adult female, about five inches long, from off the Indus Delta, 947 fathoms.

Regd. No. $\frac{63}{1}$.

20

HARPODON, Lesueur, Günther.

124. *Harpodon squamosus*, Alcock.

Harpodon squamosus, Alcock, Ann. Mag. Nat. Hist. August, 1891, p. 127: ILLUSTRATIONS OF THE ZOOLOGY OF THE INVESTIGATOR, FISHES, PL. XXX. FIG. 1.

B. 17. D. 12–14. A. 13–15. P. 10. V. 9.

The length of the head, measured to the edge of the operculum and not to the end of the produced branchiostegal rays and membrane, is about one-fifth, the height of the body about one-sixth of the total, without the caudal. The vertex of the head with numerous minute mucous pores.

Snout broad, depressed; its tip is formed by the projecting lower jaw, and its length, including the mandibular element, slightly exceeds the major diameter of the eye, which is about one-eighth the length of the head as above limited. The width of the flat interorbital space is twice the vertical diameter of the eye.

Mouth-cleft oblique, wide: the maxilla is nearly two-thirds the length of the head as above limited. Introrsely-depressible cardiform teeth in bands in both jaws; one series in the lower jaw enlarged, with barbed hastate tips, and one series in the upper jaw less enlarged; in each palatine an outer irregularly-double row of teeth, of which the anterior and external are enlarged, and a very short inner irregularly-double row; hyoid bone and all the branchial arches toothed.

Gill-openings extremely wide; the branchiostegal rays and membrane much produced beyond the operculum.

Body, posterior part of head, and cheeks covered with deciduous cycloid scales, which are less deciduous on the posterior half of the tail.

The dorsal fin arises within the anterior half of the body (measured with the caudal) almost opposite to the origin of the ventrals. The anal arises about an eye-length behind the vent, which is nearly twice as far from the gill-opening as from the base of caudal. The fimbriated adipose dorsal is situated far back, above the posterior half of the anal. Caudal deeply forked, with an inconspicuous median lobe. Ventrals long, delicate, and feathery, the longest (middle) rays reach to within two eye-lengths of the vent in the adult. Pectorals very narrow and fragile; they arise almost on the same plane with the eyes, and their longest (middle) rays do not nearly reach to the dorsal fin, being about as long as the postorbital portion of the head.

Stomach with a very long cæcal sac; eighteen large pyloric cæca in a pectinate arrangement.

Colours in life:—hyaline grey; paired fins and caudal black, visceral peritoneum black, buccal and branchial cavities partially and slightly pigmented.

Bay of Bengal, 240 to 276 and 281 to 258 fathoms.

Mature females are from 9 to $10\frac{1}{2}$ inches long; the males are from $7\frac{1}{2}$ to $8\frac{1}{2}$ inches long.

Regd. Nos. 13084 to 13095, 13209, 13210.

CHLOROPHTHALMUS, Bonaparte.

Chlorophthalmus, Bonaparte, Faun. Ital. Pesci: Günther, Cat. Fishes, V. p. 403, and Challenger Deep Sea Fishes, p. 192: Goode and Bean, Oceanic Ichthyology, p. 60: Jordan and Evermann, Fishes N. Amer., p. 541.
Hyphalonedrus, Goode, Proc. U. S. Nat. Mus. IV. 1881, p. 483.

Form of the body elongate, subcylindrical or compressed, covered with scales. Head rather long, with the lower jaw usually projecting. Mouth-cleft wide, the maxilla dilated behind. Teeth minute, in narrow bands on the jaws vomer and palatines. Eye large.

Gill-openings very wide: pseudobranchiæ well developed. Branchiostegals 10 to 7.

Dorsal short, situated in the anterior half of the body: anal short, situated in the posterior half of the body. Caudal forked. Adipose fin small.

Pectorals and ventrals well developed: the ventrals inserted at no great distance behind the pectorals, under or somewhat behind the dorsal.

Distribution: West Indies and Atlantic coasts of North America: Mediterranean: Bay of Bengal: Western Pacific.

125. ***Chlorophthalmus corniger***, Alcock.

Chlorophthalmus corniger, Alcock, Journ. As. Soc. Bengal, Vol. LXIII. pt. 2, 1894, p. 133, pl. vi. fig. 5: ILLUSTRATIONS OF THE ZOOLOGY OF THE INVESTIGATOR, FISHES, PL. XV. FIG. 8.

B. 8. D. 11. A. 9. P. 14. V. 9. L. lat. *circ.* 55.

Length of the head about two-fifths of the total without the caudal, greatest height of the body about half the length of the head.

Eye not quite so long as the snout (including the mandibular element) not quite a third the length of the head, about 3 times the width of the interorbital space.

The mandibular symphysis forms a strongly projecting, transverse, horizontal plate, of which the angles are dentiform. The maxilla reaches to the anterior edge of the pupil. Teeth minute, in narrow bands in the jaws: very inconspicuous on the vomer and palatines.

Gill-rakers of the first arch numerous, close-set, bristle-like.

The first few rays of the dorsal fin are in front of the ventrals. The adipose fin is as far behind the dorsal as the dorsal is behind the anterior edge of the pupil.

The pectorals are as long as the head behind the snout, and reach nearly to the tips of the ventrals: the latter are rather more than half the total length of the head.

Colours in spirit: silvery grey with numerous broad ill-defined dusky cross-bands; fins hyaline, the tip of the caudal and the base and tip of the dorsal black: numerous parallel oblique rows—very conspicuous on the thorax and belly—of tiny black specks with a silvery centre, resembling incipient luminous spots.

Seven large pyloric cæca.

The largest specimen is a little over 3 inches long.

Bay of Bengal, off Madras coast, 145 to 250 fathoms.

Regd. Nos. 13712 to 13715.

Bathypterois, Günther.

Bathypterois, Günther, Ann. Mag. Nat. Hist., 1878, Vol. II., p. 183; Challenger Deep Sea Fishes, p. 185: Goode and Bean, Oceanic Ichthyology, p. 64: Jordan and Evermann, Fishes N. Amer., p. 544.

Form of the body elongate, slightly compressed. Scales cycloid, of moderate size. Head low; with a long broad depressed bill-like snout, the end of which is formed by the prominent mandible. Cleft of the mouth wide; maxillary much developed, very movable, dilated behind. Villiform teeth in narrow bands on the jaws: vomerine teeth present or absent: no teeth on the palatines or tongue. Eye very small.

Gill-openings very wide: gill-laminæ well developed: gill-rakers long and numerous. Branchiostegals numerous. No pseudobranchiæ.

Dorsal fin in the middle of the back, above or just behind the root of the ventral, rather short. Anal rather short, below or just behind the dorsal. Caudal forked, its lowermost rays sometimes prolonged. Adipose dorsal present or absent.

Pectorals remarkably developed, at least their uppermost rays are isolated and enormously prolonged. Ventrals abdominal, well developed, their outermost rays usually prolonged.

No luminous spots.

Distribution: Atlantic; Arabian Sea, Bay of Bengal and Andaman Sea; Western and Southern Pacific.

Key to the Indian species of the genus Bathypterois.

I. Ventral edge of the caudal peduncle not notched:—
   1. Lowermost caudal and ventral rays enormously prolonged, nearly 3 times as long as the head in the adult, longer in the young ... *B. Güntheri.*
   2. Lowermost caudal and ventral rays moderately prolonged, the former about once and a half, the latter not quite twice the length of the head *B. insularum.*

II. Ventral edge of the caudal peduncle curiously notched: the outer ventral rays slightly, the lowermost caudal rays very slightly prolonged ... ... *B. atricolor.*

126. *Bathypterois Güntheri,* Alcock.

Bathypterois Güntheri, Alcock, Ann. Mag. Nat. Hist., Dec. 1889, p. 450, and August 1891, p. 129: ILLUSTRATIONS OF THE ZOOLOGY OF THE INVESTIGATOR, FISHES, PL. VII. FIG. 6.

B. 12. D. 13. A. 11. P. 2/6/5. V. 7-8 L. lat. *circ.* 55.

Body elongate and compressed, its height about one-sixth of the total, without caudal. Head contained nearly three and a half times in the same measure; depressed, flat-crowned, nearly as broad as deep. Snout broad, depressed, rounded, duck-bill shaped, with a median intermaxillary notch, into which a strong recurved projection of the very prominent mandible fits; its length one-third that of the head; its surface with numerous large pores. A wide mucous channel with a line of large pores along the under surface of the broad mandible. Eyes minute, situated near the middle of the maxilla, close to its edge, a snout-length apart; the orbital margins rounded and inflated. Interorbital space nearly flat from side to side. Nostrils small, superior, far in advance of the eye.

Cleft of mouth extremely wide, slightly oblique; the maxilla, which has a dilated, abruptly-truncated, hinder end, is nearly two-thirds the head-length. Villiform teeth in broad bands on the outer edges of the strong jaw-bones, and in a minute patch on each side of the expanded vomer.

Gill-cleft reaching to the fore end of the isthmus; gill-laminæ broadish; gill-rakers numerous, close-set, long, bristle-like, except on the fourth arch.

Body and head, except the jaws and front part of the vertex of the snout, covered with large, thin, smooth scales, those on the sides of the head rather deciduous, those on its crown enlarged.

The interradial membrane of all the fins except the caudal is covered with a thick, black, velvety, deciduous integument. The dorsal begins a little in advance of the middle line, and is just entirely in advance of the anal, the two fins being of nearly equal extent and height. A very small adipose dorsal in the posterior half of the tail. Caudal large and deeply forked; its lowermost ray rigid, prolonged, curved, with a spatulate tip, the total length of the ray from base to tip being nearly two-thirds that of the rest of the body.

The pectoral consists of three distinct portions:—(1) an upper portion of two detached, rigid filaments, the first of which is the longest and, though broken, reaches to the tip of the upper lobe of the caudal; (2) a middle portion of six comparatively short branched rays, diminishing in length from above downwards and connected together by a stout interradial membrane; and (3) a lower portion of five free, simple, elongated rays, which reach at least halfway along the tail.

The ventrals arise just in front of the dorsal; the outermost ray of each fin forms a long, curved, rigid, spatulate appendage, which is nearly as long as the body in the adult and longer than the body in the young.

Colours in spirit:—Head nearly black; body dark brown, with two broad, transverse, white bands, one just in front of the dorsal fin, the other near the middle of the tail; caudal white; the other fins black, except their prolonged rays, which are translucent white, with black tips. A large, opaque-white, three-lobed body shows through the bones of the crown of the head and snout, and there is a white streak along the mucous canal of the mandible.

Length of adult female 10 inches (not including the prolonged caudal ray).

Andaman Sea, 490 fathoms; Bay of Bengal, off Andaman Is., 561 fathoms; Arabian Sea, off the Laccadives and Maldives, 636 and 719 fathoms.

Regd. Nos. 11770, 13706, 14001, 14002.

In the young the prolonged caudal and ventral rays are relatively much longer than they are in the adult.

127. *Bathypterois insularum*, Alcock.

Bathypterois insularum, Alcock, Ann. Mag. Nat. Hist., Nov. 1892, p. 356.

B. 13-14. D. 12-13. A. 10. P. 2/12-13. V. 9. L. lat. 48–51. L. tr. 13.

Body elongate, its height a little more than half the length of the head, which is about one-fourth of the total without the caudal. The snout, which has the typical duck-bill shape, is in length a little more than one-third the length of the head. The very small eyes are not quite a snout-length apart. There is nothing peculiar about the mouth, but there are no teeth on the vomer. The branchial structures are identical with those of other species of the genus. The body and the head, except the jaws and snout, are covered with thin deciduous cycloid scales.

The dorsal fin begins half a snout-length behind the base of the ventrals, and the anal immediately behind the vertical through the last dorsal ray; there is a small adipose fin nearly midway between the dorsal and the base of the caudal. The two uppermost pectoral rays are intimately coherent in their basal half and reach at least as far as the adipose dorsal; the other pectoral rays, which are slender and rigid, reach at least as far as the vent. The ventral fins are very large, their two outermost rays, which are very stout and stiff, are prolonged, being about $1\frac{2}{3}$ times to twice as long as the head. The two or three lowermost rays of the forked caudal are prolonged, their length being at least one-third that of the rest of the body.

Colour black; fins hyaline grey.

Length of the adult female, $5\frac{1}{2}$ inches.

Arabian Sea, off the Laccadive Islands, 1140 fathoms.

Regd. Nos. 13187, 13188.

128. *Bathypterois atricolor,* Alcock.

Bathypterois atricolor, Alcock, Journ. As. Soc. Bengal, Vol. LXV. pt. 2, 1896, p. 306: Ann. Mag. Nat. Hist., Aug. 1898, p. 146: ILLUSTRATIONS OF THE ZOOLOGY OF THE INVESTIGATOR, FISHES, PL. XVII. FIG. 6.

B. 12. D. 15. A. 10. P. 2/12. V. 9. L. lat. 52. L. tr. 15.

Length of head a little more than one-fifth, height of body about one-eighth, of total (without caudal).

Length of snout a little more than one-third that of head, and a little more than 5 times that of eye, equal to width of interorbital space.

Few or no teeth on the vomer.

The dorsal fin arises just behind the vertical through the base of the ventrals, and nearly half its extent is in the anterior half of the body (measured without caudal): the anal arises just behind the level of the last dorsal ray: the adipose fin is halfway between the end of the dorsal and the base of the caudal: the lower caudal lobe is hardly prolonged. Upper two pectoral rays prolonged at least as far as the end of the caudal fin, coherent in basal part but not fused: outer two ventral rays thickened, unbranched, prolonged as far as 7th or 8th anal ray, not quite half again as long as the head.

Colours, uniform black, except the pectoral filaments.

The ventral edge of the caudal peduncle is most curiously notched as in *B. dubius* Vaillant, to which this species is closely related.

Length, a little over 8 inches.

Arabian Sea, near the Laccadives, Maldives, and C. Comorin, 891, 459 and 824 fathoms.

Regd. Nos. $\frac{62}{1}$, $\frac{166}{1}$.

Scopelus, Cuv., Günther.

Scopelus, Günther, Cat. Fishes, V, pp. 404, 405 *ubi synon.*

Myctophidæ (exc. *Nannobrachium* and *Scopelosaurus*) Goode and Bean, Oceanic Ichthyology, p. 70, and Jordan and Evermann, Fishes N. Amer., pp. 551, 552.

Body moderately elongate and compressed, covered with large scales of which those of the lateral line are generally the largest. Series of luminous spots run along the lower side of the head body and tail, and a luminous body often occupies the snout and the back of the tail. Head generally compressed, with the bones thin but ossified. Cleft of the mouth very wide: premaxilla long, styliform; maxilla well developed. Villiform teeth in bands in the jaws, on the palatines pterygoids and tongue, and sometimes on the vomer. Eye large.

Dorsal fin short; in, or nearly in, the middle of the back; anal short or of moderate length. Caudal forked. Adipose fin small. Pectorals and ventrals well developed, the latter inserted in front of, or below, the anterior part of the dorsal, and eight-rayed.

Gill-opening very wide, the outer branchial arch with numerous long gill-rakers. Branchiostegals from 8 to 10. Pseudobranchiæ present.

Air-bladder small. Pyloric cæca few.

Distribution: Pelagic and Nectic.

The Indian species of this genus are now known to be nine in number. Two of them, however, are represented in the *Investigator* collections only by specimens recovered from the stomach of other fishes, and are too much damaged for recognition. The remaining seven fall into the following sub-genera.

Indian sub-genera of the genus Scopelus.

I. Snout deep, short, rounded: dorsal fin just in advance of the anal: pseudobranchiæ well developed: the anal fin with as many rays as, or more rays than, the dorsal: eye large: scales smooth ... ... MYCTOPHUM.

II. Snout rather long, somewhat depressed, not rounded: dorsal fin a considerable distance in advance of the anal: the anal fin with as many rays as, or more than, the dorsal:—
   1. Pseudobranchiæ well developed: eye moderate: scales with minute spines ... ... NEOSCOPELUS.
   2. Pseudobranchiæ rudimentary: eye small. (Scales unknown) ... SCOPELENGYS.

Key to the Indian species of the sub-genus Myctophum.

I. A large luminous mass on the snout immediately in front of the orbit: pectorals short:—
   1. The pectorals do not reach to the base of the ventrals: all the phosphorescent spots are divided by a median transverse black septum ... ... *S. engraulis.*
   2. The pectorals reach just beyond the base of the ventrals: phosphorescent organs without a black septum ... ... *S. dumerilii.*

II. No large luminous mass on the snout: pectorals of moderate length or very long:—

1. The pectorals reach the middle of the ventrals: snout about half as long as the eye ... ... *S. indicus.*
2. The pectorals reach the 1st anal ray: snout about half as long as the eye ... ... *S. pterotus.*
3. The pectorals reach at least to the sixth anal ray: snout about a quarter as long as the eye ... ... *S. pyrsobolus.*

129. *Scopelus engraulis*, Gthr.

Scopelus engraulis, Günther, Challenger Deep Sea Fishes, p. 197, pl. li. fig. C: Alcock, Ann. Mag. Nat. Hist. (6) VIII. 1891, p. 120.

D. 14. A. 14-15. P. 12. V. 9. L. lat. 38. L. tr. $\frac{3}{5}$.

Height of the body about a fifth, length of the head about two-sevenths of the total, without the caudal. The eye is near the extremity of the extremely short snout, its diameter is about a fifth the length of the head and rather less than the width of the interorbital space.

Operculum thin and narrow, scarcely covering the gill-opening: posterior margin of preoperculum oblique.

Mouth oblique, very wide, the upper jaw overlapping the lower. The maxilla extends back to the mandibular joint and is not dilated posteriorly.

The first dorsal ray is midway between the end of the snout and the adipose fin and a little in advance of the root of the ventral: the last dorsal ray is just in advance of the vent. Pectoral short, not reaching to the ventral. Ventral reaching to the vent.

Scales perfectly smooth, those of the lateral line not enlarged.

Colour: black; mandibles whitish, with a broad black cross-band below the eyes.

The luminous organs are arranged as follows on each side:—

one on the preoperculum, near its lower angle:

three between the isthmus and the root of the pectorals, and one above the pectoral:

three, in an oblique series, between the pectorals and the root of the ventral, and an isolated one higher up on the side:

three between the ventrals and the vent, and two or three higher up on the side:

three in an oblique series running from the vent towards the lateral line:

eleven along the base of the anal and a little behind, and one higher up, opposite a break in this series:

four along the root of the lower caudal rays.

21

All these luminous organs are divided into two by a black septum.

A large whitish gland on the snout immediately in front of the eye.

A mature female is nearly $5\frac{1}{2}$ inches long.

Andaman Sea, 188 to 220 fathoms.

Regd. Nos. 13127, 13128.

Distribution: off Philippine Is.; Andaman Sea.

130. *Scopelus Dumerilii,* Bleeker.

Scopelus Dumerilii, Bleeker, Act. Soc. Sc. Indo-Neerl. i. Manado and Macassar, p. 66: Günther, Cat. Fishes, V. p. 410, and Challenger Deep Sea Fishes, p. 198.

D. 14-15. A. 14-15. P. 10. V. 9. L. lat. 37.

Very closely related to *Scopelus engraulis,* from which it only differs in the following characters:—

The eye is larger, its diameter being from a third to two-sevenths the length of the head and equal to the width of the interorbital space.

The first dorsal ray is rather nearer to the adipose fin than to the end of the snout.

The pectoral fin reaches somewhat beyond the root of the ventral, and the latter reaches beyond the vent.

The luminous organs correspond with those of *S. engraulis,* except that the uppermost tier of four distant organs are placed much higher up, the last two (which correspond respectively with the first and last anal rays) being on the lateral line.

None of the luminous organs have a median black septum; and the large glandular body in front of the eye is much brighter.

A specimen nearly 3 inches long, from off the Malabar coast, 172 fathoms.

Regd. No. 13730.

Distribution: East Indian Archipelago; Fiji; Arabian Sea.

131. *Scopelus pterotus,* Alcock.

Scopelus (Myctophum) pterotus, Alcock, Ann. Mag. Nat. Hist., Sept. 1890, p. 217: Illustrations of the Zoology of the Investigator, Fishes, pl. IX. fig. 3.

D. 11-12. A. 17. P. 15. V. 8. L. lat. *circ.* 30.

Length of the head about a third, greatest height of the body about a fourth the total without the caudal. Snout obtuse, its length hardly half the diameter of the eye, which is a third the length of the head and rather more than the mean width of the interorbital space.

Mouth large, moderately oblique; the jaws perfectly equal in repose; the maxilla nearly reaches the preopercular angle and is dilated at its hinder end; no vomerine teeth. Opercles large; the operculum produced into a membranous spur behind; the vertical border of the preoperculum very oblique.

Scales extremely deciduous, smooth, cycloid, their average diameter one-twelfth of an inch.

The dorsal fin begins nearer to the tip of the snout than to the base of the caudal, but behind the bases of the ventrals, which are much advanced, its last ray falls in the vertical through the first or second anal ray; adipose dorsal entire. Pectorals long, extending beyond the tip of the ventral to the first or second anal ray.

The luminous organs are arranged on each side as follows:—A series extending close to the mid-ventral line from the isthmus to the base of the caudal, and numbering four to base of ventral, three more to origin of anal, ten or eleven more to hinder end of anal, and one more at base of caudal; above this series are the following, rather more scattered—one at the angle of the preoperculum, two along the ramus of the mandible, two along the edge of the gill-opening, one on the base of the pectoral, two on the base of the ventral, three in a straight line along the middle of the flank, two above the anal, and one at the base of the caudal. No luminous organ on the back of the tail.

Nine pyloric cæca. An air-badder.

Colours in the fresh state:—Uniform silvery, with thickly scattered black specks; opercles and iris burnished silver.

Length of mature females from not quite two inches to a little over two inches.

Bay of Bengal, 98 to 102 fathoms; Andaman Sea, 370 to 419 fathoms.

132. *Scopelus pyrsobolus*, Alcock.

Scopelus pyrsobolus, Alcock, Ann. Mag. Nat. Hist. Sept. 1890, p. 218, pl. VIII. fig. 3; ILLUSTRATIONS OF THE ZOOLOGY OF THE INVESTIGATOR, FISHES, PL. XXX. FIG. 3.

D. 12. A. 13. P. 12. V. 8.

Length of the head (not including a membranous prolongation of the sub-operculum) about a third, greatest body-height about a fourth of the total length without the caudal. Snout about a quarter as long as eye. Eyes large, round, strongly convergent, bulging beyond the dorsal profile; their diameter is a third of the length of the head proper, and more than the mean width of the inter-orbital space. Mouth wide, oblique; the maxillary, which does not quite reach the preopercular angle, is slightly dilated behind. Jaws equal in front. Villiform teeth developed on the vomer. Opercles large, extremely thin, the vertical border of the preoperculum oblique.

The scales and almost all the luminous organs have been denuded: there are opaque white glandular organs still left on the caudal peduncle, both dorsally and ventrally.

The dorsal fin begins nearer to the tip of the snout than to the base of the caudal, its first ray is almost in the vertical through the base of the ventrals; the entire fin is nearly half an eye-length in advance of the anal. Adipose fin well developed.

The pectorals reach at least to the sixth anal ray.

About five large pyloric cæca. A well developed air-bladder.

Colours, apparently black. Iris and lower part of opercles like burnished silver, the opercles in the fresh state brilliantly coruscating.

A mature female is over 3 inches long.

Bay of Bengal, off Madras coast, 920 to 690 fathoms.

Regd. No. 12839.

NEOSCOPELUS, Johnson.

Neoscopelus, Johnson, Proc. Zool. Soc., 1863, p. 44: Günther, Cat. Fishes, V. p. 405: Goode and Bean, Oceanic Ichthyology, p. 92.

Neoscopelus differs from *Scopelus* in having a rather long and distinctly depressed snout; a narrower mouth-cleft, which reaches only as far as the posterior border of the orbit; a smaller eye; scales with minute spines, and an anal fin much more remote from the dorsal. The maxilla also is much more dilated posteriorly.

The argument, therefore, for recognizing it as a distinct genus is very strong.

133. ***Neoscopelus macrolepidotus***, Johnson.

Neoscopelus macrolepidotus, Johnson, P. Z. S. 1863, p. 44, pl. 7: Vaillant, Exp. Sci. Travailleur et Talisman, Poiss, p. 119: Alcock, Ann. Mag. Nat. Hist., (6) VIII. 1891, p. 129: Goode and Bean, Oceanic Ichthyology, p. 93, figs. 108, 109.

Scopelus macrolepidotus, Günther, Cat. Fishes, V. p. 414, and Challenger Deep-Sea Fishes, p. 196.

B. 9. D. 13. A. 13. P. 15-16. V. 8. L. lat. 30.

Length of the head about a third, height of the body about two-ninths the total length without the caudal. Snout broad, somewhat depressed, decidedly longer than the eye, its tip formed by the prominent mandible. Nostrils almost superior. Eye situated almost midway between the tip of the snout and the vertical limb of the preoperculum, its length about a fifth that of the head and decidedly less than the width of the interorbital space.

Mouth-cleft very oblique; the maxilla, which is dilated behind, only reaches to the posterior border of the orbit. Villiform teeth are present on the vomer.

The first dorsal ray is almost midway between the tip of the snout and the adipose fin: the anal begins half a head-length behind the last dorsal ray. The pectorals are as long as the head without the snout, and when unbroken, reach almost to the vent and as far as, or beyond, the tips of the ventrals.

The posterior margin of each scale is covered with minute spines.

Under surface with numerous very regular longitudinal series of large luminous organs: beginning with two series at the tip of the isthmus, becoming 7 or 8 series on the throat, 5 or 6 series on the belly, 2 series on either side of the anal fin, and 3 series—of which that in the middle line is very small—between the anal and the caudal.

A large air-bladder is present.

Mature females are nearly $7\frac{1}{2}$ inches long, mature males are somewhat smaller.

Andaman Sea, 188 to 220 and 405 fathoms: Arabian Sea, off Travancore coast, 360 fathoms.

Regd. Nos. 13124, 13125, $\frac{147}{1}$, $\frac{149}{1}$, $\frac{310}{1}$.

Distribution: West Indies; Madeira and Morocco coast; Arabian and Andaman Seas; off Kermadec Is.

In the Indian Museum is also one of the "Challenger" duplicates.

SCOPELENGYS, Alcock.

Scopelengys, Alcock, Ann. Mag. Nat. Hist., October, 1890, p. 303.

Head and body compressed. Eye small. Mouth very wide; the maxilla dilated behind. Acute villiform teeth, in bands uncovered by the lips in the jaws, and in the palatines and vomer. Gill-openings very wide; gill-covers complete. Pseudobranchiæ rudimentary. Dorsal fin near the middle of the body, short; an adipose dorsal. Anal fin short. Caudal forked. Pectorals well developed. Ventrals with eight rays. [Scales, if present, very deciduous.] No air-bladder. Pyloric cæca present in moderate number.

When I described *Scopelengys* I did not know *Neoscopelus* by autopsy. I now feel sure, though the specimen is in a very bad state of preservation, that it is very closely related to *Neoscopelus*.

Apart from any differences that may exist in the scales, it differs from *Neoscopelus* in having a smaller eye, rudimentary pseudobranchiæ, and no air-bladder.

134. *Scopelengys tristis*, Alcock.

Scopelengys tristis, Alcock, Ann. Mag. Nat. Hist., October, 1890, p. 303: Illustrations of the Zoology of the Investigator, Fishes, pl. VII, fig. 7.

B. 8. D. 12. A. 13. P. 15. V. 8.

Head and body rather elongate, compressed. Eye situated high up, very small; its major diameter is a little more than $\frac{1}{3}$ the length of the snout, which is about $\frac{1}{3}$ the length of the head, which is not quite $\frac{1}{3}$ the total without the caudal. Mouth wide, its cleft very oblique, approaching the vertical, with the lower jaw projecting in repose; the maxilla, which is widely dilated behind, measures more than half the length of the head; the premaxilla is a stout bone, firmly attached to the maxilla, which it equals in length. Acute villiform teeth, in rather broad bands uncovered by the lips in the premaxillæ and mandible, in narrow bands in the palatines, and in a small patch on each side of the head of the vomer; no teeth on the tongue.

Gill-openings very wide; gill-covers complete; long close-set gill-rakers on the first arch. Pseudobranchiæ rudimentary, consisting of three or four small lamellæ on each side.

The dorsal fin begins above the origin of the ventrals; the whole fin is included in the anterior half of the body measured with the caudal. Adipose dorsal rather large, fimbriated. The anal fin begins a little more than a snout-length behind the posterior limit of the dorsal. Caudal forked. Pectorals entire, about as long as the maxilla, and reaching just beyond the origin of the ventrals; they arise close to the ventral profile.

Eight large pyloric cæca. No air-bladder.

Colour in the fresh state apparently uniform black throughout.

One specimen, $6\frac{3}{4}$ inches in length, nearly mature.

Arabian Sea, off the Laccadive Is., 1000 fathoms.

Odontostomus, Cocco.

Odontostomus, Cocco, Lett. su Alcun. Salmon., p. 32: Günther, Cat. Fishes, V. p. 417, and Challenger Deep-Sea Fishes, p. 200: Goode and Bean, Oceanic Ichthyology, p. 121.

Head compressed; body compressed, moderately elongate, naked. Snout short. Cleft of the mouth very wide: premaxilla and maxilla slender, the former with a series of small teeth of equal size: the lower jaw, the vomer and the palatines with a few depressible fangs of enormous size. Eye large; the orbit of great vertical depth and with a broad transparent membranous lateral fold or wall.

Gill-openings wide: no gill-rakers: eight branchiostegals. Pseudobranchiæ well developed.

Dorsal fin short, in the middle or anterior half of the body: anal fin long, in the posterior half of the body. Caudal forked. Adipose fin small, placed far back.

Pectorals and ventrals well developed, the pectorals inserted near the ventral profile, the ventrals inserted below the dorsal some way behind the pectorals.

Distribution: Mediterranean, Bay of Bengal, Andaman Sea.

135. ***Odontostomus atratus,*** Alcock.

Odontostomus atratus, Alcock, Journ. As. Soc. Bengal, Vol. LXII. pt. 2, 1893, p. 182, pl. ix. fig. 4: ILLUSTRATIONS OF THE ZOOLOGY OF THE INVESTIGATOR, FISHES, PL. XXXIII. FIG. 3.

B. 8. D. 11. A. 26. P. 12. V. 8.

The extreme length of the square, high, compressed head is a little more, and the greatest height of the compressed tapering body is a little less, than one-fourth of the total, caudal included.

The snout has the form of a pointed wart beyond which the upper jaw slightly projects, the lower jaw again projecting a little beyond the upper.

The eyes, which are situated about a diameter apart, near the top of the head, have their major diameter obliquely vertical, and are capable of such strong rotation inwards as to bring the visual axis obliquely upwards, the orbit being walled in laterally by a stout but transparent fold of skin in its lower half.

The cleft of the mouth extends almost to the posterior edge of the preoperculum: the premaxillæ are armed with a series of close uniform serrations for the most part pointing forwards, the vomer bears on each side a sabre-shaped depressible fang nearly half as long as the head, the palatines have each an exactly similar fang succeeded by a row of close serrations, and the mandible has on each side a distant series of similar fangs of unequal size, the largest of them however being hardly half the length of those on the vomer and palatines.

Gill-cleft extremely wide and high: four gills with wide laminæ and gill-rakers inconspicuous or absent: pseudobranchiæ large.

Body covered with a glandular scaleless skin in which the lateral line appears in spirit as a white streak. Rows of white dots (luminous organs?) exist along the free border of the preoperculum and the inner border of the broad boat-shaped mandible.

The dorsal fin lies altogether within the anterior half of the body: the anal begins about half a head length behind the vertical through the last dorsal ray, and extends to the rudimentary basal rays of the forked caudal. The large pectorals arise close to the ventral profile, almost in the same plane with the ventrals, the bases of which they touch when laid back. The ventrals arise under the middle of the dorsal.

Length of the adult $3\frac{1}{2}$ inches.

Bay of Bengal, 573 fathoms; Andaman Sea, 370 to 419 fathoms.

Regd. Nos. 13434, $\frac{370}{1}$.

Family *Alepocephalidæ.*

Head almost always naked. Body usually covered with thin cycloid scales, but sometimes naked. Barbels none. Margin of the upper jaw formed by the premaxillæ and maxillæ, the former being placed along the upper anterior edge of the latter: the maxilla commonly broad and resembling that of the *Clupeidæ*. Gill-openings very wide: opercles complete. Pseudobranchiæ present.

No adipose fin: the dorsal fin belongs to the caudal portion of the back-bone.

Pyloric cæca few. No air-bladder.

This family is represented in the depths of the Indian Seas by 12 species belonging to 7 genera.

Synopsis of the Indian genera of the family Alepocephalidæ.

I. Body scaly:—
  1. Snout normal: body rather elongate: ventrals present:—
    i. Six branchiostegals: a single series of teeth on the premaxillæ, none on the maxillæ ... ... ALEPOCEPHALUS.
    ii. Seven branchiostegals: a single series of teeth on the premaxillæ and maxillæ ... ... BATHYTROCTES.
    iii. Seven branchiostegals: several series of teeth on the premaxillæ, a single series on the maxillæ ... ... NARCETES.
  2. Snout normal: body short and elevated: no ventrals ... PLATYTROCTES.
  3. Anterior bones of the head produced to form a tubular snout at the end of which the mouth is situated: body rather elongate ... AULASTOMOMORPHA.

II. Body naked:—
  1. Body moderately elongate: dorsal and anal fins of moderate length ... ... XENODERMICHTHYS.
  2. Body exceedingly elongate: dorsal and anal fins very long ... LEPTODERMA.

ALEPOCEPHALUS, Risso.

Alepocephalus, Risso, Mem. Ac. Nat. Sci. Turin, XXV, 1820, p. 270; Müller, Abh. Ak. Wiss. Berlin, 1846, p. 171; Cuvier and Valenciennes, Hist. Nat. Poiss. XIX., p. 169; Günther, Cat. Fishes, VII., p. 477; Goode and Bean, Oceanic Ichthyology, p. 35.

Alepocephalus and *Mitchillina*, Jordan and Evermann, Fishes N. Amer., pp. 452, 453.

Body moderately elongate, compressed, covered with thin cycloid scales. Head naked. Cleft of the mouth of moderate width, with the jaws nearly even in front. A series of small teeth in the premaxillæ mandibles and palatines, and sometimes on the vomer. Eye large.

Gill-openings wide, the opercles large and thin. Six branchiostegals. Gill-rakers numerous and rather long.

Dorsal and anal fins nearly equal and opposite, placed far back, in the posterior half of the body. Caudal forked. Pectorals and ventrals well developed, but rather small.

Distribution: Atlantic; Mediterranean; Arabian Sea and Bay of Bengal; Western South Pacific.

Key to the Indian species of Alepocephalus.

I. The maxilla reaches a little beyond the anterior border of the orbit, and the snout is more than a fourth the length of the head: the anal fin begins well behind the middle of the body (measured with the caudal):—
   1. Eyes of adult more than a diameter apart, and between a fifth and a sixth the length of the head: the gill-membranes overlap each other broadly: 9 pyloric cæca ... ... *A. bicolor*.
   2. Eyes of adult less than a diameter apart, and between a third and a fourth the length of the head: the gill-membranes overlap slightly: 14 pyloric cæca ... ... *A. Blanfordi*.

II. The maxilla reaches nearly to the posterior border of the orbit, and the snout is less than a fourth the length of the head: the anal fin begins exactly in the middle of the body: 4 pyloric cæca ... ... *A. edentulus*.

136. ***Alepocephalus bicolor***, Alcock.

Alepocephalus bicolor, Alcock, Ann. Mag. Nat. Hist., August, 1891, p. 133; ILLUSTRATIONS OF THE ZOOLOGY OF THE INVESTIGATOR, FISHES, PL. IV. FIG. 2.

B. 6. D. 21. A. 28. P. 10. V. 8. L. lat. 62. L. tr. 18.

Length of the head slightly more than a fourth, height of the body nearly a fifth the total without the caudal.

The length of the obtusely-pointed depressed snout is contained about $3\frac{1}{2}$ times in that of the head. The eyes, which converge anteriorly, are between one-fifth and one-sixth of the head-length in diameter, and are more than their own diameter apart. The large nostrils are situated close together immediately in front of the eye.

Mouth-cleft slightly oblique; the maxilla reaches just behind the vertical through the anterior border of the orbit. A row of small teeth in each jaw and on the palatines.

Gill-openings very wide, the membranes entirely separate and overlapping broadly; a great part of the gill-cover is formed by the broad flat branchiostegal rays, which are uncovered by the opercle from their very bases; the opercular

22

bones, which are extremely thin, are invested by the same tough black skin that covers the head; the gill-laminæ are coarse and the gill-rakers on all the arches long and lamellar; pseudobranchiæ small.

Head naked, body covered with large cycloid scales, which are deciduous everywhere but on the lateral line; small scales also invest the bases of all the fins. A scale from the flank measures about 7·5 millim. in the horizontal and about 5·5 millim. in the vertical diameter.

The dorsal and anal fins arise just in advance of the posterior third of the body (measured without the caudal), and the base of the former, which begins a little in advance of the latter, is two-thirds that of the latter in extent. Caudal deeply forked, with very numerous rudimentary rays at its base. Pectorals broad, in length a little more than the postorbital portion of the head. The ventrals arise just abaft of midway between the pectorals and anal; they are broad and reach more than halfway to the anal.

Stomach small, siphonal. The intestine, which, when unravelled, is about $2\frac{1}{2}$ times the entire length of the fish, consists of two portions, which both in structure and arrangement are quite different from one another: the anterior five-sixths is thin-walled and of small calibre, and is intricately coiled in a globular mass situated in the anterior fourth of the abdomen, the coils being held by a long mesentery; the posterior sixth is wide, but with walls so thick as to almost block the lumen (in the contracted state), the mucosa in this condition being thrown into numerous longitudinal folds; it passes straight down the middle of the abdominal cavity unsupported by mesentery. There are nine large long pyloric cæca in a pectinate arrangement.

In a female with much-enlarged ovaries containing ova nearly 4 millim. in diameter the ovaries extend back to the wide genital pore, through which they open to the exterior.

Colours in life:—Head, including sclerotic and iris, black; body uniform dull slate-blue; pharyngo-branchial mucous membrane and parietal peritoneum black.

Adult females are just under a foot in length: adult males are a good deal smaller.

Bay of Bengal, off Ganjam coast, 240 to 276 fathoms; Arabian Sea, off Malabar coast, 360 fathoms.

Regd. Nos. 13079, 13080, 13081, 13083, $\frac{309}{1}$.

The microscopic structure of the hind-gut of Alepocephalus bicolor.

In transverse section the appearance somewhat resembles that of the human vas deferens. Externally there is a thin fibrous coat containing blood-vessels, and internal to this and intimately adherent to it is a thin layer of longitudinally-arranged muscular fibres. Inside this is a layer, averaging about half a millimetre in thickness, of dense, circularly-arranged, muscular fibres. Internal to this is a submucous layer thrown into numerous wide longitudinal folds, and invested by a single row of long columnar epithelium, with numerous large goblet-cells. The submucous coat in all the sections made is everywhere infiltrated with round or oval, deeply-pigmented, highly granular corpuscles, which measure from $\frac{1}{1400}$ to $\frac{1}{2000}$ of an inch in diameter; in shape they resemble large leucocytes, but they are so granular that no nucleus can in any instance be detected.

The thick muscular coat, the dense infiltration of the submucosa with these pigmented granular corpuscles, and the large and numerous goblet-cells of the mucosa characterize this part of the intestine.

137. *Alepocephalus Blanfordi*, Alcock.

Alepocephalus Blanfordi, Alcock, Ann. Mag. Nat. Hist., Nov. 1892, p. 357: ILLUSTRATIONS OF THE ZOOLOGY OF THE INVESTIGATOR, FISHES, PL. IX, FIG. 1. (*reduced.*)

B. 6. D. 16. A. 17. P. 11. V. 6-7. L. lat. *circ.* 70.

Length of head one-third, height of body two-elevenths, of the total without the caudal.

The length of the obtusely-pointed depressed snout is barely greater than the diameter of the huge orbit, or two-sevenths of the length of the head.

The eyes are hardly half a diameter apart, with the large nostrils placed close together in front of their angle.

The mouth-cleft is almost horizontal, and the upper jaw, which reaches just beyond and rests upon the anterior border of the orbit, completely encloses the mandible on all sides; a row of fine teeth in each jaw and on each prominent palatine.

Gill-openings very wide, the gill-membranes entirely separate and only slightly overlapping; the branchiostegal rays are but little concealed by the opercular bones, and the whole gill-cover is clothed by a continuation of the thick scaleless skin that covers the head; gill-rakers numerous, close-set, broadly lanceolate, acute; pseudobranchiæ large and coarse.

Body covered with thick deciduous cycloid scales; a scale from the abdomen is nearly 5·5 millim. in the horizontal and 5 millim. in the vertical diameter. The dorsal and anal fins, which are similar in form, equal in extent, and opposite, lie well within the posterior third of the body (measured without the caudal); the caudal is deeply forked, with many rudimentary rays at its base. The ventrals arise almost in the middle of the body, nearer to the anal than to the pectorals.

Stomach siphonal; a row of fourteen very large and long pyloric cæca embraces its pyloric moiety; the intestine, which when unravelled is about twice the entire length of the fish, is arranged as in *Alepocephalus bicolor*, but the wall of the coiled up small intestine is much thicker, and the straight hinder gut is held by a stout mesentery.

Colour: head and fins black; body lavender-grey.

Length 14 inches.

Arabian Sea, off Cape Comorin, 902 fathoms.

Regd. No. 13191.

The microscopic structure of the hind-gut, etc., *of* Alepocephalus Blanfordi.

The straight large gut in this species, as in *Alepocephalus bicolor*, is remarkable for the great thickness of its wall and for its contracted lumen; only in the present case, although the circular muscular coat is conspicuously thick, it is not this but the highly glandular mucous coat that contributes most to the thickness of the wall. The great development of the glands of the mucosa, which are compact little branching follicles, is in marked contrast to *A. bicolor*, where the mucous membrane consists of simple columnar epithelium. The loose submucous coat is honeycombed with (lymphatic?) channels and crowded with leucocytes; but the large pigmented granular corpuscles which were so numerous in *A. bicolor* are here few in number.

The small intestine at its duodenal end, and the pyloric cæca, appear, in transverse sections, to be identical in structure. In both the mucous membrane is thrown into apparently permanent longitudinal folds, and contains in its depth a regular series of racemose glands opening to the surface by a longish duct.

Microscopic cylinders of glandular substance, which in stained sections has exactly the appearance of mammalian pancreas, run in the mesentery, parallel with the pyloric cæca and in contact with them.

138. ***Alepocephalus edentulus,*** Alcock.

Alepocephalus edentulus, Alcock, Ann. Mag. Nat. Hist., Nov. 1892, p. 358, pl. xviii. fig. 2: Illustrations of the Zoology of the Investigator, Fishes, pl. XXXII. fig. 4.

B. 6. D. 29. A. 35. V. 6. P. 9. L. lat. *circa* 50. L. tr. 15.

The length of the head is a little more than one-fourth, and the height of the much compressed body nearly one-fifth, of the total with the caudal included. The blunt snout is barely equal in length either to the width of the interorbital space or to the diameter of the eye, which is very nearly two-ninths the length of the head. The mouth-cleft is almost horizontal, the jaws are even anteriorly, and the maxilla reaches considerably behind the vertical through the centre of the eye. Minute teeth occur in a row in the premaxillæ and mandibles, and there are a few inconspicuous and deciduous teeth on the prominent edges of the palatines only.

Gill-openings very wide, the gill-membranes being attached to the isthmus only quite anteriorly; gill-rakers conspicuous on all the branchial arches, and, to the number of about twelve in the middle of the first arch, long and setaceous; pseudobranchiæ small. Head covered with a velvety scaleless skin; body with scales that are so deciduous as to have entirely disappeared, leaving only imprints.

The long anal fin begins an eye-length behind the middle of the body, measured without the caudal, and the shorter dorsal arises in the vertical through the sixth or seventh anal ray; the caudal is completely divided down to its base into two long feathery lobes. The small ventrals, which arise midway between the base of the pectoral and the origin of the anal, reach rather more than half-way to the latter point.

Stomach siphonal; a row of four stout pyloric cæca; intestine slightly coiled, with its terminal end enlarged and thick-walled.

Colours: head and eyes jet-black; body and fins greyish black.

A mature male is nearly 7 inches long.

Bay of Bengal, off Madras coast, 475 fathoms.

Regd. No. 13192.

BATHYTROCTES, Günther.

Bathytroctes, Günther, Ann. Mag. Nat. Hist., 1878, Vol. II., p. 249; and Challenger Deep-Sea Fishes, p. 225: Goode and Bean, Oceanic Ichthyology, p. 40: Jordan and Evermann, Fishes of N. Amer., p. 454.

Talismania, Goode and Bean, Oceanic Ichthyology, p. 41: Jordan and Evermann, Fishes of N. Amer., p. 455.

Differs from *Alepocephalus* only in the following particulars:—

The maxilla, as well as the premaxilla, has a series of small teeth. The opercles and part of the cheeks are sometimes, but not commonly, scaly. There are seven branchiostegals. The anal fin commonly begins below the posterior part of the dorsal.

Distribution: Atlantic; Arabian and Andaman Seas; Western Pacific.

139. ***Bathytroctes squamosus***, Alcock.

Bathytroctes squamosus, Alcock, Ann. Mag. Nat. Hist., Oct. 1890, p. 304: ILLUSTRATIONS OF THE ZOOLOGY OF THE INVESTIGATOR, FISHES, PL. V. FIG. 1.

B. 7. D. 17. A. 17. C. *circ.* 35. P. 10. V. 9. L. lat. *circ.* 50. L. tr. 15.

Length of the head a little more than the greatest height of the body and a little more than a fourth of the total.

Snout much shorter than the eye, which is a third the length of the head and almost enters the dorsal profile. Nostrils large, situated immediately in front of the eye.

Mouth-cleft wide, approaching the transverse; premaxilla short and slender; the broad maxilla, composed of three longitudinal plates, of which the innermost (uppermost) is movable, reaches just behind the level of the mid-orbit, and includes the mandible in repose, except anteriorly, where the latter strongly projects. Small, even, acute, uniserial teeth, recurved in the premaxillæ, mandible, palatines, and vomer, procurrent or procurved in the maxillæ. Tongue large. A row of pores along the limb of the mandible.

Gill-openings very wide, the membranes entirely separate; fourth gill-cleft occluded; gill-rakers long and close-set on the first three arches, longest on the first. Pseudobranchiæ large and coarse.

Scales large, deciduous, except on the lateral line where they are adherent and perforated. There are scales on the cheeks and opercles.

The dorsal fin begins just behind the origin of the ventrals, which are situated in the vertical through the middle of the body measured without the caudal. The anal begins in the vertical through the third dorsal ray. Both these fins have fleshy succulent bases, and the rays increasing in length regularly and steeply to the fourth, and then decreasing as regularly but more gradually to the last. Caudal symmetrically forked. Pectorals long and narrow; their longest rays equal the length of the head behind the anterior nostril, and in repose almost touch the bases of the ventrals. Ventrals broad, reaching slightly beyond the vent.

Stomach large; intestine coiled in a spiral; five or six large pyloric cæca.

Colours in the fresh state:—Head uniform deep black, body pinkish brown, fins transparent grey; buccal membrane and entire peritoneum black.

A female specimen, $10\frac{1}{4}$ inches long, with gravid ovaries, the mature ova measuring $\frac{1}{8}$ of an inch in diameter.

Arabian Sea, off the Lacadives, 740 fathoms.

Regd. No. 12869.

Besides this species the remains of two others from the Andaman Sea are in the collection. One of them may be *B. macrolepis*, Gthr., the other may be *B. microlepis*, Gthr.

Narcetes, Alcock.

Narcetes, Alcock, Ann. Mag. Nat. Hist., Oct. 1890, p. 305.

Differs from *Alepocephalus* only in the following particulars:—

There are teeth on the maxillæ, as well as on the premaxillæ. There are seven branchiostegals. The anal fin is entirely behind the dorsal.

Differs from *Bathytroctes* in that the teeth of the premaxillæ and mandibles are in several series.

Head naked. Body rather elongate, compressed, covered with scales of moderate size. Eye rather small. Mouth wide; the maxilla extending beyond the vertical through the middle of the orbit. Fine teeth in premaxillæ, maxillæ, mandible, palatines, and vomer, those in the premaxillæ and mandible pluriserial; no teeth on the tongue.

Gill-openings wide; gill-covers complete; seven branchiostegals; four gills, with narrow laminæ; gill-rakers long. Pseudobranchiæ present. The dorsal arises in the posterior half of the body and the anal is entirely behind it. No adipose dorsal fin. Caudal forked. Pyloric cæca in moderate number. Ovaries with an oviduct.

140. ***Narcetes erimelas***, Alcock.

Narcetes erimelas, Alcock, Ann. Mag. Nat. Hist., Oct. 1890, p. 305: ILLUSTRATIONS OF THE ZOOLOGY OF THE INVESTIGATOR, FISHES, PL. IV, FIG. 1.

B. 7. D. 15-16. A. 12. C. *circ.* 35. P. 10-11. V. 9. L. lat. 68.

Head broad, pyramidal, its length $3\frac{1}{8}$ to $3\frac{1}{4}$ in the total without the caudal; body elongate, its greatest height, just behind the gill-opening, about $5\frac{1}{3}$ in the same standard.

Head-bones sculptured, specially the operculum and preoperculum, both of which have their border augmented by a semimembranous striated fringe.

Snout nearly as broad as long, depressed, rounded from side to side, its dorsal and ventral profiles meeting at an acute angle; its length is a little over $\frac{1}{3}$ that of the head, and more than half as long again as the eye. Nostrils very large.

Eye rather small, its major diameter $5\frac{2}{5}$ in the head-length, and not quite equal to the width of the deeply concave interorbital space.

Mouth wide, oblique; the maxilla reaches well behind the vertical through the posterior border of the orbit. The premaxilla is a short strong bone; the maxilla is composed of three longitudinal plates, of which the innermost (uppermost) is movable; the mandible is very strong and broad, and its under surface is excavated for a wide mucous channel which opens by six large circular pores on each side.

Teeth small, even, uniform, acute; those in the jaws standing, uncovered by the lips, outside the mouth; those in the premaxillæ and mandible recurved, quadriserial anteriorly and triserial laterally in the premaxillæ, biserial in the mandible; those in the maxillæ uniserial, procurrent or procurved; those in the palatines uniserial, incurved; those in the vomer recurved, in a group of two or three on each side. Tongue large, toothless.

Gill-openings very wide; gill-membranes entirely separate; gill-covers large, complete; gill-rakers on the first arch close-set, finely pointed, and as long as the eye; fourth gill-cleft rather wide; gill-laminæ very narrow, the individual lamellæ extremely delicate. Pseudobranchiæ large.

Head naked; body covered with deciduous scales of moderate size. The lateral line runs straight along the middle of the body.

The dorsal fin begins almost in the vertical through the origin of the ventrals, which are situated a snout-length behind the middle of the body measured without the caudal. The anal fin begins two rows of scales behind the last dorsal ray. Pectorals and ventrals well developed, broad, fragile.

Stomach very large, with thick walls thrown into deep longitudinal folds. Intestine coiled in a spiral; ten very large pyloric cæca in a bunch.

Colours in the fresh state:—head, iris, body, fins, inside of mouth and gill-chamber, and entire peritoneum, deep black.

Two female specimens, measuring respectively $13\frac{1}{2}$ and $9\frac{1}{2}$ inches.

Both, when brought on board, were in a curious state of cataleptic rigor.

Arabian Sea, near Laccadive Is., 740 fathoms.

Regd. Nos. 12870, 12871.

Platytroctes, Günther.

Platytroctes, Günther, Ann. Mag. Nat. Hist. 1878, II. p. 249: and Challenger Deep-Sea Fishes, p. 229: Goode and Bean, Oceanic Ichthyology, p. 45: Jordan and Evermann, Fishes N. Amer., p. 458.

Body rather abbreviated and elevated, much compressed, covered with small scales many of which are keeled. Head naked. Mouth of moderate width: a single series of small teeth in premaxilla, maxilla and mandible: a few (two in the only known species) teeth on the vomer. Eye large.

Gill-opening wide: six branchiostegals. Gills very narrow: pseudobranchiæ present: gill-rakers long, lanceolate.

The dorsal and anal fins, which are in the posterior half of the body, are equal, opposite, and of moderate length. Caudal forked. No adipose dorsal.

Pectorals small. Each clavicle ends below in a long freely projecting spine, which is fused with its fellow except perhaps at tip.

No ventrals.

Pyloric appendages rudimentary.

Distribution: Atlantic; Arabian Sea.

141. ***Platytroctes apus,*** Günther.

Platytroctes apus, Günther, Ann. Mag. Nat. Hist. 1878, II. p. 249, and Challenger Deep-Sea Fishes, p. 229, pl. lviii. fig. A: Alcock, Ann. Mag. Nat. Hist. (6) VI. 1890, p. 307: Goode and Bean, Oceanic Ichthyology, p. 46, fig. 53: Jordan and Evermann, Fishes of N. Amer., p. 458.

D. 18. A. 17. P. 20. L. lat. *circ.* 100.

Length of the head two-sevenths, greatest height of the body, at its middle, rather more than a third the total length without the caudal. More than half of this height, however, is contributed by simple dorsal and ventral folds of skin into which neither muscles nor viscera enter.

The snout is shorter than the eye, which is a third or more the length of the head and almost enters the dorsal profile. Nostrils large, superior, nearer to the edge of the snout than to the eye.

The narrow triangular interorbital space and the occiput are sharply concave, the concavity being bordered on each side by a mucous canal with large pores. A similar mucous canal with pores runs along the preorbital, and another one along the free edge of the preopercle.

Mouth rather short but broad, the lower jaw projecting when the mouth is open. The maxilla, which is a broad petal-shaped bone, reaches to or a little beyond the anterior edge of the eye. The limbs of the mandible make a curious boat-shaped bone. A single series of small even teeth in the premaxilla and maxilla and in the front half of the mandible: a small tooth on either side of the head of the vomer.

Gill-laminæ very short: gill-rakers on the first branchial arch long, extremely numerous and close-set.

The clavicles project freely at their symphysis as a pair of spikes separated only at tip.

The vent is much nearer to the root of the caudal than to the gill-opening: the dorsal fin begins immediately above it and the anal immediately behind it.

Pectoral fin short, about half as long as the eye, its base nearly horizontal.

Scales small, cycloid: those near the dorsal and ventral profiles, and many of the others, have a keel, like the scales of many snakes.

Colours in spirit: brown; head, pectoral region, vent, and edges of caudal peduncle black. Length six inches.

Arabian Sea, in the neighbourhood of the Laccadive banks, 740 fathoms.

Regd. No. 12868.

Distribution: Mid-Atlantic; Arabian Sea.

AULASTOMOMORPHA, Alcock.

Aulastomatomorpha, Alcock, Ann. Mag. Nat. Hist., Oct. 1890, p. 307.

Head naked. Body elongate, covered with minute hardly imbricate scales. Anterior bones of the head produced into a long tube terminating in a narrow mouth. Margin of the upper jaw formed equally by the premaxillæ and maxillæ. Uniserial teeth, in the jaws only. Eye large. Gill-cover apparently complete. Gill-opening wide below, contracted above, where it does not surpass the level of the pectoral fin; four gills with narrow laminæ. Pseudobranchiæ almost rudimentary. Dorsal fin short, quite in the posterior part of the body. Pectorals and ventrals well developed. Anal fin very long. Caudal forked. Pyloric cæca few, small.

142. *Aulastomomorpha phosphorops*, Alcock.

Aulastomatomorpha phosphorops, Alcock, Ann. Mag. Nat. Hist., Oct. 1890, p. 307: ILLUSTRATIONS OF THE ZOOLOGY OF THE INVESTIGATOR, FISHES, PLATE V. FIG. 2.

B. 5? D. 21. A. 41. P. 7. V. 6.

Body elongate and compressed, surrounded from the mid-dorsal line behind the nape to the mid-ventral line behind the vent by a continuous thick succulent fold of the integuments, like, but not so wide as, that of *Platytroctes*; its greatest height, including this fold, is a little more than $\frac{1}{6}$ of the total without the caudal. Head completely covered with a thick, spongy, dazzling white, probably luminous, skin.

Head low and rather depressed, its length $3\frac{1}{6}$ in the total without the caudal; produced anteriorly into a long tubular snout, at the end of which is the small mouth.

The snout is a little less than half the length of the head, or $6\frac{2}{3}$ in the total without the caudal.

The eyes are very large and extremely prominent; the major diameter of the eye-ball is slightly over $\frac{1}{4}$ the head-length, but owing to the encroachment up to the margin of the cornea of the broad posterior orbital fold, the diameter of the exposed "eye" is only a little more than $\frac{1}{5}$ of the same standard; the true (bony) interorbital space is less than half the diameter of the eye in width.

Nostrils situated high up, above the anterior orbital angle. Mouth at the extreme end of the tubular snout, small, the jaws apparently with limited motion. The upper jaw, which projects slightly beyond the lower, is formed in its anterior half by the premaxilla, in its posterior half by the maxilla. Minute, acute, recurved teeth in a single row in the premaxillæ and mandible; no teeth in the maxillæ.

Gill-openings very wide below, contracted above, where they do not surpass the level of the pectorals. Gill-covers apparently complete; their constituent bones, including the branchiostegal rays, though well calcified, are extremely thin and fragile, and are completely concealed within a continuous fold of skin and mucous membrane. Four gills, with narrow laminæ and coarse lamellæ; the fourth gill-cleft wide; gill-rakers well developed on all the arches, moderately long on the first, short on the fourth and fifth. Pseudobranchiæ rudimentary, consisting of four or five delicate short lamellæ on each side.

Body covered with minute, hardly imbricate, cycloid scales, about $\frac{1}{40}$ by $\frac{1}{30}$ of an inch respectively in the shortest and longest diameters. The lateral line traverses the middle of the body uninterruptedly.

The dorsal fin begins slightly in advance of the posterior fourth of the body measured without the caudal; the length of its base is shorter than the snout; its rays, like those of the anal, increase gradually in length from before backwards, the longest being not quite equal to the major diameter of the eye-ball. The anal begins an eye-length behind the middle of the body as above limited, and ends a short distance behind the last dorsal ray; its longest rays slightly exceed the longest dorsal rays. Caudal symmetrically forked, its rudimentary rays very numerous, both dorsally and ventrally. Pectorals narrow, rather more than $\frac{1}{3}$ of the head in length. Ventrals short, arising immediately behind the middle of the body, as above limited, and reaching just behind the vent.

Stomach subsiphonal; intestine long, coiled in a spiral; four small pyloric cæca, arranged in a ring. Reproductive glands very large, apparently discharging in the male through a well-developed post-anal papilla.

Colours in the fresh state:—head snow-white, iris black, body chocolate, fins blackish grey; mouth, gill-chamber and entire peritoneum intense black.

One specimen, apparently a male near maturity, measuring 11 inches in length.

Arabian Sea, near the Laccadives, 1000 fathoms.

Regd. No. 12872.

XENODERMICHTHYS, Günther.

Xenodermichthys, Günther, Ann. Mag. Nat. Hist., 1878, II., p. 250, and Challenger Deep-Sea Fishes, p. 230: Goode and Bean, Oceanic Ichthyology, p. 46.

Body low, rather elongate, compressed, without true scales, but with numerous tiny more or less regularly arranged nodules which are probably luminous in function, and often also with scattered rudimentary scales. Mouth small, or moderate, with feeble jaws and small teeth in the premaxilla, maxilla, and mandible. Palate toothless.

Gill-opening wide. Pseudobranchiæ present. Gill-rakers long and numerous.

Dorsal and anal fins equal and opposite, of moderate length, placed far back in the posterior half of the body. Caudal forked. Pectorals and ventrals well developed, but rather small.

Pyloric cæca present.

Distribution: European and African side of the Atlantic; Arabian Sea, Bay of Bengal, Andaman Sea; Japanese Seas.

Key to the Indian species of Xenodermichthys.

I. The lateral line is indistinct ... ... *X. Güntheri.*
II. The lateral line is a salient tube supported by regularly arranged subcutaneous scales ... ... *X. squamilaterus.*

143. *Xenodermichthys Güntheri,* Alcock.

Xenodermichthys Güntheri, Alcock, Ann. Mag. Nat. Hist., Nov. 1892, p. 359, pl. xviii. fig. 3: ILLUSTRATIONS OF THE ZOOLOGY OF THE INVESTIGATOR, FISHES, PL. XXXII. FIG. 2.

B. 6. D. 15. A. 14. V. 6. P. 5?

Body elongate, compressed, covered with a thick, scaleless, longitudinally-wrinkled, black skin, in which scattered granular yellowish-coloured nodules are imbedded. The dorsal and anal profiles are symmetrically similar in life. The length of the head is slightly over two-sevenths, and the height of the body immediately behind the gill-opening about one-sixth of the total without the caudal.

The obtuse snout, surmounted by an acutely-pointed tubercle which projects from the prominent symphysis of the lower jaw, is not quite equal in length to the diameter of the circular eye. The eyes, which in life encroach upon the dorsal profile, are about two-sevenths of the length of the head, and are about two-thirds of a diameter apart.

The mouth-cleft is oblique, and the jaws are even in front, except for the symphysial tubercle on the mandible. The premaxillæ, which form on each side nearly one half the extent of the margin of the upper jaw, are armed with a row of minute close-set teeth, as are also the maxillæ (which have the typical Alepocephaloid structure and reach to the vertical through the posterior border of the orbit) and the broad boat-shaped mandible; no teeth on the palatines or vomer.

The gill-cleft is extremely wide, extending forwards almost to the mandibular symphysis and upwards almost to the post-temporal region; the opercle appears to be perfect, and, together with the branchiostegal rays, is enveloped in a thick membranous skin, as in *Alepocephalus*; four gills, with numerous long close-set gill-rakers on the first arch; pseudobranchiæ present.

No lateral line can be distinguished in life.

The dorsal and anal fins, which are equal, opposite, and similar, lie in the posterior third of the body, and approach within an eye-length of the long series of rudimentary rays that form the base of the deep-forked caudal. The ventrals lie well within the posterior half of the body, and the pectorals arise on the ventral profile, almost in the same horizontal line with the ventrals.

The stomach is siphonal and its pyloric end is embraced by a row of seven or eight cæcal appendages, the posterior six of which are relatively enormous; the intestine has an anterior much-coiled portion and a hinder portion which passes perfectly straight backwards, much as in *Alepocephalus bicolor* and *A. Blanfordii*, to its orifice just in advance of the posterior third of the body.

Colour uniform jet-black.

A mature female is nearly 6 inches long.

Bay of Bengal, off Madras coast, 678 fathoms; Arabian Sea, off Travancore coast, 430 fathoms.

Regd. Nos. 13193, $\frac{311}{1}$, $\frac{312}{1}$.

This species chiefly differs from *X. socialis* Vaillant, with specimens of which I have compared it, in having a longer and sharper snout, and much fewer dorsal and anal fin-rays.

I have described the ova of this fish in the *Annals and Magazine of Natural History* for November 1892. The largest ova are between 2 and 3 millim. in diameter.

144. *Xenodermichthys squamilaterus*, Alcock.

Xenodermichthys squamilaterus, Alcock, Ann. Mag. Nat. Hist., Aug. 1898, p. 148: ILLUSTRATIONS OF THE ZOOLOGY OF THE INVESTIGATOR, FISHES, PL. XXV. FIG. 4.

B. 6. D. 20. A. 18. P. 6. V. 6.

Distinguished from *X. Güntheri*, which it very closely resembles, by the following characters:—

1. The lateral line is a salient tube which runs straight down the middle of the body and is stiffened by thin subcutaneous equidistant scales: between every two scales there is a pore.

2. The snout is shorter and blunter, and the eye is rather smaller, its diameter being one-fourth the length of the head.

Length 6 inches.

Colour: uniform jet black.

Andaman Sea, 370 to 419 fathoms.

Regd. No. $\frac{375}{1}$.

This species is distinguished from *X. socialis* by the prominent scaly lateral line and by the much fewer rays in the dorsal and anal fins.

LEPTODERMA, Vaillant.

Leptoderma, Vaillant, Exp. Sci. Travailleur et Talisman, Poiss. p. 165: Goode and Bean, Oceanic Ichthyology, p. 48.

Body low, very elongate, tail tapering almost to a filament; skin naked. Head moderate, with enormous eyes. Cleft of the mouth small, the edge of the upper jaw formed nearly equally by the premaxilla and maxilla. A series of small teeth in both jaws, none on the palate.

Gill-opening wide but not reaching much above the level of the pectorals, the upper arc of the gill-arches also truncated. Numerous close-set lanceolate gill-rakers. Pseudobranchiæ present, small.

Dorsal and anal very long, ending near the caudal, the anal the longer. Caudal very small, forked. Pectorals and ventrals well developed.

Distribution: Atlantic coast of Morocco; Bay of Bengal.

145. *Leptoderma affinis*, n. sp.

Leptoderma macrops, Alcock, Ann. Mag. Nat. Hist. (6) X. 1892, p. 361, (*nec* Vaillant?): ILLUSTRATIONS OF THE ZOOLOGY OF THE INVESTIGATOR, FISHES, PL. XXXII, FIG. 3.

D. *circ.* 66. A. *circ.* 85. V. 5.

Greatest height of the body, at the shoulder, about half the length of the head, which is about two-ninths of the total.

Eye-ball considerably more than a third the length of the head and nearly twice as long as the snout.

The snout is squarish; the mouth is terminal, much as in *Aulastomomorpha*, the maxilla being vertical when the mouth is opened in a perfectly natural manner. The maxilla is very broad and consists of three pieces. The rami of the mandible are also of great breadth, except anteriorly where there is a series of small teeth. A series of small teeth on the premaxilla; none on the maxilla or palate.

The anal begins an eye-length nearer to the snout than to the base of the caudal fin; the dorsal begins about half a head-length behind the first anal ray: both fins extend nearly to the caudal. The distance of the ventrals from the gill-opening is equal to the length of the head without the snout.

The skin is naked and intensely black. In life it is uniformly covered with a thick velvety opalescent epidermis which is probably luminous in function. The lateral line, which consists of a row of pores, extends from the occiput to the caudal.

In spirit the colour is purple, the contracted opaline epidermis forming a sort of "bloom."

Length $8\frac{3}{4}$ inches.

Bay of Bengal, off Kistna coast, 753 fathoms.

Regd. No. 13197.

This species seems to differ from *Leptoderma macrops*, Vaillant, in having the body less elongate, the lateral line very distinct, and the rays of the dorsal and anal fins more numerous. It agrees fairly well with the figure but not with the description of that species, and is probably identical with it.

Family ***Halosauridæ.***

Body elongate, tapering, covered with cycloid scales: head either scaly or almost naked. Margin of the upper jaw formed by the premaxillæ mesially and the maxillæ laterally. Opercles incomplete. The short dorsal belongs to the abdominal portion of the backbone. No adipose dorsal. Anal exceedingly long. Stomach with a cæcal sack. Pyloric appendages in moderate number. Gill-openings wide. No pseudobranchiæ. Air-bladder large, simple.

Halosaurus, Johnson.

Halosaurus, Johnson, Proc. Zool. Soc. 1863, p. 406: Günther, Cat. Fishes, VII. p. 482, and Challenger Deep-Sea Fishes, p. 232.

Halosaurichthys, Alcock, Ann. Mag. Nat. Hist., Dec. 1889, p. 454.

Halosaurus, *Aldrovandia* and *Halosaurichthys*, Goode and Bean, Oceanic Ichthyology, pp. 129, 132, 136.

Halosaurus and *Aldrovandia*, Jordan and Evermann, Fishes of N. Amer., pp. 607, 608.

Body elongate, compressed; terminating in an exceedingly long, tapering, lash-like tail; abdomen rounded. Snout much projecting beyond the mouth, which is inferior and of moderate width. Facial bones with large muciferous channels; a series of luminous organs generally developed in connexion with the mucous canal system.

Suboperculum large, preoperculum rudimentary, interoperculum membranous. Gill-openings wide, gill-membranes entirely separate. Branchiostegals numerous. No pseudobranchiæ.

Eye large or moderate. Villiform teeth in compact bands in the jaws, rudimentary palatines, and pterygoids: none on the vomer. A band of hyoid teeth. Dorsal fin short, above the space between the ventrals and the vent. Anal fin exceedingly long, occupying the entire length of the tail. No caudal fin.

Lateral line running near the ventral profile, composed of scales which are usually enlarged and bear the luminous organs.

Distribution: N. & S. Atlantic, Indian, and Pacific Oceans.

Key to the Indian species of Halosaurus.

I. Ventral fins not united together :—
  1. Head naked, except for a few scales on the temples and upper part of the cheeks :—
    i. Scales on the temples only : nearly half the snout is pre-oral ... *H. anguilliformis.*
    ii. Scales on the temples and cheeks : not quite a third of the snout is pre-oral ... ... *H. mediorostris.*
  2. Head and snout scaly : half the snout is pre-oral ... ... *H. parvipinnis.*

II. Ventral fins united together by membrane [Halosaurichthys] :—
  1. Head naked, except for a few scales on the temples and cheeks ; about a third of the snout is pre-oral ... ... *H. nigerrimus.*
  2. Head scaly : not quite two-fifths of the snout is pre-oral ... *H. carinicauda.*

146. ***Halosaurus anguilliformis,*** Alcock.

Halosaurus anguilliformis, Alcock, Ann. Mag. Nat. Hist. Dec., 1889, p. 453.

Halosaurus Hoskynii, Alcock, Ann. Mag. Nat. Hist., Oct. 1890, p. 300 : ILLUSTRATIONS OF THE ZOOLOGY OF THE INVESTIGATOR, FISHES, PL. VII. FIG. 3.

B. 10. D. 11-12. A. *circ.* 175. P. 13. V. 1/8. L. tr. 13-14, between D. and V.

Head naked except for a few scales on the temples, its length about $\frac{1}{8}$ of the total, and exceeding the distance between the gill-opening and the base of the ventral fin by about an eye-length.

Length of the snout $2\frac{1}{2}$ to $2\frac{1}{4}$ in that of the head, the pre-oral portion being not quite a half of the whole.

The major diameter of the eye nearly equals the width of the interorbital space, and is contained six and a half times in the head-length and just over 3 times in the length of the postorbital portion of the head.

The maxilla does not quite reach the vertical through the anterior margin of the orbit.

The pterygoid band of teeth is very broad and is separated from the palatine band by a considerable interval.

Eight moderately long gill-rakers on the middle of the first arch, besides some small ones above and below.

Scales extremely deciduous, those on the lateral line larger and more adherent than the rest, measuring $\frac{1}{4}$ of an inch in diameter and having a small central perforation. The scales of the lateral line are thirty in number between the gill-opening and the vent, beyond which they are in contact with the rays of the anal fin.

The pectorals are slightly larger than the post-rostral portion of the head.

The dorsal fin begins about an eye-length behind the insertion of the first (outermost) ventral ray.

Seven or eight large pyloric cæca in a longitudinal row embracing the ascending limb of the stomach.

Colours in the fresh state:—body and fins uniformly dark sepia-brown, opercles silvery, throat black.

Four specimens, the largest 21 inches long.

Arabian Sea, off the Laccadive Islands, 1000 fathoms; Gulf of Manár, 675 fathoms.

Regd. Nos. 11541, 12874, 12875, 12876, 12877.

This species may possibly prove to be identical with *H. affinis*, Günther, from Japanese Seas.

147. *Halosaurus mediorostris*, Gthr.

Halosaurus mediorostris, Günther, Challenger Deep-Sea Fishes, p. 239, pl. lix. fig. C: Alcock, Journ. As. Soc. Bengal, Vol. LXIII pt. 2, 1894, p. 136.

B. 11. D. 11. P. 8. V. 1/8.

Head with some scales on the temples and upper part of cheeks; otherwise naked.

Length of the snout about $2\frac{1}{3}$ in that of the head; not quite a third its extent is pre-oral.

Eye small, its diameter is less than a fourth the length of the postorbital portion of the head and about two-thirds the width of the interorbital space.

The maxilla reaches to, or slightly beyond, the anterior border of the eye.

Pterygoid teeth separated from the palatine teeth by a considerable interval.

Numerous, close-set, longish gill-rakers on the outer side of the first branchial arch.

Scales deciduous, those of the lateral line enlarged.

The dorsal fin begins about an eye-length behind the outermost ventral ray.

The pectorals, which are extremely slender, are not quite equal in length to the postrostral portion of the head.

Colour light brown, greater part of head blackish.

Arabian Sea, between the Maldives and Cape Comorin, 719 fathoms.

Regd. No. 13710.

Distribution: off Philippines; Arabian Sea.

24

This species is distinguished from *H. anguilliformis* by the short pre-oral portion of the snout and the numerous close-set gill-rakers on the outer side of the first branchial arch.

148. ***Halosaurus parvipennis***, Alcock.

Halosaurus parvipennis, Alcock, Ann. Mag. Nat. Hist., Nov. 1892, p. 362; ILLUSTRATIONS OF THE ZOOLOGY OF THE INVESTIGATOR, FISHES, PL. XXXIII. FIG. 1.

B. 12-13. D. 9-10. P. 12-13. V. 1/9. L. tr. 14-15.

Head and snout scaly.

Length of head about an eighth of the total, and less than the distance between the gill-opening and the base of the ventral fin.

Length of the snout a little over a third that of the head, half its extent is preoral.

The major diameter of the eye is much more than twice the width of the interorbital space, is from a fifth to two-elevenths the length of the head, and nearly half the length of the postorbital portion of the head.

The maxilla does not quite reach the vertical through the anterior margin of the orbit.

The pterygoid band of teeth is short and narrow and is hardly separated from the palatine band.

The gill-rakers on the outer side of the first branchial arch are short and distant.

Scales adherent, especially on the lateral line. Those of the lateral line are but slightly enlarged, especially at the anterior end of the line, and number between 50 and 60 from the gill-opening to the vent, beyond which they are separated from the anal fin, at first by two, and then by one series of scales. An irregular series of scales in the middle line behind the dorsal fin are considerably enlarged and elongated.

The dorsal fin begins about an eye-length behind the insertion of the outermost ventral ray. The very narrow pectorals are about as long as the postorbital portion of the head.

About eight extremely short and inconspicuous pyloric cæca.

Colours: sepia-brown, opercles silvery: throat, etc., black.

The largest specimen (adult) is about $15\frac{1}{2}$ inches.

Arabian Sea, off Malabar coast, 459, 636, and 865 to 880 fathoms.

Regd. Nos. 13198, 14005, $\frac{169}{1}$, $\frac{173}{1}$.

149. *Halosaurus carinicauda*, Alcock.

Halosaurichthys carinicauda, Alcock, Ann. Mag. Nat. Hist., Dec. 1889, p. 454: ILLUSTRATIONS OF THE ZOOLOGY OF THE INVESTIGATOR, FISHES, PL. VII. FIGS. 2, 2a.

B. 12-13. D. 11. P. 14-15. V. 1/9. L. tr. 15-16 between D. and V.

Head and snout scaly.

Length of the head about a seventh of the total and considerably less than the distance between the gill-opening and the base of the ventral fin.

Length of snout a little over a third that of the head, not quite two-fifths of its extent is preoral.

Major diameter of the eye not twice the width of the interorbital space, about a seventh the length of the head and a little more than a fourth the length of the postorbital portion.

Maxilla not reaching the anterior margin of the orbit.

Pterygoid band of teeth narrow, scarcely separated from the palatine band.

Seven or eight distant, short gill-rakers—in addition to some smaller ones—on the outer side of the first branchial arch.

Scales deciduous, except on the lateral line where they are but little enlarged. Those of the lateral line number about 60 between the gill-opening and the vent, beyond which they are separated from the anal fin, at first by two and then by one series of scales. Some scales in the middle line behind the dorsal fin are enlarged and elongated, and in the posterior part of the tail these are set in a low median fold of skin.

The dorsal fin begins about an eye-length behind the outermost ventral ray. The pectorals are not quite equal in length to the post-rostral portion of the head.

The ventrals are coherent into a single plate, the union being membranous.

Five or six extremely small and inconspicuous pyloric cæca.

Colours: sepia-brown, the greater part of the head blackish.

Length $15\frac{1}{2}$ inches.

Andaman Sea, 490 fathoms.

Regd. No. 11763.

This species is very closely related to *Halosaurus parvipennis*, from which it differs chiefly in having the ventral fins united with one another, the preoral part of the snout much shorter, and the eyes smaller and farther apart.

150. ***Halosaurus nigerrimus,*** Alcock.

Halosaurus nigerrimus, Alcock, Ann. Mag. Nat. Hist., Aug. 1898, p. 149: ILLUSTRATIONS OF THE ZOOLOGY OF THE INVESTIGATOR, PL. XXXIII. FIG. 2.

B. 12. D. *circ.* 12. P. *circ.* 9. V. 8.

Temples and cheeks scaly; head otherwise naked. Length of the head about a seventh of the total and nearly equal to the distance between the gill-opening and the base of the ventral fin. Length of the snout about $2\frac{1}{3}$ in that of the head; about a third of its extent is preoral. Eyes about two-thirds of a diameter apart.

The maxilla reaches to the anterior edge of the pupil.

Teeth as in *H. carinicauda*.

Numerous long close-set gill-rakers on the outer side of the first branchial arch.

Scales deciduous: those of the lateral line adherent and much enlarged and about 30(?) in number between the gill-opening and the vent. There is a low median fold of skin, with some enlarged scales, behind the dorsal fin, as in *H. carinicauda*.

Fins as in *H. carinicauda*, but the ventrals are united with one another only in their basal portion.

Colour: everywhere uniform jet black.

One young specimen about $7\frac{1}{2}$ inches long, from off the Maldives, 459 fathoms.

Regd. No. $\frac{165}{1}$.

Family ***Muraenidae.***

To the ten genera and thirty-nine species recorded in the *Fauna of British India*, the "Investigator" has added other ten genera and seventeen species.

Key to the Indian Deep Sea *genera of* Muraenidae.

The branchial openings into the pharynx are wide slits: the heart is situated between or close behind the gills:—

1. Vent close to the gill-opening: nostrils close together in a hollow in front of the eye: jaws produced to form a long slender beak: NEMICHTHYINA:—
    - i. Pectorals present, the vent being between their roots ... NEMICHTHYS.
    - ii. Pectorals absent: vent about a snout length behind the gill-opening ... ... GAVIALICEPS.
2. Vent at no great distance from the gill-opening: nostrils distant from one another, lateral: snout not beak-like: eyes small: DYSOMMINA:—
    - i. Pectorals present, the vent being between their roots ... DYSOMMA.

ii. Pectorals absent: vent nearly three-quarters of a head-length behind the gill-openings ... ... DYSOMMOPSIS.

3. The distance of the vent from the gill-opening is either equal to or very much more than the distance between the gill-opening and the tip of the snout: the nostrils are distant from one another:—

i. Gill-openings united in a longitudinal slit: SYNAPHOBRANCHINA ... ... SYNAPHOBRANCHUS.

ii. Gill-openings separate:—

a. Nostrils superior or lateral: tongue free: vertical fins confluent round the tip of the tail: pectoral fins present: ANGUILLINA:—

α. Scaleless: the cleft of the mouth extends slightly beyond the middle of the eye:—

Teeth in a single series in the jaws; none on the vomer COLOCONGER.

Teeth in bands in the jaws; vomerine teeth ... CONGROMURÆNA.

Teeth in the jaws biserial; vomerine teeth ... UROCONGER.

β. Scaleless: the cleft of the mouth reaches the eye: teeth in the jaws in broad bands, and in a broad confluent patch on the palate ... ... PROMYLLANTOR.

b. Nostrils superior or lateral: tongue *not* free, or if free curiously truncated: vertical fins confluent round the tip of the tail: no scales: MURÆNESOCINA:—

α. Pectorals present: snout of good length but not bill-like: teeth in the mandible and maxilla practically uniserial; a single row of teeth in the vomer ... ... SAUROMURÆNESOX.

β. Pectorals present: snout very long almost bill-like: teeth in the jaws in broad bands and very sharp: a single row of teeth in the vomer. Maxilla with a broad longitudinal groove, running the whole length of the bone and dividing the band of teeth into two portions ... XENOMYSTAX.

γ. Pectorals absent: snout very long and bill-like: teeth in the jaws in two or three series, small and sharp: a long row of enlarged teeth on the vomer: *no air-bladder* SAURENCHELYS.

δ. Pectorals absent: snout very long and bill-like: small stout conical teeth in very broad bands in the jaws and vomer: air-bladder present: *lateral line indistinct* ... NETTENCHELYS.

NEMICHTHYINA, Günther.

NEMICHTHYS, Richardson.

Nemichthys, Richardson, Samarang Fishes, p. 25: Günther, Cat. Fishes, VIII. p. 21: Goode and Bean, Oceanic Ichthyology, p. 151: Jordan and Evermann, Fishes of N. Amer., p. 369.

Leptorhynchus, Lowe, Ann. Mag. Nat. Hist. X. 1852, p. 54.

Belonopsis, Brandt. Mem. Ac. Petersb. Sav. étrang. VII. 1854, p. 171.

Investigator, Goode and Bean, Oceanic Ichthyology, p. 518.

Body exceeding elongate, tail lash-like. No scales. Lateral line distinct. Vent near the gill-opening and pectorals, at the anterior end of the long abdominal cavity.

Jaws produced to form a long slender bill, of which the upper part is formed by the vomer and premaxillæ. The inner surface of the bill covered with small close-set teeth. Similar teeth on the mandible. Eye large. The nostrils of each side are close together, in a hollow before the eye. Gill-openings wide, nearly confluent. Pectoral and vertical fins well-developed. The dorsal fin begins close behind the head.

Distribution : Atlantic; Indian Ocean; Pacific.

151. *Nemichthys acanthonotus*, Alcock.

Nemichthys acanthonotus, Alcock, Journ. As. Soc. Bengal, Vol. LXIII, pt. 2, 1894, p. 136: Illustrations of the Zoology of the Investigator, Fishes, pl. XIV. fig. 5.
Investigator acanthonotus, Goode and Bean, Oceanic Ichthyology, p. 518.

The posterior third or more of the long slender body is very abruptly constricted to form a lash-like tail.

The head, rather more than four-sevenths of which is formed by the long tapering snout, is between one-seventh and one-ninth of the total. The diameter of the subcutaneous eye is between one-third and one-fourth the length of the post-orbital portion of the head, and between one-sixth and one-seventh the length of the snout. The nostrils have the usual position, and the jaws are curved at tip as in *N. infans.* Small recurved asperities in crowded bands form the dentition of the jaws and vomer.

The vent is situated immediately behind the gill-opening and the root of the pectoral fin.

The gill-openings, which are wide, are separated from one another only by a thin fold of skin.

No scales. The lateral line is marked by a series of small glistening pores which are arranged with beautiful regularity in "fives" (quincunces). The head is studded with similar pores.

The dorsal fin commences on the occiput, and is continued to the tip of the tail: in a part of its extent, somewhat less than the middle third, the long slender rays are replaced by strong short spines—like those of *Notacanthus*—interconnected by a low membrane. The anal fin, which commences immediately behind the vent, has its rays well-developed throughout,—the longest rays being considerably more than half the length of the post-rostral portion of the head.

The pectorals are large, and are half as long as the post-orbital portion of the head.

Colours: uniform dark sepia becoming black ventrally: gill-covers and fins black.

The largest specimen is over 30 inches long.

Bay of Bengal, 475 fathoms; Arabian Sea, 636 fathoms.

Regd. Nos. 13643, 14003.

This species is distinguished from all its congeners by the long series of strong sharp spines in the middle of the dorsal fin. On this account Messrs. Goode and Bean (Oceanic Ichthyology, p. 518) separated it from the genus *Nemichthys* and gave it the generic name *Investigator*, a course in which I am unable to follow them.

Gavialiceps, Wood-Mason MS., Alcock.

Gavialiceps, Alcock, Ann. Mag. Nat. Hist., Dec. 1889, p. 460, and Nov. 1892, p. 364.

Body exceedingly elongate, tail tapering. No scales. Lateral line indistinct. Vent about a snout-length behind the gill-opening, near the anterior end of the long abdominal cavity.

Jaws produced to form a long slender bill, of which the upper part is formed by the premaxillæ and vomer. Sharp teeth on the vomer, premaxillæ, and mandibles.

Eye small. Nostrils as in *Nemichthys*. Gill-openings wide, nearly confluent. Pectorals absent. Anal well developed. Dorsal ill-developed and beginning a considerable distance behind the head.

Gavialiceps differs from *Nemichthys* in having (1) no pectoral fins, (2) the dorsal fin ill developed and beginning some way behind the head, (3) the eye small, (4) the vent not quite so near the throat, and (5) the lateral line indistinct.

152. *Gavialiceps microps*, Alcock.

Gavialiceps microps, Alcock, Ann. Mag. Nat. Hist., Dec. 1889, p. 461 and Nov. 1892, p. 364.

The head, of which rather more than two-fifths is formed by the long tapering snout is between a fifth and a sixth of the total length. The diameter of the small subcutaneous eye is about one-eleventh the length of the post-orbital portion of the head (measured to the gill-opening) and about a ninth the length of the snout.

The premaxillary teeth are arranged in a single row, and diminish in size but increase in number from behind forwards, where they end in a narrow band of minute asperities: the vomerine teeth posteriorly are long and sharp and are disposed in a long, close-set, comb-like series; anteriorly they form a fine rasp-like band of minute asperities: in the mandible a row of large distant needle-like teeth stands up from an uneven band of small denticles. Gill-openings close together, wide. The scaleless integument is thin and deciduous and thickly enveloped in mucus; no lateral line is apparent. The dorsal fin is feebly developed, and, indeed, hardly distinguishable, except in the posterior part of the body: it begins about a head-length behind the head. The pectoral fin is represented by an inconspicuous knob, without any rays.

The abdominal cavity extends at least halfway along the tail. The siphonal stomach, which has its pyloric end long, tapering, and much constricted, leads into a widely expanded duodenum, which, in the single specimen dissected, is furnished with a small diverticulum near the pylorus. The vent is about a snout length behind the gill-opening.

Colour uniform black, with a silvery sheen on the head.

The largest specimen is about $14\frac{1}{2}$ inches long.

Bay of Bengal, off the Andamans and Nicobars, 1045 and 869 to 913 fathoms; Arabian Sea, off the Laccadives, 1045 fathoms; Gulf of Manár 902 fathoms.

Regd. Nos. 11662, 13201, $\frac{775}{1}$.

This species is perhaps identical with *Nemichthys infans* Vaillant (*nec* Günther), described and figured in Expéd. Sci. du 'Travailleur' et du 'Talisman,' Poiss. pp. 93 and 94, pl. vii. fig. 1, and there only doubtfully referred to Dr. Günther's type.

Dysommina.

Dysomma, Alcock.

Dysomma, Alcock, Ann. Mag. Nat. Hist., Dec. 1889, p. 459.

The branchial openings into the pharynx are wide slits. The heart is situated between the gills. The tail is exceedingly long, the vent being situated immediately behind the gill-opening and between the bases of the pectoral fins.

Tail tapering. Snout short but projecting beyond the mouth and lower jaw. Eyes very small, subcutaneous. Nostrils large, lateral, those on the same side distant from each other. Cleft of the mouth wide. Small sharp teeth in a single row or extremely narrow band in each jaw: a short row of large teeth on the vomer. Tongue not free.

Gill-openings rather small, well separated. No scales. Lateral line of minute pores. Pectorals and vertical fins well developed, the dorsal beginning immediately behind the gill-opening, the anal immediately behind the vent.

153. ***Dysomma bucephalus***, Alcock.

Dysomma bucephalus, Alcock, Ann. Mag. Nat. Hist., Dec. 1889, p. 459: Illustrations of the Zoology of the Investigator, Fishes, pl. VI. fig. 1: Ann. Mag. Nat. Hist., Aug. 1891, p. 137, fig. 5.

Length of the head, measured to the gill-opening, between a fourth and a fifth of the total. Vent situated with the abdominal pore on a large round fleshy "clitellum," immediately behind the gill-opening.

Snout short, between a fifth and a sixth of the length of the head measured to the gill-opening, round-pointed, somewhat depressed, studded, like the head and cheeks, with minute pores.

Eyes very small, their diameter about a fifth the length of the snout, deeply sunk beneath the skin. Nostrils large, the anterior tubular, the posterior simple.

Mouth-cleft wide, rather more than a third the length of the head; lips inflated, with many small pores; jaws weak. A row or very narrow band of minute teeth in the upper jaw; a row of small teeth in the lower jaw; a short row of large teeth at the fore end of the vomer.

Gill-covers formed of tough skin, in which neither bony opercles nor branchiostegal rays can be detected. Branchial arches very weak: gill-laminæ broad.

No scales: the lateral line, which consists of a row of small pores, follows the dorsal curve.

Vertical fins fairly well developed. Pectorals rather longer than the snout, rounded or truncated.

Colour brown, paler beneath; vertical fins darker, edged with white.

The body-cavity extends more than halfway along the tail, and the intestinal loop follows it. Air-bladder thick-walled, nacreous, consisting of three lobes—a large middle one with a small one on each side.

An adult female is 11 inches long.

Bay of Bengal, 112, 128, 193, 145 to 250, and 240 fathoms.

Regd. Nos. 11675, 13108, 13436, 13644–13646.

DYSOMMOPSIS, Alcock.

Dysommopsis, Alcock, Ann. Mag. Nat. Hist., Aug. 1891, p. 137.

Closely related to *Dysomma*, from which it differs, much as *Gavialiceps* differs from *Nemichthys*, in the following particulars:—

The vent is situated nearly three-quarters of a head-length behind the gill-opening, and there are no pectoral fins: the dorsal fin begins some way behind the gill-opening.

154. *Dysommopsis mucipara*, Alcock.

Dysommopsis muciparus, Alcock, Ann. Mag. Nat. Hist., Aug. 1891, p. 137.

Head a little inflated in the branchial region, tapering anteriorly; its length a little more than one-eighth of the total. The vent lies with the genital pore in an unpigmented circular depression, which is situated at a distance from the gill-opening equal to the length of the post-rostral portion of the head; the tail, which tapers very slightly, is therefore more than four times the combined head and trunk in length.

Snout acutely pointed, overhanging the upper jaw; its length is one-fifth that of the head and $2\frac{1}{2}$ times that of the small deeply subcutaneous eye; its surface is densely crowded, like the lips, with minute pores. Nostrils large; the anterior, which is tubular, is situated near the tip of the snout, the posterior is a valved foramen lying immediately before the angle of the eye.

Mouth wide, its cleft being nearly half the head in length; small sharp teeth in a single row in the mandible and a double row in the maxilla; vomer with a row of three large teeth. The mandibular teeth are small and close-set posteriorly, larger and more distinct anteriorly.

Gill-openings small, close together near the mid-abdominal line; the gill-covers are formed of tough skin, in which branchiostegal rays are faintly apparent; branchial arches weak, gill-laminæ broad.

Skin scaleless, enveloped in thick, very tenacious mucus. Lateral line a row of indistinct pores. Vertical fins confluent, the dorsal beginning halfway between the gill-opening and the vent, the anal immediately behind the vent. No pectoral fins.

The abdominal cavity extends almost to the tip of the tail, its posterior part being occupied solely by the genital glands and air-bladder.

Stomach with a long tapering cæcal sac reaching some distance behind the vent, intestine forming a single loop, the convexity of which embraces the gastric cæcum. Air-bladder a long nacreous tube extending from the occiput almost to the tip of the tail; much inflated anteriorly, and tapering posteriorly to a fine thread.

Colours in life deep purple-black.

Bay of Bengal, 240 to 270 fathoms.

Regd. Nos. 13106, 13107.

SYNAPHOBRANCHINA, Gthr.

SYNAPHOBRANCHUS, Johnson.

Synaphobranchus, Johnson, Proc. Zool. Soc., 1862: Günther, Cat. Fishes, VIII., p. 22, and Challenger Deep-Sea Fishes, p. 253: Goode and Bean, Oceanic Ichthyology, p. 142: Jordan and Evermann, Fishes N. Amer., p. 351.

Gill-openings ventral, united into a longitudinal slit between the pectoral fins, separate internally. Pectoral and vertical fins well developed. Nostrils lateral, the anterior subtubular. Cleft of the mouth very wide; teeth small. Body scaly.

Distribution: Atlantic, Arabian Sea, Western Pacific.

155. ***Synaphobranchus pinnatus,*** (Gronov.) Gthr.

Synaphobranchus pinnatus, Günther, Cat. Fishes, VIII., p. 23, and Challenger Deep-Sea Fishes, p. 253, pl. lxii., fig. A. (*ubi synon.*): Vaillant, Exp. Sci. Travailleur et Talisman, Poiss. p. 88, pl. vi., fig. 2: Goode and Bean, Oceanic Ichthyology, p. 143, fig. 164: Jordan and Evermann, Fishes N. Amer., p. 351.

Length of the head not quite a seventh of the total, and equal to the distance between the gill-opening and the vent; length of the tail, therefore, considerably over twice that of the rest of the body.

Length of the snout about a third that of the head and rather over twice that of the eye.

Mouth-cleft rather over half the length of the head. Teeth in the jaws in a narrow band with some enlarged ones anteriorly: a single short row of largish teeth on the premaxillary, and a single row of small teeth on the vomer.

Scales rudimentary, forming a diagonal pattern. Lateral line distinct. Cheeks and occiput scaly.

The dorsal fin arises about a head-length and a third behind the gill-opening, and therefore a short distance behind the anal: both fins are low. Pectorals half as long as the head.

Colour purple-black or brown.

Arabian Sea, 459 and 824 fathoms. Registered No. $\frac{171}{1}$: $\frac{318}{1}$.

In the Indian Museum are one of the "Challenger" duplicates, and a specimen from America.

Anguillina, Gthr.

Coloconger, Alcock.

Coloconger, Alcock, Ann. Mag. Nat. Hist., Dec. 1889, p. 456.

The branchial openings into the pharynx are wide slits. The heart is situated between the gills. *The tail is a good deal shorter than the combined head and trunk.* The gill-openings are separate. The muscular and osseous systems are well developed. The posterior nostril is superior. The tongue is free. The end of the tail is surrounded by the fin. Pectoral fins are present. No scales.

Snout short. Eyes large. Cleft of the mouth wide, extending beyond the middle of the eye. The teeth form a sharply prominent serrated ridge in each jaw: *there are none on the vomer.* The vertical fins are well developed, the dorsal beginning above the base of the pectoral.

156. *Coloconger raniceps*, Alcock.

Coloconger raniceps, Alcock, Ann. Mag. Nat. Hist., Dec. 1889, p. 456: Illustrations of the Zoology of the Investigator, Fishes, pl. VII. fig. 4.

Head frog-like, its length (measured to the gill-opening) is half, or sometimes a little more than half, the distance between the gill-opening and the vent, and a fifth, or sometimes a little more than a fifth, the total.

Snout blunt, shorter than or as long as the eye. Eye about a fourth the length of the head and equal to the width of the interocular space. Nostrils large, the anterior sub-tubular, the posterior above the angle of the eye.

Mouth cavernous, its cleft extending to the hinder edge of the pupil. Jaws slender, equal. Tongue short, broad, fleshy, free in its anterior third. In each jaw a row of small uniform teeth in continuous contact, except at their extreme tips, which show as minute recurved asperities on a sharp-edged ridge. No vomerine teeth. A large, oval, horny, granular plate in the fauces behind the superior pharyngeal bones. A mucous channel with numerous pores along the lower jaw beneath.

Gill-laminæ narrow; gill-openings of moderate size, a broad fold extends from their outer edge to the base of the pectoral fin.

No scales. Head with numerous black tubular papillæ. Lateral line a salient tube, with upwards of a hundred similar papillæ.

Vertical fins confluent; the dorsal, which begins above the base of the pectoral, is considerably higher than the anal. Pectorals two-fifths of the length of the head, or a little longer.

Colours in spirit: brown; abdomen speckled with black, due to the peritoneal pigment showing through.

Visceral peritoneum black. Stomach with a cæcum half as long as the body-cavity. Intestine sinuous. Only the left lobe of the liver developed. Air-bladder large, globular.

Length $6\frac{1}{2}$ to $10\frac{1}{2}$ inches.

Andaman Sea, 265, 271, and 405 fathoms; Bay of Bengal, 200 to 400 fathoms; Arabian Sea, off Malabar coast, 224 to 284 fathoms.

Regd. Nos. 11637, 11639, 11778, 11779, $\frac{138}{1}$, $\frac{142}{1}$, $\frac{150}{1}$, $\frac{776-780}{1}$.

Congromuræna. Kaup.

One species of this genus is included in the *Fauna of British India;* the "Investigator" has brought five more to light, all being inhabitants of deep-water.

Key to the Indian species of Congromuræna.

I. The length of the head measured to the gill-opening, is less than the distance between the gill-opening and the vent:—
   1. The head is at least three eye-lengths less than the distance between the gill-opening and the vent:—
      i. The band of vomerine teeth is of good length... ... *C. anago.*
      ii. The band of vomerine teeth is extremely short: series of small black dots above and below the lateral line ... *C. guttulata.*
   2. The head is an eye-length shorter than the distance between the gill-opening and the vent ... ... *C. macrocercus.*

II. The length of the head, measured to the gill-opening, is equal to or greater than the distance between the gill-opening and the vent:—
   1. The length of the snout is a fifth that of the head: the dorsal fin begins in advance of the gill-opening ... ... *C. squaliceps.*
   2. The length of the snout is about a fourth that of the head: the dorsal fin begins above the gill-opening:—
      i. Outer teeth in the jaws decidedly enlarged: vomerine teeth in a short very narrow band ... ... *C. nasica.*
      ii. None of the teeth enlarged: vomerine teeth in a very broad band of some length ... ... *C. musteliceps.*

157. *Congromuræna squaliceps,* Alcock.

Congromuræna squaliceps, Alcock, Journ. As. Soc. Bengal, Vol. LXII., pt. 2, 1893, p. 183.
Bathycongrus squaliceps, Ogilby, Proc. Linn. Soc. N. S. Wales, XXIII., 1898, p. 293.

Head, measured to the gill-opening, about an eye-length longer than the distance between the gill-opening and the vent, which is not quite one-fourth the length of the tail.

The snout, which projects far beyond the mouth, is one-fifth the head in length: it is broadish and blunt pointed. The major diameter of the very elliptical eye is not quite two-thirds of the length of the snout. The anterior nostril is a short wide tube situated on the lip near the end of the snout, the posterior is a wide foramen situated in advance of and above the angle of the eye.

The mouth-cleft is wide, extending almost to the vertical through the posterior border of the orbit, and the lips are greatly developed: the minute teeth are in bands in the jaws, and in a broad rasp-like patch outside the mouth in the premaxillary; there are a few teeth on the vomer quite anteriorly.

Gill-openings comparatively wide, separate. No scales: lateral line with small pores. Pectorals narrow, half an eye-length longer than the snout. Vertical fins confluent, the dorsal beginning a little in advance of the gill-opening.

Colour in spirit, grey, the vertical fins in their after half to two-thirds with a black edge, which in the anal tends to involve the whole fin. Pectorals hyaline. A very large air-bladder extending half a head-length beyond the vent. Visceral peritoneum silvery.

The largest specimen is 20 inches long.

Bay of Bengal, 128 and 195 to 210 fathoms.

Regd. Nos. 13693–13695, 13697, 13450.

158. *Congromuræna macrocercus*, Alcock.

Congromuræna longicauda, Alcock, Ann. Mag. Nat. Hist., Dec. 1889, p. 455 (name preocc.): ILLUSTRATIONS OF THE ZOOLOGY OF THE INVESTIGATOR, FISHES, PL. VII. FIG. 5.

Congromuræna macrocercus, Alcock, Journ. As. Soc. Bengal, Vol. LXIII., pt. 2, 1894, p. 134.

Bathycongrus macrocercus, Ogilby, *loc. cit. supra.*

Differs from *C. squaliceps* only in the following particulars :—

The head, measured to the gill-opening, is an eye-length *shorter* than the distance between the gill-opening and the vent, which is not quite a fourth the length of the tail.

The snout, which has the same form and the same relations to the mouth, is a little more than a *fourth* the length of the head.

The eye is very little more than half the length of the snout.

The mouth-cleft reaches to the posterior border of the pupil.

The dorsal fin begins above the gill-opening.

The narrow pectorals are as long as the snout.

Colour brown, the fins grey.

Length 16 inches.

Andaman Sea, 265 fathoms ; Bay of Bengal, 240 to 276 fathoms.

Regd. Nos. 11781, 11782, 13452.

159. *Congromuræna nasica*, Alcock.

Congromuræna nasica, Alcock, Journ. As. Soc. Bengal, Vol. LXII., pt. 2, 1893, p. 183 : ILLUSTRATIONS OF THE ZOOLOGY OF THE INVESTIGATOR, FISHES, PL. IX. FIG. 2.

Bathycongrus nasicus, Ogilby, *loc. cit. supra.*

Differs from *C. squaliceps* only in the following particulars :—

The head, measured to the gill-opening, is very slightly longer than the distance between the gill-opening and the vent, which is considerably more than a fourth (1 : about 3·4) the length of the tail.

The snout is a little over a quarter the length of the head and is rather sharp-pointed.

The eye is not much more than half the length of the snout.

The teeth are in two bands in each jaw, the outer band being enlarged: the vomerine teeth also are enlarged.

The dorsal fin begins over the gill-opening. The pectorals are as long as the snout.

The colour is grey: the vertical fins in their posterior third or fourth have a very narrow black edge.

Length of adult females from 10 to 12 inches.

Bay of Bengal, 128 and 195 to 210 fathoms.

Regd. Nos. 13453–13456, 13649–13692.

160. *Congromuræna musteliceps*, Alcock.

Congromuræna musteliceps, Alcock, Journ. As. Soc. Bengal, Vol. LXIII., pt. 2, 1894, p. 133, pl. vii., fig. 5: ILLUSTRATIONS OF THE ZOOLOGY OF THE INVESTIGATOR, FISHES, PL. XV. FIG. 7.

Bathycongrus musteliceps, Ogilby, *loc. cit. supra.*

Differs from *C. squaliceps* only in the following particulars:—

The snout is sharp-pointed; its length is a quarter that of the head and fully twice that of the eye.

The mouth-cleft reaches to the posterior border of the pupil.

The vomerine teeth are in a broad band of some length.

The dorsal fin begins above the gill-opening.

Colours dark brown, pectorals and vertical fins nearly black.

Length 15 inches.

Bay of Bengal, 145 to 250 fathoms.

Regd. Nos. 13698–13702.

161. *Congromuræna guttulata*, Gthr.

Congromuræna guttulata, Günther, Challenger Deep-Sea Fishes, p. 252.

Congrellus guttulatus, Ogilby, *loc. cit. supra.*

This species, if my identification be correct, differs from *C. squaliceps*, only in the following particulars:—

The head measured to the gill-opening is more than three eye-lengths shorter than the distance between the gill-opening and the vent, which is not quite a third the length of the tail.

The snout, which is blunt-pointed, is a fourth the length of the head.

The diameter of the eye is between half and two-thirds the length of the snout.

The mouth-cleft reaches to the posterior border of the pupil.

The dorsal fin begins behind the root of the pectoral fin.

Colours, yellowish brown, with series of small black dots and splashes above and below the lateral line.

Length nearly two feet.

Off Malabar coast, 636 fathoms.

Regd. No. 14009.

Distribution: Off Fiji Is. 315 fathoms; Arabian Sea.

UROCONGER, Kaup.

162. ***Uroconger vicinus***, Vaillant.

Uroconger vicinus, Vaillant, Exp. Sci. Travailleur et Talisman, Poiss. p. 86, pl. vi., fig. 1: Alcock, Ann. Mag. Nat. Hist., X., 1892, p. 363: Goode and Bean, Oceanic Ichthyology, p. 138.

Length of the head, measured to the gill-opening, not much more than half the distance between the gill-opening and the vent, and between a seventh and an eighth of the total.

Body high for an eel; its greatest height being rather more than half the length of the head.

Muciferous cavities of the head well developed, the pores on the snout and in a line running from the mandibular symphysis towards the gill-opening being very conspicuous.

Snout about twice as long as the eye and between a third and a fourth the length of the head. Anterior nostril subtubular, situated not far from the end of the snout, difficult to distinguish from the mucous pores: posterior nostril situated just above the eye.

The mouth-cleft reaches at least to the middle of the eye. Teeth large, especially on the premaxillæ and at the anterior end of the maxillary and mandible. Vomerine teeth reduced to two large ones—one behind the other—at the anterior end.

Gill-openings of moderate size, separated by an interval greater than their own greatest diameter.

Lateral line very distinct, its pores white.

The dorsal fin begins about a snout-length behind the gill-opening. Pectorals narrow, pointed, nearly as long as the combind eye and snout.

Colours purplish brown.

The ripe female is 25 inches long.

Bay of Bengal, 475 fathoms; Arabian Sea, off Malabar coast, 430 and 636 fathoms.

Distribution: Cape Verde and Atlantic coasts of Morocco; Indian seas.

This species is distinguished from *U. lepturus* Richardson, (1) by the reduced number and larger size of the vomerine teeth, (2) by the widely-separated gill-openings, (3) by the increased distance from the gill-opening of the dorsal fin.

The microscopic structure of the wall of the stomach of Uroconger vicinus.

The stomach has a lining membrane of two different kinds: in the anterior half the mucous membrane is of an almost horny hardness; in the posterior half it is soft and glandular; and the transition between the two is abrupt.

In vertical longitudinal sections of the stomach-wall, carried through the abrupt line of demarcation between the two different regions of mucous membrane, examined under the microscope, the following structure is seen:—

(1) *Common to both regions of the stomach:* (*a*) an external thin fibrous coat, one-fortieth to one-sixth of a millimetre thick, with many longitudinal bundles of muscular fibres and large blood-vessels; (*b*) a very compact thin coat of transverse muscular fibres, about one-eighth of a millimetre thick; (*c*) another very compact layer of longitudinal muscular fibres, about one-seventh of a millimetre thick; (*d*) a very thick ($\frac{3}{4}$–$1\frac{1}{8}$ millimetre) submucous coat made up of a loose mesh-work of branching and anastomosing small-nucleated cells, the meshes being filled with lymphoid cells; this coat also contains many blood-vessels, which frequently traverse in their course large, compact, sharply-circumscribed nodules of lymphoid tissue, and a great many branching pigment-cells.

(2) *The mucous membrane of the anterior part*, which is about one-eighth of a millimetre thick, appears at first like a superficial layer of pure fibrous tissue; but good sections show that it consists of a stratified epithelium with its constituent cells compressed somewhat as in the horny layer of the human epidermis. These compressed (horny) cells, however, are not flattened into plates to form a smooth surface, but are angularly concreted to form a broken rough surface. Beneath the superficial horny layer are several rows of cells of which the granular protoplasm seems to be fused into a solid mass, leaving only the nuclei distinct; and beneath this again comes fibrous tissue gradually passing into the loose submucosa.

(3) *The boundary-line* between the anterior horny mucosa and the posterior soft mucosa is very abrupt, and in every section there is seen a conspicuous thickening of the submucous coat at the expense of both the mucous and the muscular coats. The mucous coat is made up of the compact ramifications of an acino-tubular gland lined with granular, large-nucleated, cubical epithelium.

(4) *The mucous membrane of the posterior part*, which is rather over one-fourth of a millimetre thick, is formed entirely of long tubular glands packed close together, side by side, at right angles to the surface. These glands, which much resemble mammalian gastric glands, are lined with a granular cubical

26

epithelium having large prominent vesicular nuclei; they have broadish mouths, and in their deepest third they end by subdividing into two or three long sinuous branches, which lie in a plane parallel to that of the rest of the gland.

PROMYLLANTOR, Alcock.

Promyllantor, Alcock, Ann. Mag. Nat. Hist., Oct. 1890, p. 310.

Closely related to *Congromuræna*.

Body stout, with the muscular and osseous systems well developed. Tail about as long as the trunk. Muciferous cavities of the head well developed. Eye rather small. Cleft of the mouth narrow, not extending behind the middle of the eye. Villiform teeth in broad bands in the jaws and *in a broad confluent patch on the palate*. Tongue free. Nostrils lateral. Gill-openings widely separate; four gills with wide clefts. *No scales*. Pectoral and vertical fins well developed, the latter confluent. *The dorsal begins some distance behind the occiput.*

163. ***Promyllantor purpureus***, Alcock.

Promyllantor purpureus, Alcock, Ann. Mag. Nat. Hist., Oct. 1890, p. 310: ILLUSTRATIONS OF THE ZOOLOGY OF THE INVESTIGATOR, FISHES, PL. VI., FIG. 2.

The head is about a sixth, the tail is about half-a-head-length more than half the total length; the body is massive, its greatest height equals the length of the post-orbital portion of the head.

Head with its muciferous cavities highly developed, low, broad, inflated, ending in a broad, pointed, swollen snout, which is twice the length of the eye or $\frac{1}{4}$ the total length of the head, and conspicuously prominent beyond the mouth. Eyes circular, set high up on the side of the head, deep beneath a small transparent area of skin, a diameter and a half apart.

Anterior nostril a short wide tube situated inferiorly at the tip of the snout. Posterior nostril a large circular foramen just above the anterior orbital angle.

Mouth-cleft reaching slightly behind the vertical through the anterior border of the orbit; the jaws completely hidden by the very thick inflated lips. Villiform teeth in broad bands in the jaws, and in a broad, confluent, triangular patch covering the palate. Tongue free.

Gill-openings small widely separated foramina, hardly larger than the eye; four gills with narrow laminæ and coarse lamellæ and wide clefts; no gill-rakers.

Integument thick, coriaceous, scaleless, investing the vertical fins and completely concealing their rays. The lateral line traverses the middle of the body.

Vertical fins confluent; the dorsal begins a distance behind the occiput equal to the length of the post-rostral portion of the head, or just behind the level of the tips of the pectorals when laid full back. The anal begins immediately behind the vent. Pectorals small, pointed, equal in length to the rostr-orbital portion of the head.

Stomach with a *cul-de-sac* of moderate size; intestine wide, little convoluted; liver large, indistinctly lobated, embracing the œsophagus. Air-bladder very large, with very thick spongy walls and a small central cavity.

Colours in the fresh state:—body and fins uniform purple-black.

A mature female is 17 inches long.

Arabian Sea, off the Laccadive islands, 1000 fathoms.

Regd. No. 12878.

MURÆNESOCINA, Günther.

SAUROMURÆNESOX, Alcock.

Sauromurænesox, Alcock, Ann. Mag. Nat. Hist., Dec. 1889, p. 457.

The branchial openings into the pharynx are wide slits. The heart is situated between the gills. The tail is nearly as long as the head and trunk combined, and is much lower than the trunk. The snout is pointed, is of good length and overhangs the mouth and lower jaw, but is not specially prolonged. Eyes large. Nostrils lateral. Cleft of the mouth wide. Sharp teeth in a single row in the maxilla and mandible: some enlarged teeth in the premaxilla and at the anterior end of the mandible: a row of fangs on the vomer. Tongue free.

Gill-openings separate. No scales. Lateral line distinct but not conspicuous: each pore at the end of a small branch.

Vertical fins ill-developed confluent, the dorsal beginning a little in advance of the gill-opening. Pectorals well developed.

164. *Sauromurænesox vorax*, Alcock.

Sauromurænesox vorax, Alcock, Ann. Mag. Nat. Hist., Dec. 1889, p. 458: ILLUSTRATIONS OF THE ZOOLOGY OF THE INVESTIGATOR, FISHES, PL. VI., FIG. 3.

Form of the body lizard-like, especially in the adult female, the body being high with an arched back, and the tail being low, even at its junction with the trunk, and tapering.

Length of the head, measured to the gill-opening rather over two-thirds the distance between the gill-opening and the vent, or about two-ninths of the total.

The length of the snout is twice the width of the interorbital space and more than twice the diameter of the large circular eye; it tapers to a fine point, which is slightly hooked. Nostrils large, the anterior subtubular, at some distance from the tip of the snout; the posterior in front of the middle of the eye.

Cleft of mouth wide, extending an eye-length behind the posterior border of the orbit; the upper jaw overlapping the lower. Tongue free, bicylindrical, truncated. In maxillæ and mandibles a single row of close-set, equal, acute teeth of moderate size; also in the maxillæ an inner very incomplete series of similar teeth, and in the mandibles near their symphysis three pairs of canine teeth, the middle of which are very large and fit when the mouth is closed into a notch between the maxillaries and premaxillaries; four large equal canines in a row in the vomer; premaxillæ with three smaller canines, which project when the mouth is closed.

Gill-openings wide, extending obliquely from the upper border of the base of the pectoral fins to near the middle line of the abdomen; a broad flap of skin connects their anterior margin with the base of the pectoral fin; gill-laminæ broad.

Integument thin, without scales. The lateral line follows the dorsal curve and ends in the posterior half of the tail.

Vertical fins, especially the anal, feebly developed, confluent; the dorsal begins considerably in advance of the gill-opening, the anal behind a very large abdominal pore. Pectorals longer than the snout.

Colours: chocolate above, whitish or silvery below; vertical fins whitish, pectorals dark brown edged with grey.

The ripe female is 14 inches long.

Bay of Bengal, 193 and 145 to 250 fathoms.

Regd. Nos. 11672, 13648, 13703.

Xenomystax, Gilbert.

Xenomystax, Gilbert, Proc. United States Nat. Mus. XIV., 1891, p 348: Goode and Bean, Oceanic Ichthyology, p. 146: Jordan and Evermann, Fishes of N. Amer., p. 360.

The branchial openings into the pharynx are wide slits. The heart is situated between the gills. The tail is very much longer than the combined head and trunk. The gill-openings are wide and are separated by a narrow space. The posterior nostril is superior. The tongue is not free. The end of the tail is surrounded by the fin. Pectorals present. No scales.

Snout long. Eyes large. Mouth-cleft very wide, extending behind the eye, the upper jaw projecting much beyond the lower.

Teeth conical slender and sharp, mostly depressible, those in the jaws in broad bands. Maxillary with a broad longitudinal groove, running the whole length of the bone and dividing the band of teeth into two. A clump of teeth on the premaxillary. A row of enlarged teeth on the vomer.

The vertical fins are well developed and confluent; the dorsal begins a little in advance of the gill-openings.

Lateral line conspicuous. Air-bladder present.

165. *Xenomystax trucidans*, Alcock.

Xenomystax trucidans, Alcock, Journ. As. Soc. Bengal, Vol. LXIII., pt. 2, 1894, p. 134: ILLUSTRATIONS OF THE ZOOLOGY OF THE INVESTIGATOR, FISHES, PL. XVI., FIG. 5.

Length of the head, measured to the gill-opening, equal to the distance between the gill-opening and the vent, or slightly more than a sixth of the total.

The depressed and sharply pointed snout is a little more than one-third of the head in length and nearly four times the major diameter of the eye: its mucous pores, like those of the mandible and of the rest of the head, are large slits: the anterior nostril is a large sub-tubular slit situated on the lip close to the tip of the snout, the posterior is a wide elliptical foramen situated, almost superiorly, partly in the posterior and partly in the middle third of the snout. The mouth-cleft is wide, extending an eye-length behind the posterior border of the orbit, or more than half way along the head, and the maxillæ are most remarkably massive. The teeth are in broad crowded bands, acicular or caniniform, and for the most part depressible: those in the upper jaw are in two bands —an outer very broad band of large depressible teeth in four series which increase in size from without inwards, and an inner narrow band or very close-set row of small rigid teeth—the two bands being separated throughout their whole extent by a broad groove: the pre-maxillary teeth, which are much enlarged, are in a broad patch standing outside the closed mouth: the mandibular teeth are in at least five series increasing in size from without inwards, and at the symphysis, where they are greatly enlarged, they form a patch which fits into a wide notch in the upper jaw: the vomerine teeth form a short row of fangs. Tongue small and intimately adherent throughout to the floor of the mouth. Skin scaleless, glandular. Lateral line formed by a row of large brilliant close-set pores. Gill-openings wide, crescentic, separated by a very narrow interspace.

Vertical fins well developed, the dorsal beginning just in advance of the gill-opening. Pectorals narrow, pointed, more than half the snout in length.

The stomach is large, extending the whole length of the abdominal cavity, and is very distensible: the intestine in its posterior portion is coiled in a series of close pleats: only the left lobe of the liver is developed: pancreas large: a large air-bladder extending behind the vent.

Colour: body and fins blue-black; pectorals with narrow whitish edge and tip: margin of gill-opening and of all the mucous pores of the head and lateral line brilliant white.

A mature female is between 25 and 26 inches long.

Arabian Sea, between the Laccadives and the Malabar coast, 360, 406 and 719 fathoms.

Regd. Nos. 13704, $\frac{35}{1}$, $\frac{321}{1}$.

This species appears to differ from *X. atrarius*, dredged by the U. S. Fish Commission in 401 fathoms off the coast of Ecuador, only in the greater relative length of the tail, the nearer approximation of the gill-openings, and the greater length of the pectoral fins.

SAURENCHELYS, Peters.

166. *Saurenchelys taeniola.*

Gavialiceps tæniola, Wood-Mason MS., Alcock, Ann. Mag. Nat. Hist., Dec. 1889, p. 460.
Nettastoma tæniola, Alcock, Ann. Mag. Nat. Hist., Aug. 1891, p. 135, and Oct. 1892, p. 364.

Length of the head, measured to the gill-opening, about five-eighths of the distance from the gill-opening to the vent, and about a seventh of the total.

Length of the snout five times that of the eye, and contained about $2\frac{2}{3}$ times in that of the head. The nostrils are difficult to distinguish from the large elliptical symmetrically disposed mucous pores of the snout.

The mouth-cleft extends to, or beyond, the after limit of the eye, and the upper jaw projects well beyond the lower.

Broadish bands of small sharp teeth in both jaws, the band in the upper jaw subdivided by a median longitudinal toothless space. A patch of somewhat enlarged teeth on the premaxillary, separated from the maxillary teeth by a notch into which a patch of similarly enlarged teeth on the mandibular symphysis fits. Three long rows of teeth on the vomer, the outer rows very small and sometimes absent, the middle row very large. Tongue short, the edge of the tip just free.

Gill-openings of moderate size, close together.

No scales: the lateral line is very distinct and consists of a row of large pores which is continued right across the gill-cover to the occiput.

Vertical fins confluent; the dorsal begins above the gill-opening.

No pectoral fins.

No air-bladder.

Colour: black in adult life, the young silvery.

Adult females are about 24 inches long.

Andaman Sea, 265 fathoms; Bay of Bengal, 240, 270, 281 to 258 and 260 fathoms.

Regd. Nos. 13111–13113, 12467, 13098–13105, 13202–13206.

Nettenchelys, Alcock.

Nettenchelys, Alcock, Ann. Mag. Nat. Hist., Aug. 1898, p. 149.

Body stout; tail longer than the combined head and trunk. Muciferous cavities of head well developed; snout much produced, broad, depressed; mouth-cleft very wide, broad bands of small conical teeth in jaws and vomer; tongue not free; a tubular nostril situated dorsally near the tip of the snout on either side. Gill-openings of moderate size, well separated; four gills with wide clefts. No scales; the lateral line, which consists of a single row of pores, is very indistinct in the greater part of its extent. Dorsal and anal fins well developed, confluent with the broad caudal only in the basal half of the latter. No pectoral fins. An air-bladder; no pyloric appendages.

167. ***Nettenchelys Taylori***, Alcock.

Nettenchelys Taylori, Alcock, Ann. Mag. Nat. Hist., Aug. 1898, p. 150; Illustrations of the Zoology of the Investigator, Fishes, pl. XXV. fig. 5.

Head, measured to gill-opening, one-seventh the total, and half as long as the distance between the gill-openings and the vent; the tail is thus a good deal more than half the total. Snout a third the length of the head (measured to the gill-opening), elongate, broad, depressed, bill-like, the upper jaw overlapping the lower. There is a series of large pores along the upper lip, as also along each side of the lower jaw and along the top of the snout on either side, but the only undoubted nostrils are a largish tubular pair at the tip of the snout. Eyes subcutaneous, not much more than a fourth the length of the snout and not much more than half a diameter apart.

The mouth-cleft reaches behind the eye; the dental surface of both jaws is broad and is crowded with row upon row of close-set conical teeth, which are little more than villiform, though the innermost row in either jaw is slightly enlarged. On the vomer is a long broad convex band of similar teeth—about six longitudinal rows of them. The tongue is large and thick and tapers to a point; it is firmly adherent to the floor of the mouth.

Gill-openings of moderate size, lateral, well separated.

No scales. Although the mucous system and pores of the head are so well developed, those of the lateral line, which are in a single row, very soon become distant, small, and inconspicuous, though they are continued to the end of the tail.

Though the tail tapers it does not end in a point, but in a broad caudal fin, the outer rays of which are confluent only in their basal half with the dorsal and anal fins; these latter are well developed, the dorsal beginning immediately behind the gill-opening. No pectorals.

The stomach forms a *cul de sac* of great length; the air-bladder extends a long way behind the vent.

Colours: dark lavender-grey; dorsal and anal fins with basal half whitish and free half blackish.

A ripe female, 22 inches long, from off the Travancore coast, 430 fathoms.

Regd. No. $\frac{317}{1}$.

Named after Commander A. Dundas Taylor, formerly of the Indian Navy, the founder and first chief of the present Marine Survey of India.

Sub-order PLECTOGNATHI.

Family ***Sclerodermi.***

TRIACANTHODES, Bleeker.

Triacanthodes, Bleeker, Act. Soc. Sc. Indo-Neerl. iii. Japan, iv. p. 37: Günther, Cat. Fishes, VIII. p. 208.

Body elevated and compressed, with a short tail; covered with small spiny scales. No lateral line. Teeth very small, conical, close-set, from 14 to 20 in the upper, and about twenty-two in the lower jaw, in a single series, often with two or three in a second series. Anterior dorsal fin formed by from 4 to 6 strong spines. Ventrals formed by a pair of strong spines joined to the pelvic bone, with one or two rudimentary rays.

Distribution: Japan; Indian Seas.

168. ***Triacanthodes ethiops,*** Alcock.

Triacanthodes ethiops, Alcock, Journ. As. Soc. Bengal, Vol. LXIII. pt. 2, 1894, p. 137, pl. vii., fig. 6: ILLUSTRATIONS OF THE ZOOLOGY OF THE INVESTIGATOR, FISHES, PL. XV. FIG 9.

D. VI. 14–16. A. 14. P. 12-13. V. I. 1. C. 12.

Height of the body a little more than half the total without the caudal. Head and body covered with small spiny scales, which are continued—much reduced in size—on to the basal half of the fin-rays. In the young the spinelets of the scales are embedded each in a fleshy papilla.

Eye very large.

Spinous dorsal well developed; the first spine, which is the longest, is rather shorter than the spine of the ventral fin, which is a third the length of the body without the caudal. All the spines are rough with small barbs.

In the axil of each ventral spine is a small filamentous soft ray.

Colour in spirit: in the young blue-black, the papillæ white: in large specimens mottled black and white.

Largest specimen rather over $3\frac{1}{4}$ inches long.

Bay of Bengal, off Madras coast, 145 to 250 fathoms; Andaman Sea, 185 fathoms.

Regd. Nos. 13709, $\frac{369}{1}$, $\frac{370}{1}$.

The peculiar delicacy of the tissues and the large goggle eyes proclaim this fish to be an inhabitant of the depths.

Halimochirurgus nov. gen.

Body low and moderately compressed but not elongate, except the snout, which is produced to form a long curved perfectly tubular organ, with the mouth near the end, remarkably like the surgical instrument known as a catheter. Tail short. Skin everywhere covered with small villiform and capillary spinelets. No lateral line.

Mouth small, placed superiorly and transversely, near the end of the tubular snout. A row of minute conical teeth in each jaw.

Gills pectinate. Gill-opening a narrow slit in front of the pectorals.

The spinous dorsal consists of two large spines. The soft dorsal is short and almost opposite the anal.

Each ventral consists of a huge spine articulating with the pelvic bone.

The mandibular symphysis is sharp and very prominent beyond the mouth, but there is no barbel.

This curious fish is undoubtedly a very close relative of *Triacanthus*, but has, at the same time, well-marked affinities with *Monacanthus* and *Anacanthus*.

169. ***Halimochirurgus centriscoides***, Alcock.

Halimochirurgus centriscoides, Alcock, Proc. Asiatic Soc., Bengal, July, 1899, p. 78.
Illustrations of the Zoology of the Investigator, Fishes, pl. XXXI. fig. 3.

D. II. 13. A. 12. P. 11-12. V. I. C. 12.

Greatest body-height not quite half the length of the tubular snout, and a fifth the total length without the caudal.

Snout tubular with an upward curve, ending in a point formed by the mandibular symphysis. On its upper surface, a short distance from its end, is the transverse mouth, well inside of which are two broad curtains of mucous membrane—one connected with each jaw—forming an inner valvular orifice. A row of minute distant conical teeth in each jaw.

Eye large. Nostrils small, in a hollow immediately in front of the eye.

Skin covered with granular, villiform, and capillary spinelets, which also extend some way on to the fin-rays.

First dorsal spine situated above the ventrals, and equal in length to them but hardly so stout: its length is about nine-tenths the greatest body-height. Second dorsal spine about seven-tenths the greatest body-height.

Each ventral fin consists of a long stout movable spine having a movable catch-joint with the pelvic bone. All the spines are rough.

Caudal not quite two-fifths the length of the snout.

Colour white, with a silvery sheen.

Length a little over $4\frac{3}{4}$ inches.

Off Cape Comorin, 143 fathoms.

Regd. No. $\frac{781}{1}$.

The delicacy of the tissues, the large eye, and the contents of the stomach show that this fish came from a considerable depth and from the bottom.

Addenda [to Family Stomiatidæ].

Astronesthes, Richardson.

Astronesthes, Richardson, Ichth. Voy. Sulph., p. 97: Günther, Cat. Fishes V., p. 424: Goode and Bean, Oceanic Ichthyology, p. 105: Jordan and Evermann, Fishes N. Amer., p. 586.

Phænodon, Lowe, Proc. Zool. Soc., 1850, p. 250.

"Body rather elongate and compressed, scaleless, with the vent situated at no great distance from the caudal fin. Head rather compressed, with the snout short and with the cleft of the mouth wide. Teeth pointed, unequal in size, two pairs in the upper jaw and one in the lower being long curved canine teeth: maxillary finely and subequally denticulated: vomer with a pair of small fangs: palatines with a single series of small pointed teeth, similar to those of the tongue. Eye of moderate size. A fleshy barbel is suspended from the centre of the hyoid region. Dorsal fin rather long, opposite the interspace between the ventrals and the anal: caudal forked: pectoral and ventral fins well developed. Series of luminous dots run along the lower side of the head body and tail. Gill-opening very wide, the outer branchial arch with minute gill-rakers: pseudobranchiæ none: air-bladder none. Stomach caecal" (Günther).

Distribution: Atlantic: Indo-Pacific.

122 *a*. *Astronesthes* sp.

Illustrations of the Zoology of the Investigator, pl. XXXV. fig. 3.

A very small but perfect specimen of *Astronesthes* was taken, off the Travancore coast, in 224–284 fathoms.

It does not agree with any of the described species, but is nearest related to *A. niger*, from which indeed it seems to differ only in having (1) the ventrals placed further back, (2) the anal fin shorter—consisting of only 12 rays, and (3) the barbel very much thicker, and of nearly equal thickness throughout.

As it is obviously immature I do not describe it: possibly it is a young *Astronesthes niger*.

Synopsis of the Indian genera of Stomiatidæ.

[To be substituted for the *Synopsis* on p. 146.]

I. Hyoid barbel free: pectorals well developed: teeth on the palatines and vomer:—
   1. Body elongate: skin mapped into hexagonal areolæ: dorsal and anal fins opposite to one another and situated close to the caudal ... Stomias.
   2. Body of moderate length: skin perfectly smooth and scaleless: dorsal fin above the space between the ventrals and the anal ... Astronesthes.

II. Hyoid barbel attached to the mandibular symphysis: skin smooth and scaleless:—
   1. Pectoral rays reduced in number: no teeth on the palate ... Malacosteus.
   2. Pectorals absent: teeth on the palatines ... ... Photostomias.

INDEX.

LIST OF PUBLICATIONS ISSUED BY THE TRUSTEES OF THE INDIAN MUSEUM.

	Rs.	As.	P.
Account of the Deep-Sea Brachyura collected by the R.I.M.S. Investigator. By A. Alcock, M.B., C.M.Z.S., F.G.S.	6	0	0
Account of the Deep-Sea Madreporaria collected by the R.I.M.S. Investigator. By A. Alcock, M.B., C.M.Z.S., F.G.S.	4	0	0
Catalogue of Archæological Collections in the Indian Museum, Parts I and II. By J. Anderson, M.D., F.R.S., &c.	4	12	0
Catalogue of Coins of the Indian Museum, Parts I to IV. By C. J. Rodgers, M.R.A.S., M.N.S.	24	0	0
Catalogue of the Indian Deep-Sea Fishes in the Indian Museum. By A. Alcock, M.B., C.M.Z.S., F.G.S.	5	0	0
Catalogue of Mammalia in the Indian Museum, Part I. By J. Anderson, M.D., F.R.S., Part II. By W. L. Sclater, M.A., F.Z.S.	6	0	0
Catalogue of Mantodea in the Indian Museum, Parts I and II. By J. Wood-Mason, F.Z.S., &c.	2	0	0
Catalogue of Moths of India, Parts I to VII. By E. C. Cotes, and C. Swinhoe, F.L.S., F.Z.S., &c.	5	12	0
Echinoderma of the Indian Museum: Ophiuroidea collected by the R.I.M.S. Investigator. By R. Koehler	10	0	0
Figures and Descriptions of Nine Species of Squillidæ from the Collection in the Indian Museum. By J. Wood-Mason, F.Z.S., &c. Edited by A. Alcock	2	0	0
Guide to the Zoological Collections Exhibited in the Invertebrate Gallery of the Indian Museum. By A. Alcock, M.B., C.M.Z.S., F.G.S.	0	10	0
Guide to the Zoological Collections Exhibited in the Reptile and Amphibia Gallery of the Indian Museum. By A. Alcock, M.B., C.M.Z.S., F.G.S.	0	3	0
Hand List of Mollusca in the Indian Museum, Parts I, II, and Fasciculus E. By G. Nevill, C.M.Z.S., &c. Index, Parts I and II. By W. Theobald	7	4	0
List of Batrachia in the Indian Museum. By W. L. Sclater, M.A., F.Z.S.	1	0	0
List of Snakes in the Indian Museum. By W. L. Sclater, M.A., F.Z.S.	1	0	0
Monograph of the Asiatic Chiroptera and Catalogue of the Species of Bats in the Indian Museum. By G. E. Dobson, M.A., M.B., F.R.S., &c.	3	0	0
Monograph of the Oriental Cicadidæ, Parts I to VII. By W. L. Distant, F.E.S. ...	£. 2	2	6

The above can be obtained from the Superintendent of the Indian Museum, Calcutta, and from Messrs. Friedlander & Son, 11, Carlstrasse, Berlin.

Other Publications sold by the Superintendent of the Indian Museum (*also obtainable from Messrs. Friedlander & Son*). Issued by the Director of the Royal Indian Marine.

	R.	A.	P.
Illustrations of the Zoology of the R.I.M.S. Investigator, 1892. Fishes, Plates i–vii. Crustacea, Plates i–v ...	12	0	0
1894. Fishes, Plates viii–xiii. Crustacea, Plates vi–viii. Echinoderma. Plates i–iii ...	12	0	0
1895. Echinoderma, Plates iv-v	2	0	0
,, 1895. Fishes, Plates xiv–xvi	3	0	0
,, 1895. Crustacea, Plates ix–xv	7	0	0
,, 1896. Crustacea, Plates xvi–xxvii	12	0	0
1897. Fishes, Plate xvii. Crustacea, Plates xxviii–xxxii. Mollusca, Plates i–vi	12	0	0
,, 1898. Fishes, Plates xviii–xxiv. Crustacea, Plates xxxiii–xxxv. Mollusca, Plates vii-viii ...	12	0	0
,, 1899. Fishes. Plates xxv-xxvi. Crustacea, Plates xxxvi–xlv	12	0	0

Zeitfracht Medien GmbH
Ferdinand-Jühlke-Straße 7
99095 Erfurt, Deutschland
produktsicherheit@kolibri360.de